SINGER OF LIES

Borgo Press Books by Michael R. Collings

All Calm, All Bright: Christmas Offerings
The Art and Craft of Poetry: Twenty Exercises Toward Mastery
Brian Aldiss
Dark Transformations: Deadly Visions of Change
The Films of Stephen King
GemLore: An Introduction to Precious and Semi-Precious Gem-stones
The House Beyond the Hill: A Novel of Horror
The Many Facets of Stephen King
Naked to the Sun: Dark Visions of Apocalypse
Piers Anthony
Scaring Us to Death: The Impact of Stephen King on Popular Culture
Singer of Lies: A Science Fantasy Novel
Wordsmith, Part One: The Veil of Heaven: A Science Fantasy Novel
Wordsmith, Part Two: The Thousand Eyes of Flame: A Science Fantasy Novel

SINGER OF LIES

A SCIENCE FANTASY NOVEL

by

Michael R. Collings

Emeritus Professor of English
Seaver College
Pepperdine University

THE BORGO PRESS

An Imprint of Wildside Press LLC

MMIX

CONTENTS

CHAPTER ONE

Adjunct 746D42M—who had chosen to call himself *Erik Baan-feld* during conscious times—startled awake. His first perception was shock...mindless shock that sizzled vivid white-noise up and down his spine, blanketing all other sensations with its electric jolt.

His second was isolation.

The Jack!

He slapped automatically at the back of his neck, knowing even as he did so that his questing fingers would not find the smooth ceramic plug that interfaced with him, directed him, *made* him.

Only when his fingers curled around nothingness, tickled by loose strands of hair along his neck, did he begin to register the third level of perception.

His ears were jangling like alarm claxons, alerting him that sometime very recently cabin pressure had abruptly and significantly changed. Beneath the insistent clangor, he heard nothing...at least nothing that he could interpret unJacked. His lungs burned against the arc of his ribs, a sure sign that he had been holding his breath much longer than even *his* body was designed to endure. The sullen, metronomic throb of blood in his neck and temples only added to his profound sense of unease.

He forced his eyes open. Everything was dark.

Too dark. Too silent. Too warm.

Erik couldn't even define quite where he was. He remembered unplugging in his cubicle the night before, just after Marquette had dismissed him. Now, here, suddenly, nothing read as familiar. He blinked. Jacked, he would have shifted into the infrared or ultraviolet spectra, depending on which the computer decided was necessary. But now there was nothing. Just darkness. He blinked again, and gradually his eyes adjusted to the darkness, if not to the chaos of sharp angles and erratic shapes surrounding him. He had unJacked in his cabin, *but this wasn't his cabin*. He was not in his cubicle. He was sitting on something, but it was not upright. Even against the confusing matrix of unfamiliar shapes—even without the assurance of either Jack or Marquette—he could sense his body tilting at a crazy angle.

Something inside his mind—*his own* unJacked *mind*, he registered, and that merely added to increasing sense of unease—clicked, and unfamiliarity jerked itself into a sort of familiarity. He was in his console chair. In the command center. Seated next to Marquette.

He darted a glance sideways. He couldn't see the Spacer's tall lanky figure bent confidently over the control panel, and Erik's panic boiled up anew. He tasted coppery fear at the back of his tongue. His throat tightened even more, threatening to choke him.

Programmed responses, he reassured himself...but knowing a thing intellectually did not make it easier to bear. He forced his eyes away from the tilted back of Marquette's chair. He could do nothing until he had Jacked in. His free hand felt along the panel to his right, unerringly found his console Jack, jerked it toward himself, and pressed it roughly into the socket—barely larger than his thumbnail—at the base of his skull.

He closed his eyes. After the instant of dissociation that he knew was coming but hated nonetheless, he melded with the onboard computer, which immediately stimulated the appropriate brain cells and triggered the mechanisms that allowed the organism that called itself *Erik Baanfeld* to function normally. Or at least as normally as the radically atypical circumstances permitted.

He blinked several times, scanning the cabin as he did so until his eyes shifted to an appropriate light-perception level. He released his pent-up breath, felt himself forced into a semblance of calm as electrical impulses worked on taut nerves and muscles. As if it were a matter of his own choice, he drew a deep breath. His ribs hurt. The air rasped at the back of his tongue, overlaying the coppery tang. He was used to the stale flatness of recycled oxygen, but now he smelled heat and melting plastics and burning insulation and pungent fluids spilled across the canted deck.

His mind flashed from level to level, working through the flight regs that dictated his next actions. As an adjunct, he had no access to the portion of the computer responsible for ship maintenance and control. That belonged to Marquette alone. And the bits of data he could glean from his peripheral scanning systems were not sufficient for him to understand entirely what had happened.

His lower lip trembled. He touched a stud on his console. Impulses raced through his Jack. After a moment, the calmness returned.

Marquette would take charge soon. Then everything would be all right.

Until then, Erik set about organizing his most recent memories. He closed his eyes.

He had had a long talk with Marquette the night before; or, rather, Marquette had talked *at* Erik for a long while before dismissing him with a curt "Good night, Baanfeld." At least he had deigned to use Erik's self-designated eke-name, after weeks of referring to him by serial number or simply as "Junk." Spacers often not only accepted but overtly relished their superiority to the adjunct-clones bred for ExServ missions. Some Spacers, in fact, considered junks as little more than unnecessary baggage. They sometimes endured the presence of the junks with only thinly disguised ill will; occasionally a Spacer didn't even bother with that much courtesy. Marquette was no worse than most, better than some. But only his Spacer training and the implants that kept Erik comfortably passive and subservient had prevented Marquette from striking Erik on more than one occasion.

Surprisingly, the night before, Marquette had been loquacious, nearly affable. He had actually spoken openly, as if Erik were another human being, not a walking-wet-ware computer-link fathered by frozen tissues, mothered by a mechanical crèche, and nurtured on synthetics. The moment had presented, Erik decided, an uncomfortable twist from business as usual.

As soon as Marquette had dismissed him, turning his attention at once to the control console, Erik had retired silently—and with a throbbing sense of relief—to his cubicle. He had been growing edgy about his first official planetfall, when they would finally set foot on the world they had been observing. He had tossed restlessly on his hard narrow bunk, waiting wide-eyed through long, uncounted moments until, despairing of naturally resting in the ship's artificial night, he thumbed a stud on the control panel that connected him to the computer and slid easily away....

Until the alarm.

An unexpected spike of panic sliced through his mind. He raised his right arm and adjusted the compu-link. In the silence, he heard the welcome whisper of slick tunic against cushion. The compu-link increased the current flowing through his Jack. He turned another knob. The panic dissipated, then disappeared. He flexed the fingers on his left hand and reached out. They brushed the smooth, warm surface.

The alarm.

He reached out again. This time his hand struck the sharp edge of a sharply accordioned panel. The bare metal scraped a layer of skin from his knuckle. In a movement at once childlike and ingenuous, he sucked at the drop of blood on his knuckle. The pain disappeared. Careful to avoid cutting himself again on the edge, he explored the crumpled panel with his fingertips, trying to figure out what it was. It felt frustratingly familiar. There should be.... Yes, there it was. He brushed a knob, then depressed it. A red light glowed along the upper edge of the console.

Blood-red light reflected from shining metal surfaces all around him. The light was dim but strong enough for him to make partial sense of what surrounded him.

The place was a shambles.

His heart thudded uncomfortably. He felt a free-rush of adrenaline that was both frightening and unfamiliar. He thumbed the compu-link knob another degree or two. The descent from approaching panic to calmly disinterested objectivity was accomplished—as always—so smoothly that he barely noted it.

He studied the cabin.

He was strapped in his seat-module at the compu-link console. His seat was tilted oddly, as if some insane muscleman had wrenched one side up with a crowbar and wedged it that way, but Jorge Marquette's lay almost on its side. Erik still could not see Marquette's body or face; at least with the stimulation from the compu-link flooding his mind he no longer quite so desperately needed the physical presence of the Spacer to reassure him. One of Marquette's arms hung limply in sight, though, apparently caught in the restraint webs. Even in the faint light, Erik saw that the arm and hand were cruelly twisted; one finger seemed bent completely backward. Erik thumbed his own restraint web, but his hand slipped on the buckle. He had to try a second time before the restraint released. The instant the web opened, he slid to one side. His lungs seemed to expand forever as he sucked in air. In spite of its scorched taste against his tongue, his lungs demanded more and more, now that they were freed from the throbbing tightness that had stretched across his chest. He choked back a cough.

He started to move toward Marquette but was stopped by an insistent tug on his socket. He turned, sighed heavily, Jacked out, and watched the compu-link wire retract. It looked alive. It always did. For an instant, he felt the jarring isolation that accompanied disconnect, then he felt another uncontrollable obsession, another imperative working on him. A Spacer was in trouble. He must help.

He took another moment, though, to run an internal check on his own body. His head ached and his left temple throbbed, but his hands and arms moved freely. He stretched. His legs were numb but functional. He was all right.

Marquette was not.

Erik could only partially wriggle through the wreckage around his module, but he could reach far enough around the command seat to touch Marquette's temple. He felt a large patch of something thickly crusted and dry, but there was also, thankfully, a pulse—it registered as a slow, barely perceptible ebb and swell beneath Erik's fingers, but it was definite. Erik wrestled his way across the narrow cabin, barking his shin on a thick metal bar that he could not remember being there before. The crimson emergency light bathed everything in blood. He twisted carefully around the side of Marquette's module, found the buckle, and released Marquette's harness. Even though apparently unconscious, Marquette moaned when Erik unwound the web from the man's twisted arm. Erik handled the injured arm as little as possible. He needed to see what was wrong and Jack-in for further help before he dared do anything more. One wrong stress, and he might cripple Marquette permanently. Neither of them could afford that. He rose, took an instant to gain his bearings in the radically altered interior of the cabin, and leaned across an overturned terminal to touch the auxiliary power switch. A wash of relief flooded him as strong, bright, white light flickered then flared through the cabin.

At least the electrical systems were undamaged...and the computers. He shivered as he thought of the consequences had all of the main systems—especially the compu-link—been damaged. His right hand touched his socket lightly, as if unconsciously reassuring himself that an essential part of himself was still there. And still functioning. He felt a momentary need to Jack-in, a compulsion so strong that his knees threatened to buckle and sweat broke out on his upper lip.

He wasn't designed for this sort of thing. He wasn't designed to take charge. That was the Spacer's job. He was only supposed to... to....

A sharp pain lanced across his forehead. When it passed, his mind felt clearer, calmer. He had to check on Marquette, help Marquette, get Marquette back on his feet.

He turned his attention to the man. He knelt as close to the twisted seat as he could and cautiously enlarged a long rip in the man's sleeve. Beneath, the skin was furrowed where something metallic had sliced it. Erik studied the angle of the arm. The forearm was broken. Compound fracture. A splinter of bloody bone protruded through a ragged tear in the flesh. Beneath the layer of blood—dark and also crusted, so whatever had happened must have happened hours earlier—Marquette's flesh was dead white. Erik felt under what remained of the console for the emergency kit. Splinting and binding the break would be tricky, but necessary.

For this, he needed help. He glanced up, located the secondary Jack on Marquette's console, Jacked in, and felt his mind spinning through options, almost instantaneously calling up the medlog. *Compound fracture,* he thought, and the instructions appeared, as if printed in vivid red on the air six inches in front of him.

He worked rapidly, reviewing passages from the medlog at each stage, calling up step-by-step illustrations and instructions for emergency treatment of compound fractures. Palm against this pressure point to slow the bleeding (by now, fortunately, there wasn't much), pressure here for the splint, wrap this around and tuck against the self-sealing edge—he worked silently, mechanically. Except for the rapid movements of his fingers and an occasional vibration in the Jack-lead, he might have been a statue, cunningly contrived and painted to imitate a human.

He was so absorbed in the task at hand that he didn't notice when Marquette regained consciousness.

"Wha...where...?"

Marquette's face contorted with pain. His forehead gleamed pale behind a swath of blood smeared outward from his temple. He reached awkwardly to support his broken arm. Erik put a restraining hand on Marquette's good arm, keeping it away from the bindings until they had time to set. In the tension of the moment, neither seemed aware that a junk had touched a Spacer uninvited, let alone that the junk had—however implicitly and wordlessly—given the Spacer an order.

"Compound fracture, sir," Erik said tersely. "Messy, but I think okay." He completed the binding and pressed the sedative module to Marquette's upper arm. The flesh turned red for a moment, then faded to pale white again. Already, though, the pain lines were dimming in the man's face. "Can you stand, sir?"

Marquette stared at Erik, as if he had never seen the Adjunct before. Then he nodded once. The movement was studied, as if Marquette had kept it to a minimum to avoid unnecessary pain...or to reassert his control over the junk and the situation in general.

Marquette raised himself on his good elbow, winced, and sank back. "Then again," he said with a fleeting trace of the grin that had reputedly captured women's hearts in every port, "maybe not."

Erik nodded and Jacked out. He wanted to stay with the compulink, at least long enough for Marquette to take charge again, but there was no way he could support Marquette while attached by the lead to the control panel. He watched the lead retract; it snaked smoothly away, with little more than a whisper of metal against metal.

With Erik's help, Marquette eased himself from the wrecked seat. When he shifted his weight, however, he winced again.

"More sedative, sir?" Erik asked. He felt his separation from the compu-link even more clearly now that he could not call on the medlog for immediate help. Maybe he should have attached Marquette to the link. Maybe he should have done a full body scan on Marquette. Maybe he should have....

Marquette carefully shook his head once. "No need," he said through pinched lips. He tried another step, winced again, and bit his lip hard enough to draw blood. "Ankle feels sprained. Won't support me." He held his arm out—there was a command embedded in the gesture, one that need not be articulated to be obeyed.

Erik slipped under the outstretched arm and helped Marquette find his balance. He became a living crutch for the heavier man's full weight. Together, they made their way through the wreckage toward landing hatch, Marquette steering unerringly in spite of the chaos of metal, plastic, and wire. When they stood before the arced steel plate, Marquette nodded permission to Erik. Erik reached with his free hand and punched the power switch. It jammed. Erik had to jiggle it a few times before he was rewarded with a sibilant rush of incoming air.

He shifted under Marquette's arm as they crawled through the hatchway. Sweating from the exertion, hurting vaguely from his own bruises and scrapes (nothing as bad as Marquette's, though), and hungry to be back where he could re-connect with the compu-link that accompanied him during so many of his waking hours—that helped him forget occasionally that he was only a Adjunct, an organic adjunct to the scout vessel under the command of a fully human Spacer—Erik straightened. As he did so he pulled Marquette up with him. Breathing deeply from their exertions, they looked out over the world that cradled the damaged ship.

Erik's first impression registered a mindless blur of undifferentiated green—green everywhere. In spite of the fact that orbital bioscans had told them what to expect, the shapes and colors of the thick vegetation seemed eerily, hauntingly familiar. From where he stood, Erik could identify sprawling trees that had to be variants of terran oaks and dense patches of greenery that were either current bushes or something so close that the differences between them would be negligible. For meters around the ship, the ground was stubbled with short, sturdy grass...except, of course, where the crash had ripped great gouts away and exposed knots of iron-rich red soil.

The seeding-ship sent centuries before had obviously fulfilled its mission competently; the scene reminded Erik of holos of one of Earth's wildlife refuges.

Before Erik had a chance to study the landscape more closely, Marquette abruptly slumped, groaned softly through clenched teeth, and fell back against a scarred panel.

"Rest here, sir," Erik said. "I'll get the foam." Erik settled Marquette more comfortably against the scouter, then returned to the control cabin. He passed through what was left of it to the central corridor, turned left, and opened the medical cabinet. The crash had shaken the entire craft severely—white-wrapped packets of supplies lay scattered like untidy snowdrifts across gray metal shelves, but most of the medicines seemed at least usable. Erik grabbed the nearest foam dispenser and hurried back.

Outside, he knelt beside Marquette and adjusted the wrappings on the injured arm. Marquette bit his lip but made no sound, closing his eyes and turning his head to rest his temple against cool metal.

Erik applied the foam to the wrappings. In the stillness of the clearing, its hiss sounded as loud as a rocket's throaty roar. Erik noted absently that his ears had stopped ringing; apparently there was no permanent damage. He worked cautiously, covering not only the injured arm but the shoulder as well, spreading the foam outward across Marquette's chest. When it hardened, the cast would immobilize the arm, eliminating the need for a sling until more complete medical steps could be taken.

By whom? Erik thought. That was one question of many that he did not yet have the courage to speak out loud.

The anesthesia in the foam began working, deadening the pain as it penetrated bindings and skin and filtered a relaxant into Marquette's blood stream.

"Better, sir?" Erik asked.

Marquette nodded. "Some."

The man seemed, indeed, noticeably more relaxed than he had been only moments before. Some natural color had return to his cheeks, and his lips no longer looked like thin gray slashes in a craggy but otherwise featureless white surface. Marquette was doing his part, resting as comfortably as possible given the situation. Erik returned to the scouter.

Beyond the medical cabinet, debris clogged the passageway. The aft compartments must have ruptured upon impact. Struts twisted like knotted cords across the entry to the computer terminal and the sleeping quarters. A long, thin rift sliced across the ceiling panels. If the ship had had a spine, it was now shattered...and the body it was supposed to control lay paralyzed, bent and stiff and useless. In spite of the warmth inside, Erik shuddered as he stared around, his eyes registering the jumble of spilled containers, crumpled bulkheads and sprung seams. If he had remained in his bunk after the alarm had sounded, he would be trapped there now...or dead. He backtracked along the corridor.

If they needed anything from those compartments, Erik decided, it would mean long hours of backbreaking work, even with what machinery they could salvage from elsewhere in the ship.

"And that means *me*, not *us*," he reminded himself, thinking as much of Marquette's arm as of his own status. Marquette's wrenched ankle probably wasn't serious, but that arm would be useless for weeks at least, months perhaps. Erik shrugged. Time to worry about that later.

The forward areas seemed less damaged than the aft. That part of the ship was, after all, designed to absorb most of the shock of an emergency landing. If the ship's spine had ruptured, at least its skull was intact and, apparently, some critical parts of its brain. His quick scan swept the mess and clutter that only the night before had been a compact, efficient, almost obsessively neat control cabin. He noted particularly the complex banks of computer terminals, most of which he was only vaguely familiar with and many of which were now probably little more than so many useless lumps of crushed metal and scorched plastic and fused wires. The skull might be intact, he thought, and partially functional, but massive areas of the brain inside were certainly dead.

Erik muttered against their bad luck and went back outside. For a long while, he studied the wreckage, wandering aimlessly back and forth along the ragged edge of the small meadow that had served—however accidentally—as landing field. They had struck one of several low hills jutting from the dense, surrounding forest like humped backs of some great sleeping beasts. Erik noted the thick trunks of a number of nearby trees, some of them nearly the girth of the scouter. If the ship had hit even a hundred meters further down slope, he realized, there would probably have been substantially more damage.

In spite of the smell of burning insulation that permeated the ship's internal air system, there was no indication from the meadow of any external fires. Marquette must have remained in control most of the way down. Then something had gone wrong. Marquette had called Erik forward. He remembered a bit more now—harnessing himself into his seat and bracing against its padded back—but nothing after that. During the crash, or shortly thereafter, something must have torn loose behind them, knocking Erik unconscious and smashing into Marquette with enough force to break his arm.

Erik climbed a few steps up the slope behind the scouter's tail section. From there a jagged, stony ridge continued up the slope, rocks jutting like broken, uneven teeth. Spines of sharp gray granite-like rock, glistening with minute crystals, had ripped the craft open; a number of them had shattered into rubble. Trails of pulverized stone and ragged bits of metal lay strewn on the ground, marking the scouter's path.

From the top of the ridge, he glanced around. The place looked peaceful enough. They could be in worse situations, he thought, surprised at his relief. As far as he could estimate, given Marquette's intentions when he began the descent, the settlement they had scanned from orbit the day before (already it seemed like years) probably lay several day's march away, so there should be no problems with potentially hostile natives...yet.

His mind returned to more immediate problems. They would need some kind of shelter soon. He looked at the twisted remnants of the hull. They could stay in there tonight, cramped perhaps, but safe. Tomorrow, he would have Marquette instruct him in how to set up something roomier and more comfortable. After all, they would have to stay here until the rescue team arrived—and that could be months unless the signal went through just right. Erik hunched against an odd outcrop of rust-red rock and contemplated their situation, mechanically tabulating credits and debits like an accountant.

First, the most serious debit: Marquette was injured. Erik didn't think there was anything seriously wrong with the Spacer beyond the fracture and the twisted ankle, but he was not a trained medic and even Jacking in would give him only theoretical knowledge, not practical. Plus, Marquette could easily have suffered internal injuries, perhaps a concussion. Who knew what could go wrong inside a human body as abused as Marquette's had been?

On the credit side, though, the medical cabinet was undamaged and accessible, and the Jack still functioned. He might be able to help Marquette, at that, or, minimally, take some steps to keep the Spacer's injuries from worsening. He would have to clear the corridor at least as far as their quarters to get to extra blankets stored there. It was warm now, in what seemed early afternoon, but the vegetation he saw everywhere suggested cool nights; the area certainly wasn't tropical. Their uniforms were durable enough, even when torn here and there, but they were not designed for warmth. At the very least, as soon as the foam set completely, he would have to help Marquette wrestle back into the cramped command center. Until then....

"Junk." Marquette sounded stronger, more like his old self. Erik jumped up, brushing coarse-grained dust from his pants, and made his way carefully down the slope.

By the time he reached Marquette, the man was on his feet, balancing his weight against the scouter. He looked alert and more in control than he had earlier. "How does it look up there?"

"Not good, sir. The ship's ripped open, most of the rear caved in."

"Okay," Marquette said, settling again into the habit of command, even if his crew only consisted of one grass-green sub-junior-grade linguist-analyst Adjunct on his first assignment for the Ex-Serv. "Here's what we do. Shelter, food, supplies. Rescue beacon. General scouting of the area in case there are any settlements we hadn't located. Tomorrow...."

He fell silent. Erik felt a small glow of pride—Marquette's list paralleled his own precisely. Not bad for a first-timer...and a junk. His training had settled in deeper than he knew.

Marquette tried to straighten further, then his small reserves of strength gave way and he slumped back against the scouter.

"Not yet," he said, breathing heavily. "By tomorrow, though...."

Erik nodded in mute agreement. After all, Marquette was in command. He was the experienced Spacer, the human, with enough planet-side experience to see them through. The junk was only there to help when help was required.

Marquette shivered. The reflexive movement sent ripples of pain across his face.

"Come on, sir," Erik said, "Get inside, at least. Worry about tomorrow...tomorrow."

Marquette nodded, cautiously shifting his weight until Erik bore most of the stress. Together they clambered through the hatch.

The air inside tasted fresher now. Erik could nearly ignore the pungent burned smells, but he did feel a distinct chill as they climbed out of the sunlight. He helped Marquette slide to the deck, then spent a frustrating and nearly wasted fifteen minutes trying to set the cabin in order. Righting their consoles, straightening out the hash of restraints and buckles, getting one securely enough onto its base to support Marquette—by the time Erik was finished, he was sweating and panting. And the job had barely begun, he noted as he glanced around the cabin.

"Junk," Marquette said. "Help me up. I've got to see how much damage the console sustained."

There they were again, the unmistakable notes of assumed superiority, of command. For a few moments it had been slightly unnerving but exciting, Marquette speaking to him almost as an equal.

Oh well. Erik straightened his shoulders. Situation back to normal.

It took some doing before Marquette was comfortably seated. As soon as he was able, the Spacer turned his attention to the ship. His good arm swept smoothly across the console, fingers punching and probing, twisting through knots of burned-out wiring and fused insulation.

Erik stood around for a while, pushing this, pulling that, holding a handful of wires taut as Marquette requested.

Then, suddenly and surprisingly, Marquette swiveled to face Erik, his chair grating and wobbling just enough to make Erik reach out to steady it.

"Junk, you must be tired. We've had a helluva day, and I got to sleep through most of it. Go on out and take a breather. I've got things under control here. We have auxiliary power, lights, even controlled environment if we need it...at least for a while. Until tomorrow, for sure. Go on outside, see if there's anything interesting."

"Yes, sir," Erik said. But he was speaking to the scarred back of Marquette's chair; Marquette had already turned and focused his attention on the complexities of the command console.

Outside, dusk had nearly settled. The air blew cool but not cold across Erik's bare arms. It held a surprising crispness, the faintest hint of a promise of snow. He closed his eyes, savoring the sensation of moving, fresh air across his face. Somewhere there was water nearby. He could feel a tang, a sharp moistness that his genetically Earth-bred senses identified as running water, probably a stream.

He opened his eyes, orienting himself to the smell. He walked across the clearing toward the edge of the forest. The trees cast deep shadows that obscured everything beyond a few meters.

He felt a tingle of caution—after all, this *was* an unknown place, an unknown world, and he was pulling further and further away from the ship and his Jack—but the draw of the smell was unaccountably strong. He closed his eyes again, concentrating on sounds. Maybe, just maybe, he could hear the rustle of water against stones—or possibly it was only leaves rippling in a faint breeze. He laughed softly, opened his eyes, and walked beneath the shadows.

Marquette's initial scans had shown no dangerous indigenous animal life, but even Erik knew that preliminary scans were of necessity notoriously spotty. It was hard to cover an entire planet with one scouter in only a couple of scans. He walked carefully but not fearfully.

A few paces into the forest, he stopped and turned. The daylight had almost disappeared from the clearing. The scouter, canted against the hillside, glowed orange in the dying light of an eerily terran sun. The clearing lay silent, still.

"Just a bit further," Erik said quietly. "Not all the way to the stream tonight, but a little further anyway." He had, of course, never been allowed to go camping, had in fact been designed to dislike too much open space, but right now he been ordered away from the scouter, from Marquette's precise movements as he repaired what could be salvaged of the scouter's systems.

Later, maybe in a week or so, Erik would have his chance to be the expert, but for now....

He walked on, following what seemed an animal trail, or perhaps just a coincidental series of breaks in the thick brush. At first the air was silent. He became aware of his own breath, soft but nonetheless harsh-sounding against the backdrop of silence.

Then there was something else.

It was faint at first, not even a whisper, just enough of a sound to make him stop and cock his head to one side, straining to identify the odd disruption in the stillness.

It was barely there, a rustle that sounded distant yet threatening, like something very large moving far away. He glanced over his shoulder toward the scouter. He could see nothing but the dusky boles of massive trees. The clearing—if it was where he thought— had disappeared.

The sound, that satiny, sibilant whispering, seemed louder now.

Somehow, he had let himself get disoriented in the near-darkness. He started to run, then yelled "Stop," surprising himself with the loudness of his voice. "Stop and think. Don't go running off crazy."

He closed his eyes, breathing deeply and shutting out the sound (louder now, drawing nearer, getting bigger). Then he opened them, concentrating every sense on the remaining shreds of light. He turned his head slowly, trying to pierce the shadows enough to see beyond the nearest trunks and clumps of brush.

There. Was that a glimmer, a not-quite-shadow? Was there something silvery gleaming just beyond that huge bole? He took several steps, then searched the darkness again. Yes, there was definitely something there.

He moved, locking his gaze on the silvery gleam that grew with each step until it resolved into a battered, curving shape hunching in moonlight. It was the....

With a ferocity that terrified and froze, part of Erik's mind screamed at him—a part that he had not suspected in himself, that part that had while unJacked still subliminally kept track of the progress of the whisper-rustle moving toward the clearing.

"RUN!"

He ran.

He stumbled over roots and branches, caught his trousers in brambles, once barely missed tumbling over a rock and probably smashing his skull in the process, but he ran. He passed the monstrous oak bole, trying not to notice how errant shadows twisted after him like alien creatures.

The sound was louder now, but still distant, even more frightening because of its quiet intensity. Without knowing how, Erik knew that whatever caused the sound was huge, deadly.

He ran faster.

By the time he stumbled through the hatchway, the sound had already disappeared. He stopped, one foot in the ship, and turned, testing the air.

He was greeted with silence. The feeling—the threat—was gone. Or at least so far distant that Erik could no longer perceive it. He slipped into the ship and closed the hatch behind him. That made him feel better.

"Nice walk?" Marquette asked without turning around. He was deep in repairs, his shoulders hunched over disembodied panels and decapitated studs. He hadn't missed Erik, hadn't worried about the encroaching darkness.

"Yes, sir," Erik said, fighting to keep his breath and his voice steady. He walked over to the other seat and sat down, mechanically fastening the landing restraints.

He watched Marquette's hand moving confidently over the panels. The man seemed not to notice that one arm was immobilized. Or, if he noticed, he wasn't letting something as minor as a fracture interfere with his work. Erik wondered whether he should mention the...*thing*...to Marquette.

He decided not to. Not yet, anyway. After all, he hadn't actually *seen* anything. Maybe it was just a case of an overactive adrenal system (have to check that with the med-kit, he thought), or too little sleep, and certainly more stress than he was used to.

He closed his eyes just for a moment, settling back into the seat-module. He would rest for a while. Then he would see if he could help Marquette somehow. Maybe he would tell Marquette about it tomorrow. Marquette would know what to do.

He slept.

.

CHAPTER TWO

As things turned out, he didn't say anything to Marquette the next morning, either. He started to once, but didn't.

By the time he roused, Marquette was already busy at the console. For all Erik could tell, the man had worked through the night. What had been shapeless snarls of wire had taken on a semblance of organization, with leads laid in groups across twisted, smoke-stained surfaces.

In fact, Erik realized, the small sounds of Marquette working had awakened him—like a mouse scratching in the wall would wake a worried mother immediately, or the crinkling of a candy wrapper halfway across the house might rouse a boy from his dreams.

He had almost smiled in his sleep, yawned, and tried to stretch, then felt his flight harness cutting into his shoulders.

"Strange," he started to say, his voice little more than an audible murmur, then stopped when his memory-gears clicked in.

The crash.

He glanced over to the other module. The day before, he had braced it upright with a length of alloy pipe he had found hanging across part of the corridor. It was unsteady but had held up so far. Marquette, engrossed in his work, seemed not to have heard Erik's voice.

Maybe he hadn't, Erik thought, not sure whether to be grateful or not. At least he hadn't made a fool of himself by waking up and thrashing around before he remembered why he was sleeping in restraints. Marquette wouldn't have done that, he was certain. He watched the man work. Even with one arm immobilized, the man was deft and graceful. His good hand flickered like lightning across the damaged board, his long, tapered fingers splicing, tying.

"Good morning, sir," Erik said finally.

"Uh-huh," Marquette mumbled as he stretched his good arm across the console, his spine visible beneath his tunic as he arced away from the padded back of his seat.

Erik unbuckled the restraints and stood, stretching the way he liked, noting as always that his fingers just missed touching the ceiling. Marquette could easily press his palms flat against the cold metal.

"How is it going, sir?" Erik asked, working to loosen knots in his aching back and stiff neck.

"Okay," Marquette said. He was obviously not in a communicative mood.

"Sir," Erik began, "last night I...." That was as far as he got. What could he say? *Hey, Marquette, sir, last night I did this really dumb thing, see. I wandered away from the ship and forgot to take any bearings. And then it got dark, you know, really dark. And I got scared and heard this whispering sound and it got really scary and I ran back to the ship and almost fell down. Do you think there's a dangerous animal out there?*

Put that way, it sounded pretty foolish. And he hadn't seen any evidence of another living thing out there besides himself. He'd better wait.

Marquette either hadn't heard his false start or was so involved in intricate repairs that he choose not to answer.

Erik hung around, watching over the back of Marquette's seat, occasionally reaching for a tool or pulling on a wire, whatever Marquette requested.

Finally, though, he tired of inaction. "Sir, may I go outside for a bit."

"Uh-huh."

Outside, the light seemed blinding after the dimness of the control room, but wonderfully blinding, as if his eyes, designed to accommodate to multiple intensities of light and shadow, had punched through to an entirely new level of perception. Everything—the individual leaves on the trees, the single blades of grass, even the few wispy clouds scattered across the deep sky—seemed crisp, outlined with vibrant, almost *living* color.

And the air!

Erik breathed deep draughts, catching whiffs of tangy smells that reminded him of Earth, years before, when he had been allowed a brief visit to one of the reserves, along with his squadron of Adjuncts. But here, on this world, no one had to queue up for permission to breathe such wonders. You just walked outside and the reserves met you at your doorstep.

He wandered around the clearing for a few minutes, noting in the clear light a few small (and, to him at least, totally unidentifiable) tracks in the soft soil at the edge of the forest. The wildlife returning, he figured, checking out the strange, hard, glittering invader squatting silently and coldly in the middle of their territory. The tracks were probably made by something like ground squirrels or field mice, whatever the seeding ship had carried as cryogenically preserved ova...or perhaps remnants of life forms that the planet had originally evolved.

Erik felt a sudden chill as the subtle sounds of the night before re-played through his memory. Whatever made that noise, it was bigger than a ground squirrel or a field mouse. For a second he almost back went inside the scouter and told Marquette about the sounds. But finally, he didn't.

Instead, he ran. He jogged around the clearing, clambered over the gnarled fingers of rock that had disemboweled the ship, slipped down the other side, and resumed running along the fringes of forest, keeping just outside the shadows in the early morning sunlight, reveling in the freshness and the warmth on his skin. He ran the circuit until he saw black spots and his sides ached and the blood pounded in his temples, then he walked three more rounds, cooling down, then did half-a-dozen bends and straightened, shaking his head to clear his vision.

He went inside to rummage in the supply cabinet for breakfast.

He thought about taking the food packets outside and building a fire—*you know, really roughing it*—then decided against that. Instead, he pressed the heating tabs. By the time he carried the packets to Marquette's console, breakfast was hot and ready.

Probably because of his run, Erik savored the taste of the synthetics this morning. Marquette, he noted, merely picked at his meal, paying more attention to the console than to his food. Erik finished quickly, slightly amused at Marquette's diffidence. It was probably a result of sitting passively in here, breathing this stale, burnt air, not getting any exercise, Erik thought, then remembered Marquette's arm and ankle. The man had managed to work for hours now on delicate, heavily damaged circuitry, with only one mobile hand.

"Sir," Erik said, his voice subdued. "Can I do anything to help?"

Marquette leaned back in his seat, his face visibly pinched and tired.

"Nope. Just finished. At least, it's as near finished as I can make it." He ate a forkful of food, chewing slowly and thoughtfully, his mind far from noting the texture or quality of the fuel he had just consumed. "I've pulled up about quarter power, not enough to lift off, of course, but it will give heat and light for quite a while. I can't make much else work. I'll have to use the secondary homing beacon to send our distress signal; the one here is totally burned out. Otherwise," he turned abruptly and—most unaccountably, Erik thought, considering their situation—grinned, "we're in rotten shape."

Erik laughed, taking Marquette's grin and subsequent laughter as tacit permission to join in.

After they finished eating, they moved outside, neither of them quite ready yet to tackle the job of pulling wreckage from the aft compartments. Marquette limped slightly, but his ankle obviously must have felt better. He seemed to enjoy the scenery, but less enthusiastically than Erik. Maybe being a Spacer for so long, he had lost his sense of....

"What's that?" Marquette asked, breaking the silence.

"What, sir?"

"There, beyond that stand of trees."

Erik stared through the pattern of shadow and sunlight, trying to spot whatever had caught Marquette's attention. The man was famous for his keen eyesight. Erik, on the other hand, either through design or through a minor flaw in his construct, was just shy of having to wear correctives. His eyes were good enough for active Ex-Serv duty but had suffered the occupational hazards of unrelenting scholarship.

"I can't see anything, sir," Erik finally admitted. "Just trees."

Marquette grinned without looking at Erik. "That way you miss the forests, don't you, Junk?" he said, using the intentionally insulting Spacer term with something oddly like affection. "Come on."

But Erik *had* seen the right thing, it turned out—nothing. Beyond the clearing that was now their unofficial home, maybe half a kilometer into the forest, a second clearing yawned in the dense growth.

The only problem was that there shouldn't have been one there.

"I didn't notice much yesterday," Marquette said, rubbing at the cast that immobilized his arm, "but I don't remember seeing that at all."

Erik nodded, checking the ground as they threaded through the underbrush toward the second clearing. It was roughly half the size of the one where the ship lay—obviously smaller but still too large not to have been noticed earlier.

What was worse, Erik realized, it cut directly across the trail he had followed the night before.

He pulled ahead of Marquette, running to the center of the clearing, then turning to stare at the Spacer as he pushed aside several of the low-lying bushes. Beyond Marquette, the ship gleamed harshly in the morning light—at precisely the same angle Erik had noted last night.

But now, the ground was violently torn up, ripped open as if it had been plowed. The trees standing on the border of the clearing seemed to lean inward, toward the forest itself. Erik knelt by one—a birch-like sapling maybe two centimeters in diameter, trailing his fingers down the roughened bark, noting where something had cut into tender wood. The roots has been pulled loose on the clearing side, as if someone—or some-*thing*—had tried to uproot the tree and very nearly succeeded.

He straightened, brushing dust and pulverized fibers from his hands.

"Well," Marquette said.

Without speaking, Erik retraced his steps to the center of the clearing, reconstructing what he had seen the night before.

He was sure that this was where he had stopped, where he had turned and looked for the ship, feeling again that moment of panic when he could see nothing. He glanced to his right, to his left, getting his bearings, then closed his eyes. In the darkness, he re-created the scene, vague banks of darkness here and here and here, trees and underbrush too distant to be more than shapeless shadows. The glimmer of the ship there, through that almost invisible cleft in the foliage.

And off to the left, just a pace or two out of line-of-sight with the ship, the huge oak bole that....

His eyes flew open. The bole was gone. It had stood just inside what was now an empty, open space. He ran to the spot. There was nothing. No remnant branches or twigs, no leaves, not even a depression in the ground where massive roots would have to have descended toward bedrock. He dropped to his knees, digging in the loamy surface soil. He felt nothing but earth—no jagged tips of roots where the trunk had been ripped away. Nothing.

Either something had destroyed it completely, or....

"Sir, let's get out of here," Erik said. Without looking back, he headed for the ship, barely aware of the noise Marquette made in passing through the growth. He didn't stop until he was standing in scouter's shadow. He waited, staring at the smooth metallic skin of the ship, until Marquette laid a hand on his shoulder. Erik jumped.

"What's wrong?"

"Nothing, sir. That is—I don't know. Last night there was this tree, a huge thing. I heard a funny whispering and it spooked me and I started back toward the ship. I passed by the tree and it seemed to... reach for me. Sir."

He waited for Marquette's derisive laughter, but none came. When he looked at the man, he saw only concern.

"Did you hear anything else last night?" Marquette asked finally.

"You mean after I came back to the ship, sir? No, sir, nothing."

Marquette shrugged. "Whatever did that had to have made a lot of noise in the process. I was up most of the night and didn't hear anything either. But then these things are pretty well insulated." He slapped the side of the ship. Erik felt a proprietary warmth as the sound rang through their clearing and echoed back at them.

"Still," Marquette continued, "we'd better keep a close watch from now on. I wouldn't want to tangle with anything that could do that in only a few hours."

He started inside the ship, then turned and looked directly into Erik's eyes.

"No more wandering off alone, Junk. And from now on, where we go, we go armed."

CHAPTER THREE

The rest of the day was hard. After half an hour of further wrestling with the disaster inside, any worries about possibly lurking alien creatures sank deep beneath a second skin of sweat. Since Marquette was still favoring his ankle and couldn't use one arm, Erik ended up handling most of the heavy work.

Between breakfast and lunch—or what passed for lunch, since neither of them were willing to halt long enough for any formal preparations—Erik, with Marquette's occasional help, had managed to clear only a few meters of the worst wreckage, manhandling with difficulty twisted bulkheads and fragmented sheathing that a larger man, or a stronger, or more dexterous one, might have moved with half the effort.

The expenditure of effort was worth it, though, because shortly after lunch, Erik managed to clear one of two critical entryways—the one to the aft computer terminal. He had no more than wedged the heavy door inward when Marquette wordlessly slipped past him and settled himself at the console, ready for a long siege of repair work, if necessary, in order to activate the emergency rescue beacon.

Erik shrugged, and then continued pushing and prodding and grunting and sweating, hoping to clear the entry to their quarters before nightfall. Another night in that command chair up front, he thought, and he would be finished. Just thinking about it made his back stiffen and twinge.

So he worked doggedly, not stopping for an afternoon meal, carrying load after load of warped and mangled metal and plastic outside and stacking debris as neatly as he could beneath the curve of the ship, not questioning his own impulse to tidiness. As he passed the computer, he could hear Marquette at work—tools clattering, current crackling, Marquette occasionally cursing as he wrestled with the monitor or keyboard. The one sound that Erik constantly hoped to hear—Marquette's voice speaking over the communicator or, failing that, the steady buzz of the tracking beacon—never materialized.

It was almost nightfall before Erik told himself he had done enough and allowed himself to quit. The cabins were now accessible, although it was still an uncomfortably tight squeeze into his. That was all right, though—for once his slight build was an advantage rather than otherwise. He made one last trip through the ship, picking up lingering bits of detritus, wondering how much labor would be necessary to put the craft into working order—or if it were permanently grounded. Perhaps it would lie like this for...well, for years, centuries even, until soil and small stones washed up along its sides, spilled over the top, created new beds for generations of grasses, then brush, finally perhaps even oaks—and the clearing would be dominated by a new hill, more rounded than most, smooth of side and oddly symmetrical.

He laughed at his own idiotically romantic imaginings. Long before that could happen, of course, the rescue team would arrive. If nothing else, the team could salvage most of the ship's interior, maybe even the hull itself. Then all that would be left of Marquette's and his brief, unanticipated stay would be a ragged pit just beyond one of the shattered granite spines. Nothing more.

This time he shrugged, then threaded his way through the narrow opening into his cabin. There was power, he noted as he threw himself on his bed, heedless of the disarray within the room. The light glowed more dimly than usual, and the floor canted noticeable, but otherwise everything seemed reasonably normal. The air was all right, fresh and bracing, finally free of the pervasive burnt-insulation smell he had almost grown used to. Either the environmental controls were functional and recirculating the air, or it was being replenished through the open hatchway....

He leaped up and squeezed into the passageway, not noticing as he ripped the leg of his service trousers on a sharp projection along the door jamb.

The hatchway!

It was still wide open, a spot of shadow circumscribed by the seeming-brightness of the ship's interior. Night had fallen, and he had nearly forgotten to close the hatch. What if...?

He checked over his shoulder. Marquette couldn't have seen. From here, the computer terminal was hidden. Anyway, Marquette hadn't budged for hours. He would probably stay at the job until....

As if tuned into Erik's thoughts, Marquette stuck his head around the corner, his face split into an almost puerile grin. Judging from the silly cast that grin lent to the Spacer's face, he had done something either very good or very bad.

"Sir," Erik began.

Marquette cut him off. "Pour the drinks, Junk, help'll be here soon! Everything's working back here. I'll be able to activate the beacon this evening, when the window for transmitting is best."

Erik thought briefly about grabbed Marquette's good arm, pounding the man on the shoulder, dancing around him in a wild swirl, and whooping with delight, but settled more rationally for a vigorous nod of his head and a face-splitting grin of his own.

"Hold it," Marquette said, suddenly serious. "How long do you think it will be? Before someone gets here"

"I don't know, sir." It surprised Erik that Marquette had even framed such a question, especially to him. "You're the Spacer, sir, not me. Perhaps a month? It didn't take us much more than that to get here, sir."

"Good guess, but wrong. You're forgetting one thing."

"What's that, sir?"

"Politics."

Erik stared at Marquette. "What?"

"Politics—you know, one-upmanship among those in power, that sort of thing. We've got a lot of new planets to survey, a lot of lost colonies to return to the Comity. After all these decades, you would think that one of them could wait a month or so more. But since we are okay, the ship damaged but available as shelter, and our supplies intact, we'll probably get second priority. Hemmings' ship is the nearest; it would take him almost a month just to finish up what he's doing, then he could start preparations to come out and pick us up. It could be even longer, depending. Until something happens, Junk, we wait. Paid vacation, if a bit rough."

"But, sir, what if—"

"'What if' doesn't count in this case, Junk. Right now our situation is stable. If things change, we get on the beacon again and report. In an emergency—a *real* emergency, life or death—Hemmings could be here within two weeks. But then, if the emergency were that threatening, it wouldn't matter much to either of us whether the rescue team got here in two weeks or two months or two years, would it? So for the time being, we wait. And we enjoy some peace and quiet."

Erik walked over to the command console and sank into his chair. Marquette followed. Erik noted that the man's limp was hardly noticeable now. He sat for a while, staring at his console, occasionally fingering a knob or an unlit panel. Then he smiled. "You know, sir, this may work out well for us, anyway."

"How?" Marquette asked.

"We're here, sir, planet-side, on the spot, before originally scheduled. Computer analysis of the settlement isn't complete yet. Neither is the linguistic scan. We had only just activated the Ear when...when whatever went wrong did. But I have enough preliminary data to know how to approach the first settlement. The first indication of linguistic change places this settlement at a stage roughly paralleling...."

"No you don't, Junk," Marquette interrupted. "None of that linguistic crap. I'm still not convinced that Halvorson's ideas hold much water. I've commanded four resettlement missions without worrying about noun conjugations or verb declensions...."

"It's the other way around, sir, noun declen—"

"Whatever." Marquette dismissed Erik's interruption with a wave of his hand. "I *know* that the old-fashioned scans work—percentages of high-technology metals in surviving structures, land-use patterns, things like that. Listening into conversations from up there and deciding from their grammatical quirks whether the natives will greet us with open arms or closed fists, well, that I'm just not so sure about."

"But University Control said that I was to—"

"Yeah, after *all* Halvorson's tests were run. Not before. And certainly not with only a few hours of raw data to play with. Nope, Junk. We stay here. No contact until Hemmings or someone else arrives. Then we work through his computer."

"But, sir—"

"But nothing, Junk" Marquette said, swinging up to his full sitting-height and looking down at Erik. "But nothing. I command here. There may be only two of us, but I—"

The chair jerked and almost twisted out from under him. The cabin lights flickered, died. The crimson emergency system cut in. A second later it faded, and the main power came up again. Marquette scanned his console, punching a button or two, checking for malfunctions.

"Power still okay," he said in a single, quick breath.

"What was that, sir?" Erik said.

"No idea. The ship could be shifting. Settling."

"Didn't feel like settling to me. Sir," Erik added the last word only a moment later than would have been natural.

"Nor to me," Marquette admitted. His hands flew over the console, and a screen just above his head lit up. For a moment it glowed green, then settled into a complex pattern of light and dark. Marquette reached up and adjusted it. The pattern cleared, showing an external view of the ship, from the hull back along the fractured spine to the tail.

"What's that, sir?"

"Huh," Marquette grunted, his concentration riveted on the screen.

"That projection, sir, like a radar dish. I didn't see it today."

"Beacon screen. Extruded when operational, designed for vacuum, but works okay planet-side." Marquette spoke absently as he began to scan the area around the ship.

Erik watched, silent and helpless. This was Marquette's specialty—this was his ship and he knew it throughout. If there was anything out there....

"There!" Erik said suddenly, the words out before he knew he intended to speak.

"What?"

"A...like a shadow. Left, left, sir!"

Marquette swiveled the scanner. The picture on the screen shifted back from the clearing to the hull of the ship. When the emergency beacon screen was centered, Erik yelled, "Stop! There."

Marquette stared. "What *is* that?"

"I don't know, sir. It's...it's like a moving shadow. Is it possible to get a clearer image?"

Marquette tried, jiggling this switch, turning that knob. "No. No good. Not enough light. Our infrared is out, so it can only pick up what light is there. Maybe if I enhance it...."

As he reached toward the console, the shadow on the screen moved. It flowed up and across the dim gleam that was the ship, a wash of blackness without shape or feature. Marquette's hand slapped the console, depressing a single stud. Somewhere, a wild whine arced through the sky.

Then the shadow drew back as quickly as it had appeared, disappearing into the surrounding night.

But the beacon screen was gone.

The hull was smooth, as virginally smooth as if nothing had ever been there at all. Somewhere in the back of Erik's mind, he registered the unnerving datum that the thin, shrill sound had suddenly stopped.

Marquette sat bolt upright, staring at the screen as if his eyes could change the images it showed.

"That's impossible. That installation was designed to withstand...." He was silent for a moment, then continued. "Well, that's it, Junk. Regardless of what happens, we're stuck here now. At least until Hemmings can get here...*if* he gets the message. It was only a short burst. And somehow, even if he does get it, I don't think he will be setting out tomorrow."

He sat, head tilted back, staring at the unmoving images on the screen.

"What the hell was that?" Erik finally said. "Sir."

"Don't know. Reports on this place don't cover any shadows with the strength to twist duralloy fittings right off at their base. In fact, our reports don't indicate any large animal life at all, other than what the seed ships brought.

"Damn it, this was supposed to be an easy trip," Marquette continued, his voice dropping so that he sounded more as if he were talking to himself than sharing in a conversation. "Just test out that idiotic idea, give a surface-rat Junk a taste of ExServ life, then...."

He stopped, his face actually reddening slightly, a phenomenon normally unheard of in Spacer-Adjunct relationships. "Hey, I'm sorry. I didn't mean it like that. It's just that we—the Spacers, I mean—the Exploration Service, we've been working these worlds for years now, with a pretty good success rate. And now University Central steps in and tells us that they've had this wonderful new brainstorm that will make us obsolete except as orbit-jockeys. Just high-class Junks ourselves." He caught himself again. "Sorry again. Nothing personal, you know. You're a pretty good guy in a pinch, for a...."

He turned toward the screen again, watching intently. Erik tried to answer. Nothing he could think of would work, nothing would sound other than like a whining acceptance or an equally whining denial. He knew—everyone at University Central knew—how resistant the ExServ was to change. But he had hoped that his weeks with Marquette had changed at least one Spacer's mind.

Finally he shrugged and shook his head. He couldn't tell if Marquette had seen the slight movement or not.

They sat in mutual—and mutually uncomfortable—silence for nearly half an hour before Marquette said quietly, "Looks like it's gone for good, whatever it was."

He looked over at Erik. "Go on, hit the sack. You've done a yeoman's job today clearing things out. I'll sleep here. If our friend comes back, maybe I can think of some way to discourage any more return visits."

"If you don't mind, sir, I'd rather...," Erik began.

"Come on," Marquette said, his voice soft and conciliatory. "It's the least I can do after what I said. Anyway," he continued, rubbing at the cast on his arm, "this is so uncomfortable that I doubt I'll sleep much anyway tonight. I'll call if anything happens. Promise."

All that seemed left for Erik was grace under pressure: "Yes, sir. But sleep if you can."

"Okay. Anyway, there's not much chance anything will happen tonight. I'll probably be bored out of my mind."

"Yes, sir," Erik answered as he rose and walked toward his cabin. "Bored and nothing to do."

Just after he fell asleep, however, grateful for the familiar contours of his bed, he discovered how wrong they both had been.

CHAPTER FOUR

This time, Erik actually and acutely *felt* the crash—only it wasn't a crash, he told himself groggily as he stumbled from the litter-strewn floor toward the passageway. It couldn't be a crash. They were on the ground. The ship had already crashed.

Another bone-shaking jolt threw him through the doorway and slammed him against the opposite bulkhead. At the last moment, he twisted, taking his weight against his shoulder and upper back. The pain woke him fully.

"Sir!"

"Here!"

Marquette's voice rippled from the control center, urgent, commanding—overlaid with an almost tangible tension.

Erik hurried forward, stumbling over heaps of supplies from the now re-sprung doors of the medical cabinet. All of his work, hours of back-breaking work yesterday, all for nothing. The place was a shambles again. Maybe even worse than before.

He lunged into his seat just as the ship jolted violently again—left, right, then an unaccountable quivering along its spine.

"What is it, sir?" he asked, slapping his harness across his waist.

"Our dark friend's back," Marquette said. Erik glanced at him. He was pale, even in the sickly light of the control center, pale beyond lingering pain from his arm or his ankle. Sweat beaded along his temples and upper lip, and his good hand trembled as it rummaged across the board in front of him. Erik had never seen him like this, not even during the most difficult moments of duo-training and actual flight.

Blood oozed wetly from a wicked slice along Marquette's scalp.

"You okay, sir?"

"Shut up. We've got work to do." Marquette began firing instructions at Erik. For a frantic moment, Erik thought he had forgotten everything he had ever known about the ship's controls. He sat, staring at his hands, at the console, as if they were both unintelligible alien growths.

"Move it, Junk!" Marquette rasped. Erik jumped, his hands flying to his Jack and manipulating the plug, then hovering over panels of dials and studs, mutely (and almost unconsciously) following Marquette's directions.

Above his head, a screen sizzled with static. Erik glanced up. Marquette noted the movement. "It's taken the scanners completely. Nothing shows from outside."

"Why didn't you call me sooner, sir?"

"No need. And no time. It just came. I was here, luckily, working through some circuits. Hasn't been more than two, three minutes."

"What are you doing now?" Erik asked.

"Trying to divert current from emergency life-support to hull. Maybe shock the creature. Scare it. Kill it."

The plan, fragmented as it was, might have worked. It *should* have worked. It did in all the vids he had viewed during training, Erik thought, just as a another jolt from outside tipped the hull at least ninety degrees to his left, then flipped it back, through, and well beyond its original position.

Like a planet-rover driver trying to work a wheel loose from mud, he thought, an instant before his seat ripped completely loose, spun once in the air, and crashed against the bulkhead.

* * * * * *

This time, waking brought neither darkness nor silence. An unusual and somehow threatening gray light filtered into the control center from somewhere, and behind the throbbing and pounding in Erik's own head, he heard muffled moans. His left hand slapped to his neck. His Jack was still in place but nothing was coming through. He set and re-set it, but still nothing. Finally he removed it and let it drop to the floor.

He tried to sit up, discovered that his chair had canted against what was once the wall, pinning him down.

He worked his right arm free, flexed a cramp out of it, then fumbled with the belt release. It gave way, and he slammed against the metal of the wall. Stunned, he sat still for a moment, then pushed with his shoulder and arm.

The seat was heavy, but gave way. In a moment he was free.

The ship tilted at a wild angle, tilted halfway out of square. Marquette's seat, hastily jury-rigged the day before, had, like Erik's, sheered completely off its moorings. Even in the dim light Erik could see Marquette's leg bent, twisted beneath wickedly sharp wreckage, blood staining the man's uniform.

But Marquette was alive. The moaning Erik had been hearing verified that.

He crouched over the confused mass of metal and plastic and flesh, tugging at the heavy command chair. It wouldn't budge.

"Marquette, sir," he whispered, his voice echoing hollowly, "can you hear me?"

There was no answer, beyond the uninterrupted moaning. Erik twisted around the bulk of the chair and into the passageway, rummaging through the medical supplies, grabbing whatever looked like it might be useful, scraps of first-aid training films and procedural tapes and Jacked-in exercises re-playing in his brain.

No help there this time, he thought frantically. No more Jack for a long, long time.

He set the supplies on the floor, crouched beneath the edge of the seat, and pushed upward with his shoulder. The module rose slightly, then stuck. Marquette was too heavy for Erik to lift completely—and moving him like this might prove fatal.

He grabbed a med-kit from the floor, upended it, and searched through its contents until he saw the gleam of a scalpel.

He palmed it even as he began working himself around the far side of the chair, insinuating himself between Marquette's body and the bulkhead.

It was totally dark there. He could feel the warmth from Marquette's body—an uncomfortable, fervid warmth that reminded him forcibly that this was the closest he had ever come to his team-mate without permission. He reached, the scalpel blade nested in his hand as he inched it over the contours of Marquette's twisted body. He felt the slick smoothness of uniform, the warm, damp stickiness of what must be blood—too much blood.

And then the coarse webbing of Marquette's restraint harness. His fingers followed it down an inch or two, tucked around it, making sure there was a bit of space beneath. Then he began cutting.

The harness was designed for impact security. It didn't cut easily. All the time, Marquette moaned mindlessly, unaware of what was happening, barely holding on to a remnant of consciousness. Erik's hand grew slippery as he strained, twisting his own arm unnaturally to get the blade into position, his legs and shoulders and back first aching, then cramping and freezing as unendurable minutes passed. He shut his eyes, shut his ears to the incessant moaning, concentrated all of his being into his fingertips, into the tiny muscles sawing with the scalpel at the belt, fraying it strand by strand.

It snapped.

Marquette's body dropped. Its dead weight pressed against Erik, grinding him into the bulkhead. He felt Marquette shift slightly, a small movement, but enough to indicate some volition—and perhaps not too many new injuries.

He wormed his way out, sheathing the scalpel in his palm again and pulling his hand back across the unknown territory of Marquette's chest. When he could stand, he pushed on the chair again.

This time, it gave completely, falling back over the rubble of the console, freeing Marquette.

"Can you get up, sir?" Erik whispered urgently, kneeling over the man.

Marquette lay where he had slumped when the chair gave way. He did not move. Something about the laxness of his shoulders, the way his head lay propped against one arm, eyes staring blackly into nothingness, frightened Erik.

"Marquette. Sir! Come on. We've got to get out of here!"

Nothing.

He knelt closer, feeling along Marquette's exposed arm. No indication of any breaks. He lifted the arm, slipping his head and shoulder beneath it and pulling upward. If there was any injury to Marquette's back, this could do it for him—but there was no alternative. It was absurdly useless to wait for an ambulance here.

Marquette groaned, then seemed to understand what Erik wanted. Erik heard one foot shuffle through the debris, then Marquette's body heaved upward, as much through the man's efforts as through Erik's. Together, they struggled back to the hatchway. Erik noted how heavily Marquette leaned against him—the leg was possibly fractured, at the least terribly sprained.

"Here," Marquette croaked before they were halfway from the seat to the hatchway, now almost waist-high on Marquette, and even closer to Erik's shoulders.

"Okay," Erik agreed, helping the man lower himself against curve of the bulkhead-floor.

"Broken?" Marquette hissed through clenched teeth.

"I'll check, sir."

Erik ran his hand down Marquette's leg, desperately trying to remember more than a scrap of first aid training, wishing he could simply Jack-in, wishing he had reviewed the manual when they first understood how serious their situation could be, wishing that none of this had ever happened. If only he had spent that night studying, preparing for unexpected but perhaps inevitable complications, instead of uselessly sleeping while Marquette worked at the console.

But wishing didn't help.

Right now, he had a real, flesh-and-blood emergency, and no amount of wishing would make the hideously deforming swelling in Marquette's leg disappear. Erik still didn't know for sure if bones were broken, but decided to treat the injury as if they were.

For the second frustrating time, he rummaged through medical supplies thrown into a jumble in the middle of the passageway, returning with the plasticast foam and another scalpel.

"Hold on a little, sir," he said. Marquette nodded mutely, his eyes again little more than blank openings into pain and darkness.

Erik slit the seam of Marquette's pants from knee to cuff, then pulled the material away. Now that he could see the leg, he was even less sure of a diagnosis. The surface was badly swollen, to be sure, and heavily bruised, already darkening along the shin, the skin shiny, white, and taut. He began spraying the foam, circling the leg carefully, noting peripherally the tension leaving Marquette's muscles as the anesthetic took effect.

Within moments, the job was complete. He made Marquette as comfortable as possible, scrounging some clothing to serve as a makeshift pillow.

"Rest, okay, sir," he said. The anesthetic would probably make Marquette dopey—covering that much body tissue directly should. If it didn't, the shock-reaction might. At any rate, he was probably better off asleep for a while. Marquette's shoulders tensed as if he were about to try to stand, then slumped. His eyes closed. After a moment, his ragged breathing began to even out.

Erik waited a few more minutes. Then began exploring.

First, he had to find out about the *light*.

All of the internal systems seemed blown. Nothing worked, not even the battery-operated telltales in the passageways and cabins. The familiar glow of emergency by-pass systems on the console had long since died. In truth, it should have been pitch black inside the scouter.

But it wasn't.

From somewhere, a gray, dusky light filtered through the wreckage. Erik worked his way into the passageway, beyond the openings to the computer terminal (he noted in passing that no one, not even Marquette, would be using that terminal for quite a while). Just aft of their cabins, he found the source of the odd light.

The ship had split like an over-ripe melon at the first incision of a knife. The hull had apparently already been torqued to an inordinate tension by the crash, and when the...the *thing*...managed to break it in one crucial place, the metal had apparently sheered in a jagged line from midpoint back, as far as Erik could see.

Unless the metal had been intentionally *ripped* open.

The way the scouter was angled, the rip lay more along the side than the top. Either that, or oncoming daylight had deterred the creature. Otherwise it would have continued its work, opening the fissure, insinuating itself inside, destroying and devouring....

Erik shivered. *Enough,* he cautioned himself. *Don't borrow more trouble. You've got enough already.*

He returned to Marquette. Even in the poor light, the man seemed deathly pale, his eyes, though partially closed, still seemed mere slits of darkness against chalk-washed cheeks.

There was nothing more he could do in here, Erik realized. First priority had to be getting Marquette and himself out of the scouter, suddenly transformed from refuge into something like a prison. If they were still inside when (*not* "if," Erik realized; the creature would surely come back)—*when* the creature returned, it could finish its job on the hull and pick them out like so many peas in a pod. The simile struck him as both ludicrous and appallingly accurate. He pushed down the impulse to laugh, afraid that to begin would lead to hysteria, ending any chance he had of acting rationally and effectively.

He wished again for a Jack and almost turned to try the console once more.

Instead, he concentrated on the hatchway. Already damaged in the initial crash, it might fail entirely. Then his only option would be to cut his way through the rip in the hull, a long and difficult job at best, especially if he could find no power source for the cutters and other tools on board, almost all of which relied upon ship's power or auxiliaries.

"Well, here goes," he said, pressing his thumb against the hatch's control panel. He almost screwed his eyes shut, but decided that was childishly inappropriate. Not looking wouldn't make things work differently, just as sitting back and wishing wouldn't make the Jack work, wouldn't make Marquette's leg heal, or wouldn't get them off this planet and safely back to ExServ Central.

The hatchway worked.

Incredulous, Erik watched it slide upward, curving over his head and flooding the dim compartment with brilliant light. He heard the muted hum of its battery-run safety release; then the hum ceased. Shielding his eyes with his hand, he stared out of the opening. Morning, probably, at least that was what the quality of light suggested. He stared intently.

No dark shape blotted out the sun. Whatever that thing was, it might be light-sensitive, and most likely was nocturnal. That meant they had at least several hours to find shelter—as far from the scouter as possible.

He hitched himself up and worked his way over the edge of the hatchway, trying not to think about having to pull Marquette out later, not without doing even more damage to the Spacer's much-abused body. But, Erik decided, they would manage somehow, that was certain. Given the alternatives, they *would* manage. But the maneuver might be neither easy nor comfortable.

Outside, the air was still, as if even in bright sunlight any wildlife close by remained frightened by the creature's night-time rampage. The air surrounding the scouter shimmered with dust as Erik dropped to the ground. He walked along the length of the scouter, part of his mind assuring him that the danger was long past and would not return until dark. Another part, however, gave his eyes and ears continual instructions to watch and listen, to concentrate on the distant shadows crouching deep within the thickets of trees.

As he walked, he stumbled over the oddly uneven ground, not understanding fully what was happening until he stopped to draw a deep, cleansing breath.

He looked at the ground more objectively, more analytically.

What he had unconsciously dismissed as merely rough spots in the meadow had to be in fact the creature's trace, gigantic gouts of earth thrown up as if by bombs, no so much distinct, discriminate shapes as ragged wounds scraped into the living earth itself. They ringed the ship, crossing each other and re-crossing until the meadow was as scoured as the mysterious clearing he and Marquette had explored the day before. The thing had been there quite a while, Erik realized, probably moving under the cover of darkness, out of sight of the camera, considering its approach until it realized that it would have to begin by destroying the sensory projections ....

Erik stopped cold, physically and mentally, a shiver spiraling up his spine. He was assuming that the creature was rational, that it was capable of thought.

If that were true....

He turned and ran back to the hatchway, shouting Marquette's name. They had to get moving, fast. Otherwise, they were no better than walking dead men.

He reached the hatchway, grabbed the edge with his hands and threw one leg over into the ship. Just as he moved to slide into the cabin, he heard a harsh voice behind him.

"Halt!"

CHAPTER FIVE

He froze.

The words were a command, undeniable and definite.

A native.

Erik knew that without turning around. He had known, he realized with a sudden intake of breath, even before he heard that single word. He had felt a presence unidentifiable on a conscious level.

A native.

Somehow, in the stress of crisis, he had managed to forget that possibility. He turned slowly and stepped out, hands held away from his sides in what he hoped would prove a universal signal that he was not about to reach for hidden weapons. He stepped down to the ground, then moved a meter or so away from the ship.

The man stood half-hidden in the shadow of an oak near the edge of the clearing. He seemed huge, inordinately tall and equally heavily muscled . He wore crudely tanned animal hides and held a roughly fashioned spear ready to throw.

He moved into the sunlight and spoke again. As he did, Erik became aware that he had intuitively translated the first sounds into Standard as "halt." But the man opposite him was *not* speaking Standard. The sounds were familiar, though, and when the man repeated them, Erik found that he could make sense of them.

"Who are you?" the stranger demanded. "What do you here?"

Erik tried to respond. He couldn't fit the words into a linguistic context yet, although he could follow what the native was saying. His mind worked feverishly, sifting through the many permutations of pre-Standard languages he had committed to memory: which was *this*?

The stranger repeated the questions, punctuating them with an undoubtedly meaningful gesture—the spear now pointed directly at Erik's chest.

Erik tried to answer, using Standard. "We are visitors. My friend is hurt. Can you help us?"

The man did not respond. Instead, he moved closer, never losing the tense stance of a fighter. Erik had never seen such concentrated power, not even in a Spacer. The man was huge, but nowhere flabby. Erik could see the ripple of muscle beneath the shaggy outer wrappings. The man looked as if he could rip Erik in two—make that *two* Eriks into *four*—without even breathing hard.

And right now, it seemed as if he intended to. Erik stood motionless. Marquette was apparently still unconscious; there were no sounds from inside the ship.

The native approached the scouter. Now he seemed cautious, wary.

He motioned to Erik again. "Alone?"

Erik tried to respond in something resembling the other's distorted, antique semi-Standard.

"Yes..., uh..., no. One." He held up an index finger and pointed over his shoulder, wondered as he did so whether he should have decided to bluff the giant and say that there were several more inside. He rapidly decided that candor would be best. The stranger would discover soon enough that there were only two of them.

The other man approached closer, lowering the spear fractionally.

"Where is the other?"

"Hurt." The words came more easily now, nearly instinctively, since he still hadn't quite identified the underlying structures of what he was hearing.

"Bring him."

Erik shuddered as he turned his back on the native and struggled into the open hatchway. His shoulder blades twitched, as if expecting a spear thrust at any second.

The sudden darkness blinded him momentarily. He felt his way through the shambles, his eyes only gradually adjusting to the flush of light along the split hull. Marquette was still in the command center, stretched out by the wreckage.

Erik knelt beside the injured man, raised one of his arms, and tried to lever Marquette up. He couldn't. Weight and angle worked against him. Finally he resorted to pulling, trying to be careful of Marquette's injured arm and leg. Marquette groaned once, then fell silent.

Erik managed to get Marquette into the shaft of light at the hatchway, then turned to face the native.

The man had not moved. He stared for a moment at Erik and at Marquette's unmoving form. Then, with a sudden movement, he thrust the spear butt into the ground, apparently satisfied that he had nothing to fear from the odd duo he had discovered. He seemed not to notice the alien nature of the ship.

Instead he strode to the hatchway, shoving Erik out of the way with a single movement of his forearm. He reached in, cradled Marquette's shoulder, and with an apparent tenderness that momentarily stunned Erik, lifted Marquette out and laid him against the side of the ship. Without a word, the man backed to his spear and resumed watching.

For a few minutes he contented himself with simply looking around. At one point he approached where Erik was standing, reached out, and touched the light fabric of Erik's uniform. Something about it apparently amused him, since he grunted what might have been a guttural burst of laughter. He was far more impressed, however, by the thin metal webbing around Erik's waist—his flight belt, with the ExServ insignia engraved on the buckle.

Still the stranger did not speak, however. He began walking along the scouter, occasionally flicking a glance at the vessel, once or twice almost reaching out to touch it. Finally, however, he returned to his position near Erik and Marquette.

Behind him, Erik heard a small sound. Marquette was stirring. Erik knelt toward the Spacer, saw awareness flickering in the Spacer's pain-filled eyes, and hastily explained what was going on.

"A native," Marquette said, looking up and focusing with difficulty on the form standing nearby. "Evaluations?"

"None yet, sir. He's barely spoken so far, but I haven't seen or heard anything to contradict the original readout. His size is a surprise. Probably a local evolution—increased height and musculature might possibly be an advantage in a semi-barbarian society dependent upon physical strength and stamina for survival. This one may be abnormal, but somehow I don't think so. He carries himself erect, no slumping to hide his height." Erik realized that he was sounding like so many of the textbooks he had memorized but couldn't keep from shifting into professional mode. This was, after all, why he was here.

"There's no evidence of technology, though," he continued. "The spear tip may be metallic, but if so it is obviously hand-formed. Most likely the colony cannibalized their ship long ago, using whatever scrap metals they could break off the main structure. The spear tips and other metal remnants might be looked on as emblems of manhood or authority. They might carry religious significance, also. He was interested in my metal belt. He seemed awed by the mass of the ship.

"He's friendly enough, mildly curious, not particularly surprised to find us here. We'll have to play it as it lays, I'm afraid, sir."

Throughout this whispered monologue, the native remained immobile yet alert, concentrating on Erik and Marquette, his face an unreadable blank.

"Help me up," Marquette said, command filtering into his voice again.

Erik helped him rise hesitantly to his feet. The foam had solidified, allowing Marquette to move, albeit slowly and carefully, without jostling his leg. There was no overt evidence of a fracture, but Marquette's ankle was badly swollen again, and he favored it heavily. With Erik's help he managed to walk a few feet from the wreckage, toward the middle of the clearing. He looked around for something to use as a staff. When nothing presented itself, he straightened painfully, resting most of his weight on the uninjured leg. Erik moved away, just enough to leave Marquette standing alone, near enough to reach out if he needed help. Marquette did not notice Erik's maneuver, however, or chose to ignore it. Instead, he faced the stranger, who had watched their slow progress with an expression of mild interest.

"I am Marquette, Exploration Service. I am in command. As you see, we are forced to remain here. Our vessel is incapable of flight. I would appreciate any help you might give."

Marquette's command of historical dialects was feeble, the pronunciation slurred, and several words did not come through precisely as he had intended, but the native seemed satisfied. Erik could not tell whether the native understood anything or not; certainly Marquette had not been speaking in the man's native and apparently unique dialect, relying instead on the archaic Standard that had served so well on so many other worlds.

But the stranger nodded, strode toward them, looked them up and down, and motioned with a massive hand.

"Metal." He gestured toward the ExServ belts. "*Prattlinga* do not wear such things."

Erik looked at Marquette.

"What did he say?" Marquette whispered without taking his eyes from the native.

Erik translated, all but the odd word *prattlinga*. It sounded frustratingly familiar, but he still could not quite place it.

Slowly Marquette nodded and began awkwardly, one-handedly unfastening his buckle. Erik loosened his own belt, slipped it from his waist, and handed it to the native.

"Those." The man pointed to their collar insignia. Erik's quills,

Marquette's starbursts…within seconds, both disappeared with the belts beneath the ragged furs.

I was right. Erik thought, *metal is significant, if not sacred. We are outsiders; therefore we have no right to it.*

"Weapons?" the stranger demanded, more a command than a question.

Marquette swallowed before beginning to answer. "No, we've...."

To his own amazement, Erik heard himself interrupting. "Yes, that is, we have hand-weapons. Only for protection against...."

Now he broke off, aware simultaneously of Marquette's glare and the obvious evidence around them that whatever they might have had was woefully inadequate against their earlier visitor.

The native glared at Erik. "Get them."

Once again, Erik climbed through the hatchway, returning seconds later with two web holsters, each wrapped around a standard-issue weapon. He looked at the bundles. Neither had ever been at his waist; in spite of everything that had happened, it hadn't even occurred to him to arm himself. And Marquette had been too injured to think clearly.

What a mess he had made of things. And worse, he wasn't certain that even Jacked in he could have done much better.

The man did not study the weapons, as Erik had figured he surely would. Instead he thrust them into his clothing, presumably into a pocket or bag held around his waist. Erik wondered why the weapons should interest him so little, particularly if he were a hunter or a warrior. Surely something so obviously superior to that wooden spear would....

"Prattlinga, come." The command cut Erik's introspection short. The native was heading toward the edge of the forest.

Suddenly Erik realized that the light was wrong—he had assumed morning when in fact the sun was low in the opposite sky. The crush the night before had rendered them unconscious for longer than he had thought...now night was moving quickly on. And the fellow wanted them to follow into the forest, away from the safety of the ship.

Erik started to argue. After all, Marquette was hurt, perhaps seriously, and obviously incapable of traveling any distance without damaging strained ligaments in his ankle, re-breaking the fracture in his arm, or making worse whatever might have happened to his leg—or all three. But Marquette motioned for Erik to remain silent.

And Erik remembered—there was no safety in the ship, either.

"Is there an encampment, a village somewhere close?" Marquette stumbled over the words, then caught himself and continued more confidently. "I am hurt. I need help," he called toward the retreating figure.

As before, there was no indication that the native understood. He did not answer. He did not even respond to the sound of Marquette's voice. He had already started threading through the dark shadows of shrubs and brush. He did not look back. Marquette signaled for Erik to support him.

"Why the hell did you tell him about our weapons?" he whispered, although there was no chance that the barbarian would overhear them. "We could have come back, armed ourselves, stood up against...."

"Against *this*," Eric said, gesturing toward the torn-up ground. "A flyswatter against a sonic bomb. Anyway, it just seemed...oh, I don't know. It seemed important to tell the truth. Sir."

Marquette grunted and leaned against Erik's shoulder. The man was far too heavy for Erik to help much. All he could do was act as crutch until they could find a better substitute. For the moment, he struggled along, trying to help as much as possible but aware that his movements constantly threw Marquette off stride, forcing the injured man's weight onto his ankle or jerking his arm involuntarily. Erik was simply too short. The inches he lacked were precisely the ones he needed to help the Spacer effectively.

Together they struggled out of the clearing and into the green-black coolness of the forest. Erik was too concerned with Marquette's injuries to notice the surrounding trees and shrubs, beyond superficial glances now and then. He was briefly impressed again by the similarities between this forest, an isolated patch of greenery on a planet far removed in time and space from Earth, and the reserve forests back home.

But most of the time he saw nothing. He was growing warmer, in spite of the shade and the lateness of the day, sweating with the effort of supporting Marquette. The few patches of meadow they struggled through seemed unbearably hot. Marquette suffered even more, although he remained silent. They tacitly agreed to waste no energy talking, not even whispering. Their guide was setting a demanding pace, even for a two-meter-plus athlete, healthy and uninjured. Alone, Erik might have had difficulty keeping up with the man. Now, it was impossible. Gradually, they fell behind, until their guide became only a dim shadow among darker shadows.

CHAPTER SIX

Marquette obviously felt the strain more with each step. His face lost its normal coloring, draining to a pasty white around his eyes. His breath sounded ragged through lips waxy and compressed in pain. A few minutes more staggering through the thick brush, and his determined silence was broken by moans and sharp intakes of breath as his injured foot struck unevenly on the ground.

We can't keep going at this pace, Erik thought. *Much more of it and Marquette's body will be beyond what little medical help I can give.*

He was ready to call out to their captor, to plead, beg for a break. He swallowed several times, wetting his dry throat, hoping to catch enough breath to make himself heard. He squinted through the dusky shadows, focusing his whole attention on the patch of moving darkness ahead.

Suddenly, his plea became unnecessary, even before it was breathed.

Something crashed in the distance, a thunderous crash as of a huge creature careening through trees and shrubs, shattering ancient boles and uprooting gnarled trunks. Erik threw a wild glance over his shoulder.

"Come on, sir," he whispered urgently to Marquette. "We've got to get out of here."

Marquette seemed oblivious to the sounds. He struggled against Erik's demands, his eyes glazed and his breath even sharper. Caught in the web of pain, he was unaware of any danger.

Erik didn't know precisely the source of the sounds drawing nearer behind them, but apparently the native did. As if a wraith, he melted into the darkness, becoming part of the mists and shadows, disappearing into the gray-green depths. Erik started to call out, but bit his lip before any sounds forced their way out. Except for the thrashing behind them—closer now—the forest was silent. Erik instinctively recognized the silence of fear and hesitated to break it—

not only because any shouts from him would undoubtedly bring the creature down on them more quickly (as if it were not already stalking them), but also because he felt an imperative need for silence.

He pulled Marquette, wrapping his arm around him and dragging him forward. For the first time since leaving the scouter, Erik did not listen to Marquette's moans.

"Hurry," he whispered in a voice made harsh by fear and urgency. Their captor had disappeared; for all Erik knew they were alone in an alien forest, unarmed and injured, exhausted, and in mortal danger from an unknown beast or beasts indigenous to an unknown world and hence unimaginable to them. He remembered the shadow he and Marquette had seen on the screen the night before, the way it had flowed over their scouter, splitting its solid-metal hull. Remembering quickly re-kindled the fires of fear. He propelled Marquette toward a thinning in the line of trees to their left.

They had been paralleling a river bed for some time. Erik had dimly heard the rustling of water but forced the sound from his mind. Now, in the silence of terror that surrounded them, the rippling sounded like a waterfall, a disharmonious counterpart to the crashing behind them.

Erik turned toward the river. His thirst was urgent and the torture of listening to running water almost more than he could bear; but right now, he had other hopes. The promise of relative safety, perhaps of using the river as a barrier beyond which the unknown thing might not pass drove away all thoughts of thirst. They half-ran, half-stumbled through the underbrush, Erik wrenching Marquette through interwoven branches studded with wicked thorns that shredded their uniforms and drew beads of blood. The thorns gleamed long, sharp, and white.

Finally, they broke through to the river. Erik could make out low cliffs on the opposite side, vertical heights broken by black shadows. Caves? He couldn't be certain, but the cliffs rose from the other side, beyond the river, beyond the maze of low shrubs and vines that choked this side of the riverbed. He started to maneuver Marquette through the brambles and bush separating them from the river when unexpectedly, frighteningly, a heavy hand grabbed his free elbow. Erik stifled a reflex scream as he recognized the native's face emerging from the shadows. The man seemed to know where he was and what to do. Releasing Erik's elbow, he darted through obscure openings in the growth, heading toward the river. As he ran, he threw two words over his shoulder at Erik.

"*Grendel*. Run!"

There was no mistaking their urgency. The man recognized whatever followed them...and feared it. Erik felt an odd familiarity to the first word but had no time to think through.

He ran, but even in the extremity of the moment, he hated to prod Marquette any more. The man's face was bloodless, a ghostly mask floating above the red-stained blue of his tunic, now purple and black in the twilight. The makeshift casts had cracked, opening deep gashes in the plasti-form, dark with shadow, perhaps with blood. The man's breath was ragged and gasping, too fast and too shallow. But there was no alternative.

"Faster, faster." Erik didn't try to explain. Marquette seemed to intuit their increased danger, however. He steadied himself, squeezing his hand against Erik's upper arm as if to telegraph his awareness. He bit his lower lip until blood flowed onto his chin. He tried to hurry.

That was their undoing.

Marquette suddenly groaned out loud, stumbled, and nearly fell, jerking Erik roughly to his knees. Behind, the crashing grew louder, more purposeful. Erik thought he could *hear* the creature's breathing, even above the shattering of living wood and Marquette's tortured gasping. Whatever had their scent was not particularly fast (or at least didn't care to *move* quickly), but it was devastatingly powerful. Erik knew...believed...hoped...that they could find safety if they could make it to one of the black-lipped caves ahead and above in the cliff wall.

He also knew that Marquette would never make it.

The man had already taxed his body beyond all rational limits. He quivered with pain, weaving toward total collapse.

Erik himself was trembling, but somehow found the reserves to prop and pull Marquette to his feet and renew their slow progress to the river bank.

Out of nowhere, he heard a human cry, an agonizing cry embodying defeat, submission, and fear. It was, he realized, startled and dismayed, himself.

"Help!"

The word had torn from his throat, given birth through its own volition. For the first time since the three had passed through the depths of the forest, the native looked back. He raised a brow, either in surprise or exasperation—Erik could not tell which, nor did he care, as long as the fellow would give him a hand with Marquette. The native took a step or two toward the struggling men. He hesitated, listened, then swung around, his attention riveted on the noises shattering the peace behind them. He decided, apparently, that there was time. He ran to Erik and Marquette, grabbed Marquette under the arm, ripping the foam-cast from the injured man's shoulder and chest as he did so but giving no heed to the man's uninhibited scream of pain. Together, Erik and the native dragged Marquette toward the river.

Now Erik could see the water. Beyond the forest, the sky was lighter, glowing a deep blue but still verging on nightfall. The breeze whirling over the riverbed carried unmistakable smells of evening. At any other time, Erik. would have stopped and filled his lungs with refreshing sweetness, but not now!

The river was shallow. Crossing should present few difficulties. Erik could see swirls of white foam brushing glistening brown rocks. Further out, the foam glowed crimson and gold as it reflected the setting sun. The water couldn't be more than ankle deep, knee deep at most, regardless of the miniature rapids. Only a few paces more.

Then they were in it. Erik saw dry moss encrusting the rocks just before they splashed into the river. The water was low, retreating from the heat and drought of a dry summer, perhaps. He didn't care. He only hoped that the narrow river would slow, if not halt, the creature.

The rocks were firm and for the most part offered solid footing. Icy water swirled around their ankles. Here, straddling the shallow current, the air was cold, biting through his sweat-laden clothing. Erik shivered, feeling beads of perspiration catching and holding bone-chilling air. Only a dozen meters or so away, the cliffs rose beyond a narrow strand of coarse gravel.

They splashed on.

Erik might almost have begun to enjoying it.

Instead, abruptly, the noises in the forest intensified and fractured into a mind-grating wail. The native stiffened but did not look back. He seemed anxious to hurry their already precipitous progress through the water. Whatever followed them had given warning; it knew where they were and it was near enough to howl in triumph.

The crashing stopped as suddenly as if Erik had become instantaneously deaf. In the silence, the murmuring of the water seemed a roar. Marquette's hoarse breathing rose and fell, like some ragged respiration from the hidden bowels of the planet itself. Without understanding why, Erik released his grip on Marquette long enough to fling a glance over his shoulder. Something was there, poised in the darkness at the edge of the tree-line, an indefinable blot of blackness, unresolved, undefined beyond the merest suggestions of serpentine limbs and glowing eyes. Even so, the subtleties of the outline suggested ultimate terror.

Erik whirled to face the cliffs, throwing himself slightly off-balance as he did so. That, coupled with a burst of speed from the native, gave Marquette a half-spin.

It was more than the man could endure. Perhaps he slipped on a patch of algae on a rock. Perhaps he simply gave in to pain, fatigue, despair. Perhaps he finally capitulated to the utter hopelessness he had to have felt.

At any rate, he went down. He pitched forward into the water and lay there unmoving, his head turned just enough for him to breathe. Erik could see his breath as it ruffled the water just below his lips.

Erik leaned down and grabbed Marquette's arm, hauling the heavier man up while bracing to regain—and retain—his own footing in the swirling water. He felt the sting of tears in his eyes, along his. cheeks. A wordless cry floated above his head.

As if their sudden plight were a prearranged signal and its silent stance at the forest's margins part of some carefully orchestrated scene, the blackness beneath the trees howled, its cry drowning Erik's entirely. With an undulating movement, the shadow leaped from under the overhanging branches and the open brushy areas, its weight crushing the plants that had so effectively hampered Erik's few moments before. It moved slowly, but with absolute power. And now it moved silently.

Erik did not see the thing coming. When the creature echoed his own cry, he grabbed Marquette's collar and shoulder, pulling and screaming into the silence: "Help me! I can't lift him by myself."

The native appeared not to notice. He was calculating, his eyes flicking like a serpent's from Erik to Marquette, then back into the gathering darkness.

Suddenly he gripped Erik's arm and forced him through the river and toward the shore. Erik struggled, screaming incoherently. He could not, would not leave Marquette. He broke the native's grip, more through luck than skill, and splashed back toward Marquette's inert form, refusing to look up from the swirls of red-gold foam, from the blue of the Spacer's tunic. He felt rather than saw the sinuous approach of the thing from behind—and did not dare confront it directly. He dared only splash closer and closer to Marquette. He was only a body's length away, an arm's length, within grasping distance!

And a glittering something snaked redly through the air and buried itself in Marquette's sky-blue tunic. The blue bubbled red, then water caught the color and danced in crimson among the rocks, merging with the reflected scarlet of the sun.

Erik stopped, stunned.

The native splashed past him, grabbed the hilt of the knife, and jerked it from Marquette's body. The blade was slick with red-black blood.

More blood spurted from Marquette's wound, unhindered, unstoppable. Erik stared. The native grabbed him again and spun him toward the cliffs. Deeply shocked, Erik could not fight against the man. He allowed himself to be herded through the water to the far side of the river up a shallow rocky bank and onward toward the blackness of one of the caves

He did not register the approach of the creature nor see it settle over the kaleidoscope of crimson and blue in the center of the river. Nor did he notice as the rippling of the river was joined by a deeper, more frighteningly organic sucking and slurping.

Somewhere between the strand and the cliffs, Erik pitched forward and fainted.

CHAPTER SEVEN

Erik Baanfeld abruptly woke again to silence...but this time to a silence modulated by flickering fingers of light.

He was lying against the cool, rough wall of a cave. In the center of the cramped space, a small fire glimmered across chunks of some reflective stone. The native sprawled against the other wall, apparently asleep. Even at rest, he exuded an undeniable aura of strength and capability.

Not far from the man's head, a ragged circle of black defined the opening of the cave. The fire light was dim enough for Erik to see a single star winking in the darkness. He suddenly felt very much alone, isolated, far from everything he once thought he understood.

He lay still for a few minutes longer. He noted that for the first time since leaving the scouter he could breathe silently, without pain. He leaned his head against the stone, allowing his eyes to close, savoring the solidity of the earth, the quiet of the night.

Then his eyes flew open and as rapidly narrowed.

Marquette!

He listened intently for a second, but there was no evidence that the creature might still be lurking outside. From the smell of the faint breeze blowing into the cave, from the silence and darkness beyond the opening, Erik somehow knew that hours had passed since he had left...since he had been *forced* to leave Marquette dead or dying in the river.

He swung his head silently until he could stare directly at the native. He did not even have a name by which to call this...this *thing* in human form that could so easily and coldly slaughter another human being. And now Erik was unarmed and in the barbarian's power, while the native surely had more unknown armaments secreted within in his clothing. Erik had not seen the knife before it flashed into Marquette's helpless body; who knew what else the savage might be carrying?

No, Erik realized, he had no chance to stand against the native. Perhaps if he could escape while the man slept, disappear into the darkness, blend into the night and get far enough from this cave to find a hiding place until morning, then he could retrace their steps—surely there must be a visible trail marking their frantic passage—and find the scouter. Once there, he could try to jerry-rig an emergency signal and barricade himself in the wreckage to wait for rescue. There were supplies—sufficient food and water at least—and he could rig some kind of protection against the thing, if it should decide to return. He would be rescued, then he would report to the ExServ what had happened. Perhaps...probably, if he had any hand in it, the order would be given to wipe this colony out. Perhaps Command would realize that this world had regressed too far, that there was no way these...these *primitives* (no, Erik remonstrated with himself, that word is too neutral, too tame) could ever take a place again in human society. He would warn ExServ. He would see to it....

He shifted his weight. A rock dislodged and rolled onto the floor. The slight sound seemed hideously loud in the silence. Erik forced himself into immobility, barely daring to breathe, trying to will his heart to stop pounding and his blood to cease throbbing through his veins.

The native did not stir.

Slowly, Erik allowed his pent-up breath to escape, silently, swallowed by an even greater silence.

Yes, that would be the best plan. Back to the ship. To food, shelter, comfort. To familiar surroundings. To safety.

Except....

Except that he would have to get through that forest somehow. He shuddered inwardly—this time, however, careful not to allow the movement external expression. He didn't want the native to wake up yet.

He could do it, though, he could find a way through the forest, regardless of the unnamable thing that lived there, regardless of his fear of what might be in the deep shadows. He would have to do it. It was the only way to make something worthwhile out of Marquette's death. He would have to do it, and he would.

But how could he find the scouter?

The question cut through the passionate spinning in his mind. Did he know where to go? He had been so concerned with Marquette, so involved in a flight for survival (so futile, as the event turned out, for Marquette), that he had not consciously noted the path they followed. And after leaving Marquette, he had himself been unconscious; who knew how far the native had carried him from the spot where they had crossed the river.

He cursed himself for being all sorts of a fool. *Some space-Junk you* are! he thought contemptuously. *First mission, and you don't even keep enough sense about yourself to watch where you are going.*

From then on, it was easy to relive the events of the preceding day, seeing in every decision, every action criminal foolishness and fatal stupidity. Fatal for Marquette, perhaps soon for Erik himself.

If only....

Point by point he retraced his decisions, falling deeper into a morass of guilt and depression.

He groaned. Then stiffened. He shot a glance across the cavern. Still no movement from the native. Well, if he was ever going to get away, now would be the time. He lifted his head away from the wall, feeling the strain on shoulder and back muscles. Inch by inch he pulled away until he was sitting. He winced as tender spots, bruises, and pulled muscles in his arms and back complained.

For a few moments, he was content to sit, tensing and relaxing muscles, working the stiffness out as best he could.

Then he braced a hand against the coarse grit covering the floor of the cavern and stood. Silently, he hoped. He detected no sounds, other than the faintest scraping of his boot heels. Just to make sure, he remained standing, motionless, barely breathing, for a long time.

There was no movement from his captor. He stepped toward the opening, slowly, cautious in the extreme. He was going to make it!

"Stop."

The single word was scarcely more than a whisper, yet it flooded like icy water on the beginnings of a flame. Erik's shoulders slumped, his knees trembled, and he turned to face the man. He did not even consider the possibility of dashing through the entrance and out into the night. He did not know the terrain; the enemy did. He had no source of light, other than the hope that starlight would light the cliff face while he climbed down—*how far?*—to safety; the enemy had fire. He was bruised and stiff; the enemy, almost languid in his arrogant power and strength. He had no chance; the enemy had all chances.

Erik limped noisily back to the wall. He had not noticed it before, but his right ankle was sore. Not sprained or broken, probably; it just complained from the maltreatment of his race across the water, or more likely, during the native's climb to the cave entrance, Erik no doubt slung over his shoulder like a sack of grain. He sat down heavily, slumped against the wall, removed his boot, and inspected the ankle. A bruise showed just above the bone, but there were no other signs of injury. It might be tender for one or two days but not dangerously so.

Methodically, without looking across at his captor, Erik put the boot back on and leaned against the wall. He focused on the small fire, trying not to think of what had happened, what was happening, what might have been.

A movement across the room caught his attention. The native had sat up, reached into a niche behind him, and tossed a few bits of wood onto the fire. Then he resumed his original position, to all outward appearances asleep and unhearing.

He won't catch me like that again, Erik promised himself angrily. *I may be small, I may be unskilled, but I will learn. He won't destroy me.*

For an hour, Erik stared at the man, memorizing every shadow, every fold of the fur garments, every knot of muscle in the exposed forearms and thick legs. As he studied the face, he inexplicably lost his anger: slowly, irrevocably it drained from him. There was nothing in the man's face—at least in this moment of sleep—to suggest the cruelty Erik knew that he had seen.

And there was nothing to support Erik's initially frantic desire to see the man and his entire community wiped out.

Finally, Erik spoke.

"Why?"

He was pleasantly surprised at the strength in his voice. The small cave amplified the sound, making it strong and precise. But there was no response. He spoke again.

"Why?"

The man raised heavy lids to stare at Erik. After a few seconds he braced himself on one elbow and returned Erik's question:

"Why?"

Erik realized that the man was not simply parroting him. The man was asking a new question, unrelated to Erik's. He expected an answer; could Erik give him one?

"We must," he finally responded, although the words were more a mutter than a statement. Then, more strongly: "It is our duty, our assignment, to study worlds for re-entry into the community of humanity. It is important, essential. We cannot let you and others like you remain living like this."

He knew how patronizing he sounded. He hated himself for falling back on the pre-programmed response like a first-year student stumbling unprepared through an oral exam. But he had nothing else at hand, nothing else to say.

And besides, the man had seen the scouter, apparently understood what it represented. Obviously all memories of the Union had not died out here, as they had on other worlds. The people here, represented to be sure by this single individual at this moment, would recognize Erik (and would have more easily recognized Marquette) for what he was—one from beyond the stars, from the by-now quasi-mythical universe that had sent them here and abandoned them. They knew, Erik was sure, and now he had to work them back into a position of trust.

Apparently the native was willing to accept Erik's response for the time being. He sat silently, as if dissecting the answer word by word.

But Erik was not satisfied. He leaned away from the wall, then stood. Favoring his bruised ankle, he walked to the fire, now little more than embers in spite of the scraps of wood the man had tossed onto it. He looked across the circle of stones, down at the native, imposing even when recumbent, and repeated his own question:

"Why?"

The man looked up at him, and Erik felt small, as he had in Marquette's presence and in the presence of all seasoned human Spacers at both the Academy and the University.

"He could not have lived. We are too far from the village, and his wounds were too serious for the kind of traveling he would have to do."

"But we could have carried him up here. We could have...."

"No, we could not. We would have died with him. We did not have the time. And he had given up. He would not have lasted this far. If his wounds did not prove fatal, his loss of will would have. I had no choice."

Then, after a moment: "He did not suffer."

This last was spoken in a different voice. There was an unaccountable gentleness in it, a sadness almost.

Underneath that tone, however, Erik heard an assurance and a confidence that he found disconcerting, yet he could not find words to counter it. What the man said was obviously wrong, morally and ethically wrong. Even granting that Marquette might have died, a thing Erik was unwilling to grant, they should have helped him. They should have tried.

Erik returned to his seat at the opposite wall, suddenly tired, weak, and shaking.

"What is your name?" the native asked.

"Baanfeld. Erik Baanfeld." Erik's voice emerged dull and rasping. He did not even consider identifying himself by his Adjunct number.

"Your duties?"

"Word study." Erik had intended to say 'linguistics analyst', then realized that his mind did not contain the word-analogues for the archaic version of Standard the other man was speaking. What he actually said might even have been best rendered as "word work."

"What is that?" the other asked.

"I was designed to study languages in lost colonies, to see how much the languages have changed over the centuries. Then the Ex-Serv can tell how far the people have moved from where they were." Erik didn't stop to consider how much of the answer the native might understand. He did not want to think, to question himself about anything. He responded blankly, as if in shock.

"Ah, yes. That would explain your facility with our language. I wondered about that."

Erik looked up and met the other's eyes. "What's your name?" he countered.

A shadow passed over the native's face. "I cannot say. It is forbidden. You are not of the Folk. And even among them, only a few know my true name. Most call me Weard."

Guardian, Erik translated instantly, and then felt curious at his certainty. "Where...?" Erik began, but Weard cut him off.

"We must travel far tomorrow. Sleep now. You are safe. You must rest."

Erik did not want to sleep. He wanted to find out more about Weard's people. Were they the only group on the planet? How had they survived? Where were they? How soon could he get back to the scouter and work on the rescue beacon?

And other questions crowded the back of his mind, vague and ill-defined but insistent.

What had seized Marquette's lifeless body back at the crossing?

What had nearly destroyed the ship, then tracked them through the forest?

Were there other things like that in the forests of this world?

But Erik did not ask them. Weard had closed his eyes again, whether in sleep or in mock-watchfulness, Erik could not guess. He did not dare try another escape; curiously, he had lost the impelling need to *try* to escape. So far his captor had seemed reasonable, even civilized. But Erik did not know how far he dared push the man.

He leaned against the wall and closed his eyes, inviting sleep.

Just as darkness fell and he drifted into sleep, he stiffened and clenched his fists until his knuckles stood out white against the drawing shadows.

That man had murdered Marquette.

CHAPTER EIGHT

Light burned his eyes. He swung his head to the side, only to strike something rough, cool, and dully cutting. His eyes opened.

Where was he?

Heart thudding, he leapt to his feet, almost cracking his skull on a squat stalactite. A cave?

Then memories flooded him, uncontrollable and unwilled.

Marquette. The native, Weard.

Their odd conversation during the deepest hours of the night.

Now it was day. The sun had broken above the scraggly line of trees across the river, just enough to pierce the cave's mouth and strike his face as he had slept. Erik rubbed his eyes with his fists, stretched, and—thoroughly awake—looked around.

There was no sign of Weard. The fire circle was cold and gray, long dead. The man was not visible, nor were any of his belongings. It was as if Erik was now and had always been alone in the cave.

He crossed the gritty floor and peered out, allowing himself a few seconds for his eyes to adjust to the harsh light. The sun on this planet gave off a slightly whiter light than did Sol. As a result, everything seemed more sharply defined, more clear-cut than he would have expected.

After the confusion of the crash, their capture (*What other word could I use?* he wondered), their headlong flight, he had not noticed. But in the peace of this morning, the translucent clarity startled him. He could see forever, it seemed.

He avoided looking directly below, however. There would be nothing left, he knew—no ragged remnants of blue, no backwash of browning crimson caught in a rock-crusted pool. But he couldn't face the river, not quite yet. Even the peaceful rippling of water would seem too much a condemnation.

Instead, he let his eyes follow the horizon. The forest continued unbroken through the one hundred and eighty degrees of his line of vision. To the left and right, the cliff face continued, a rugged, ragged monolith of fragmenting stone that glistened in the morning light. Further along, on both sides, the cliffs swept back in sweeping arcs. Where they disappeared, they seemed as smoothly unscalable as they did here. He had no idea what might lay on top of or behind the cliffs.

He could distinguish only the nearest trees. Most seemed deciduous, much like the ones they had marched under yesterday—at least, the rounded crowns suggested oak-types. Occasionally an isolated spear of darker blue-green reminiscent of terran pines thrust upward. With a little imagination, and more than a little squinting, Erik could almost transform the vast greenery into a cityscape complete with turreted structures, spires, domes.

Further away, the green-blue-green merged, faded, grew to gray. At the farthest limits of his sight, he thought he could see a low chain of mountains, or else jagged clouds. He could not tell which. The land looked to be level, with only scattered mounds or rises, such as the one where the scouter now lay abandoned.

All in all, Erik had to concede, the place was inviting and pleasant enough...if you could ignore the veiled threats implicit in the unbroken foliage. If one black serpentine thing could live there hidden and undisturbed, then so could others.

Finally, drunk with the vistas extending beyond him, Erik found the courage to look down.

His first reaction was disbelief.

How had he ever been maneuvered up those rocks! No wonder he had bruised his ankle. The cliff face was sheerer than it had looked the day before, even taking into account Erik's panic at the time. Not even the native, with all of his readily apparent strength, could have carried a dead weight up the cliff. Erik must have recovered consciousness, at least enough to move mechanically where he was told to move. Still, it must have taken unknown reserves of strength, adrenaline, and constant prodding by Weard to get him up. He was intensely relieved that he had no memories of the experience.

Below, the rivulet murmured innocently...insolently. There was no evidence of the tragedy. No signs marred the placid flow of water, save a broad sweep of crushed scrub-brush along the far bank, where the thing had....

Erik broke off. He didn't want to think about that any further.

"Baanfeld. Here."

The voice caught him unaware. He looked to his left. Not two meters away and slightly below the narrow ledge where Erik perched, Weard's head poked out of another cave entrance. The native gestured imperiously. Erik had no alternative but to cross over.

His ledge continued beyond the cave entrance for three-quarters of the way. He had little trouble clinging to the rough cliff-face and inching along, feeling with the toe of his boot. He did not look down.

He had never done much mountaineering. But after all, the ledge was broad enough and stable.

Then the ledge ended. Erik's foot abruptly slid on the angled rock, spilling sand and gravel-sized bits of stone off the ledge. He heard them skitter down the cliff face, even heard them plunk onto the solid rock beneath.

For a second his heart stopped. He froze.

He gripped the cliff face until his fingers turned white, paralyzed in place. His breath tore from his throat as he clung there, one foot planted on rock, the other dangling in air." H-h-help," he finally managed. "What do I do?"

He couldn't see Weard; the slip had caught him facing toward the first cave. He heard the other man's clothing as it rubbed against crumbling stone, even imagined he could hear his breath in the sudden silence.

But Weard said nothing. Erik strained, still clutching the rock face.

For all he could tell, he might be alone, suspended between earth and sky.

Then, somehow, he moved. Only a finger at first, but he moved. He pulled his foot back toward him, until he felt the ledge solid again beneath both feet. Then he breathed deeply, thinking frantically.

He could go back—to what? If he couldn't manage this short a climb, how could he hope to climb down the sheer face.

There was obviously no other opening from the first cave; if there were, Weard would have stayed there. And the man *had* successfully crossed.

So even if the ledge did give out sooner than he had expected, there must be a way over to the second cave. And apparently Weard wasn't going to tell him what it was. Erik pushed his foot over the edge again, then lowered it slightly, just enough to let it drag down the face. There. A crack, a toehold. Then another. Centimeter by centimeter he lowered himself, until his left foot struck an outcropping that signaled the entrance to the second cave.

He had made it.

When his feet finally rested again on the solid outcrop, he looked up, expecting to see something—approval, perhaps—in Weard's eyes.

Weard was not there.

During the entire time, Weard had remained silent, offering neither encouragement nor guidance. It would have been easier and infinitely safer, Erik thought bitterly, if Weard had at least given him occasional instructions. But no, he had said nothing And now he had disappeared, apparently not even caring whether or not Erik crossed successfully. He felt anger growing inside—a deferred anger that was part the experience of the past few moments, part his fear, part his frustration at Marquette's death.

Furious, Erik entered the second cave, a substantially larger cavern than the one in which they had spent the night. It extended further back as well, disappearing into shadows. Weard squatted in the center on the gravelly floor, ripping with his teeth at what seemed a length of dried meat. He looked up, pulled out his knife, cut a piece off, and tossed it to Erik. Erik caught it one-handed, watching Weard closely, still seething with rage.

Actually, his emotional state was as shocking as anything else that had happened. Junks weren't supposed to be capable of rage or of ecstasy—nor of any conscious emotions beyond irritation and pleasure.

He glanced down at the hunk of meat. It was some kind of jerky, rudely preserved but presumably edible and, with luck, nutritious.

He started to speak, but Weard cut him short. "Eat."

"Not until you...," Erik began, not sure even as he spoke what threat he would utter, what words would express his anger and contempt and fear.

"Eat."

Weard made no movement, other than to shift the jerky in his hand. But Erik read a warning in that small gesture. He sat where he was and began chewing on the jerky tentatively.

Whatever beast had given its life to provide the morsel had been foully mistreated. It smelled—and probably tasted—worse than last week's garbage. He bit. The strip was strongly flavored, but not with any spices or condiments Erik had ever tasted before. His throat tightened, and his stomach threatened rebellion, but he chewed carefully, his eyes never leaving Weard's face. The stringy fibers were permeated with the acrid taste of rancidity. Erik swallowed convulsively, forcing his stomach to remain calm. He swallowed again.

Suddenly, startlingly, he became aware of hunger—a deeper emptiness in his stomach than he had ever felt before—and remembered how long it had been since last he ate, how far he had run, how strenuous their flight had been. With that realization, the jerky ceased being quite so obnoxious; the flavor shifted gradually from rotting meat to merely unknown and alien spices. Erik began eating, chewing slowly and stolidly, matching Weard bite for bite as they squatted across the dimly lit cavern from each other.

The silence lasted for a long time. Part of it was hunger, of course, but Erik could tell that Weard did not want to talk. *All right, I can oblige you there, too*, he said to himself.

They sat for minutes longer. Then Erik shifted; his legs were falling asleep. The silence bothered him more and more. Even Marquette, for all of his moodiness and taciturnity, could be counted on for an occasional remark. Finally, he could stand it no longer.

"What now?" he said pointedly.

"Home." Weard seemed a man of few words—and usually only one at a time. Erik wondered at the ease with which they had spoken during the preceding night, but did not press the point.

Weard rose, apparently satisfied with the dismal breakfast and ready to go. He turned toward the back of the cavern and disappeared into the shadows. Erik waited impatiently for him to return. Presumably he had something of value cached back there. Instead, the hollow voice echoed out to him.

"Come, prattling. We go."

Erik scuttled across the cave, around a neck of granite, and into a low tunnel. The way was dark, dimly lit only occasionally by pockets of phosphorescent minerals that Erik neither recognized nor had time to explore. Ahead, the lumpy blot that was Weard continued briskly, as if he could see in the near-darkness and were unencumbered by an alien less capable than himself. Erik refused to call out. He hurried along, reassuring his tiring, shaky body that the way must be relatively smooth, since the bobbing shadow ahead seemed unconcerned with any sudden dips or cracks. For the most part, that was true. Through the march in the tunnel—which to Erik seemed hours long, until his thighs quivered with exhaustion and his back screamed for a chance to unfold and hold itself upright—he came close to losing his balance only once or twice. Each time, a steadying hand against the wall was all that he needed, and he was off again.

Weard remained ahead during the entire march, not once slowing (at least not for Erik's benefit), not once glancing behind to check on his...follower. Erik was confused as to his actual status. He had assumed *captive* the night before, especially after Marquette's murder. Captive, with an interesting admixture of slave, perhaps. But if so, where were the ropes, the chains, the bonds to insure that he did not escape. Or did Weard realize from the start what Erik was finally beginning to understand...that there was no place for him to run to.

On the other hand, Erik could not quite believe that Weard was willing to accept him—much less treat him—as an ambassador of good will from the Comity, regardless of Erik's truncated statement of purpose the night before. In fact, the man seemed most inclined simply to ignore Erik, or at best to treat him as a necessary nuisance.

So they continued, Weard far in front, Erik keeping up with considerable difficulty, but perversely determined neither to call for help nor to fall so far behind that he would lose sight of Weard. He remembered his experiences with the track coach in Training. To small to be effective at most of the contact sports, he had chosen track, partially on account of his litheness and speed; partially because it was essentially a loner's sport. He was not particularly good—better, perhaps, than most, but not unbeatable. He had rarely finished first, just often enough to keep his place on the team. Usually, he could be counted on for a strong second, and a few critical points where they were most needed. He had never finished last. And he was not about to begin doing so now. He kept up with Weard in spite of the darkness, the grueling pace, his body's constant complaints, and the man's obdurate silence.

Finally, after interminable marching, mostly to the unpleasant accompaniment of his memories, Erik noticed that the tunnel now angled upward slightly—and that Weard had disappeared!

He ran up the tunnel, recklessly, knowing that what he was doing was stupid at best, possibly fatal at worst, but forced to run nonetheless. When he at last caught sight of Weard, Erik noted that the fur garments the man wore were ringed with pale silver light, that he could see clearly the lank hair, the knotted arms and legs. Beyond Weard, light of some sort was streaming into the tunnel.

It was daylight. Erik smiled. He had not been sure what to expect—an underground commune of ill-kempt troglodytes, perhaps, or a morlockian civilization beneath the earth's crust. Still, he admitted, he was relieved to be on the surface again. Apparently they had climbed up to the top of the plateau of which the cliff face formed one side.

From the entrance to the tunnel, the landscape did not look appreciably different from what Erik had already seen. The same Earth-type vegetation predominated, although here and there a form defied classification. The spire-like piney growths were more frequent (did that mean that the climate up here would be cooler than in the valley? It seemed possible), and the general sense of green was altered to include more blue-green, more dusty gray-greens. The forest was also not as spacious and open as the one below. There was more underbrush, knotted and clumped, in spots virtually impassable. The terrain was far more rugged, with suggestions of hills, valleys, perhaps actual mountains further away.

He could not see the sun; it was still behind the cliff face, which even here rose above them for some hundred meters. But the shadows, both of the cliff itself and of the isolated trees dotting the rocky slope in front of them, suggested that the sun was nearly overhead, and that it would break over the crest of the ridge momentarily. About noon, then.

Weard seemed satisfied with their progress. He stopped for a moment to survey the terrain below them, then threw himself against a smooth slab of rock that had broken off the cliff face, fortuitously landing without breaking. Within seconds, Weard was apparently asleep.

Erik did not trust him. The pose was too much like the one from last night. Perhaps he was truly asleep: if so, he was a light sleeper, then, and the first sound from Erik would bring him to full consciousness. Or perhaps he was not asleep, but merely playing with his captive. He might even let Erik get halfway to the protective shadows of the trees before calling to him, or even more likely, sending that knife through his back. Erik sat down, trying to enjoy the cool shadows, wondering what was to come.

He didn't have long to wait. After perhaps ten minutes, displaying an ease and grace surprising in one of his size, Weard rose and began walking, following the base of the cliffs. He did not speak to Erik, but Erik rose also and followed. They paralleled the cliffs, keeping well above the forested areas for most of the day. The sun silvered above the rocks, hot and white, more piercing than Erik was used to but not overly uncomfortable. It was larger, whiter, hotter than Sol, even to the naked eye, but also much farther away. But then it would have to be, or this place would not have been colonized. The Old Empire had been very careful where she placed her children.

CHAPTER NINE

The afternoon wore on, growing hotter. Erik began to tire. Occasionally he thought he could see trails cutting through the edges of the forest, within the welcome shadows. Each time, he became more aware of trickles of sweat on his forehead and down his back.

He would have asked about the trails, even asked that they follow one, had he dared. There must be some reason, he decided, why Weard refused to leave the heights, as uncomfortable as they were. The path they were on was rough and unkempt. They scrambled over man-sized boulders and stumbled through fields of rocks too small to climb over, to large to step over easily, too closely packed to skirt. Erik's bruised ankle began to throb; he found it easier to empathize with Marquette's suffering the previous day—on those rare moments when he allowed himself to think of anything.

He was breathing heavily. The sun bore down unmercifully on the reflective rocks, parching him. His uniform darkened with sweat, with dirt where he had rubbed against rocks, with flecks of blood where sharp edges had abraded his skin when he had stumbled. Weard stayed ahead, still uncommunicative, still marching as if he had been on his feet only a few minutes. Erik could see no traces of sweat on the fur garments, even though they must have been more stifling than his own clothing.

But in general, he was surprised to discover, he was in relatively good shape. His ankle hurt but was functional. He was tired, although not yet to the point of mindless fatigue that he had felt day before. He was hungry, but not yet hungry enough to tackle the remnants of the dried meat stuffed into his pocket.

He was thirsty. That was the major drawback. He needed water. It had been almost a day and a half since he had last drunk. Much longer, and he would face serious difficulties.

Finally, when the sun entered the last quarter of the sky, Weard turned away from the cliff face and climbed down from the piedmont into the forest. The change in temperature shocked Erik, but it was a welcome shock. His thirst lessened almost immediately, although still remaining a nagging reminder that all was not well. This was not just another training hike through the trees.

As soon as they entered the forest, Weard became instantly more alert. His hand played restlessly near his side, as if to be near the knife or whatever other weapons he might have concealed about him. The spear was now lowered into a defensive position, Weard's fingers taut and ready around the thick shaft. Erik could not see any immediate necessity for such precautions—but then, he had not seen any yesterday either, and he had been seriously, almost fatally, mistaken. Perhaps life-forms indigenous to the upper ranges were even more formidable than those in the valley.

He sincerely hoped not.

They continued as before, Weard leading the way, never seeming aware of his follower. He remained silent, not even grunting instructions to walk quietly, to be observant, or to keep close. Erik did all three, however, regardless of any lack of directions. Weard did not offer to supply Erik with a weapon; Erik did not ask for one. Still unsure of his position, he dared not make any demands which might later jar with his rank on the world where he now found himself hopelessly stranded. He did, however, pause just long enough to grab a long, thin, strong length of wood. At the least it would serve as a staff, an aid in walking; at best, if necessary, he could use it as a cudgel. True, he had little experience with such a weapon (again, and not for the first or last time, he cursed his education—then tempered the curse with the realization that his training had not been designed for this purpose. He had had survival training but had not really believed that he would need it.)

He hefted the staff once or twice. He could at least lay on an enemy with vigor if not with particular skill.

Weard apparently did not notice Erik's weapon. By now the sun was nearing the upper edges of the trees. The cool winds of evening were rising, refreshing, yet ponderous with dark memories. Soon night would fall. Somewhere behind them, a noise echoed, startling Erik. Was it...?

Weard halted for a moment, listened, shrugged, and continued on his way. Whatever it was, Weard did not sense danger in its presence. Again and again, Erik heard noises, some as familiar as the night songs of birds (and not a few of those surprisingly reminiscent of terran songs), others unfamiliar and startling in their alienness.

Still they continued, increasing their speed if anything. Erik had not thought it possible for him to move faster than he had been, yet the prospect of remaining alone in the darkness was more than he could face. He knew with dead certainty that if he fell behind, Weard would leave him, just as he had left Marquette, perhaps with the same small incision between his ribs. He pushed himself with more cruelty than he ever could have used to urge Marquette...and somehow managed to stay close behind his captor.

Again and again, he imagined hot breath and cold eyes on his neck, he became half-convinced that sinuous black appendages were undulating toward him from the shadows, that a monstrous blackness was settling on him. Only by force of will did he keep from delaying just long enough to turn his head and look...and by doing so lose sight of his guide. Even now Weard seemed more than half shadow, so silently and swiftly did he move.

Night fell.

Through the tattered crowns of trees, stars glittered. To the left, a moon crescented dimly. With the coming of night, the strange sounds increased. Still Weard continued unerringly, never confused, never hesitant which branching of the convoluted trail to follow. And Erik followed, more exhausted than he had ever been.

Suddenly Weard halted. Half-blinded by fatigue and by the sweat spilling into his eyes despite the evening cool, his sight a reddening blur throbbing in time to his frantic heartbeat, Erik almost careened into him.

"Home."

The guttural sound floated softly on the air. Erik almost stumbled, then leaned against the smooth trunk of a tree, the darkness pounding, the silence devoured by his rasping breath. He panted deeply, feeling his knees tremble, his hands sweating. Then he pushed away from the tree and shouldered his way through the last few feet of thorny bush, catching his sleeve on a protruding ranch and ripping it to the elbow. Finally, he worked his way to Weard's side.

They stood on a low bluff overlooking a river valley. In the starlight, the river wound like liquid silver through a dark meadow. The water glimmered, sinuous and mercurial. A memory surfaced unbidden, lines Erik had studied for his coursework years ago, about crisped brooks

> Rolling on orient pearl and sands of gold,
> With mazy error under pendant shades
> Ran nectar, visiting each plant, and fed
> Flowers worthy of Paradise which not nice art
> In beds and curious knots, but Nature's boon
> Poured profuse on hill and dale and plain....

True, the darkness hid much from sight—golden sands and orient pearl—but Erik drank in the peaceful beauty of the place.

"Where...?" he began. Weard silenced him with a gesture.

Further into the meadow, well beyond the river, a quincunx of lights glowed, midway between the river and a darker line where the forests resumed. Each center of light included many individual flecks, as if houses clustered about some focal point. The middle glow was larger than the four surrounding it.

Weard started down the bluff, with Erik following only a few steps behind. The trail here was hard-packed and smooth, worn by the passage of many feet. As it approached the base of the low bluff, it leveled and widened slightly, meandering through stunted willowy growth about a meter high. Unwillingly, Erik slowed, unable to force his pained muscles any faster, too overcome by the coolness of the night, the moistness of the air, and the distant glimmering of lights to re-create the sense of panic that had served him throughout the day. He fell behind—only a step or so at first, then several.

Suddenly he started as he realized that Weard had disappeared into the night. Nothing—no movement, no sound—disclosed the man's presence. He began to walk faster, then to run as emptiness crashed onto him.

And then, thank God, there stood Weard, his feet making ripples in the river's quiet flow, leaning on his spear and watching. Erik saw the starlight glittering in the man's deep eyes. For an instant, Erik almost believed that the man was smiling, that his teeth caught the moonlight and cast it back toward Erik.

And then he stumbled.

It was nothing, really. Just a well-worn root, rounded and smooth and barely two or three centimeters above the path. But in Erik's near-panic and mind-crushing fatigue, it was enough. He fell. One hand flung out to break his fall, grabbing at the vegetation lining the path. Instantly his palm flamed as it swept across dark leaves.

Nettles. Or something very like them but far more painful. For a second, he felt his flesh peeling away in blackened sheets, exposing raw nerves.

He almost screamed. The sound began and he clamped it down. But too late. At the slight break in the silence, Weard looked down at Erik, concern and possibly disappointment flickering across his face. His eyes dimmed; the smile—if it had in fact ever existed—disappeared. The man watched Erik for a full minute. For some reason, Erik could not pull his body upright onto the path. He just lay there, cradling his injured hand and staring back.

Weard shrugged, turned, and continued on, still without saying a word.

Erik scrabbled to his feet, his panic and fear suddenly dissipated, even the burning in his palm forgotten. He brushed against another nettle, and another, and barely noticed. Somehow he had made a serious mistake. All of his efforts had been negated in some unknown—and eminently unfair—way. He had done his best—more than his best. And now....

He wanted to run to Weard, to lay his swelling hand on the other's shoulder and apologize, plead, beg, explain—whatever it would take to erase the error. Whatever this particular error had been. But he could not.

Instead he followed silently, imitating the other's care as he left the nettles and splashed into the river.

For several meters between the hedge of nettles and the river, the soil was thickly carpeted with grass. Erik's feet relished the moist coolness. The air, heavy with vapor, partially satisfied his thirst.

Then he was into the water. Weard was nearly across, stepping from stone to stone. This river was much deeper than the one they had struggled through the day before, deeper and noisier, with a more mature-sounding rumbling. Someone had apparently set the rocks in the bed, large rocks which humped far above the water level and provided a dry—if occasionally tenuous—passage. The opposite shore was much like the first, soft, with lush growth. There were no nettles, however.

Weard was waiting on the far side. Still without speaking, he watched Erik's slow progress from rock to rock. Once a slight misstep coupled with increasingly untrustworthy muscled threatening to spill Erik into the river. He scrabbled to stay on the boulder, scraping skin from his palm but ignoring the pain since, in his present fatigue he would have no hope of swimming to either bank safely. And somehow he knew, again, that if he fell, Weard would do nothing to rescue him.

He worked his way to his feet again, mostly through sheer will power, and jumped to the next boulder, and the next. Finally Erik reached the far bank, and watched as Weard turned, walked silently upstream for several meters, knelt on a flat, smooth rock jutting into the current, and dipped up water in what seemed a metal cup. At least it glinted like metal in the dim light.

Weard drank deeply, then, as if remembering the wraith-like figure behind him, thrust the cup into the folds of his garment.

Probably some kind of relic, Erik concluded, too sacred for profane eyes—for *Junk* eyes. Even he noted the bitterness in his imagery.

In turn, Erik walked to the rock, knelt next to Weard, and scooped a handful of water to his mouth. He spilled most of it, but what remained in his palm was cold and sweet. He returned his hand again, again, enjoying the sensation as the water washed away the hot stickiness in his throat and the lingering fire on his palm. He splashed the last double handful on his face and neck, closing his eyes with pleasure.

"No more. Come now," Weard said. For the first time in their march from the caverns, the man had actually acknowledged Erik's presence and had waited long enough for Erik to catch his breath and feel a modicum of solid comfort.

"Thank you, sir," Erik said.

Weard did not answer.

Instead, he began walking away from the river. Erik looked up. The lights had disappeared. The village—or villages, whatever the separate spots of light had been—had disappeared. Other than an infrequent flicker that could have been firelight or reflected moonlight on some smoothly polished stone, the meadow stretched darkly onward. Erik thought he could see a dark line cutting through the grass, but could not be sure.

They crossed the meadow without any further interruptions, almost without sound. Erik was startled by the quiet peacefulness of the place, by the grasses growing almost thigh-high, waving silently in the night, their tips silvered by hints of night. The two men moved quietly but quickly.

As they walked, the dark line Erik had noticed grew, becoming taller, solidifying until it emerged from the darkness as a wall or fence several meters high and extending into the night on both sides of the path. After only a few moments more of walking, they finally arrived at the edge of the wall. Erik discovered that the wall was in fact a barrier of thorns and brambles.

The barrier was not alive, not a hedge of growth as the nettles had been. Instead, they were great dead specimens, heaped together like the bones of slaughtered animals, forming a palisade impassable even for one as tall and as strong as Weard. They glistened whitely. Erik could see sharp thorns, many of them eight or ten centimeters long, gleaming wetly as if individually polished. Dark smudges of a thick viscous liquid smeared the tips of many. Weard pointed to one such thorn and spoke a single word.

"Poison."

Erik nodded. This was a protection for the settlement, as effective on this world (presumably) as force-beams and laser-grids on the Worlds of the Comity. Effective, probably, even against the amorphous monstrosity of the lower forests, should such things exist here on the damper, cooler upland ranges.

Weard followed the wall of thorns to the left. It rose unbroken to perhaps five meters above the ground, so thick that no hints of light now filtered through, no sounds, no smells.

Then Weard stopped. To Erik's untrained eyes the spot looked no different than any other they had passed, but Weard grasped a thick branch and twisted it out and down. The branch gave way and with it a section of the barrier slid outward, opening a narrow passageway. Weard gestured. Erik should precede him.

Erik entered the darkness of the tunnel, oppressed by the knowledge that meters of painful death poised over him. He did not know whether any of the thorns along the passageway had been smeared with the poison; he hoped not. He heard Weard entering behind him and glanced over his shoulder. The man pulled the brambles closed, twisting another branch to lock them in place. He moved quietly past Erik and resumed the lead.

The passage was short, only about four meters—but dark. Not until they were safely outside (or inside, since the barrier enclosed considerable space) could Erik see again. From this level, and this close, the quincunx of lights had disappeared. Instead, Erik saw that he was standing on the outskirts of a settlement, although he had no way of estimating accurately either its size or population in the dimness of the night. Sets of outside fires threw gaunt shadows over buildings and ground, blurring everything into a surrealistic glare of black and orange.

They approached the nearest structure, a hut set close to the wall. There was no light, no sign of life.

"Wait," Weard whispered, his voice carrying but somehow barely disturbing the overall stillness.

He disappeared into the shadows. Erik waited, impatient but determined to study the place as closely as possible in the few minutes he might have. If he were ever to escape....

Beyond him, the main settlement stretched far to each side. In the center stood a single structure, isolated from the others by bare ground, a low fence of unfinished stakes, and a wide path circling it. On four sides, apparently purposefully aligned, probably with compass points, clustered knots of smaller buildings. The closest was just to Erik's right. He counted fifteen buildings in the group, per-haps as many as twenty. Each seemed large enough to house a fam-ily comfortably. All appeared made of stone or wood, with thick thatched roofs, squat doors, and slatted windows. There seemed to be no glass in the windows, since each was mere blackness without any reflection from the outside fires. Everything was scaled just slightly too large for Erik, suggesting that Weard's height and bulk were not unusual among his people. Erik shuddered, suddenly feel-ing like a child let loose in a playground built strictly for adults. The buildings seemed large, heavy, unfamiliar.

He could see only a few people. The others were probably sleeping. From the almost inaudible murmur coming through the nearest window-opening of the hut into which Weard had disap-peared—a guard hut, Erik had decided—Weard was apparently making his report. Presumably there would be other entrances to the enclave, other sentries posted about the circuit of the barrier, other darkened huts huddling almost against the poisoned thorns of the skeletal, bleached white brambles.

Within the settlement, an occasional silhouette crossed between Erik and a distant fire. Muted light guttered through windows at ir-regular intervals. Perhaps not everyone was asleep after all, he de-cided, trying to imagine what sort of cottage industries, social gath-ering, intimate exchanges might be taking place behind the closely set slats. But he could not. He had no clues to follow.

Far off, he could hear low sounds, as of cattle. The settlement was not as silent as he had thought at first. His own heartbeat had dropped to a normal rhythm and the pounding in his ears had ceased; now that he was concentrating, he could hear more than he anticipated. It sounded, in fact, as if livestock were clustered in the darkness to his left.

Overlaying everything else was a sense of squalor, of filth and decay that stunned Erik. He told himself that much of the feeling was probably due to the constantly flickering light, dim and unreli-able, that emphasized shadows and made the ragged, rough texture of the huts even more barbaric and distorted the outlines of the few people in sight until they resembled great hulking clots of darkness against the firelight.

All in all, the place looked like a scene from a recidivist's night-mare.

And the smell!

Outside the thorn barrier, the air had been sweet, fresh, invigo-rating. Within, however, that changed quickly. The thorn walls hindered the evening breezes; the air near the barrier hung heavy, unmoving, and musty, with an acrid undercurrent that Erik felt certain came from the poison smeared on the ubiquitous thorns. Elsewhere hints of wood smoke (agreeable enough, perhaps, in other circumstances) mingled uneasily with more than hints of decaying meat, rotting vegetable matter, animal manure, and human sweat. Erik paled, remembering with distaste the hunk of jerky lumped in his pocket. What he smelled now promised little in the way of a reprieve.

At that moment, Weard reappeared, stepping from the depths of the guard hut. He motioned for Erik to follow before setting off across the meadow toward the cluster of huts—small, rough-hewn, unprepossessing even to Erik's untrained eye—on their left. They reached it, entered through a gateway in a low, ragged fence surrounding the complex, and threaded their way among the separate structures. Up close, they seemed even smaller, barely large enough for one or two people. And they were huddled discomfortingly close together. He hoped fervently that which ever one they were headed for would be clean and well ventilated.

They passed a handful of huts before Weard paused in front of one to all externals just like every other one. Weard looked down at Erik.

"Erik Baanfeld, for tonight, you will sleep within my house. Come."

CHAPTER TEN

Erik entered.

It was dark, musty, and potently odorous. He stumbled over a clump of something on the floor: it felt like a bundle of cast-off clothing and smelled worse. Behind him, Weard rummaged on a shelf near the door, did something which produced a rasping sound, as of two pieces of wood being scraped together, and held out a thin stick of wood flickering feebly with a dim yellow flame.

A sulfur match, from the stench of it that quickly permeated the small room. Erik had read of such things, even seen pictures of them but had had never actually seen one working.

Weard touched the flame to a bit of filament extending from a greasy candle nearby. The resulting glow lit the hut with a warm golden light foreign to Erik, whose life had been spent among electricity, glow-globes, laser-lights, and such.

But candles! For a moment he was appalled and depressed by the regression implicit in the artifact.

Candles! Probably formed from the melted and rancid fat of *animals*.

And yet, in spite of his distaste, for just a brief moment, almost as flickering and ephemeral as the candle itself, he felt an oddly comforting sense wash over him as the candle bathed the interior of the hut in that curious golden glow.

Then he saw the cabin clearly, and any lingering nostalgia dissipated.

The aboriginal lighting arrangements were nothing compared to what else he saw around him.

Scattered here and there, rough planks studded the walls in no apparent order or arrangement. On some, vessels of clay or stone lay next to wooden implements. On others lay tight rolls of furs and hides; on still others, lumps of shadow and light that he could neither clearly see nor place.

Six or seven spears were braced in a corner. None of them bore metal tips. Nearby, an assortments of bone knives hung from leather thongs strung through holes in their hafts. In the center of the opposite wall stood a large but rudely constructed cabinet, like an old-fashioned wardrobe from the histories. It was made of rough, untreated wood, except for a heavy, mottled hide that partially covered the front. Inside, Erik caught a glimpse of shapeless furs.

The main room was small, perhaps three meters square. Three doors opened onto it, each outlined with unfinished wooden jambs and lintels, and each closed off with well-worn hides. Weard motioned toward one of the doors. Erik pushed the hide aside, momentarily surprised by its unexpected pliancy and softness. He entered the second room. Weard followed closely, bringing the candle with him.

This room appeared to be a sleeping chamber. It was even smaller than the main room. There were no windows, although multiple cracks in the walls allowed a hint of cross-ventilation. The floor, like the floor of the main chamber, was packed dirt. A cot made of wood laced with strips of hide stood against one wall. Thick furs, like those hanging in the wardrobe in the other room, covered the bed.

There was only one other piece of furniture in the room, a small table, its legs obscured by hides hanging down to the floor. Weard placed his candle on the table, illuminating a pitiable small pile of...books! Erik stared but did not dare to step over to inspect them. He had tacitly assumed that the colonists had lost the ability to read, since they had obviously lost so much else. He stared at the books, trying to make out as much about them as he could in the dim, flickering light.

From across the small room, the bindings looked old, to be sure, but certainly not centuries old as they would have to have been if they had come with the original colonists; and the visible pages were much thicker, more primitive-looking than pages in the books Erik had seen. So someone, somewhere, relatively recently, must still have been making books. That conclusion was promising.

Weard took no overt notice of the books. He turned to the bed and reached up to a shelf almost hidden in shadows near the ceiling. He pulled down a bundle and tossed it to Erik.

"It gets cold at night." he said, then turned away.

Erik looked around. There was only the one bed, and that obviously belonged to Weard. The floor near the roughly curtained door was smooth and level, worn hard by the passage of many feet. The spot would have been uncomfortably small and cramped for Weard, but for once, Erik's slight construction—*build*, he corrected himself—was a definite advantage. He unrolled the bundle, which turned out to be tightly rolled pelts, their fur matted and crushed but still invitingly soft. He spread one out, stretched himself on it, and threw the other over him, cringing as the tanned inner surface touched his skin. As he had feared, the smell was overpowering. He sighed.

Weard turned at the small sound. Out of the corner of his eye, Erik saw the man straighten. Again, that hint of a smile played about Weard's mouth, too faint in the candle light for Erik to be sure. Then Weard took a step toward Erik, knelt, and pulled the fur off, flipping it high in the air and letting it fall, fur side down, against Erik's body. This time, he felt the fur itself, chilled by the night air but already warming, capturing his body heat and holding it in.

"Thanks," Erik said.

Weard stiffened, his face impassive as stone and cold as the red-stained, roiling waters where Marquette had died. Weard stood without a word and stepped back to his cot. He removed his outer garments, those cumbersome and bulky coverings of fur that would have broiled Erik under the hot sun of mid-day. He folded them carefully, setting them on the same shelf above the bed—the only shelf in the room, Erik noticed.

With his outer garments removed, Weard seemed slightly smaller, marginally less barbaric, less oversized. He wore a tunic of thin leather. In the darkness it appeared to have the texture of a fine velour, and was a deep, rich brown with overtones of gold. The material was well-prepared, for it seemed as pliant and soft as Erik's own uniform—and as durable, if not more so. Erik moved beneath the fur, fingering the long tear in arm of his tunic, feeling tufts of unfamiliar fur thrusting through other rips and tears in his uniform and pressing against his flesh.

Suddenly, Erik was overcome by acute physical fatigue, numbing mental weariness, and a deep confusion that left him staring fixedly at the ceiling. Every time he thought he had something figured out, he would discover some new datum that confounded and unbalanced him: Weard's unexpected knowledge of outer worlds; his obvious concern for Erik's feelings during their night conversation in the cavern, then his unbroken silence and coldness during their day-long march here; the obvious barbarism of the settlement itself, now the stack of books and the clothing. It undermined too many of his expectations.

A creaking drew Erik from his distracting thoughts. Weard had sat down heavily on the bed and undid the thongs which held his sandals against his feet. Barefoot, he stood and removed a leather pouch from his waist. Erik could not see what was in it, since Weard carefully turned his back to him before bending and depositing the pouch—or perhaps only its contents—behind the hangings on the table. Then Weard blew out the candle. In the darkness, Erik heard the man's movements as he finished undressing, followed by a series of creaks and groans from the cot.

For a moment there was silence. Erik stretched, pillowing his head in his arms, trying to think, trying to sleep. The ground was hard and cold but not damp. And actually, he realized, it was not all that cold, either. The furs insulated him well. The darkness was broken intermittently by flickering lights making their way through gaps in the outer walls, glowing from the dying central fires or from candle light in nearby huts.

When Weard spoke, it startled Erik, both by the break in the stillness and by the unaccountable gentleness in the man's tone.

"Have you need?"

"What?" Erik said, immediately aware of how childish it sounded.

"Body-need. Must you...?"

"Oh," Erik said, suddenly aware of an uncomfortable and increasingly urgent pressure in his bladder. He raised himself up and rested on his forearm, turning toward Weard's voice. "Uh, yes, I do...I must."

Another series of creakings welled up from the other side of the room. With a rasp, Weard lit another match and touched its head to the candle. Erik blinked in the brightness, taking several moments to register the other man's nakedness. In the candlelight, he seemed measurably larger, the muscles of his chest outlined and sharp as he sat on the cot, the hide covering tossed carelessly across his thighs. Erik could see the man's legs and feet, thick knots of muscle and sinew at eye level, only a meter away. Weard leaned over, reaching under the cot and pulling something out. It scraped against the dirt floor.

He motioned. For a second, Erik did not understand—and then he flushed, feeling blood pounding into his face.

It was just a large, bowl-shaped thing, possibly clay, possibly hollowed-out wood darkened by use and by the insufficient light the candle cast on it. Erik realized that he had assumed...that he had been thinking of...that it was *unthinkable* for any civilized being, even a Junk, even to consider....

Again that half-smile played over Weard's features. This time Erik was sure he had seen it, and his flush deepened. For some reason he wanted Weard to think well of him. There was no justification for such a wish, of course, particularly since the man was a murderer, a barbarian, a cruel taskmaster who had exhausted and almost deserted Erik during a forced march that in retrospect had no real purpose. He obviously despised Erik, felt superior to him, and now found him contemptible and amusing.

But all of that made no difference. Erik was drawn to the man, feeling a growing respect that had no referents in Erik's consciousness. He recalled that single cry when his hand struck the nettle, the look of disappointment that flashed across Weard's face, to be supplanted almost immediately by coldness and wariness. He couldn't risk another mistake, another hesitation that would....

Weard stood, the momentary expression again suppressed behind a mask of indifference. Unconcerned by his own nakedness he looked down at Erik, the expression in his glinting eyes unreadable. He pushed the bowl with the side of his foot and shoved it over to the far wall, then turned and stood there, his back to Erik.

Erik closed his eyes and swallowed dryly, hearing the splattering sounds and smelling the pungency of urine overlaying the other organic odors that suddenly sharpened and assailed him like hidden enemies waiting in the shadows.

Then there was silence, a slight vibration in the hard-packed earth, and the familiar creaking. Erik looked over. Weard was almost invisible, his body a lump beneath the fur coverings, his head hidden from Erik's view by the edge of the cot. There was no movement.

"Now you."

It was less offer than command. Erik threw back the edge of his fur and stood, carefully ignoring Weard, and walked toward the bowl. He fumbled with the fastening of his trousers.

For a terrifying moment, he could do nothing. The need was there, the building pressure—but nothing would come. And then, when it did, it seemed as if he would never, could never stop. Each passing moment embarrassed him further, took him further away from his world of hygiene and polished metallic cleanliness and inviolable privacy into this...this outpost world without even the rudiments of....

He finished.

Without turning, he spoke into the darkness of his shadow on the wall, "Is there someplace I should...."

"Leave it. Tomorrow. Now, sleep."

The candle light died. Erik turned and stepped over to his makeshift pallet.

As he sat heavily on the ground and started to pull the robes over him, Weard's voice broke the silence. Again Erik felt that occasional, fragile undertone of concern and care that vied with the other man's distance and coldness.

"It's warmer without clothing. Especially boots. Let the feet breathe."

"Thanks." Erik shrugged out of his tunic, shivering as the cool air washed across him. He pulled off his boots and socks, setting them against the wall near the head of his sleeping area. Then he stepped out of his trousers. His briefs glowed whitely in the fragmented light that filtered through the walls. He rolled trousers and tunic into a tight bundle, then set them next to his boots and crawled between the furs.

He lay for a long while, staring into nothingness, feeling warmth filtering through his body. He tried to plan, to think, but the smell of urine intruded into his thoughts, a constant, acrid reminder of yet another mistake, another failure. He wondered how he would ever sleep with that stench filling his lungs, but weariness overcame his worst fears. Gradually he lost awareness of his surroundings and began floating in a nebulous haze of warmth and softness.

Just before he entered into dreams—or perhaps just after—he seemed to hear a voice speaking quietly: "Sleep well."

He slept.

CHAPTER ELEVEN

Awakening the next morning was as much a shock as it had been the day before. Sunlight filtered gray shards through uneven cracks in the walls, the half-light spinning furiously off dust motes. Erik could see clearly, however, even in the dimness. Weard was gone, as was the roll of fur he used as an outer garment. Erik was on his feet in a second, wincing as stiff muscles complained at the sudden movement. He was not used to sleeping on bare earth, but surprisingly, he found himself refreshed and rested—in good spirits, really, as he stretched and unkinked and yawned heavily.

He shivered in the morning coolness, wishing to crawl back under the sleeping furs for just a few more moments. But that was impossible. He must...well, he wasn't sure what, but he couldn't lie around all day. He pulled on his trousers and tunic, shivering even more as their damp coldness struck his skin. His socks were stiff and matted; for a second he considered wearing his boots without them, then decided he couldn't. He had no idea what physical demands might be made of him, and he couldn't risk blisters. Still, the socks felt unclean and scratchy as he pulled them on.

Dressed, he stood and looked around the room. Everything else was as it had been.

Well, almost everything, he realized, feeling his face redden. The large bowl was gone from the far wall, as was the heavy-hanging acrid smell that Erik remembered from the night before. The candle, half-burned and streaked with black, stood on the small table. Beside it, the books beckoned.

But before exploring any further, Erik knelt down and smoothed out his sleeping furs, rolling and folding them as he walked across the narrow room, trying to make the bundle as neat as it had been when Weard handed it to him the night before. He could barely reach the shelf, but by bracing one foot on the side of the cot and lunging with the other, he boosted the bundle up. Satisfied, he stepped down to the floor and turned toward the table.

He picked up the first book. There was no title on the obviously hand-stitched leather cover. He flipped it open to the first page. There was no fly-leaf, either; apparently the people here chose not to waste paper on such useless frivolities. Instead, the first lines of a solid block of thick, black text stared at him, a title printed in heavy block letters across the top of the page like a sentry guarding what was to follow.

His hands trembled so violently that he nearly lost his grip on the thin volume.

Beowulf!

He hadn't expected to see that name—but finding the book here, in a warrior's hut, helped to answer so many questions. He would not have been surprised to see a badly copied technical manual, salvaged and reproduced as an heirloom, possibly unread and unreadable. Or a volume detailing the legal system on a colonial starship, preserved as an anchor with the past. But *Beowulf?*

At the same time, Erik felt a wash of relief. Seeing the words spelled out, the lines marching stolidly across the well-worn page, he had finally placed the language-variant. That ancient epic stemming from a time almost beyond human memory was among the few surviving documents of a barbaric past when all men lived as Weard lived now, not out of choice but out of necessity. It was, also, a mythic time, a heroic time, when warriors slew monsters and then gathered in the great mead-hall to celebrate their victories in songs and lays—*that*, he recalled, was the world of Beowulf.

He looked around at the stark interior of the hut. Somehow, he had not extrapolated from his studies of the text of the poem, years ago, seated at sterile and pristine library terminals, anything like this, the harshness and barbarism he had experienced so far.

His eyes dropped to the page.

Yes, there it was, in a reasonable transcription of the original writing:

> *Hwæt! We Gardena in geardagum, þeodcyninga,*
> *þrym gefrunon, hu ða æþelingas ellen fremedon.*

> Behold! We the Spear-Danes, in days of yore of
> the kings of the people have heard renown; how those
> princes displayed valor....

His mind swung instinctively into the chanting rhythm of the lines.

He scanned the book. The letters resembled pre-Collapse English, with lost letters ('Þ' and 'Ð,' for example) unreconstructed. The letters were not computer printed, certainly, but they didn't seem hand-formed either. They were ill-shaped, rude, and coarse, some broken along edge lines, but they were uniform. The colonists must have built some kind of rudimentary press. Still it was a curious chance that had preserved this particular book when so many others, more applicable to the problems of a colony's survival, had presumably perished from accident or neglect.

Erik set the volume back on the table and picked up the second one. This one didn't even have a title-page. He checked the binding, but there was no sign of mutilation. The text simply began. He glanced at the corner, but there was no pagination. The volume seemed to be a portion of a history of the First Dark Ages, although he did not recognize it specifically. It, too, was printed in the same odd characters as the *Beowulf*.

Okay, that explained some of the general configuration of this society, at least as far as he could define it—the emphasis on warrior-hunters; the barbaric village huddled behind a thorn-wall palisade; the modifications in the language itself, including Weard's calling-name—*guardian* in Old Anglo-Saxon.

He set the second book down, careful not to scratch the worn leather cover, arranging the two as they had been before he touched them. For the first time since waking after the scouter crashed, he felt that he had discovered some valuable information. He just had to figure out how to use it.

On an impulse, he knelt and pushed back the curtains hanging below the table. In the dark recess, he found a small cabinet, enclosed on three sides. The fourth side, facing him, was covered by a second, thinner curtain. He pulled the hanging to one side and let light spill into the cabinet.

It was empty.

Whatever Weard had placed there the night before was gone. Most likely it had been the pouch or its contents—the metal cup and metal-bladed knife probably.

Contemporary analogues to the arm-rings in *Beowulf*? Erik let the hanging fall back, obscuring the hiding place. He straightened and walked toward the doorway.

The outer chamber was empty. In the daylight he could see the furnishings better than he had the night before. Weapons hung on walls, lay stacked singly and in groups on shelves and on the hard-pack floor. Bundles of furs and other garments lay scattered among odd assortments of equipment cluttering the room. A few candles perched on the shelf near the exit, next to a wooden box that probably held matches.

No one seemed to be around, although Erik assumed that the other two interior doors opened onto sleeping chambers similar to Weard's. Most likely this hut, and perhaps this entire section of the settlement, was reserved for warriors of Weard's age and status: bachelor, young, possibly newly elevated to the ranks of the warriors. This could be a common-room. And in the wardrobe....

He stepped toward the single piece of furniture. It was well made; unlike the walls of the hut, it showed no cracks. The planks fit closely and securely, and were polished to a high gleam. The fur hanging in front was thick and soft and unusually beautiful, patterned in dark swirls of rust and black.

He reached toward it slowly, gathering courage to pull it aside.

"Prattling!"

The word was simultaneously a naming and a command. Erik's hand jerked back as if he were a child caught trying to raid a sweets-capsule. He swung to face the doorway.

A figure stood outlined in white light, the details of his face blunted by the silhouetting effect of the sun rising behind him. It didn't sound like Weard, although the man's size and shape roughly fit.

"It is not permitted."

The voice cut through the air, coldly and openly contemptuous, something he had not yet heard overtly in Weard's voice.

"Come!"

Again, the word became command. For the speaker, it was obviously unthinkable that anyone would dare not obey. Erik didn't. He caught sight of a stone-tipped spear hanging loosely in the speaker's hand and chose not to argue the point.

As he headed for the door, the man tossed one of the furs at him, gesturing for him to throw it over his shoulders like a cloak. It would help disguise his uniform, he understood. He would seem less a stranger.

Outside, he squinted and shielded his eyes from the bright light—he hadn't realized how pitifully dark the huts were, even during the day. The morning sun had just cleared the upper fringes of the thorn barrier. He looked around.

The place was larger than he had assumed the night before, with almost double the number of buildings he had estimated. Still, there were the four primary encampments within the perimeter of the palisade, each with its complement of wooden huts. In the center, the single structure seemed larger, more imposing—if such a term could apply to a roughly dressed, thatched-roofed building only marginally larger than the largest of the huts. It seemed more set apart, more consciously isolated.

The mead-hall, Erik realized. From *Beowulf.* What was it now? Yes, *Heorot,* the palace of Hrothgar the King.

His guide was leading him through the southern encampment toward the central building. The man was tall, perhaps a shade taller even than Weard, and muscular, from the back looking enough like Weard to be his brother. But then that was to be expected. The colonists would have had a limited genetic pool, and after four or five centuries with no infusion of new genes, everyone might begin to exhibit the more dominant characteristics. And here, size and strength seemed definitely linked to survival.

They walked past a few clusters of people, at first only young men like Weard and the guide, and later older men and an occasional woman. The women, he noted, were as statuesque as the men, tall, attractive, and strong. As they passed everyone turned away from Erik and his guide.

All right, Erik thought, *now I'm invisible as well as an alien...a true Junk.*

The mead-hall (he insisted on calling it that if only to help him remember the geography of the encampment) was clearly their destination. A small knot of men—mostly older, white-haired, wrinkled, but still powerful-looking—stood in the narrow yard between the fence and the building itself.

The guard approached the fence, then stopped. "Go."

He pointed with the tip of his spear toward the group of men. Erik stepped through the gateway. As he approached, the men separated into two groups, forming a narrow path. *Gauntlet,* he thought. Passing between the clusters of old men, he became more forcibly aware of his short stature, his litheness in contrast to the bulk surrounding him. It had been bad enough working with Spacers like Marquette; but here.... Even in their old age, these men had retained an undeniable sense of power and strength. No one spoke.

He finally reached the entryway. The doors hung open, great double doors of some dark-grained wood that had been polished to a metallic sheen. Without looking back, straightening himself and standing just a bit taller, he entered.

A voice spoke from the shadows to his right. Weard was waiting there. As Erik stepped into the darkness, the man grasped his elbow—only later did Erik realize that it was the first time Weard had touched him since pulling him from the stream and away from Marquette's dying form. The man whispered harshly.

"Be careful. This is the final test."

Final test? Then Erik had been right. Ever since his capture, he had been tested—and last night, first at the nettles and later in the hut itself, he had somehow partially or completely failed.

This was his last chance.

CHAPTER TWELVE

Weard stepped in front of Erik, preceding him into an inner chamber. The place seemed huge—its squat exterior had been deceptive. It was lit from above by a series of opaque skylights of some material Erik could not identify, and flanked on one wall by an enormous stone fireplace easily large enough for Erik—for a handful of Eriks—to stand in upright. Around the walls and scattered across the room were rough wooden benches, smoothed and polished on the seats more by use than by design. At the far end, a low wooden dais rose a few centimeters from the hard-pack. On it stood a warrior.

A Warrior.

That was the only way to describe him. He was taller than Weard, taller than Erik's unnamed guide, and more mature than both. He wore the same garments as everyone Erik had yet seen, with no hint of adornment except for a thin silver band about each upper arm. Later, when he stepped closer, Erik saw that the bands were made of a steel alloy, a product of lost technology far more valuable as an honorific than any native silver or other metals might be.

The man's hair was long and dark, with occasional shots of white. This was *the* warrior, a warrior among warriors, who commanded respect and obedience even from Weard. The closer Erik came to the man, the less confident he felt, the more like a guilty child.

Behind Erik, the double file of older men shuffled in, taking their seats as if in a pre-arranged order on both sides of the hall.

Weard spoke first.

"Æthele, I bring the Stranger."

Weard gestured for Erik to step forward. When Æthele spoke, it was to Weard, not to Erik.

"Where are the relics?" His voice—the intonation, the voicing of consonants and vowels—carried the unmistakable timbre of ritual; not surprisingly, he spoke using the language Erik had come to think of as the common tongue for the settlement. Erik wondered yet again what was happening, what invaluable clues he was missing in the interchange.

As soon as the sound of Æthele's voice ceased in the hall, Weard stepped forward, pulled out the leather pouch hidden beneath his cloak and slowly, ceremoniously opened it, reached in, and removed several items. These he laid one at a time across the wooden floor of the dais, at Æthele's feet. The glare of light from one of the overhead panels fell directly on the objects, shimmering reflectively from metallic surfaces.

Erik recognized two holstered weapons and two ExServ flight belts, intact, just as they had been when Weard demanded them. There were no weapons on the belts, only a short-range communicator and small packets of tools designed for use at the computer terminal. Nothing of any immediate help, even if Erik could by some chance lay his hands on them. Next to the belts lay his service insignia...and Marquette's.

The warrior lifted up one of the flight belts, holding it high over his head, the sunlight glinting from the polished webbing. Then he lowered it and stood silently, studying Erik.

Finally he spoke: "Who are you?"

Erik was unsure how to answer. He had approached the truth with Weard, and undoubtedly the younger man had related everything of their conversations to the older. He would continue on that path.

Briefly, nervously, he outlined his mission to the planet and its sudden, disastrous conclusion, his role in the Exploration Service, the ultimate purposes of the ExServ, and his own presence on the planet. He avoided any complex explanations of his status as an Adjunct. And he said little of Marquette's death, since he did not yet trust himself to put the experience into words, nor could he gauge his audience's reactions to the bitterness, anger, and frustration welling in him. It would be safer to stay as objective as possible. He was allowed to continue uninterrupted, although occasional sounds of approbation (usually in passages narrating Weard's actions) or disbelief (in those passages relating to Erik's own life) echoed from the old men. Gradually he reached the climax of his narration and his appeal.

"Our purposes are of the highest," he concluded, struggling to incorporate his peroration into the grammar and syntax of the archaic dialect and fearing that he would come across merely as prolix and rhetorical. "We of the Ex-Serv come unarmed. There were no war-weapons in our ship. Those…"—he gestured to the holsters still lying on the dais, still glinting in the light—"…were only for protection, not offense. Even now I stand before you without a weapon, without means of defending myself or inflicting injury upon your people. I am here as your servant, to prepare you for the changes which must come. The Comity is eager to recover her colonies, her children abandoned by others so many generations ago, to lead them, to help them enter into a union of peoples which now embraces the habitable worlds of our system. I come peacefully, willing to help you with all at my disposal."

His final words met with a long and distinctly uncomfortable silence.

To each side of him and behind him, Erik heard muffled shuffling, as if some of the old men were nervously awaiting their headman's responses. Weard was absolutely silent and unmoving, standing slightly behind Erik, just within range of his peripheral vision. Only the warrior on the dais seemed to move as his eyes darted over Erik, continuing his uninterrupted assessment of the stranger before him. The eyes seemed intent on finding a point at which to penetrate Erik's body, his mind, his soul.

Erik waited for the response, his breath caught painfully somewhere midway between lung and throat. The success of his mission, perhaps his very life, depended upon the decisions reached at this moment. Yet when Æthele finally spoke, it was in a different tone—and to different effect—than Erik had anticipated.

"You think us primitives and barbarians, don't you, young man?" Suddenly, the harsh gutturals of the language disappeared, although more than faint traces of an alien pronunciation remained. The word forms were much closer to the norms of pre-Collapse English than Erik was used to hearing from Weard and the guide. Vocabulary, syntax, structure were all more sophisticated than any utterances he had yet heard.

Now the voice hardened. Erik felt the steel biting into Æthele's words. "You think us barbarians and fools, eager to relinquish the lives we have forced this world to give us, to turn our selves, our families, our futures over to an unknown and foreign power. This *Comity* you speak of, what is it that we should wish to affiliate with it? Is it merely another empire, commanded by force and threatening to overrun our world should we refuse your offer?"

Erik was startled by the alteration in the man, yet part of his self-control returned within seconds. The shift in linguistic patterns had momentarily disoriented him, as surely had been Æthele's intention. Now, however, he spoke forcefully and clearly.

"We are not instruments of force, sir. The choice is yours"—not precisely the truth, Erik thought ruefully, remembering occasional savage incidents on other planets. But then those other ExServ missions had not had quite the intimate awareness of the needs and desires of the former colonies that Erik might be able to provide here. He could mediate between the Comity and this world, resolve any differences in advance.

"The choice is yours," he continued. "We come merely to extend an offer by which you might return to the level of civilization and progress which your fathers knew. You have memories of such worlds, I am sure. You have retained the speech of your fathers. You have books which tell of worlds which have been. Now you have the chance to learn of the worlds which are, of advanced societies which you may join."

Æthele studied him for a moment before answering. "You come, then, to lead us into the light of progress and civilization, to raise us from the dust in which we now choke, and carry us to the stars?"

Erik wanted to shout a resounding *yes* but held back, literally biting his tongue until pain washed through his body. The irony and sarcasm in Æthele's voice were too profound to miss. He straightened and assumed what dignity he could under the circumstances.

"Sir?"

Æthele shifted the direction of the dialogue once more. "You are a man of the Comity, is this not so?"

"I am of the Comity, yes, sir."

"You have had the advantages of civilization and progress for... for how many years, now?"

"Twenty-three, sir. I am twenty-three Standard years old, roughly the equivalent of twenty among your own people, given the variances in orbit and...." He stopped, his face reddening as he recognized the lecturing, condescending tone he had assumed. "I am twenty-three," he continued. "I was nurtured by the Comity as an Adjunct, educated for my services at University Center and the Exploration Service Academy, if that is what you mean."

"It is. That is sufficient. Now, what have you to offer us?"

Erik began again, relieved that he would have a second chance to present the ideals of the ExServ and the Comity, to argue more persuasively (now that he had had a chance to think things through more fully) than he had before. He began speaking, only to be cut off immediately by Æthele.

"No. You misunderstand me. I asked what *you* could offer us. You personally, Erik Baanfeld, Emissary of the Wondrous Worlds

Beyond and Missionary of the Gospel of Civilization and Progress." Again the steel-edge irony cut through the room, shocking Erik in its intensity. He felt his cheeks redden. "What have *you* to present to us?"

"But I'm only an Ad—," Erik began, then stopped. He swallowed hard, feeling a sudden chilling draft originating somewhere behind him and blowing across the back of his neck. This question represented the critical point in his mission, perhaps in his life. He must answer it properly, honestly, convincingly, or lose any measure of acceptance he might thus far have achieved. Out of the corner of his eye, he saw Weard flick a glance at him then return to his unmoving, stone-like posture.

Yet what could he say?

"I have training in languages and...."

"We have but one language here," Æthele said harshly, "and we have neither need nor desires for others. We understand each other. We speak the common language among the people, reserving the high tongue for the confines of this building alone. We need no scholars. Our books are few and well understood by all. No, that is not sufficient. What more can you offer?"

Erik thought frantically—wished desperately for a terminal and a Jack to tell him what to say. This kind of dialogue had not been imagined during Training. But he must not lose control now. "I have knowledge of computers and of communications devices."

"Again useless," Æthele said, condemnation heavy in his voice. "We have no such things. Indeed we barely retain memories of them. When we must communicate with other settlements, we send out swift runners bearing writings, or for far journeys, riders. Our network is sufficient for our needs. Have you other skills?"

"Well...I have medicines and other supplies in the wreckage of my ship. With a small party, I could return and bring them to you. I could alleviate pain and suffering, decrease the frequency of illness, save lives which might otherwise be lost"—unbidden the image of Marquette, bandaged and swathed in foam, rose in Erik's mind. He closed it out.

"Again you misunderstand me, *prattling*." Erik had heard the term before, but had not until now considered its possible meanings. Now the full weight of disdain implicit in it registered. The inflections were unmistakable. He was a thing of no merit or status—less on this world even that he had been as a Junk on his own—until (and unless) he proved otherwise.

Æthele continued. "You misunderstand me—willfully, I begin to fear. You come to us, claiming to represent a society far superior to our own. You urge us to welcome you with trust and confidence, promising wonders and marvels.

"But we already know of these marvels. They were promised us once before, and those promises were not kept. *Our* fathers were brought here to a promised world, then abandoned by *your* fathers, by 'civilized' men who nonetheless nearly destroyed their own worlds, if I understand your account correctly. Now you have managed to salvage some remnants of this dissipated Empire from the ruins, and armed with these machines and devices you come here to demand—oh, politely to be sure, and with all deference—that we once more enslave ourselves to a political entity which has already once proven false to us.

"You imply that the men of the Comity—*Empire*, by another name, for all we know or care—are superior to us, to the out-world savages who have managed somehow to scrape out an existence on this rude world. You, who are smaller and weaker than the least of our sons and are by your own account among the least of your own people, who claim to have such great stores of knowledge, but can produce nothing of worth to us—why should we believe or trust you? Why should we sever our ties with generations past and ally ourselves with the hope of the unnamed stars beyond? We have enough here for us. Do we need more?"

Erik stared, disoriented by the polite vehemence of the speech. But he had no time to plan a clear rebuttal. From all sides now, new voices rose, old and cracked or ringing with the vigor of maturity, hurling questions at him:

"Can you fight with spear?"

"Can you fashion arrows of flint, or shape flawless shafts, or fletch?"

"Can you follow hidden trails in the starlight?"

"Can you find water during the scorching summer days?"

"Can you...?"

"Can you...?"

Erik whirled, trying to isolate individual interrogators but the questions flew too fast for him to pinpoint any single sources. He spun on his heels, encircled by the men, taller and heavier than himself, stronger and more ruthless, at home on a world he had never imagined, let alone experienced. They raised no fist to him, bared no weapons, but he felt the contempt and hatred for his kind echoing from them.

With a single sound, Æthele regained control of the men. They fell silent and retreated into the shadows along the walls.

"Can you do any of these things? These are the services which are essential for us here. We have no need for your science, your civilization, your progress...unless you can show us how your knowledge can fit into our world. *You* are the Stranger, the Alien, not we. The burden of proof, I believe, falls upon you."

Erik had to make an answer, yet there was none. From the perspective of this world, Æthele was right.

Oh, he was a fair hand in combat sports, or at least had been at University Center. He had even tried once or twice to gain some proficiency with a bow and arrow. But he had no illusions about his competence. Anyone in the room—probably anyone in the entire settlement old enough to more than toddle—could outperform him any day. He knew little about hunting, less about rural living, nothing at all about the particular skills necessary here.

But he couldn't simply accept their indictment of his world. There *was* good in it. He *could* bring much to these people, if only they would let him.

It was up to him to make them let him. That was his mission now. All else paled before it. Inadvertently he had become First Contact. As an Adjunct, he was untrained for the position, unprepared to accept it, but the choice had been taken from him. He was here, had spoken to them, had—wisely or unwisely, that made no difference now—exposed them to knowledge of the Comity. He could not have done otherwise, he knew. He had not the ability to pass as one of them, nor the physical makeup to do so, even had he tried. He had been open and honest.

And they had returned the compliment. They had been honest and frank. Æthele put the matter concisely.

"Ours is a stable society. Only a few of us, those of this Council and our brethren in Councils in other settlements, know fully of our past. We have preserved records that outline the history of the original colony, beginning with the founding of *this* enclave and moving through the slowly dawning realization that the men and women who settled here had been cruelly and ruthlessly abandoned, without the supplies and technologies they had been promised. Suddenly, they had to survive on a world to which they were not suited, which they did not understand, with no help, absolutely no help from the worlds beyond the stars. Many died. Many despaired and ceased their struggle.

"But a few refused to accept defeat. They were our true fathers, those committed survivors. They banded together, determined to create a way of life that would wed them to the alien soil that imprisoned them. And they did.

"They hid much of the knowledge of the past from their children, including the histories of the Empire, the worlds beyond. They would not have their children grow up dependent upon myths and legends of supernaturally wise beings who would one day return to take them by the hands again.

"No, we rejected that past. We created our own. There were a few books. By chance, one of the colonists was a scholar. He provided the model for the world we created. Only we of the inner Council, those of us within this hall at this moment, know that everything you have claimed is true. Oh, perhaps not everything, but we can accept the existence of the Comity, the ExServ, the missions to abandoned colonies.

"But outside this hall, there is a different world, with a different history, different traditions, even a different language. It is a world which died on Earth two thousand years before the earliest intimations of an Empire, one which had ceased to exist except for the broken lines of a single decaying manuscript preserved and copied diligently by antiquarians and scholars.

"But it was the one world which would allow us to survive. *Beowulf* provided our structure for living, our government, our morality and ethics, our language. Our people read the poem *as life*, and live their lives as poem.

"Not verbatim, of course, but in large measure. Within these walls, in the presence of these few men, I am one kind of person, rational, cultured perhaps, even progressive, as we define the term. But during every other moment of my life, I am a chieftain, a Germanic Ring-giver, Warrior of warriors, barbarian, savage.

"Do not misunderstand me this time, Erik Baanfeld. We do not play at being savages. We *are* savages. We must be, to survive, just as our people must be to survive."

He thrust an outstretched arm toward Erik. The sun reflected coldly off the metal bands on his arm.

"Just as you must become to survive."

Erik's presuppositions crumbled. Nothing he had experienced, studied, even heard about had prepared him for such a situation. A catastrophically regressive culture, consciously retrograde in all essentials, led by men who were fully aware of what they were doing.

And he must somehow persuade them to reverse the direction of centuries of hide-bound tradition—of lies and deceit, of making human beings recapitulate conditions that died out millennia before. But what could he possibly do about it?

Æthele was speaking again. The violence in his voice had disappeared, leaving only a hint of sadness.

"Erik Baanfeld, we would wish that you and your colleagues had never found our world. We are content here. True, this is a dangerous and violent world, but we have made our compromises and accommodations.

"Now you threaten to shatter that.

"If you wish to survive in our world, here are our conditions. You must become one of us. Outside of this council, you must cease being a member of the Comity. You must never mention it, never refer in any way to worlds beyond, to technology, to science, to knowledge beyond that which would be natural to one of our world. You must speak our language, wear our clothing, eat our food, making no attempts to introduce into our lives elements which you feel are superior or more 'civilized' than ours.

"If you fail *once*, you will be killed. Quickly, efficiently, as a danger to the community. No second chance. Is that clear?"

Erik nodded numbly. Killed, just as Marquette had been. Mercifully, perhaps, but surgically removed.

"Furthermore, you must make your own way within our society. No place will be given to you. You claim that your Comity has much to offer. Your proof shall be your survival. We have no room for those who cannot contribute to the safety of the Folk. Do you accept these conditions?"

Erik nodded again. He had no choice. Then he cautiously asked the important question.

"Sir, my ship lies within a two-day's march. Is it permitted that I return once to it to...?"

"It is not. The lowlands lie outside our control. We rarely venture there"—here he cast a pointed glance at Weard, who stiffened even more, if that were possible. He looked back at Erik without so much as a break in the rhythm of his speech. "And when we do, we do so only briefly. We cannot spare the men to see you safely through the dangers. You must remain here. That is the condition I lay down in exchange for your life. You may not return."

"Yes, sir."

Æthele turned his attention to the men behind Erik, motioning them forward with an imperious wave of his hand, a movement more in keeping with his chosen role as Ring-giver than that of an enlightened governor.

"These are my words. The *prattling* Baanfeld may remain with us, become one with us. He is to receive no special treatment—neither helpful nor hindering. He is as one of our own children, untrained, inexperienced. However, one must bear responsibility for him. Is there one willing?"

No one spoke. Erik felt his face grow hot as he realized the enormous burden he might become to one of them. That one must not only supervise his activities, constantly monitoring him for any signs of relapse into his old patterns of behavior; but, perhaps even more difficult, his warden could also become his executioner. The old men murmured among themselves before, one by one, they hesitantly withdrew into the shadows. Finally only Erik, Æthele, and Weard remained in the light near the center of the hall.

"I accept him, sir," Weard said. Erik shot a darting glance at his one-time captor, now apparently guardian in law as well as in fact. The face turned toward Æthele was as expressionless as the stone face of the cliffs overlooking the river where Marquette had died. Erik could not determine whether Weard had accepted him out of duty or pity.

"So be it," Æthele intoned. He nodded slightly, his eyes angled over Erik's shoulder. Behind him, he heard the creaking of the huge double doors and the shuffling of feet as the Council filed out. One old man remained near the dais for a moment, then disappeared into the deeper darkness behind it, returning within a few seconds bearing a bulky bundle which he dropped at Erik's feet.

Passing by Erik's shoulder, the old man continued across the hall and out the doors, swinging them closed after him. Erik heard the double doors shut, a bar dropping across their width.

Æthele let the silence linger for long moments. Weard still did not move. Finally the Ring-giver spoke.

"You must leave your out-world coverings here. Some have seen it already, but that could not be helped. When you leave here, however, you must be garbed as one of us."

He nodded to indicate that Erik should do so immediately. Without pausing, Erik tugged his ExServ tunic over his head, conscious of his tousled hair as the soft material pulled up and off. He looked up at Æthele, who gestured toward Weard. Erik folded the tunic with as much ceremony as he could muster and handed it to the man.

Then he removed his boots, balancing on one foot as he pulled the boot from the other. He pulled his stained and matted socks off, rolling them together and stuffing the roll into the toe of one of the boots, embarrassed by the dampness, the dark stains, and the pervasive odor that three days of wear had given them. He handed the boots over to Weard, who solemnly accepted them and carefully laid the tunic on top of them.

He removed his badly torn trousers, slipped his only marginally less damaged underwear down and stepped out of them, handing them in turn over to his guardian. Piece by piece, he shed his identity as a member of the ExServ of the Twelve Worlds Comity, until he stood naked in the shaft of light, outlined by silver brightness in the morning sun. He felt defenseless and weak, vulnerable, even though only Weard and Æthele were present to witness the moment.

He felt rather than saw Æthele assess his arms and chest, the musculature of thigh and leg. A quick glance passed between the dais and the shadows behind him, although Erik could make nothing of its meaning. Perhaps they judged him to small, too weak to survive; perhaps they were wondering how long he might manage to last in their world. He shivered, his bare flesh cool and the blood animating it abruptly cooler yet.

He watched Æthele closely, hoping to catch some more definite sign in the man's face or eyes.

"Kneel, prattling," Æthele commanded. Eyes pinioned on the man on the dais, with no support from either side or from behind, Erik dropped heavily to one knee, then to both. The hard-pack floor might seem smooth and featureless to Weard and his people, but to Erik, its gritty roughness felt like tiny knives cutting into tender flesh.

"Head bowed," Æthele added, "to show respect, and to show fear."

Erik did so, curling his head downward until his chin pressed uncomfortably into his chest and his throat felt so constricted that for an instant he nearly panicked for lack of breath.

"Clasp your hands behind your back."

Feeling increasingly vulnerable, as if his nakedness were not sufficient to humiliate him, but knowing that his one alternative to obedience would probably be death, he obeyed.

Someone—Weard, it had to be, since everyone else had left earlier—approached from behind. The desire, the need, the utter *compulsion* to look back was strong; it demanded all of Erik's concentration to withstand. He stared at a single glittering mica fleck on the ground between his knees, memorizing the way it winked the sunlight back to him, staring at it until his eyes began to water and blur. He concentrated on remaining stone-still and urged his body not to move, not to breathe. If he could have, he would have stilled the beating of his heart and the surging rhythm of his blood.

Behind him, leather creaked ominously, a warm current of air eddied against his back, and he felt Weard's massive presence close to him. When the words came, they were a whisper as soft as breath, barely carrying to Erik's ears. They were harsh, yet not harshly spoken.

"For your life, prattling, do not dare move."

Erik stiffened even further. His body—chilled and trembling only moments before—felt now as if it were aflame. His shoulders burned in the fragment sunlight; sweat dropped heavily from his forehead, from his chin, even—absurdly—from the tip of his nose. Sweat streamed down his ribcage and pooled in the darkness between his legs.

Weard's hand gripped Erik's wrists, pinioning both of his hands against the now-painful arc of Erik's spine. Weard pressed harder, immobilizing him. With Weard's full weight grinding Erik's wrist bones into the soft flesh of his back, and compressing his buttocks into the aching flesh of his calves and ankles, Erik doubted that he could move if he wished to, and wondered half madly if he would ever move again.

"Remember," Weard whispered, and this time the word was impregnated with threat and consequence.

A cold edge touched the back of Erik's neck. He stifled an involuntary shiver as flesh tried to draw back from what he instinctively knew had to be the unsheathed blade of Weard's knife.

It touched again, more firmly, scraped lightly across Erik's skin, caught with an instant of shock on something hard and equally metallic—the half-centimeter wide circumference of his Jack—and then with what had to be a single movement, vicious and deft, outward and upward virtually simultaneously, Weard excised the Jack itself, ripping it from the inorganic conductors that had been built into Erik's flesh.

He thought he was going to die. Or lose consciousness. Or at the least faint. The pain, through mercifully brief, was intense beyond anything he could have imagined. The instant the bloody Jack thudded to the dirt floor, and perhaps only a second or two before Erik would have toppled to his side, Weard's arm shifted from his imprisoned wrists to his shoulder, and the bulk and weight of his guardian-captor helped him to rise shakily to his feet.

From the dais, Æthele had watched the operation, unmoving and distant. Erik later doubted that the warrior had so much as blinked—and he half feared that had he convulsed, collapsed, or bled to death right there at the man's feet, Æthele would have watched with the same dispassionate silence.

Weard pressed something—a damp cloth pungent with aromatic oils—against Erik's neck and as Erik breathed the redolent air, he felt a blessed numbness work its way from the wounded neck upward and downward. Again he almost staggered, this time from relief, but Weard's body unobtrusively supported his own.

Erik had no idea how long they stood there, two figures so close that they might almost be a single mutant meta-human, rigid and unmoving beneath the eye of the warrior on the dais.

Finally, however, Erik drew a deep breath and straightened. Weard withdrew his supporting arm, and Erik raised his head—amazing that there was no pain, either surface or internal!—and looked up at the dais.

Æthele nodded again. Weard disappeared into the shadows for a few moments. Erik locked his gaze on Æthele's, refusing to so much as waver, straightening his shoulders and back until he stood at attention. Weard returned and laid a tightly wrapped on the edge of the dais. Æthele gave unspoken assent, and Erik knelt down to unroll the bundle. It contained several articles of clothing. He picked up a loincloth and slowly, gingerly stepped into it, careful not to upset the cool cloth on his neck as he tugged sinewy ties tight across his right hip. The leather under-tunic was not as soft as Weard's had appeared. He had not yet earned such comfort...or perhaps he was expected to make his own, if these did not suit him. The outer furs were coarse and stiff, matted, dirty, and heavily redolent with decay. Erik's empty stomach lurched as he threw the ragged edges over his shoulders.

He squatted on the hard-packed earth, understanding without being told that he must not balance himself on the dais, and separated the laces of the leather sandals, then sat back and wove them around his feet, trying to remember as best he could how Weard's looked, glancing once at the other man's feet and ankles to check crossings and knots.

Finally, fully clothed, he stood before Æthele. He was more shocked than anything by the realization that his neck barely hurt at all and was in fact subliminally itching as it began to heal. While Erik thought that some of the medications still stored in the scouter might have cut the pain as quickly, he knew that none of them could have begun the healing process so quickly.

Teaching these people something new might be more difficult that I imagined, he thought, quickly turning his attention back to the dais as Æthele began to speak.

"You are now one with us. Your trial begins." The warrior had returned to the archaic tones of the language-construct which served for all normal communications. "From this moment on, you will be constantly watched. If you pass this test, we may consider again the suggestions you have made about your world. If you fail, we will cleave unhindered to the old ways, refusing in any manner possible any subsequent overtures by your colleagues from off-world."

Erik replied in the same tones, haltingly at first; the abrupt return to archaic forms, especially following so closely on the physical and psychic shock of the loss of his Jack, had been as disconcerting as Æthele's initial switch to pre-Collapse English.

"How long will the test endure?" His voice surprised him, much stronger and resonant than he would have expected. It almost seemed to echo from the darkness surrounding them.

For a long while, Æthele did not answer. He looked closely at the ExServ belt still hanging from his hands, then at the stack of clothing Weard again held. He stepped down from the dais and took the clothing, then turned his back on Erik, and walked silently away, stopping only once to pick up the remaining insignia lying on the wooden planks. Then, taking with him the sum of everything that had once represented Erik Baanfeld of the ExServ, he disappeared behind the dais. Standing in the glow of the sun as it filtered through the ceiling, Erik could see nothing beyond the darkness. He could, however, hear a faint sound, as of metal on metal, or tumblers, perhaps, in an old-style lock. A door squealed open, closed, opened again and closed. Then there was a final, definitive click. Yes, he decided, hidden back there was a metallic lock of some kind.

When Æthele returned to the dais, his hands hung empty at his side.

Taking a deep breath, Erik repeated his question. "How long will the test endure, sir?"

Æthele looked at him gravely and, it seemed suddenly to Erik, sadly. "For the rest of your life, prattling. For the rest of your life."

CHAPTER THIRTEEN

Erik followed Weard outside into the bright glare of daylight, both momentarily blinded after the hall's darkness. They stood at the great doors, allowing their eyes to readjust before they stepped out.

With that step, Erik Baanfeld, scholar and Adjunct-Spacer, Comity servant, ExServ para-officer, ceased to exist. In his place stood the prattling, the untried, the untested, garbed in stinking animal hides, a bloody rag wrapped around his neck, standing in the shadow of a warrior as a child might hide behind its father for protection.

Weard turned and walked toward one of the compounds, Erik at his heels, still shaky but recovering, surprised to find himself not significantly debilitated by his ordeal. No one in the compound paid any attention to them. By now most of the people must be in the fields working, Erik thought, or involved with day-to-day tasks here in the enclosure and too engrossed to look up—or more likely, they had been warned by Æthele *not* to look up. He wondered what covering tale the Elders had circulated to account for him.

They walked to the same part of the settlement Erik had been in the night before. He studied it more closely, aware of its sudden importance in his life. He had left it that morning expecting...well, he was not sure what, but surely not the sentence that had been passed. He returned to it condemned to spend the rest of his life there.

However long *that* might be.

They threaded through the clusters of huts, Erik's eyes watering in the combination of bright sunlight and harsh wood smoke billowing from cooking- and work-fires. Odors strong and ripe rippled across him; he had neither time nor inclination to discover specifically where they came from. All too soon, he feared, he would be intimately familiar with the peculiarities of the place.

Once inside Weard's hut, Weard took some coarse black bread, a hunk of oily strong-smelling cheese, and a dipper of cold water from a shelf and handed them to Erik; but in spite of Erik's assumption, the sparse meal was not prisoner's fare. Erik ate every bit as well, and as much, as Weard, who squatted silently across the room. Erik gradually realized how hungry he actually was, how long it had been since he had eaten his fill, but he did not dare ask for more.

Finally, Weard stood and said, "Come this way, Erik."

For a moment, Erik stared, confused at hearing his eke-name name spoken in a voice such as one might use with a colleague, or a friend. He pulled himself to his feet and followed Weard into the sleeping chamber.

Stripes of brightness cutting across the floor and walls provided enough light to see. Weard stood by the cot, his legs almost touching the small cabinet supporting the books—books now subtly more important than before.

"Let me look at your wound," Weard said, even as he was removing the cloth from Erik's neck. The man held the impromptu bandage for Erik to take, while he studied the back of Erik's neck. He must have approved of what he saw, since he grunted, took the cloth from Erik, left the room for a brief moment, and returned without the rag.

Weard studied Erik for a moment.

"Take off your clothes. Let me show you how to do the bindings properly."

Erik pulled the rank furs and tunic carefully over his head, then untied the sandals, frustrated and angered when the thongs slipped into awkward, knotted tangles around his ankles. Weard laughed— and Erik suddenly felt in some degree, however small, however temporary, part of this place. Weard was treating him as a human being, not as a sub-human Junk or an alien under an indeterminate sentence of death.

Still smiling, Weard inspected Erik's clothing. He retied the loincloth, shifting it subtly until it fit smoothly on Erik's hips. He replaced the tunic, tightening it here and there, shortening several of the ties, cutting away a bit of leather with his knife. Gradually, the clothing welded itself to Erik's body. The Council had probably scraped together the cast-off garments of fast-growing boys. Adults were too large for Erik to have worn their clothing, and the tunic chafed at the shoulders and arms, as if broken in by a body-structure Erik's size but still immature and consequently differently proportioned than Erik's. Just walking from the hall to the compound had been enough to start small abrasions where rough seams bit into his skin. Under Weard's conscientious touch, however, the hides became more supple, comfortable even, and allowed a freedom of movement Erik hadn't anticipated. He looked at Weard, his surprise openly expressed on his face.

Weard smiled, then the smile disappeared, replaced by the closed-mouthed solemnity of yesterday's forced march through the forest. Erik shivered. Weard bend forward and spoke, again almost whispered, the urgency of his words chilling in Erik's ears.

"We have had centuries to refine our techniques. We are committed to this style of dress by the requirements of survival on a planet with few resources, and by the requirements of the culture we have created. It may seem crude to you, but it meets our needs well. It *is* harsh and rough, but it is also sturdy and protective."

Erik nodded, looking down at the intricate knots decorating Weard's calves. He had much to learn, it seemed. And his education was beginning immediately. His superficial sense of superiority, bolstered by his initial discovery of how uncomfortable and ill-fitting the clothing was, diminished as the garments smoothed over his shoulders and sides, becoming almost part of his skin.

Weard knelt and began retying the sandals. An irritated spot that threatened to blister was eased, and the thick leather soles shifted slightly under Erik's tender feet. Knots of tension in his ankles and calves disappeared as well.

Weard straightened and faced Erik, severe now, and unsmiling.

"I have shown you once. You must now care for yourself. Perhaps I have exceeded my instructions in helping you, but I would have you begin your test as one of us, with some of the knowledge that even our youngest children possess. If you fail to check the knots, though, or make them too tight or too loose, you might injure yourself and become useless. That must not happen."

Erik nodded. To be crippled here would be tantamount to a sentence of death.

"Now remove your clothing and retie it," Weard ordered, stepping to the other side of the room.

Erik obeyed, methodically stripping and laying the garments carefully on the bed.

"Roll them," Weard said, giving an occasional word of advice as Erik rolled the bulky clothes into a compact bundle.

He concentrated on each movement, forgetting his nakedness, becoming as a newborn child in his single-minded attention to the smallest details of a world he did not yet understand.

"Now dress again."

He began pulling and tugging, tying and twisting as he remembered Weard doing, constantly aware of his tutor-executioner's attention. He struggled to keep his hands steady.

When he finished, he looked up at Weard. Weard barely glanced at Erik. "Again."

For the third time, Erik stood naked, stripped not only of clothing but increasingly of any means of defining himself. This time, because he was more comfortable with the complexities of knots and ties, he was simultaneously conscious of Weard's eyes at his back, and his pulse pounded and his face grew hot and flushed.

"Now dress."

He did so, keeping his back to Weard as much as possible.

When he finished, the warrior inspected Erik closely, then muttered, "Satisfactory, for now."

Disappointment cut through Erik. He had hoped for more. Weard gestured and left the hut. Erik followed. They walked through the compound, skirting small groups of young men.

"Many are absent," Weard explained, "since the defense of the Folk requires constant vigil. Thus far, we have managed to restrict the *grendela* to the lower forests. Yet they constantly attempt assaults here, on the upper plateau. Our young men guard against them."

"Grendela?"

"The beasts of the first night of our journey. Great shadowy beasts, with many arms. They are fearsome, voracious, devilish. And difficult to kill...impossible for a single man to stand against, almost so for fewer than five or six."

"And that's why we ran?" Erik began, then fell silent.

"Yes."

For a long while, they stood near the center of the warrior's area. The sun beat down, hot and unbroken. Rivulets of sweat beaded on Erik's forehead, smudging the dust on his temples. His clothing was uncomfortably hot. In spite of his care with the bindings, his feet itched where leather rubbed against them.

Without speaking, he bent to adjust the knots. When he straightened, Weard met his glance and nodded approvingly. Erik noticed that the other man had also loosened the fastenings on his cloak, throwing the bulk onto his shoulders instead of letting it hang over his body. Gratefully Erik followed his lead, baring his legs and chest to the sun. Within moments he was cooler yet wonderfully warmed and heartened by the heat on his bare skin.

They continued on, leaving the central compound and heading for a large enclosure in the shadow of the thorn-bush palisade. The area was cordoned by a low fence, barely waist high to Erik, clearly intended more as a warning than as a true barrier. Inside, a handful of young men were practicing—at least that was the only interpretation Erik could place on their activities. Several were paired off, thrusting at each other with spears, warding blows with heavy leather shields. The air surrounding them was stifling with heat and dust. Weard led Erik to the closest pair. In an undertone, the man explained the finer points of the exercise. Erik tried to listen but found himself caught up in the drama of the encounter. The two might be just practicing, but to Erik's eyes they seemed deadly serious. The tip of one spear was tinged with scarlet, and the man standing opposite the spear was breathing hard, a slowly widening splotch of red staining the gray of his tunic, but he did not seem slowed by the wound.

The two circled, spear bracing against shield, shield against spear. Erik lost track of the time, so engrossed was he in the exhibition. The two warriors continued, thrusting, parrying, deflecting, occasionally striking, drawing blood from yet another wound.

"Is this some kind of grudge match?" Erik finally whispered as one of the combatants landed a staggering blow on the other. "Or a fight to the death?"

"What do you mean?" Weard also spoke in a whisper.

"It looks as if one of them is trying to kill...."

The wounded man thrust hard, his spear pinioning the other's shield in the dirt.

Weard shouted, "Enough."

The two disengaged immediately, pleased grins creasing their faces. They were panting in the heat. As they approached Weard, Erik could smell the strong odor of unwashed young bodies, of perspiration caked into untanned leather, of exertion and strain...and blood.

"Well fought," Weard said, clasping each of the two in his strong grip, just above their elbows. Weard wore two intricately engraved metallic bands in precisely the same spots—marks of rank or valor, Erik decided. The younger fighters were unadorned. They were novices, eager to earn the right to shed blood for the community.

"Well fought," Weard repeated, smiling. Neither replied. Up close, Erik decided that they were young, only fourteen or fifteen but already close to Weard's stature and musculature. From a distance, their rough clothing, ragged hair, and tanned faces had misled Erik into thinking them adults, as had their strength and agility.

These were mere boys. At their age, he had barely begun serious study at the University, had never fired a weapon, even in sport. Yet these two were trained and efficient killers. As they stood in the circle, breathing hard and sweating, each bore shallow wounds from the other's spear. And the blood was still spreading across the wounded boy's clothing.

"My cousins," Weard said. "They are of an age, ready to take their places on the patrols."

"Brothers?"

"Yes. Why?"

"They seemed so serious, deadly, trying to kill each other. And one is hurt."

The wounded boy slumped, shouldering against his brother. With a nod, Weard released them and they trudged toward the huts, one leaning slightly on the other's shoulder but both ramrod stiff and walking proudly.

"Of course," Weard said somberly. "We do not fight for pleasure or for sport. We fight to live. When we practice, it is as if we were facing any beast of the wilderness. If we do not kill it, it will kill us."

Erik's eyes widened in shock. Then Weard smiled. "Of course, the elders do not allow too much bloodshed on the practice field. And they step in immediately if emotions run too high. We must train our youth to be fierce and protective, but we do not wish to sacrifice them to our own pride and lack of foresight.

"If, on the other hand, the elder in attendance decides that one of the combatants is shamming, he may signal for the battle to continue, or he may step in and face the slacker himself. Then blood will certainly flow. A laggard might spend some time in the recovery huts. But he will learn. When one of us grasps a spear..."—as he spoke, he gripped his own—"...and faces an enemy, he must be ready to kill.

"I am proud of my cousins. They are sons of one father and of one mother. They were born in the same hour from one womb. Yet when they fight with one another, they can forget the ties of blood. Neither has been disciplined by an elder. And neither has been more than scratched by the other. When they have gained a few more pounds, when they have had their mettle tempered by combat, they will be of great service to the Folk."

Erik stood silently for a few moments. Then he turned away and walked toward a small two-sided hut near the edge of the fence. In the shadows, he saw neat rows of stone-tipped spears, thrusting clubs, stone knives, and leather shields.

He entered the shadows, inspecting the row of weapons. The spears towered above him even though they had barely been head-high to the brothers. He ran the tip of one finger along the surface of a hide shield. The leather was taut and stiff, hard to the touch, probably impenetrable to anything but a direct thrust from a powerful arm.

He lifted the shield from its shelf, surprised at its weight. He slipped his arm into the leather straps on the wooden frame. The straps fit loosely around his upper arm and forearm. There were no buckles to adjust the fastenings. His shoulder felt the strain of the unaccustomed weight, especially since there was no way to distribute it more evenly.

The shield extended from his shoulder almost to his knees, awkwardly large and cumbersome, not at all the light, maneuverable defense it had seemed in the hands of the brothers. And yet this was just like the ones they had used. It was simply too massive for him, too heavy.

He put it back, rubbing his shoulder afterward. He continued through the arsenal. The knives were too long for him to use, other than as rude bayonets. The clubs, huge knots of wood, would impossible to wield effectively in any kind of battle.

Finally, he turned away from the racks and walked into the sunlight.

Weard had not moved. Slowly Erik walked toward him. "I understand."

Weard nodded approvingly. Words were not necessary. The prattling knew there was no way he could become proficient in weaponry. He was too old, for one thing; at his age, men had already served years on patrol, had perhaps already aided in killing a grendel. No one would allow an untried stranger to accompany him on a hunt. The prattling was simply too small, too unskilled, too dependent.

And he knew it. Weard felt a small flush of pride that Erik could recognize his limitations and not struggle against them.

In the distance, the two brothers emerged from their hut, still shoulder to shoulder. One was naked from the waist up, a band of white encircling his chest. From where he stood, Erik could see that the bandage was already stained, just under the heart. The youth's skin glowed, however, brown and glistening in the sunlight. Laughter floated through the stillness to touch Erik's ear. The two disappeared into the enclave.

"That blow would have killed me."

"Yes," Weard agreed curtly. "Had you survived long enough in battle to receive it."

Erik made no answer—there could be no answer. With an abrupt tap on Erik's shoulder, Weard signaled that they should move on. They walked through the practice field, beyond the weapons hut, to a broad stretch of gray-green grass. Two more young men were wrestling barehanded, weaponless, almost naked. An old man stood nearby, occasionally muttering under his breath, even more rarely rasping a command or cry.

Weard and Erik approached, not speaking. These were no trained warriors. They were boys, children. They seemed no more than ten or so, yet they were already Erik's height and probably outweighed him. They were men in physique and power, boys in experience and age. They scuffled silently, with none of the groans and grunts Erik was used to in training rooms. They fought in silence, as if afraid that a listening enemy might lurk nearby.

Weard moved next to the old man. Erik followed, his steps grating on the bare earth; neither of the wrestlers gave any indication that they were aware of his presence.

Weard and the old man whispered for a few seconds, then the elder stamped one foot on the ground.

"Here!"

The boys broke their holds, straightened, and faced him.

As they spotted Weard, they grinned outrageously. Erik began to realize that chance had thrown him in with someone well liked, admired, respected among the Folk. And, he also began to understand, someone superlatively trained in the critical arts of survival.

The two boys ran toward Weard, showing none of the self-control and self-discipline of the older fighters. Then the elder uttered a single, harsh word. They halted, crestfallen, and stood at an exaggerated attention.

"Flan and Tir," Weard said, pointing to each. Erik recognized the names as words: *Arrow* and *Glory*. These must be public names, more hopeful than substantive—but the hope was coupled with obvious pride and power.

The boys nodded to Weard and glanced at Erik as their names were spoken, interest and curiosity moving in their deep-set gray eyes.

Weard turned to Erik and laid a hand on his shoulder. "Erik Baanfeld," he said. The boys bowed slightly, inclining little more than head and shoulders, as if uncertain of the stranger's status yet aware that anyone standing with Weard might be important. Still, Erik saw, they had looked at him, assessed him, taking in his slight stature and lack of heavy musculature. He thought he detected a flicker of contempt...disbelief, perhaps, in their eyes.

In the meantime, Weard turned his attention back to the old man. "With your permission, I would speak with Tir and Flan alone."

The old man bowed stiffly from the waist and left, muttering to himself.

Weard motioned for the two boys to come closer. Erik felt a shuddering of anticipation.

"How long have you two been wrestling?" The two looked at each other.

Finally Tir spoke up, diffidently, as if awed by Weard's attentions. "One year, sir."

"Both of you?"

"Yes, sir. We are of an age, Flan and I. We have been friends since birth."

Weard looked toward Erik.

"And you, Erik. Have you wrestled?"

"Some," Erik said. "Yes, I have. At the Uni..., uh, yes, sir."

"Would you like to work out with Tir or Flan?"

Erik nodded tautly. He wasn't deceiving himself. He had been well trained at the University and at the Academy. Given an opponent close to his own size, he could make a good showing. But against these stripling warriors, he knew he had little chance. They were good: they were wrestlers, not just uneducated Junks rolling about in the dirt.

Still, he had no alternative. He had to make the try, if only to prove something to himself. He would do the ExServ no good by refusing; in fact he dared not refuse for fear of losing the tenuous respect he sometimes felt from Weard.

"Which one?" Weard asked.

Erik thought for a moment, studying his opponents. They were closely matched, nearly of a size and weight. Flan seemed a fraction taller, but Tir was an equal fraction heavier. Both were formidable, even if not yet in their teens.

Finally, for no reason he could define, he chose. "Tir."

Better *Glory* than *Arrow*, he thought. Flan backed off. Tir stepped toward the grassy area.

Weard helped Erik remove his cloak, stripping away the knots Erik had so carefully mastered that morning, loosening bindings with an ease and speed that seemed impossible. Within seconds, Erik was as nearly naked as his opponent, wearing only his loincloth, his bare feet warm against the earth.

At Weard's signal, Erik moved forward, balancing on the uneven ground. He approached Tir.

"Signal when you are ready," Weard instructed. Erik took a few breaths to study his opponent. The boy was tall and stocky. The only advantage Erik could count on would be speed, perhaps...and deter-mination. He nodded for the contest to begin.

With a yelp, Tir leaped toward him. And just as abruptly, the contest was finished.

Erik lay in the dust, a knotted forearm pressing into his throat. The hand clenched into a fist, and Erik blacked out.

When he opened his eyes, Tir and Flan were standing nearby. Weard knelt near his head, tense and withdrawn. Erik sat up, winc-ing as he moved his ankle. The strain had not bothered him since the night before; now, after the violence of Tir's attack, tendons were again screaming in pain. Erik went white but refused to shame Weard by reacting to the pain. He sat for a moment, breathing hard.

"Are you all right?" Weard asked.

"Fine," Erik managed to say between deep gulps of air. "Short-est fight on record."

Weard's lips cracked into a grin.

"Probably. I didn't even see it. I was blinking."

Erik stared at him for a moment—was that a joke?

"Can you stand?" Weard's voice cut through Erik's bemuse-ment.

"I think so."

Weard stepped back, leaving Erik alone on the field. Erik hoped that the strain from his ankle did not show too visibly on his face. Tir and Flan were watching him closely, as if eager for signs of weakness. Erik saw a fleeting image of a wounded deer being torn to pieces by savage wolves—some hidden memory from a tale read and memorized long before, no doubt—but the explanation gave him little comfort. Well, he thought, I won't give them anything more to jeer at me about.

He raised himself slowly to one knee, favoring the injured ankle as much as possible. So far, so good. He steadied himself, settling his uninjured foot deeply into the dust. Then, with a single smooth movement, he stood.

At least he should have. That was the scene he had sketched for himself. Unfortunately, his ankle refused its assigned role. With a pinched cry he toppled forward as an unexpected spasm shot up his leg, convulsing muscles and searing his mind.

He looked up, sweat beaded on his forehead. Weard did not move. To his right, he heard whispered words as Flan and Tir walked away.

"Prattling."

"Adl."

Erik's ears barely seemed to register the sounds, but his mind translated them, feverishly grabbing something other than the pain as focus and center. The terms barraged his sick consciousness with his failure. *Prattling*—child, no, worse than child, someone useless to himself or to the community.

And *adl*, diseased, a walking sickness that must be destroyed lest the whole become infected.

Erik could not meet Weard's eyes. The two remained motionless beneath the scorching sun. Erik felt his shoulders and back burning, unused as he was to having his bare skin exposed. Finally, he heard Weard move away. The man's feet barely scuffed as he left. Erik was alone.

He rolled back onto the dry earth, staring at the blinding sun, blinking away black spots, then shading his eyes with one hand.

He had failed. There was no doubt of that. He had perhaps even alienated Weard through his failure, although he couldn't be sure. At the very least, Flan and Tir would spread the word, not only of his defeat in the wrestling match but of his weakness in the face of pain. And everyone would shun him. Any good he might once have done the ExServ and the Comity had suddenly transmuted into harm. On this world, he was worse than a Junk. He was nothing.

He sat up, feeling twinges of pain even from that small movement. No one remained on the practice fields. In fact, he could not see anyone anywhere in the settlement. It was as if the entire community had withdrawn itself from his shame. He looked about for something to help him stand.

The shivered shaft of a spear lay not three meters away, half in the shade cast by the weapons hut. He raised himself to one knee, favoring his ankle again, then to his feet. He was prepared this time for the ripping agony; he went even whiter and bit his lip but neither cried out nor fell. It was too late, he knew, but at least he could convince *himself* that he was capable of withstanding the pain. He dragged himself over to the shadow, then grabbed the smooth shaft, and, using it as a makeshift crutch, picked up his cast-off clothing and made his way back the edge of the practice compound.

He stopped just beyond the gate. Where should he go? He was not one of the warriors; did he have any right to share Weard's hut? But where else could he go? He didn't have his bearings yet, nor did he know much about the settlement.

He struggled through the maze of huts until he arrived at the one he recognized as Weard's. He stumbled in, crossed the main room, and entered the sleeping chamber. His bundle was still on the shelf where he had put it that morning.

With a deep sigh, he reached to pull it down. It was a long reach for him; even normally he would have had to stretch, but encumbered by the broken spear-haft, he over-extended and pitched forward, straddling Weard's cot, re-twisting his ankle, and striking his head against the rough wall.

And there was pain, and tightness, and darkness.

CHAPTER FOURTEEN

When he awoke, he felt something cool on his forehead. He tried to blink. A moist cloth covered his eyes. Without moving, he surveyed his sense impressions. He lay on a cot. Beneath a light robe—soft fur against his skin—he was naked.

He lifted his hand and tried to remove the cloth. Another hand caught his, a smooth hand, cool and damp. It was not Weard's.

"Who are you?" Erik asked without removing the cloth. His head ached, and even in his self-willed blindness sharp splinters of light flickered behind his eyes.

"Feorm," came the soft reply, as soft as the hand that still held his, as soft as the flesh that curved around his palm. A woman's voice. She sounded young; her voice was gentle, unlike anything he expected to hear speaking to a prattling, an adl.

"Where am I?" He felt rather than knew that he was no longer in Weard's sleeping chamber; and even if he had not, he understood enough of the customs here to know that a young woman would not have enter the warrior's compound.

"You are in a hut near Families. I will care for you."

He raised his hand again. This time she did not stop him. He removed the cloth and tried to look around.

At first, he could see nothing. The hut was dark; what light entered through the open doorway merely blurred the outlines of sparse furnishing. Feorm had settled back into shadow. He could only trace her hazy outline.

He tried to sit but fell back on the cot, dizzy and sick.

"What happened?" he finally asked, his throat throbbing and his voice cracked.

"You have been ill for three days. You fell and struck your head. While you were unconscious and fevered, your injured ankle became again inflamed. Your fever broke this morning, and you have been sleeping quietly all day. I hoped you would awake before nightfall. It is almost sunset.

"There is great strength in the daylight sun. And dark power in the night. I am glad that you are awake now."

"Three days," Erik murmured.

"But you are recovering," Feorm said. "I have cared for you."

As she spoke, she leaned farther back into the gathering darkness. Even though his eyes had cleared, Erik could see no more of her than the hand resting lightly on the edge of the cot. The hand was young, well-formed, roughened perhaps by hard work, but still deeply attractive.

He tried again to sit up, succeeding this time. The pain in his head subsided to a mild ache as he leaned against a roll of fur propped against the wall. He could see his leg, the ankle swathed in gray bands, uncovered and resting a few inches above the cot, propped securely on a small pad of some dark material. He moved his leg gingerly, steadying himself for the pain.

The leg moved freely. He twisted his foot, testing the tendons. They too felt healed.

He looked his surprise at the silent figure sitting in the darkness.

"We have some skills in healing," the disembodied voice said, "and the sprain was not as bad as we feared at first. Poultices brought down the swelling and herbs removed the soreness and the heat. Soon you will be able to walk, although you must be careful for several days yet."

Erik shivered as the evening coolness played over his bared chest and shoulders.

The woman raised her hand and touched his upper arm. "Rest now." The hand retreated into shadow. Erik lay back and pulled the fur coverlet higher for its warmth—but even with his captured body-heat, the coverlet seemed chilling after her touch. Through the open doorway, the sun became a red and orange sliver of light against the palisade, then disappeared. Twilight deepened even as he watched, bringing distant night into the settlement. The last vestiges of light danced through the doorway and died. From another angle, the intermittent glimmerings of an open fire gradually replaced the sunlight, but the interior of the hut remained black. He could no longer even see the hand.

"Who are you?" he finally asked, ashamed of his silence and admiring her patience.

"I have said."

"I don't remember."

"Yes. The fever. I am Feorm."

Feorm. Erik's mind resumed its old habit of thought, interpreting the name: "Hospitality." He did not know the woman, did not know what she looked like (or at least could not remember through the feverish haze of the past three days), had only heard her voice—but the name was appropriate, even if it was only her public name.

"Yes," he said softly. "But who are you? Why do you tend me?"

"I am...." She broke off without finishing the thought.

Erik waited, but she refused to speak further. "Why do you take care of me, a prattling, an adl, an outsider you have never seen before?"

There was an even longer silence before her voice threaded through the night.

"I am promised to Weard. We are to marry. I have loved him since we were children together. He has asked that I watch over you and I agreed. Now I must go. There is bread and water here."

She lifted his hand and set it gently on a small bench near the head of the cot.

He had been wrong, he realized, in thinking her hand rough. It was not. He could feel its strength, but its smoothness penetrated to his bones, calming and soothing on one level, stirring him on another. She pulled it away quickly.

"If you need anything, call. I am in the next hut and I will hear you."

She stood and left. Erik still did not see her clearly, beyond a swift outline in the glowing doorway, a lithe and graceful outline, tall and slender.

He let his head fall back against the pillow. The night wind curled through the doorway and whispered along the chinks in the rough walls. He shivered, hoping that he would not have to spend winter in this place. He pulled the soft, clean-smelling furs against his cheek and slept.

* * * * * *

During the night the fever returned. He remembered little of that night, or the next, or the next. At times he slept deeply; at other times he cried out and tried to get up from his bed and run from amorphous creatures that haunted his dreams; never did he fully awake. Each time someone was there to help, to talk him gently back to deeper sleep, to restrain him and soothe his fears. Some times it might have been Feorm; other times it was a younger male presence whose voice and touch Erik thought he knew but could not define in his dreamy state; once Weard came, and his deep voice resonated reassuringly through Erik's dreams.

Someone had lifted his head and helped him drink when he was thirsty and had sat beside him on the narrow cot and fed him broth from a metal spoon that burned between his lips and almost roused him into life. It must have happened several times, although he could barely distinguish between those actions and the dreams that stalked his sleep.

He felt the pressing need and ran down stark white corridors, knowing that he was lost and almost crying but running anyway, turning after turning, panic rising as each new vista showed itself identical to the last. He wore his ExServ uniform, its sky-fresh blue the only spot of color for ever and ever. He had to find a urinal or he would lose control and shame himself. He ran on, feeling the need grow stronger as the corridors stretched further and further, without doors or window, until he could not stop it and he groaned and the corridors grew dark and cold and he was naked and an icy wind froze his back and legs and his feet. Arms supported him as release exploded. He smelled the pungency of urine and almost woke again. But still he slept and dreamed.

At first, *Marquette visited him often, his uniform hanging in tatters from fleshless bones, his eyes eaten away to staring darkness and the flesh of his cheeks sunken and rotting—but it was Marquette, with a deep, festering wound in his chest and his teeth bared in a leering, skeletal grin and his hand reaching toward Erik, reaching and reaching.* And Erik would scream, and eventually the vision would transmute into a woman, tall and dark and beautiful, who would also reach out to him, and her touch was warmth and life, and the dream would fade until the next time. And when it came again *it was bright daylight beneath a canopy of deep green leaves, and Marquette's death-ravaged face seemed more wholesome and alert, his uniform torn and dirty but not yet blooded, and his chest whole and clean. Her warmth seemed less necessary to dispel the guilt and fear.* Each time it came, the fear lessened and her presence deepened.

Finally, Marquette stopped coming. The last time, he *looked as he had at Academy, tall and strong, a Spacer whole and complete, healthy and alive. He merely stood and smiled, nodding once, then—*

Erik slept deeply and uninterruptedly for many hours. When he dreamed again, *it was not Marquette and blood and death, but someone he had known before, Kyren, the first girl he had loved (even though she had not loved him, not as deeply at any rate, and they had parted before he could gather the courage to tell her and she had known that he was only an Adjunct anyway). They were camping in a reserve near home,* he dreamed, *although she would never have gone alone with a Junk into the wilderness.* But in the dream *they were camping, and she wore shorts and a thin blouse that pulled across her breasts when she moved. She was shorter than he and blonde and beautiful, and once she touched his fore-head with a hand that seemed ice to his fire. Together they ran along forest paths, laughing wildly into the emptiness. He watched the movement of her back and buttocks and thighs swelling beneath her clothing and wondered what she would look like naked.*

And she was, suddenly and startlingly naked as she climbed a rocky slope, stood poised at the top, then dived, floating birdlike and cutting ice-green water without a splash.

He stood on the rock, as naked as she and as unashamed, and watched her the darker blue that was body move beneath the lighter ice-blue water. And then he was still naked and falling toward her, his dive carrying him forever outward from the cliff and yet she was beneath him, outlined in the water. He floated above her, floating and flying and diving at once. She rolled onto her back, her breasts making small flurries in the water—and it was not Kyren at all but someone taller and stronger, heavier but not bulky, with long black hair floating in the water like a negative halo surrounding the brightness of her face. He fell closer...could almost touch her, could feel her breath on his lips and throat and breast. He felt fullness in his groin and then fire and then water....

Water soothing on his arms and neck and chest. Water cooling the warmth on his belly and thighs. He struggled upward, gasping as if drowning even though his panicked breathing brought great draughts of icy air.

"I'm sorry." A voice said, and the voice belonged to someone tall and dark and beautiful leaning over him, washing him. The water was warm but cooled rapidly in chilly air, and she seemed to be apologizing as he lay against the furs and panted, catching his breath in choking gasps that had nothing to do with temperature gradients but lingered onward from his dream.

"What ...."

Fingers pressed against his lips, and the voice continued.

"Rest. It is not yet dawn. The fever returned, but has again broken. You ...."

Someone spoke, quickly and quietly from another part of the hut, but Erik could not see who it was or understand what was said. He barely heard Feorm as she answered in quick, short phrases, but he could feel an undercurrent of tension in the fingers that turned suddenly cold on his lips.

The fingers left and hands dried his body, then pulled something soft and smooth and warm over him.

"I'm sorry," he murmured, but to him it sounded like the crashing of thunder against a summer sky. "Did I...? I didn't mean...."

He closed his eyes to the world.

"Sleep." Her voice was gentle again. He drifted toward sleep, but this time he remembered.

He had seen her face and hands and smile.

"Feorm," he whispered, not aware that someone sat silently in a corner of the room. The unseen youth stiffened and half rose at the word but, finally, chose not to move or to speak.

This time, Erik's drop into sleep was deep and natural and healing, and he did not dream at all.

CHAPTER FIFTEEN

Morning was inclining well toward noon when he woke again. And when he did wake, this time it was suddenly and completely, to a heart-stopping fear. His eyes flew open and he sat bolt upright on the cot, the robe falling unnoticed away from his chest. For a moment he did not register where he was. His hand surged behind his neck, probing for his Jack. Then his fingers stilled, and his heartbeat slowed. His sleep had been the most restful he had experienced since the crash. He could not remember dreaming. Nor did he know for certain how long he had lain in bed.

For a second, though, even after his eyes were open and had taken in his surroundings, Erik half-expected to hear Marquette's voice ringing from the walls of the scouter.

He shook his head to clear his thoughts. And then realized that this was the first time in...*in how many days*, he wondered, that he had even thought about Marquette. With that realization the force of his memories flooded over him.

Marquette was dead.

And if he could not cope with whatever faced him next, he might be just as dead.

If Weard or Æthele or any of the other warriors—or perhaps even one of physically precocious youths—decided he was a danger to the people, they would dispose of him as dispassionately as if he were a gnat bothering them in the heat of a late summer day. He pushed the thought aside, refusing to see visions of swirling water or a blue ExServ tunic studded with spreading red.

A slight scraping sound drew him from his reflections. He looked up to see a figure silhouetted against the light streaming through the doorway. For a flickering second he half-hoped that it was Feorm, then he saw the massiveness of the body, the hand outlined as it clenched the shaft of a spear. It was Weard.

The man entered without speaking, stationing himself near the foot of the cot but still within the wedge of light. He stood there, not speaking, studying Erik's face, the lines of stress now nearly erased, the flickering suggestions of curiosity, nervousness, and...fear.

"How...how many days?" Erik finally asked, his throat dry and rough.

"Six. This is the seventh."

Erik straightened further up, resting his head against the wall of the hut. The coverlet slipped down to his waist, but in the increasing heat of the day he felt no need to huddle under it.

"That was not well done, my friend." Weard's voice rumbled through the small room. For the first time, Erik noted how out of place the man was inside any man-made structure, particularly this small, rough shelter of unfinished walls and sloping thatched ceiling. For that matter, how out of place he was anywhere except the wilds of the plateau and the lowlands. Weard was formed for rugged living. He had no need to be indoors.

Weard was apparently waiting for Erik's reply, but he could think of nothing to say. The indictment was just. There was no defense. In the disconcerting moment of truth, Erik had barely heard the rest of Weard's statement.

Suddenly Weard unbent. His hand loosened on the spear and the giant figure lowered itself onto the foot of the cot. Erik shifted his legs, relieved to find that he could manipulate his ankle with minimal discomfort. How had they done that? Even with the best medical aid in the Comity, a sprain like this should have taken more than a week to heal.

Before he could ask Weard—before he found the courage to do so—the man spoke again, this time in a milder voice, with a hint of warmth unusual for him.

"You did much damage on the field, my friend, and not just to your head and your ankle. Much damage and little constructive work. Word has spread. Only a few know who you truly are, but all have heard of the small-limbed stranger who does not understand the ways of the Folk. And all have heard of your childish cry of pain."

He stopped, seemed to be lost in thought. He laid one massive hand on Erik's leg, bridging the unthinkable gap between them with that single action, forming a link in brotherhood.

"Erik," he finally said, in a voice deep with concern. "You probably have no true idea of what you did there, or of what you did that night in the nettles—why I suddenly became harsh."

As if how you treated me before was not harsh, Erik added to himself, trying not to let his feelings show.

"You must think us barbarians, inhuman, unfeeling, cold, and eminently dangerous. And you are right. We are all of those things…and more. We must be. We must survive, and in order to do that, we have had to lose much that was gentle and warm, much that our fathers perhaps shared with yours."

For a moment, Erik saw Marquette's body again, one hand bobbing limply in the current as frothing water broke over a small rock. He had not remembered noticing the hand before. Memories of his dreams washed over him and he shuddered.

But he could not speak. He nodded, accepting Weard's words dispassionately, reserving final judgment.

"You are thinking of the other one? Marquette?"

"Yes." In spite of his surprise at both the question and the perception behind it, Erik felt bitterness like black bile flowing into his inadequate single-word response.

Weard looked at him more intently, as if unprepared for the invective loaded into that single sound.

"It was for the good of the Folk," he said simply.

Erik understood at once that that was as close to an explanation or apology he would ever receive from the hunter. Marquette had been sacrificed to some greater good that Erik did not yet accept or understand. For Weard, however, that was sufficient.

"Yes." This time, the bitterness drained out, replaced by tired resignation.

Suddenly Weard straightened and paced along the narrow end of the room. He seemed about to speak, stopped, paced again, then said one word.

"Come."

Something about the sound warned Erik. This was the old Weard, the warrior who had spun a glinting knife into Marquette's body—not the Weard of the careful hands adjusting bindings to avoid a raw place on the skin, or the possible friend seeing to it that another friend is cared for in illness. This was a Warrior-Hunter of the People, and his wishes were not to be ignored.

Weard's single word was more than suggestion, less than command. Still it stirred Erik immediately to action. He threw back the fur coverlet and stood. Aware of his nakedness, he began glancing around for his clothing. A small, ragged bundle huddled on a low bench near the wall. It stank, and it turned out to contain only one well-worn, thin garment, a tunic of some material Erik did not recognize.

He looked his unspoken question.

Weard nodded grimly. Erik slipped the coarse garment over his head, cringing at the roughness of the material, wrinkling his nose again at the unsubtle odors that permeated it. Sweat, filth, and decay co-mixed to create an effluvia of fear and despair.

"You are not of the Folk," Weard intoned. "You have no skills as a warrior or hunter. We cannot give you of our substance; that we need for ourselves, in order to survive. Until you become a useful part of our world, you must live with what we can spare."

Again, Weard's tone was cold and dispassionate. Erik wanted desperately to find some bit of human warmth in the words but knew that the effort would be wasted. At this moment, Weard spoke for Æthele and the Council; in spite of his own fears and cares for Erik, the man was restricted by his official role.

Erik nodded. He thought he saw a reflecting glint of understanding in Weard's eye before the man turned and left the hut.

Stepping out, Erik squinted at the sun low in the sky even at noon. In spite of the present heat, winter was coming. The breeze fluttering his tattered tunic suggested cold and ice as it ruffled the thin bit of animal hide against Erik's ribs. He hugged himself, more out of nerves than cold. Glancing up, beyond the thorn barricade and cresting the ridges to the north, he saw flecks of color as if deciduous trees were beginning to put on autumn tones.

"Weard," he asked as they crossed the compound. "What do you call this?" He gestured inclusively toward the settlement.

"This is Festburg."

Strong fortress—a name both appropriate and threatening.

"What about the planet?"

Weard paused in mid-stride and looked down at Erik. "That question should not have been asked."

Too late, Erik understood and nodded. Other planets would be anathema—to specify this one would presuppose the existence of others...and of the Comity.

"What do you call this place?" he asked.

"This is Folk-heim, the upper plateau. There are five other settlements, all newer, all more than five-days' march from here."

"*Folk-heim*," Erik repeated. *Home of the People*—but not his folk, nor his home. By now they had reached an area unfamiliar to Erik, lying at the distant edge of the settlement and as far from Weard's hut and the warrior's practice field as the thorn-barrier would allow. Looking up at the flat expanse between himself and the barrier, Erik thought for a moment that it was another practice field; then he shook his head. That was behind him, literally and figuratively. He glanced over his shoulder. In the distance, obscured by the sunlight diffracted by clouds of dust and smoke, he could make out clusters of fighters wielding swords and shields against their brothers in arms, but no less intent on victory for all of that.

No, Erik shrugged, he would probably never be going there again.

Weard stopped in front of a small, battered structure, the dingiest Erik had yet seen. It looked more like a child's lean-to than something constructed by—or for—adults. The low walls seemed random collections of cast-off timber, splintered, ragged, spongy with patches of dry-rot and blackened with age. The gaping spaces between them had been stuffed haphazardly with drying tufts of moss and brush. Beyond it stood a fence, also low, but apparently far sturdier than the hut itself. From behind the fence floated a curious bleating sound.

Weard struck the lintel of a makeshift door a sharp blow with his spear. The structure shivered visibly under the force of what for Weard was merely a light tap. From the blackness inside, a hoarse voice croaked.

"Who's there?"

Weard did not answer. He struck the lintel a second blow, harder. Bits of scruff loosened from the roof and floated down like snow. Erik heard scuffling, as if something heavy were being dragged across a dry riverbed. The sound—and the association—made him uncomfortable. He edged closer, until he could see around Weard.

The figure that appeared in the doorway was thick-set and short—shorter than any adult Erik had yet seen. The man's head bent forward, as if searching the ground for treasure trodden underfoot by proud, erect warriors. One shoulder humped above the other; an arm curled against the man's side.

Erik studied the apparition...and it resolved into recognizable lines. A man to be sure—Erik had not really expected otherwise—but one whose body was cruelly crippled and broken. Even in his brief time among the Folk, Erik had become so attuned to tall, strong, massive musculature that the sight of the twisted body shocked him in silence.

"neMonn," Weard said curtly, gesturing toward the figure. *Not-man*, Erik translated, or *no-man*. One who was and is no more. A Junk. Like me.

Weard abruptly turned on his heels and strode toward the main compound, leaving Erik standing alone in the sunlight.

neMonn struggled out of the shadows, scrabbling sideways, crab-like, toward Erik. For the first time since leaving the University. Erik found himself looking down at another adult. He felt absurdly tall, strong, well-formed; then cut off that fruitless line of thinking as a withered hand clutched the air in front of him.

"So you are the new one," neMonn said, his eyes moving appraisingly up and down without requiring any commensurate movement of neck or head. "Welcome." There was no missing the curiosity in the voice—or the sincerity of the welcome. Erik nodded a reply, surprised at the man's interest in him.

neMonn made his way back into the hut, motioning for Erik to follow. Once inside, they lowered themselves to the earth and sat for a few minutes, quietly, in the dark. Erik felt a sudden tension, unspoken but heavy between them.

Finally neMonn spoke.

"Do you know who I am, where you are?"

"No."

"Ah. I thought so." He thrust his chin awkwardly sideways, toward the compound. "They don't speak of me much any more. They did once, though, when I was a Warrior. By the gods, yes! They did once!"

He leaned against a wall. As he did so, the light filtering through cracks in the walls struck his face, casting it into sharp relief.

neMonn was a young man!

His body was twisted, his hair matted, long, and filthy, his eyes sunken into his skull and circled by a web of fine lines. But he was not old. Beneath layers of dirt and scaly patches, his skin was tight and smooth. His good arm was round and muscled. He might not be much older than I, Erik thought but did not speak. He allowed himself to blink his amazement. Then he looked again, more searchingly, noting the angles of body squatting in shadows, the twisted arm with its claw-like hand held tightly against the torso and the left leg, stiff, withered, and drawn, throwing the whole body off balance.

Erik opened his mouth to speak when a shrill voice called from outside. With an ease that startled Erik, neMonn pulled himself up and shuffled out.

"Come," he said, his voice again rough and rasping.

Erik followed him. In front of the hut, just inside the fence, stood a boy. Having become used to the burliness of the Folk, he wasn't surprised when the boy turned out to be tall and heavy-set, nearly the size of a teenager on one of the Twelve Worlds, although perhaps only seven or eight Standard years old.

neMonn motioned to the boy with a quick slice of his head. "One of our wards."

"What do you mean?" Erik asked quietly. neMonn didn't answer; instead he shuffled toward the fence and pushed against a rough gate hung on leather hinges. Erik followed.

Inside the gate, neMonn followed the fence line for a dozen meters or so before entering the shadows cast by a long, low building that Erik had not noticed before. The building stood open on three sides; it was really only a single wall facing into the northern winds, with a roof supported by smooth poles. The ground inside was littered with musty straw.

Even though Erik had never seen anything even remotely like it, he recognized it as a barn or shed.

He looked up and searched the open expanse between the shed and the thorn barrier. On the far side, almost invisible beneath the thorn-wall, a clump of furry animals moved restlessly in the skimpy shade of low shrubs. Erik didn't recognize the animals, but they were presumably a major source of food and clothing for the Folk. The shed would protect the flocks during cold winter nights.

neMonn caught at his elbow and pulled him toward the shed. There, Erik saw three more youths, only slightly older than the one standing nearby, sitting in a tight circle just inside. They did not look up at him or at either of his companions. neMonn made his way silently into the shadows and settled on the dank straw. Erik followed.

The four boys formed a circle, with neMonn at the head, facing across the pasture. Erik dropped into the empty space at the foot.

The boys ranged in ages from eight or nine to early teens, he later discovered. The older one was not much smaller than Flan or Tir.

The boys did not pay any attention to Erik beyond curious glances as he emerged from the hut with neMonn. Then they shifted their gaze to the crippled form at the head of the circle. In a low voice, husky but strong, neMonn began chanting. One by one the boys joined in, their voices blending in a variety from thin, high soprano to sometimes resonant, sometimes crackling bass.

It took Erik a few moments of concentrated listening to understand the words. This was a lay, a heroic poem, a saga of warriors and battles—but whether a remnant carried with the colonists from Earth or a re-creation of one of their own struggles, Erik could not tell. The words were archaically inflected, even more so than the rest of the common-language.

So, neMonn was a teacher. He had scrabbled a place for himself among the Folk, a minor place, perhaps, but sufficient for a crippled, former Warrior to survive. He could not fight; therefore he could no longer dwell with warriors, wear their garb, sleep in their huts, eat their food. But he could teach, could instill in the impressionable minds before him the glories of warfare and the grandeur of battle that was essential to the survival of the Folk. And he could oversee his charges as they in turn tended the flocks.

Even neMonn could perform those limited tasks. And Erik was, perhaps, fit only to be his helper.

CHAPTER SIXTEEN

The rest of the day passed unmercifully slowly. At first Erik enjoyed sitting in the shadow of the shed listening, feeling the archaic rhythms pound in his brain and throb in his blood, sinking further into the glories of a language he had long ago learned and now was learning to love. As a singer, neMonn was untrained, however, that much was clear even to Erik. Often he stopped at awkward places, as if he had forgotten the next lines. More frequently he stumbled over lines, missed alliterative passages, faltered in the throbbing four-stress beat that sounded like the crash of waves and thrum of thunder echoing in Erik's ears. And the boys were little better, managing to keep in rhythm only occasionally, and then more accidentally than intentionally.

Still, there was something about the experience, the barbarism of the setting, the rugged authenticity of intonations so different from the recorded reconstructions Erik had once studied. From the first moments, he was lost in the music.

Too soon, however, neMonn ceased, his voice trailing irresolutely into silence. Erik looked over at the man. In answer to Erik's questioning glance, neMonn merely raised one shoulder in a mangled shrug, as if to apologize for the limits of his knowledge.

"That is all for today."

The boys leaped to their feet with the triumphant cry of school children everywhere and everywhen at the close of classes. Stumbling over each other in their haste, they ran into the sunlight, chasing each other, playing mock-warfare with sticks stacked against the fence.

"Come on," neMonn said. "Now our work begins." For the rest of that long, hot, and utterly miserable afternoon, Erik tried to adjust to this new assignment. On the surface, the work was not difficult—even neMonn experienced little difficulty in keeping the flock from scattering, from milling against the low fence and breaking through into the inhabited areas of the stockade. That was not the real problem. The animals (whether native or colony-bred, Erik could not tell—and he couldn't very well ask neMonn for clarification) were definitely herd animals. Where one led, others followed. Most of the time, Erik or one of the boys ran around the far side of the herd, yelling and swinging arms, frightening the timid beasts back into the lengthening shadow of the palisade.

The work was not difficult. But it was hot and sweaty. No grass grew in the animals' enclosure, and the few shrubs crouched too low to provide shade for the herdsmen. With the sun beating down on him, Erik soon felt the heat and weight of even his minimal clothing. He longed to strip the tunic off and run bare-chested but did not dare do so until the others did. If this was another test, he wouldn't fail it.

The worst part of the task, however, was feeding the creatures. He hadn't realized it before, but a herd of any size obviously required food from outside the enclosure. And these animals were voracious, tearing into bundles of dry grassy stuff that Erik and the others carried in—load after load throughout the long afternoon.

Only once did neMonn allow them a break, and then only long enough for a quick breath of air outside the enclosure and a drink of icy water from a clay vessel. Erik relished the taste, the touch of the water against his dust-caked throat. Following the lead of the others, he poured his final dipper over his head, reveling in the drops that filtered through his hair and straggled down his back.

For much of the time, Erik remained isolated and alone. The four boys avoided him, although they glanced at him curiously when they thought he would not see. neMonn remained aloof as well, treating Erik with the same diffident objectivity that he showed toward the boys. Erik did nothing to elicit commendation—but neither did he merit reprimand.

By late afternoon, however, he was exhausted. He was unused to running, to breathing harsh dust mingled with the stench of animals, to hauling scratchy bundles of fodder and dumping it in the feeding areas. His thighs quivered from fatigue beneath a layer of fine, gray dirt that clung to his body hair like mist—but his ankle was holding up well, he noted, proud of that accomplishment at any rate.

Suddenly, so rapidly that he did not quite understand how it had happened, he and neMonn stood alone in the compound. The four boys had melted into the twilight like wraiths and were gone.

"They live in Families," neMonn explained. "They will return tomorrow. But we must finish for the evening. Usually I do this alone, so tonight I am grateful for your help."

They rounded up the herd, bullying the animals into the shed. At first Erik was not sure how two herdsmen could keep the herd beneath the shelter. In the heat of the day, the animals had proven unbearably fractious, running in all directions whenever Erik tried to move them. But in the twilight, they became more docile, moving into the shelter and huddling against the wall as if grateful for the minimal protection from whatever dangers lay beyond the palisade. One by one they disappeared into the darkness. Finally, there was no sign of them except an undercurrent of contented bleating.

"That was easier than I expected," Erik said, breathing heavily and relieved that the day was over.

"Yes. Two can handle them much better than one. But they are well trained, and they feel winter coming on. In a few weeks, we will barely be able to force them from the shed. Still, it was well done."

Erik felt an unaccustomed warmth spread over him, one having nothing to do with sunlight or campfire. He had done the job well. He had been praised.

neMonn grabbed Erik's elbow. "Let's go on in. Later, after the first snowfall perhaps, we will go to the hall for warmth when it grows too cold for our hut. But for now we remain here. I because I no longer merit to drink and sing with the Warriors, you because you have never belonged there."

He paused.

Erik was surprised at the length and intensity of neMonn's words—the longest single speech the man had directed at him all day. For a moment he did not know how to react.

Suddenly he understood the unstated message in neMonn's final words. "You know about...," he began, cut off by a quick gesture of the other man's hand.

"I know what I know. Nothing else is needed." Then neMonn laughed, a clear, piercing laughter filled with good spirits in spite of adversity. And Erik laughed with him.

They returned to the hut. It took neMonn only a moment to kindle a small fire from coals tardily glowing in a rock-lined pit. For a quick moment, the wretched hut seemed gilded in the light of the few sticks neMonn used to feed the fire. Then he tossed something else onto the flickering flames. A heavy, stifling, noxious odor seeped through the hut, invading corners and permeating the air.

Dung.

Erik had smelled enough during the day to recognize it immediately. Possibly sun-dried and cured, probably at least partially combustible, but dung nonetheless. The insecurity of his position communicated itself to him forcefully with each breath. Like neMonn, he would receive the least and the worst—until he had proven himself.

They ate sparingly of heavy bread studded with husks from whatever grain had gone into it. There was a chunk of dried cheese, hardened nearly beyond recognition, but plenty of cold water. Erik felt hungry but satisfied after their meal, eaten as they squatted near the fire. neMonn said nothing the whole time, concentrating on his food. Erik followed his lead.

Afterward, neMonn sat back, curling his twisted leg beneath him.

"Well, prattling, one day over."

"neMonn," Erik said softly, purposefully not looking up from the embers. "My name is Erik. I prefer it."

neMonn sat silently. Then he laughed clearly and sharply, and his face lit up with pleasure. "You speak for yourself. I hadn't expected that..., Erik. Yes, that's settled. Now let's sleep."

Erik nodded his agreement, his eyes heavy and his muscles complaining.

"I'm ready."

"Good," neMonn said. He stood, using the sheer force remaining in his good leg to lever his body upward. Erik watched the operation with respect. Even though seriously injured and obviously crippled, neMonn was still physically formidable—Erik reminded himself not to trust too completely in the other's apparent good humor, at least not yet. Not until he knew more about neMonn.

In the meantime, neMonn had pulled down a wad of ragged bedding and spread it as a pallet on the naked earth.

He glanced up once at Erik, and Erik was surprised to see something bleak—humiliation, shame, apology—glinting in the dark eyes.

"Once I had more to offer guests. Before..."—he shrugged his shoulder, letting his crippled arm bob and twist and speak the words he chose not to utter—"...I would have offered you soft furs and a cot. Now, this is all."

"It's fine," Erik said, wondering nonetheless. Thus far, he had suffered no particular hardships among the Folk, sleeping either in Weard's cabin or in the healing hut. Now, he knew, things were about to change.

neMonn arranged the furs, reserving the largest and least tattered as a covering. Then he walked outside. Erik followed. They moved through darkness until they were far downwind from the rest of the Festburg, and relieved themselves before returning. Erik noted absently how natural the act seemed; six months ago—six *weeks* ago—he would not have even considered urinating against a rough-cut wall. Now, it seemed as natural as breathing.

Inside, neMonn sprinkled a handful of water over the glowing coals. For a moment the hut grew miasmal with the stench of smoldering dung. Erik wondered how he would manage to sleep without vomiting. Then neMonn poured water on the fire, just enough to douse lingering embers but not enough to flood the pit. He seemed to know what to do, since in a few moments the smell dissipated a bit. Still, Erik stood close to the doorway, turning for a surreptitious breath of cleansing air. neMonn made his way to the far side of the hut and threw back a solid panel. Through the opening, early stars twinkled over the thorn palisade outlining a darkly velvet sky. A breeze threaded through the hut, further cutting the effluvia of dung, until Erik felt more comfortable.

"Enough?" neMonn asked quietly.

"Yes."

"It does get a bit strong in here. But in the winter, we'll be grateful just for the smell, because it may convince us that there is warmth even when none exists. So far, though, I haven't needed that small comfort."

"How long...?" Erik began, then stopped, unsure of protocol.

There was a long moment, broken only by neMonn's harsh breathing.

"Almost a year. Several months in a healing hut, during the worst of winter. I moved here when spring came. It was clear by then that...."

Erik could almost make out the other's form in the darkness. It seemed that neMonn looked at his arm, his leg, then across to Erik.

He straightened and continued.

"...That I could not hunt again. So I chose to tend the herds and teach what small skills I have."

Again, there was a long silence before he continued. "I have not yet lived here through a winter." Erik could hear fear in the voice, fear and pride and resolution. neMonn would die before making demands on the Folk. He was, in his own way, as remarkable as Weard or Æthele, as much a part of this culture, as completely dedicated and committed to it, willing to accept its harshness as well as its strengths. Erik felt a new strength in himself as he watched the man.

Then neMonn moved, pulling the wooden panel to and closing off the hut. He crossed the room and dropped onto the pallet. Erik heard the rustling of clothing, then neMonn's deep breathing, clearly an invitation for the uninvited stranger to share what little hospitality the hut offered.

He crossed and knelt, trying to remove his sandals by feel, cursing under his breath when one of the bindings knotted and refused to loosen.

Suddenly he felt a hand on his. neMonn reached over and, using his good hand, undid the ties. The thongs dropped to the ground. Erik removed his other sandal, careful this time to keep the bindings from tangling. The sandal came off with unexpected ease.

He pulled his tunic over his head and rolled it into a pillow against the rock-hard dirt. Then, wearing only his loincloth, he slid onto the pallet, uncomfortable at his proximity to another body.

He had rarely shared accommodations with anyone. Even at University and the Academy, dorms had provided a modicum of privacy in the form of beds and lockers.

And he had not been with females enough to feel comfortable with someone else this close. For a moment, his dream surfaced, and he saw the lithe form cutting through ice-green water; then it receded, leaving him tense and jumpy.

He could feel heat radiating from neMonn's body. It juxtaposed with the chilling breeze on his naked shoulders. He shivered. There was a touch in the air of frosted skies and snowy winds. For the first time, he seriously questioned whether he would live to see the spring or not.

"Cover up well. It will be cold tonight." neMonn's hand brushed his arm as the man flipped the fur higher.

"Thanks."

Erik lay back, staring at the nothingness where a ceiling would be if he had light enough to see. He remained motionless, replaying memories—Marquette lying in the icy stream recurred with depressing regularity, intercut with flashes of Marquette dead and decaying.

neMonn was apparently asleep. His breathing was soft, deep and regular, almost impossible to hear. The darkness seemed preternaturally quiet to Erik, used as he was to the constant movement of the Academy, to the artificial day-night schedules.

Here everything was silent. For the first time he was neither so exhausted nor so ill that he merely slept. He listened to the utter silence, broken only by whisperings of sound:

A cough, far off and muffled.

A rustling from the shed, a single bleat that sounded like the animal equivalent of a snore.

A branch popping in a fire.

Beyond that there was nothing.

On an impulse, he stood, barefoot and naked to the waist. Gooseflesh wrinkled on his arms and shoulders and back. He walked to the door anyway, feeling the dirt floor as the hard-pack pressed against soles already noticeably tougher than they had been a week before.

Outside, he drew a quick breath, as much in surprise as from the biting chill.

The night was gorgeous.

He hadn't expected that, but there it was. The sky overhead reflected deep blue, just avoiding blackness by the merest hint of light and color. The stars glowed like...well, he couldn't think of anything appropriate as a comparison, but they glowed with fervor and intensity. He could see none of the constellations he had learned as a child, but he had not thought he would. He was far from any familiar space.

Instead, he simply watched the individual points as they glittered, enjoying the quiet, the peace.

"Erik."

The sound was pitched to carry to his ears but not to disturb the rest of the enclosure. It was neMonn's voice.

Erik turned toward the hut before answering. "Out here. Looking at the stars. It's beautiful."

"Come in. It is cold. You must rest for tomorrow." Erik let out a pent-up breath that became shudder as the cold forced its way into his awareness. He shivered.

"Okay."

He entered the darkness, feeling something bleed from him as he drew the lingering rankness of dung, sweat, and dirt into his lungs. He had become frighteningly cold.

He slid between the furs, grateful for their trapped heat.

"Roll against me," neMonn said quietly. "You must be freezing."

"It's okay," Erik began, "I'm...."

"You're freezing and shivering and you will be no good for work tomorrow unless you warm up quickly. That was foolish, Erik, and I won't let you add one foolishness to another."

Erik understood the sound of truth. He rolled on his side and pressed his back against neMonn's.

He lay for a long time, unable to sleep. He wanted to thank neMonn for his kindness to a stranger; he wanted to know how much neMonn knew of him and his situation, how much Weard or Æthele had told the man. He wanted some reassurances that he might eventually hope, and that he might learn to fit.

Finally he broke the silence, his voice a whisper in case the man was already asleep.

"neMonn, I...."

neMonn's voice came even more quietly. "Do not speak. Tomorrow will be difficult. Sleep."

He slept.

CHAPTER SEVENTEEN

The next morning, when Erik awoke, neMonn and the others were already outside. Erik levered himself up, flexing stiff arms and aching muscles, and cursing softly at his new accommodations. He threw on his clothing and laced his sandals, then stepped out into the cold morning air.

The sun was not yet up; long shadows still hid much of the Festburg. A thin line of mist swirled around the huts, obscuring their rough stone foundations. His breath condensed as a puff of vapor. It was cold—colder than it had been the day before.

"Come!"

neMonn's voice startled him.

Erik turned to see the man and his young charges waiting impatiently by the fence. neMonn stood motionless, but the youths stamped their feet and curled fists into the warmth beneath their arms.

"Come! We have no time to waste." With those words—clipped, enigmatic, and abruptly unlike his tone the night before—neMonn shuffled toward the palisade, followed by the boys. Erik caught up with them and fell in line behind Daroth, the youngest. They made their silent way through Families, then on toward the barrier. At a signal from neMonn, the two oldest boys, Cempa and Cwealm, ran ahead and pried open the passageway. Erik noted how carefully the boys handled the compacted bushes and their poison-smeared thorns.

When the path was clear, neMonn resumed the lead, passing between the deadly walls and into the open air beyond, followed by Daroth, Brond, Erik, and finally the brothers, Cempa and Cwealm. As Cwealm emerged from the opening, he pulled the bushes back into place. When the small party finally stood on the damp grass of the meadow, all that remained of the passage into Festburg was the hint of a shallow indentation in the thorny wall. Erik was not sure he could find it again if he were alone.

But he had no leisure to think about that. neMonn set off across the meadow with his curiously arrhythmic lope, his crippled leg barely impeding his speed. The others followed, the younger two running about and yelping in their energy and exuberance. At the stream, someone splashed water on Erik's legs as he stopped to look back at the settlement. The water stung in its coldness, but by the time he turned, everyone was marching seriously ahead.

But maybe Daroth's hands glistened just a little, as if they were inexplicably damp.

Erik smiled.

They crossed the meadow at its narrowest point, then entered the forest. Erik shivered as he passed the shadows and into the piercing chill beneath the trees. Here the early beams of the sun had not yet penetrated, and the cold of night lingered long into mid-morning.

neMonn led them along a path to a clearing perhaps ten minutes into the forest. Here they stopped. In the clearing sat what seemed at first to be small huts clustered near each other. Erik approached the closest one.

It was not a hut, he soon discovered, but a stack of long, thin sheaves of twigs and branches, some dead and brown, others barely wilted, but all bearing leaves like rumpled shrouds. The sheaves were bound tightly with withes, then interwoven to create beehive-like structures. They were made of the same plant Erik had spent the previous day feeding to the animals. He glanced around. There must be fifty of the stacks—quite a reserve of fodder from the perspective of harvest-time, but he wondered how long it would last during a harsh winter.

neMonn signaled Erik to move closer. The boys had already begun untying the bindings on the nearest stacks.

"These are winter stores for the animals," neMonn explained. "We gather the branches from the haelo, the tree of riches. When properly cured, the branches stay nutritious for months and can be handled easily. During the warm days, we bind the branches so they will cure and so we will not have to carry them so far when they are fresh and wet and heavy. Now, with the coming of the cold, we bring them into the Festburg. We must hurry. If we do not store enough, the animals may starve. This will be a severe winter; I can feel the Breath of the North even now. Come, we must work."

The boys were already struggling out of the clearing, laden with bundles of sheaves held together by long strands of cured hide. Daroth was nearly invisible, bent almost double beneath the huge load he had strapped to his back. Only his bare legs and sandals showed as he disappeared into the shadows. neMonn gestured peremptorily to Erik.

Without a word, Erik began dismantling the conical stack nearest him, piling bundles of brittle branches awkwardly on top of each other, tying them together, and boosting them onto his back. Soon the sweat beaded on his forehead in spite of the chilly air. He wished for a band of some kind to tie around his head as the sweat trickled stingingly into his eyes, blinding him and forcing him to blink continuously.

Nearby, neMonn grunted as he shouldered a massive bundle of branches. Erik noted with chagrin that even with a nearly useless arm and leg, the man easily carried twice what Erik could manage.

"No matter," neMonn said, interpreting Erik's glance. "You will grow stronger, and you will learn."

They set off through the forest, retracing their steps to the Festburg.

At first Erik did not think much of the task. Here at least was something constructive he could do. Soon, however, he realized that the job's simplicity hid an unpleasantness he had not anticipated.

He began to sweat freely. Carrying rustling, dry bundles was different than tossing individual branches onto feeding piles. As he worked, his clothes grew matted and cold with perspiration, abrading his skin where the haelo rubbed. Layers of skin felt as if they must be peeling away but Erik was powerless to do anything about it. He could not stop, could not unship his burden—to do so would be to fail at the easiest task Weard could give him. He would have to succeed.

So he continued. The ten-minute walk back to the compound lengthened interminably. Before finishing the first load, Erik was winded, and yet the work day had barely begun. neMonn still walked briskly and the boys were out of sight.

Erik halted and hitched the pile higher onto his shoulder. The movement relieved some of the chafing but dislodged a shower of tattered leaf filaments onto his hair and eyebrows and—worse yet—down his back. Lodged between skin and matted clothing, the haelo leaves itched unmercifully.

The trip (the first of who knew how many) was already torture. Erik was not used to the physical exertion—weeks in space had taken their toll regardless of specified daily exercise periods, and since the crash, he had not exactly been preoccupied with isometrics or aerobics.

And there was something else.

The leaves smelled heavily of some pungent oil. They reminded Erik of menthol, like eucalyptus. Apparently the curing process only partially leached the oils.

Now he discovered that he was apparently allergic to them. As the brittle filaments caught against his skin, they grew soft with sweat and warm with Erik's body heat. The oils bled from torn edges. Wherever they touched his skin, they burned, like a mild sunburn at first, then hotter and hotter. He felt his skin reddening, warming, heating uncomfortably, perhaps even blistering.

Halfway to the Festburg, Cempa and Cwealm passed him, running and laughing at some hidden joke.

"Probably laughing at me," Erik muttered. "I must look like an idiot."

"What?" neMonn stopped several steps ahead and waited for Erik to catch up.

"Nothing. Keep going."

The boys disappeared behind Erik. In spite of the remnant chill, they had already shed most of their clothing and were wearing only their loincloths. He envied them.

He continued on somehow, hoping that the first load would prove the worst. He had not known what to expect; now he knew.

Fortunately, the burning reached a certain point and stopped. It bothered him neither more nor, unfortunately, less. He worked most of the morning carrying load after load, until the heat nearly stifled him, until his shoulders quivered and his legs trembled, until he too had shed his heavy outer clothing and toiled on. He became a half-naked savage working like a beast of burden on a world so sunk into barbarism that the inhabitants had no idea of wagons or sledges.

He no longer spoke nor answered neMonn when the other tried to ask how he was.

By noon he was exhausted. His shoulders and back burned scarlet from the oils and the sunlight, as did the backs of his legs where hanging branches had flailed like whips. His feet were threatening to blister, even after Erik had twice adjusted his sandals, tying them exactly as Weard had done. He was hungry, his lips and throat were parched, and his whole body seemed ready to collapse.

As he heaped a stack of branches onto a growing pile not far from the hut where he and neMonn had slept, neMonn called.

"Enough. We will eat now."

Erik gave the branches a final shove and stumbled toward neMonn, who tossed a bit of cloth over Erik's shoulder and back.

"You are overheated now. It seems hot to you, but the air is still chilled. Do not take a cold. If you do, you will be left to die. The people have neither the time nor the skills to waste on us."

Erik nodded but was disconcerted to hear neMonn speak so easily of "us," especially in such a negative context. Before he could say anything, neMonn turned, gestured, and disappeared into the hut.

Erik followed. neMonn went to the shelf on the far wall and took down a wooden platter that had not been there when Erik left. It held a few pieces of ragged meat—an indiscriminate rusty brown, unhealthy looking and even more unhealthy smelling. In the dim light, it looked as if portions of the meat were moving—Erik chose not to examine it any closer. There were also hunks of crumbling cheese and half a loaf of hard bread. Erik sniffed cautiously and was rewarded with a pungency that burned his nostrils.

neMonn called the boys. One by one they entered and sat around neMonn. With infinite care, he sat the platter onto the floor.

Those scraps are intended for us all, Erik thought with a sinking feeling. It had seemed barely enough for two—even if one could stomach it in the first place—but now he realized that the meager portions had to feed six! He watched neMonn divide the bits of meat and cheese, then slide a helping toward each boy, using a slice of bread for a plate. He gave them most of the food.

Then he broke the last scrap of cheese in half and slivered the bit of meat. That and a crust of bread remained for the two adults.

Erik choked back a bitter remark. He had made the obvious connection. The boys would always be better fed than either he or neMonn. The boys were of the Folk. They would grow into warriors and hunters. And they would eat with their families at breakfast and at night; this starvation portion was only the mid-day meal, intended perhaps to teach them to endure the stress of hunger.

But he and neMonn were not warriors and had no potential to become so. At best, they might hold their own when the harvests were good and the Festburg filled with provisions. At worst, they could become definite liabilities during the winter. When food became too scarce....

"Sometimes they cannot send even this much," neMonn said softly, as if reading Erik's thoughts.

Erik gulped the scanty meal, his hunger nearly masking the cloying aftertaste of badly cured meat and softening the clotting hunks as the bread rasped against his throat. This was only the beginning. Worse might well follow.

As soon as he could, Erik jerked to his feet and ducked out of the hut. He stumbled toward the barrier, away from the sheds where animals bleated their unthinking contentment, away from the Festburg, from Weard, from....

If only he could get away from everything.

In spite of his best efforts otherwise, he returned in memory to the flight through the lower forest, to the monstrous beast, and to Marquette and Marquette's death. His eyes welled with unwept and unwanted tears as he remembered....

"Erik."

The voice came low and soothing. Erik almost feared to turn.

A hand touched his shoulder. He flinched in pain, then stiffened as the hand pulled away. Had he been tested again...and if so, had he failed again? How could he survive like this, how could he become one with a people whose weaknesses outmatched his strengths, whose bodies were indefatigable and impervious to strains his own found overwhelming? How could he live when each moment became a crisis of life and death?

The tears withdrew unspilled to some secret place deep within. His face became as stone.

He turned.

Weard stood a pace away. He watched Erik for a moment then handed him something.

"For the inflammation," he said, indicating a gummy mess wrapped in long, broad leaves. "This relieves the irritation."

Erik accepted the gift but said nothing, made no movement.

"Go with neMonn. He will take you to the stream and show you how to wash away the oils, then rub this on the redness. It should help."

With that he left, marching toward the warrior's huts. He did not look back.

Wearily Erik returned to neMonn's hut. He heard a murmur of voices spilling from inside, a murmur that subsided as his shadow crossed the doorway. neMonn and the boys were still sitting in a circle as they had been when Erik left.

There was a space next to Daroth—Erik's place.

He crossed the room, leaned over, and spoke softly into neMonn's ear, as if ashamed to be overheard.

"Weard said you would help me."

neMonn glanced at the poultice and nodded. He gave rapid orders to the boys to continue the work, then stood. Together they left the hut. Erik began to explain what Weard had said, but neMonn broke in.

"The poultice is good. Other of our men find that the haelo leaves burn them also."

Erik noted with silent gratitude the use of the words *other* and *men*: at least neMonn, and perhaps Weard, recognized his determination to fit in. And perhaps this weakness was not his alone—apparently others suffered allergic reactions to the heavy oils as well.

The two walked through the Festburg and out. They crossed the meadow in silence and followed the streambed south, away from the settlement and in the opposite direction from the haelo clearing. The water deepened as they walked until, just as the palisade disappeared behind a low shoulder of grass-covered earth, the streambed spread out into a pool. One end was roughly dammed with bristling branches and layers of river clay.

Boulders at the far end heaped on each other in a natural diving platform.

neMonn stopped but Erik continued on, skirting muddy margins and ducking beneath low hanging branches. neMonn watched but said nothing.

As if dazed, Erik reached the boulders and climbed, moving as if he knew the surest way, the safest foothold, even though he had never seen the place before.

When he reached the top, he stepped to the edge, his toes hanging over a sharp break in the granite, and stared down.

The water rippled blue-on-green, then unbroken green as trees bent in the breeze to overhang the water.

For a moment, he almost saw.... And for a longer moment, he almost launched himself into open air to float and fly and finally rest on the surface of....

He looked away, suddenly fearful of the spell the water seemed to cast on him and of the half memories it stirred.

"Our children bathe here and play during the warm summer days," neMonn said from across the pond, his voice raised only a little from his normal speaking tones.

Erik stared as if he had just awakened from a deep and troubling sleep. neMonn acted as if he knew that something was wrong but had no idea what or how to combat it. He motioned impatiently for Erik to rejoin him, again acting as if he hoped that he would not have to climb the boulders and retrieve his wayward ward.

Without a word—and without another glance into the water—Erik retraced his steps and within moments stood by neMonn where the stream entered the pond.

"Well climbed," neMonn said. "You looked at home up there. Have you...?"

"No!" Erik said curtly. Then again, in a more conciliatory tone, "no."

More than a little mystified by Erik's actions—and reactions—neMonn led Erik to the water's edge, then lifted the cloth from his back to expose the inflamed skin.

"There is redness," he said as he laid cool hands against warm skin, "but no blisters. It must feel as though you had fallen into a fire-pit, though. Even the redness can be as painful as flame."

He knelt and soaked the cloth in water and, with surprising gentleness, washed away the oils without abrading the damaged skin any further. Gradually, the bathing became a gentle massage; as neMonn worked, Erik felt knotted muscles relax as his skin cooled.

Too soon, neMonn finished.

"Now," he said, "I will apply the healing. Don't flinch, it might sting a little."

It stung. More than a little. As neMonn touched the gummy stuff to his back, Erik felt as if he had been struck by a flaming torch. In comparison, the rash was a mild itch, nothing to worry about at all. He felt welts rising along his spine where drops of the stuff slid unhindered, scorching as they followed the curve of his back. But he did not flinch. He bit his lip, hoping that neMonn could not detect the movement, hoping that the agony would go away.

Gradually the flames died to ashes, then the ashes grew cold and gray. Finally there was numbness. The stuff had done its work.

"Now bathe," neMonn directed. "Wash the poultice off yourself and your clothes or it will cause greater hurt than the haelo."

Erik removed the rest of his clothing, dropping them into the water as neMonn instructed. Even as he did so, he felt a wonderful relaxation spreading through him.

Feeling neMonn's eyes on him, he splashed into the cold water until he was waist deep and scrubbed with clean sand until both he and neMonn were satisfied that the poultice had been thoroughly removed.

Suddenly Erik ducked his head under the water and kicked off, swimming for the sheer joy of movement. For a few seconds, he was transported home, to Earth, to the University and the Academy. He loved swimming, a skill not appreciated by most Spacers.

Too soon, he heard neMonn calling to him, but instead of returning he swam in the opposite direction. The pool was small; within a few strokes he was beneath the boulder overhang, treading water in deep shadow. The water *was* green, but he could still see his legs and feet clearly. On an impulse he pulled himself out of the water.

"Erik! Don't...!" neMonn began, but Erik was already scrambling up the rocks and standing at the top, legs together, arms out, his lungs pulling in great draughts of air as the wind dried the water on his body. He stared straight ahead, thinking of—or perhaps not thinking of, but feeling about—Marquette and home and Feorm and the beautiful, unknown woman of his fevered dream.

Without looking, he keeled forward, straightening at the last second and cutting the water cleanly.

The pool seemed even colder than it had before. His breath all but froze in his paralyzed lungs, and for a moment that lasted a lifetime he knew deep-set fear—fear that his muscles would not respond to his commands, that he would sink beneath the surface until he merged with the green depths below, that he would never rise again but continue down and down and die in dark, icy depths.

Then his head abruptly broke the surface, and neMonn was standing impatiently at the shore waiting for him.

He swam as close to the edge as he could, then stood, shook once and reveled in the scattering of crystal drops that flew from his hair and body, and slowly walked out. He looked for his clothes but could not see them.

"There," neMonn said before Erik could ask him, pointing to a rock that glistened in the sunlight some feet away. His clothing was spread over its surface, clean and also glistening, no longer matted.

He looked at neMonn.

neMonn started to say something, then apparently changed his mind. Instead, he shrugged, then gestured to Erik's things before speaking. "I washed them while you swam. They should be dry enough to wear soon. The sun is hot there."

"Why...?" Erik had been too preoccupied with the sheer pleasure of swimming to notice neMonn washing his garments for him, but now he could only imagine the pain the man must have felt in levering himself down, crouching on the rocky edge, finding a precarious balance for his crippled leg, and then leaning further over the pool until he could reach clear water and scrub the bulky things.

Instead of responding, neMonn simply handed Erik his sandals. The leather felt damply cool, as did the thongs. Still naked and beginning to shiver slightly in the clear air, Erik knelt to retie the bindings on his calves as neMonn first watched, then nodded his slow approval after Erik had finished.

"You have learned well."

"Weard taught me well. He made me understand how important it was that I...."—Erik took a deep, quivering breath, aware that with the next phrase he might be signing his death warrant—"...That I become one of the Folk."

neMonn looked straight into Erik's eyes for a long moment before answering. "That will never happen, my friend. You are not one of us. You may survive—you may even live long enough to see me buried and hear the warriors, my former fellows, sing one last dirge over my body as flames consume me. You may. But you will never be one of us."

He looked over his shoulder at the boulders clustered on the opposite shore. He shook his head once, twice.

"You are different."

He reached over and traced the lines of Erik naked shoulders and chest, following the overlay of muscle down the ribs that showed starkly through Erik's pale flesh.

"You are not strong enough," neMonn continued. "You have a child's body. It is strong enough, for a child, but your body will not grow, as Daroth's and Brand's will grow, as Cempa's and Cwealm's have grown. You will never be able to hunt in the wilds alone, or bend a champion's bow with the strength needed to send an arrow to its home."

He dropped his hand. Something died as he severed physical contact with Erik, and neMonn retreated a pace or two, then stopped and allowed his eyes to pass objectively and appraisingly over Erik's body. Again he shook his head.

"You are a kind man and, I think, a good man. But you are not of the Folk."

He walked to the rock and retrieved Erik's clothing. He held them out to Erik. They were not yet dry and hung clammy, cold, and alien-seeming from Erik's hands.

"No," neMonn continued. "You are not as we are. You are not one of us."

CHAPTER EIGHTEEN

It was still early afternoon when neMonn and Erik returned to the Festburg. The boys were nowhere in sight, but the ragged heap of haelo branches had grown conspicuously larger.

"Are you ready to begin work again?" neMonn asked as they arrived near the shed.

Erik stretched his arms in front of him, then high above his head, arcing his back until his spine almost crackled. Where the oils had irritated his skin, it felt taut and warm but not painful. He twisted his torso from one side to the other, then back. He felt deliciously relaxed after his swim.

"Let's go."

The routine seemed less burdensome in the afternoon than it had that morning. In fact, the work seemed almost pleasant. Erik made it a point to observe neMonn, Cempa, and Cwealm closely, noting more carefully how they tied their bundles, how they hunched the haelo sheaves higher on their shoulders than he had done, shifting the point of balance subtly but significantly. He imitated the others as closely as possible, refining and adjusting his burdens until he was carrying nearly as much as they. He left his back bare, as they did, and was not bothered by bits of chaff catching in his clothing and abrading. The oils did not seem to bother him any more, either. Whatever was in the poultice was effective not only in healing but also in preventing.

By the first hints of evening, he was physically exhausted but enormously pleased with himself. He and Daroth were the last two still in the glade, loading the final bundles. The forest had already sunk deep in shadow, and even Erik, untrained for such sensations, could easily smell the freshness of water and greenery hovering on the evening breeze. Daroth wordlessly boosted his bundle, then for some reason waited patiently at the edge of the clearing until Erik had adjusted his bundle and caught up with him. Together they walked into the shadows that covered the trail.

"How are you called?" Daroth suddenly asked when they were perhaps half way back. His boy-treble voice sounded soft in the silence. And with that question, Erik realized that he had not yet given any of the workers his name. He had not been asked, not even by neMonn.

He started to say simply "Adjunct 746D42M," but halted before any sounds emerged. That was how he had been called in the Ex-Serv, he thought, but was that *who* he was? And was it the name by which Æthele, Weard, neMonn, and the others could ever think of him as one of the Folk?

He thought for a long moment.

Baanfeld—*Place of Bones,* in the language of the Folk. Erik winced inwardly at the ironic twist that had retained his chosen name unaltered and largely unintelligible for two thousand years, only to thrust him into a society where it could again speak meaningfully. And yet—and here was the next ironic twist in what was coming to be a convolution of twists—what name could be more appropriate for him here. Especially if he faltered once in living up to the requirements imposed on him by Æthele.

"Baanfeld," he said finally. "Erik Baanfeld."

Daroth nodded but remained quiet until they left the forest and began the final stretch of the trail across the meadow.

"That is not a warrior's name," he stated finally. "No. That is a name of death."

The boy's voice was somber, grave. Erik stopped and stared at the young man. Daroth returned the stare, then suddenly his gray eyes sparkled, even in the dimming light, and all traces of concern died from the youthful face.

"I shall one day be named *Freca* and *Frea*," Daroth said, the words a simple declaration that somehow Erik could not find it in himself to doubt. He translated the words: *warrior* and *lord.*

The boy continued. "And then, when I am very old and very famous as a warrior, I shall be *Infrod*, the old and wise one. All will seek me out at the Councils. And I shall remember you, Erik Baanfeld, 'Place of Death', when I look out of my hut toward the mountain crests that will be home to my own death."

He stopped and looked again at Erik, briefly this time, but intently. "I see Death in your eyes, where there should be Life. But I do not know whose death I see."

Erik was startled by the intensity of his words—so startled that he stumbled and overbalanced, almost dropping his load of haelo into the waist-high grass.

With that Daroth laughed, as if life itself were the greatest and best of jokes, and loped across the meadow, running as if he had no unwieldy burden strapped across his shoulders. Erik remained where he was, his brow furrowed in thought, then he shrugged his shoulders to straighten his load and, drained of energy, trudged on.

As soon as Erik entered the Festburg, someone Erik didn't know pulled the bushes back into position to secure the compound against the night. Erik continued toward the hut, depositing his bundle along one side of the heap. He shook his head, brushing leaves and detritus from his hair, then dusted his clout, picking away a few twigs. When he entered the hut, neMonn was not there. Nor were the others. He went to the corner where he slept and rummaged in the darkness, finally finding his tunic. Throwing it about his still-naked shoulders, he walked into the night.

Across the settlement, fires glowed like a handful of stars scattered on the blankness of space. He could see the slow, tired movement of people clustering around their individual fires. He shivered, breathed deeply once or twice to clear his head and lungs, then set off across the bare ground.

When he passed the fence marking the boundary of Families, he half expected a challenge. He simply assumed that he would have no place there and would be turned away. Instead, to his surprise and relief, everyone merely ignored him. For all that his passing disturbed the routine of the evening, it was as if he simply did not exist. He sidled to the nearest fire, drawing as close to the heat and light as he dared. No one spoke to him. No one turned him away, but neither did anyone invite him closer.

After a few minutes, he stepped back into the shadows and threaded his way through the rest of the compound. He had no concrete idea where he was going or why, other than nursing a vague hope of locating neMonn or possibly Weard.

He passed a dozen huts, wandered around small clusters of people, seeing the children and the women really for the first time. The women were strong, many as sturdily built as the men although usually not quite as large. They were not beautiful by ExServ standards, Erik realized, but they were certainly pleasing and handsome in their own way—a way he was beginning to appreciate.

He continued on aimlessly until he drew near the central hall. By the far side of the building, partially hidden by shadows, he thought he saw a familiar figure. A woman. Graceful and lithe.

Feorm.

She was speaking to another woman, whose face was similarly hidden in shadows and whose form was swathed in a long cloak—

but there was something about her, some echo of memory suggested by her stance or by the way she held her head or gestured with her hands just so. Erik stared nonplussed. He had never seen her, he was certain of that—yet he felt as if he knew her.

He circled around the hall, following the well-worn path by the low fence. Just as he turned toward the women, Feorm laid her hand briefly on the other woman's shoulder. They stood for a second or two, then the second figure turned and hurried away. Erik was about to shout after her when something warned him to remain silent. Feorm did not leave. She stood where she was, staring at some indeterminate point just above the edge of the thorn palisade.

Erik moved quietly toward her. So far, she gave no indication of having seen him or heard him. He stopped a few paces behind her, stopped, and whispered her name, although so softly that she could not have heard. As if she knew that he was there and was partly shamed by his presence, she lowered her eyes and began to walk away, down the long side of the hall and into the darkness of its shadow. On an impulse, Erik raised one hand to catch her attention. He wanted more than anything to speak to her. He wanted to thank her. She had been gentle and good. She had helped him, an outcast. She had....

A sharp blow from behind, just behind his ear, knocked him to the ground. Even as he felt hard-packed earth scraping his knees and elbows, even as his forehead struck ground with a solid *thump* that rattled him even further, his scanty training kicked in and he rolled away, twisting sideways as he did so. His ears rang with ranks of broken static, and his neck seemed to have buckled under the impact.

From the darkness, a leather-shod foot struck his ribcage, stinging and bruising, but at the same time, Erik recognized that it had been a glancing blow, purposeful, calculated to give pain but not to break bones. He tucked his head into his shoulders and rolled again and waited for another kick. That surprisingly did not come.

Out of the corner of his eye, he saw Feorm disappear around the corner of the great hall. Her silhouette was incised sharply by a single distant fire. The flames—and the pain in his ribs—blurred his vision as he squinted and blinked against the darkness. She did not turn back. Apparently she had not seen him, nor had she heard the sounds of struggle.

As she disappeared, Erik shook his head, making the ringing shift decibels and frequencies, and looked up.

Two men stood over him, their outlines black and indistinguishable.

"Who...?"

The foot kicked again, bruising his thigh and sending a new current of pain down his leg.

"Shut up." The voice was low and threatening, almost a whisper. The two figures leaned down and jerked Erik roughly to his feet. His leg felt as if it were paralyzed, and his ribs throbbed in unison with his with the frantic thrumming of his blood.

Flan and Tir—*were they always inseparable?* he found an instant to wonder—pulled his arms over their shoulders and dragged him out of Families, into the shadow of the palisade as far from the huts as possible and on the opposite side of the Festburg from neMonn's hut. Erik vaguely understood what direction they were heading, but hadn't the slightest notion why. Why they were dragging him out there—why they had attacked him so brutally without warning.

Neither of the youths spoke as they moved further and further from the fire-lights. Erik tried once more to ask what they were doing, but a sharp elbow to his stomach effectively silenced him. He had not fully caught his breath when they stopped, released their grips on his arms, and unceremoniously threw him to the ground. He stared up at them. In the near-darkness, their faces were vague blanks studded with two deeply black holes that were their eyes.

Flan spoke first.

"*Adl* have no place in the Festburg. You do not belong here."

Tir spoke up so smoothly that it was almost as if he were completing Flan's thoughts; as had Flan, he seemed determined to infuse as much contempt as possible into his words. "*Prattlinga* do not speak to the women of the Folk. Especially not to the wife-to-be of a warrior. Not to the wife-to-be of Weard."

Erik struggled to his knees, then to his feet. They let him. Finally, he stood shakily in the darkness, his back almost against the thorny wall.

"I only wanted to thank her...," he said. His voice trembled with pain, and he hated himself for betraying that weakness. At the sound of words, Flan struck viciously, back-handed, slicing sharply across Erik's cheek.

The blow sent him reeling sideways. He stumbled, fell, and instinctively rolled away from his attackers. He scraping his knees again, as well as his chest and thighs as he skidded in the coarse dirt. When he looked up, his face was less than a hand's breadth from the palisade. A wickedly curved, black-daubed thorn angled toward him, only inches from his eye.

Suddenly he thought he understood.

This was Death. What had Daroth said? *There is Death in your eyes.* And was this what the boy had meant? Did they mean to pinion him on the poisoned thorns and leave him hanging, dying and dead, for the crime of having whispered a single name?

Erik pushed himself away from the barricade, then struggled to his knees again. This time they did not let him stand. When he tried to lever himself up, Tir struck him again, sending a fist smashing against Erik's shoulder. Flan followed up with a kick that drove Erik off balance and back to his knees. He tried to return the blows but succeeded only in enraging his attackers. More blows landed, more kicks struck ribcage and arms and legs, and then Erik was down again. This time he caught himself in time and remembered to roll away from the thorns, toward the distant glow of fires.

For a third time, he tried to make them understand, to talk sense to two young men who unaccountably seemed almost insane with fury.

"What did...?" he spat bloody phlegm, swallowed hard, and tried again. "What did...I do... to make you...want to...to kill me?"

Tir squatted down, his broad hands hanging loosely, arrogantly, between his knees, his face so close that Erik thought he could see starlight glimmering in the youth's eyes. When Tir spoke, his voice was even softer than before, filled with the quiet, certain death of a venomous serpent.

"I was there, *adl*." Again, the final word was a taunt and a curse. "I saw."

"Saw?" Erik managed to say. His mouth and jaw hurt, he could barely draw air, and his head ached abominably. The ringing in his ears had long since reached an unbearable pitch. "Saw? Saw what?"

Tir only stared at him. The tendons in youth's hands tightened until they seemed like charged bands of tempered steel hanging before Erik's eyes. Erik tasted blood on his lips, felt its salty heat on his face, and his legs and chest throbbed metronomically, but he did not dare to wipe the blood away or shift his aching body. Somewhere, though, he found the strength at least to stare back, to match Tir glare for baleful glare.

When Erik trusted himself to speak again, he pitched his voice as near to Tir's as he could, allowing the venom of his own pain to burn through. *"Why are you killing me?"*

Tir blinked, apparently surprised by Erik's question. Then he lapsed into impassivity again, his hands still motionless. His voice rang harshly as he spoke. "I was in the healing hut, *prattling*. Weard requested me to sit with you during the night, to call Feorm should...should you have any need. I saw. I *saw* you...." His voice had risen in volume and pitch before he stopped suddenly. His fingers curled into fists, inches from Erik's bruised face, and he fell silent again.

Erik raised himself up onto his elbows, cringing at a sharp pain in his chest. But what was happening before him was far more important at the moment. Tir could hold the key to his surviving through this night—or dying right now. He wasn't sure how to handle the boy, but clearly Tir was struggling against something difficult, perhaps impossible, to express or to understand.

Erik spoke clearly and sharply, each word distinct. "I was ill. I had a fever. I do not remember. *What did I do?*"

"You...." The fists knotted, released, and knotted again, as if it was all Tir could do to keep them under control. He tried again. "You screamed in your sleep. Your face was wet with sweat and tears, and you spoke strange sounds I could not understand. I went across the way to ask Feorm to come and help you. When she... when she entered...." The boy's right fist raised, paused, trembled in the air, and fell with a sharp *crack* against the bunched muscles of Tir's thigh.

Erik waited this time. He wasn't going to help the boy any further. Tir would have to speak his anger, confront it on his own.

"When she entered..."—Tir repeated, leaning even closer, his breath hot against Erik's torn face, his face twisted with unutterable fury—"...you, *adl!*, you lay naked before her!"

Erik blinked, confused and disconcerted. "But I was ill, the blankets must have slipped off. I didn't...I don't remember...."

"*You lay naked before her,*" Tir breathed—and Erik suddenly realized must be going on. Tir loved Feorm, too. Perhaps not in the same way as Weard, certainly not as overtly and as sexually. His feelings must be more like the intensity of puppy love or a boy's first emotional crush, heightened by the hero-worship he simultaneously felt for Weard. Erik had, however inadvertently on his part, embarrassed Feorm and had thereby tarnished her purity—or at least Tir firmly believed he had.

Erik tried to smile reassuringly. The attempt hurt. "It was only the fever, Tir, and...."

Lightning-like, Tir's right hand opened, whipped out, and struck, as silently and death-dealing as the serpent Tir had resembled. He struck a dizzying blow across Erik's already bleeding cheek, knocking him back prone on the ground. He hunched even closer to Erik, intimidating by his bulk and by a white-hot fury that Erik still could not understand.

"You were naked, *adl!* Naked! And spear-hard!" Tir flushed

violently as he spoke the words, but Erik could see nothing of the boy's face in the darkness. "*Filth!* And when she touched you innocently to cleanse the fever from your flesh, *you spilled your seed*! You defiled her presence then with your filth, and you defile the Festburg now with your life!"

The dream!

Erik wanted to cry out, to explain, to expiate himself. The fever, the stress, his loneliness...and the dream. But the right hand descended for a final time, curled tightly into a fist, and Erik remembered nothing more.

* * * * * * *

neMonn found him. It might have been minutes or hours later. The last few fires were dying; most had already died. The dark huts huddled quietly in their enclosures, and no visible movement broke the stillness. The air, and the ground, and the night were unbearably cold.

Erik had barely regained consciousness, shivering uncontrollably when someone touched his arm. Instinctively, Erik lashed out, for the instant not comprehending when his fist connected, not with solid muscle and taut skin, but with withered flesh and twisted bone. neMonn. When he realized whom he had struck, Erik wept from the pain and for the shame—half-remembered shame and now new, present shame.

neMonn felt Erik's forehead, acting at first as if merely anxious that Erik had taken some hurt from the exertion of the day and perhaps fainted. Erik felt the man's hand brush lightly across his temple, felt it slide through something damp and warm and sticky, saw neMonn hold his hand up and stare. In the fading fire-glow, neMonn's hand was ruddy and stained with something black...with blood.

"No!"

Erik barely heard the word, barely felt neMonn shake him and ask urgently what had happened.

Erik tried to move, but the pain forced a cry instead as ribs, neck, and head shot spasms throughout his body. For a moment—or for many minutes, he was never certain—he lost any sense of what had happened or who the figure kneeling over him was, and retreated into a gentle, welcome numbness as the wash of pain overwhelmed him. Gradually, though, he heard a voice, a continuous voice spilling sounds but not words. The sounds rose and fell like a desperate litany against the night.

And then the sounds made sense, and they were coming from his lips, through his aching throat and he was repeating the same words again and again. "They beat me, I only wanted to thank her, they didn't have to, I didn't know, I didn't know, I only wanted to...."

neMonn crouched and braced his crippled arm beneath Erik's shoulder. Pushing up with his strong leg, supporting Erik as much as he could, he finally worked Erik to his feet.

They were standing about halfway between the thorn wall and the nearest of the huts. Dimly Erik realized that Flan and Tir had apparently not intended for him to die immediately—they had not thrown him bodily onto the poisoned thorns. Instead they had left him bleeding and hurt, exposed to the cold of night. That meant something, but he could not quite grasp what. He tried to hold himself erect, but the pain increased with his effort. He too a step toward the huts. He felt neMonn's arm around him but for some reason he could not feel his own foot touching the ground. He stumbled, righted himself, and tried once more to walk. Even as he stumbled the second time, still supported by neMonn, he lost consciousness.

* * * * * * *

When light came, Erik started to open his eyes, then stopped. He was stunned by at the pain shooting from behind them, exploding in his brain like seeker-rockets over a battlefield. He tried instinctively to throw his hand over his eyes and shut out the light and the pain, but the sudden thrust of new agony in his shoulder and chest froze the movement. From somewhere on the other side of the room, neMonn spoke.

"Lie still."

Erik made himself relax, obeying what seemed a reasonable idea in any case.

"What happened," he whispered. "I remember...."

"Be still. From what you have revealed in your murmurings during sleep, you have made a mistake. A grave one. Nearly a fatal one, had I not found you. By morning you would have been dead. As it is, a day of rest may perhaps make you whole."

"I remember.... Feorm.... I wanted to...to...." Erik stuttered into silence.

neMonn's voice grew somber, his words almost lost. "I don't understand all of what happened, but you must never attempt to speak to her. Ever. I should have warned you. She is of the Folk; you are not. She is strong and healthy and will bear children to support and defend us. You could not. You are *adl*, a sickness; you are *prattling*. You have no voice, no body, no purpose here."

"What else did I say?" It was suddenly important to Erik that neMonn not know everything—and critically important that he not know the identity of Erik's attackers.

"Not much. You made little sense. But I am surprised that someone would beat you this severely. Feorm *is* wife-to-be to Weard, and last night you tried to speak to her, you—*adl* and *prattling*. This should not have happened. But for one to try to kill you...?" neMonn made the statement into a question, punctuated by a solemn shake of his head.

Erik shifted on the hard ground. In spite of his best efforts, deep groan escaped from between thin, tight line his lips had become.

neMonn spoke gently and quietly.

"Do you know who it was? Who beat you?"

"It was...." Erik gulped and braced himself for the lie. "Dark. It was dark. I was...confused. I don't know."

"I see."

For a long time, neither spoke.

When Erik again broke the silence, he stared up at the splintered roof instead of turning toward neMonn's voice. His own voice was hard as granite and coldly bitter. "I have no place, no rights, no life except what is granted me by the Folk."

"That is so."

"And when they choose, they can tear even that from me."

"That is also so. It is as it must be. Our life is harsh, and we must be harsh to merit it. If you survive—if you wish to live—you must find a place in it. *Your* place."

Now it was neMonn's turn to fall silent. The pause lasted so long that Erik nearly drifted into uneasy sleep. Even so, he was never entirely sure that he heard neMonn, or that he heard correctly if the other did speak.

"Erik, I will say this once and only once. I know that you are not from...here." The pause echoed meaningfully. "I do not want to know more than I have guessed. But I hope that you win. I hope that you live."

"I will," Erik promised himself, hesitant to break the stillness, to give even that much indication that neMonn had actually spoken the words. "I will."

CHAPTER NINETEEN

Erik rested that day. neMonn ordered him to do so, but in any case, he was clearly too bruised and too stiff to carry haelo stacks. neMonn expressed some concern over the ugly purple bruises on his ribs and legs and the long, shallow cut that ran raggedly across one cheekbone, but after a close inspection in daylight, he was relieved to find that Erik's injuries looked worse than they were.

Erik slept fitfully during the day, waking often, each time increasingly restless and nervous. By twilight he was up and moving, walking in tight, jerking circles around the herdsmen's hut, trying desperately to sort through the events of the past night.

He couldn't remember everything Tir had said, but he had retained enough to convince him that the youth was caught in an impossible conflict. Tir obviously idolized Weard, and therefore, consciously or not, Weard's woman as well. He might be able to handle the sight of Feorm dispassionately washing an insensate body, even a naked one, but not something that brought too closely to the surface his own unspoken but probably deep-felt longings. If Feorm had become the focus of Tir's own developing sexuality, the boys' attack on Erik could be far more personal than either of them knew... or cared to consider. If he could avoid Flan and Tir until the latter's anger was replaced by more mature thought and understanding—and, of course, avoided any further exchanges with Feorm—Erik figured that might have a chance to live through the next weeks and months.

After all, he decided finally, he *did* have an advantage over the youth. In spite of Tir's inordinate strength and size, his precipitous actions strongly suggested that he was still barely more than a boy emotionally, contending for the first time with an adult's physical needs. It had been Erik's misfortune that his disturbing, fevered dream—and his body's unconscious response to it—had stimulated a crisis without his even knowing it and consequently without his being able to prepare for it.

By the time night had fallen completely, Erik had reached his decision. Although still stiff, his bruises taut and painful, and his cheek stinging whenever he moved the muscles of his face, he felt more at ease. He would handle *this* situation on his own.

Inside the hut, neMonn was eating. The portions sent over that evening had obviously not been intended for two to share, and to Erik the implicit message seemed clear: He had not worked that day, therefore he would not eat.

For a few moments he had been aware only of a buzzing, sullen anger, then the anger had drained away leaving in its place a solid resolve to persevere, to win, to show...*them*. He had risen to his feet and shakily but determinedly stalked outside.

In spite of his pains, he felt stronger than before, cleansed in some important way, ready to stand on his own feet. Now, for the first time, he had a strategy since the crash; for a change, *he* had made a crucial decision about his own life.

He stopped at the far edge of the fence, watching and listening to the stillness. He scanned the complex patterns of stars hanging cold and crisp in the wintry sky. Somewhere out there, he thought, was Earth, and the University Center, and the Academy—where problems suddenly seemed much easier than he had ever thought them to be. He sighed deeply.

"Erik Baanfeld."

A quiet voice interrupted his thoughts. He turned—more quickly than he had intended, his hands ready to ball themselves into fists—to face an approaching figure. Within seconds, he forced himself to relax. It was Daroth.

"Yes," Erik answered.

"neMonn wishes you to accompany him tonight."

"Where?"

"To the hall."

Erik did not respond; there seemed nothing to say.

"Well," Daroth insisted, his usually genial voice overlaid with a touch of impatience, "will you come? What should I tell him?"

"Tell him I will come."

The boy set off in a lazy lope toward the hut. He disappeared inside for a moment, then reappeared, waved half-heartedly toward where Erik stood, and then ran on toward Families. Daroth had probably heard stories about last night; certainly he could not miss the physical evidence that someone had handled Erik roughly...very roughly. Even he, the youngest and most affable of Erik's temporary co-workers, seemed to have revised his estimate of Erik's status downward.

Erik sighed, winced, sighed again, and slowly approached the hut. neMonn was waiting for him in the doorway.

"Tonight you will come with me to the Hall. You will sit with me in the warmth and the light and listen to the songs of the Folk," neMonn said in an unusually formal tone. Then, almost as an afterthought, he said something more, his voice dropping to a hoarse whisper. "Tonight, there will be snow."

They paused long enough to throw their thin sleeping-blankets over their shoulders as cloaks, then walked slowly together toward the center of the Festburg. Quietly, neMonn told Erik what they would see and how he must act. "Here, of all places, it is imperative that you be careful. What happened last night could become a pleasant memory in comparison...if you have any memories left. Remember that you and I, we do not exist in the most important ways that the Folk define existing. We will sit and listen and then leave. We are allowed that much. Nothing more."

As they neared the Great Hall, Erik could see golden light spilling through the great doors that, for the moment, stood braced open. The ground nearby glistened as if coated with frost, but Erik could the warmth of hearth-fire on his face long before they entered.

Within, the men of the Festburg had gathered, Æthele and the Elders nearest the fire roaring beneath the monstrous stone mantel, the others—including Weard—ranging near or far in order of their rank. A few older youths stayed back in the shadows; they were not yet blooded, neMonn has explained before entering, but they were old enough to merit a place in the Hall, however distant and humble. Prominent among them, Erik noted, were Flan and Tir.

Flan ostentatiously feigned indifference as neMonn and Erik entered, but Tir looked up sharply, his features outlined in stark planes by the firelight. Erik returned his stare calmly, noticing with a wave of relief tinged with nervousness that now, here, within the Great Hall, in the open glare of the blazing fire, and in full sight of the assembled warriors, the boy looked uneasy, almost afraid. By the time Erik was fully inside and surrounded by light and warmth, the boy had dropped his gaze to the floor. He chose not look up as neMonn and Erik crossed between him and the fire on their way into the farthest depths of the hall.

No one else appeared to have noticed their arrival. They sidled along the farthest wall, finding a corner in the deepest shadows. In spite of the roaring fire and the accumulated heat of the warriors' bodies, it was chilly there. But Erik could at least imagine that he still felt hints of the fire. He leaned back against the wall, shrugging deeper into the worn folds of his cloak.

Near the fire someone was singing—or chanting, at first Erik couldn't quite tell which. For a few minutes, he could barely distinguish words, let alone understand the rhythms of the song, but as his ear became attuned to the sounds and to the undercurrent of noise surrounding him, he began to understand first words, then phrases.

The man was reciting a poem-song about battles and warriors, monsters and heroes. His voice might once have resonated throughout the Great Hall—and even now Erik heard traces of timbre and force—but now the voice sounded cracked and hesitant, gradually dropping so low in volume that it grew difficult for Erik to follow. He could understand nothing of the final lines of the song.

"That is Iren," neMonn whispered when the voice broke off completely. "He is a great hunter, even as an old man. He sings first now. Gamol, our Singer, died a month ago, but there were none trained to replace him. We have sent messages to the other settlements, but we fear that we will have to live many months without a Singer. Each warrior will Sing as much as he can remember of the ancient songs, but few among them have great skills in Singing."

Erik noted the pronoun: *them.* Like himself, neMonn was not part of the larger group—he no longer belonged.

neMonn shifted uneasily when a second voice broke the silence. The new song was even more hesitant and fragmentary than the first, trailing quickly into nothingness. A third voice, then a fourth sounded in the Hall. Erik caught himself nodding, jerked awake, and wondered how long he had been dozing. The fire had burned down to coals; the cold on the other side of the wattled wall behind him was stealing more insistently into his bones. He feared to move, knowing that his arms and legs would tingle at the slightest motion. His head ached, and his cheek stung when he tried to whisper to neMonn and ask how long they would have to stay. In spite of the fragmentary warmth from the fire, Erik suddenly wanted to be far away from this place, where his status as outsider—as no-man—was so evident and so damning. neMonn was staring fixedly ahead, toward the knot of warriors, and Erik understood that he must not break into the man's concentration. He would have to stay where he was until neMonn chose to leave.

Nearer the fire, yet another voice was chanting. Erik thought perhaps that it might be Weard's but he couldn't tell for certain. He listened to the faintly hypnotic rise and fall of the voice, more alert than he had been only moments before, and half-mesmerized by rhythms that seemed simultaneously hauntingly familiar and stridently alien. Again and again new voices took up the chants until finally Erik was startled to hear neMonn's voice rise next to him.

It was surprisingly strong and fervid, impossibly different in Song from the guttural croaking Erik was used to. In the dying firelight, the flickering shadows, he realized, no one could see the twisted arm or the crippled leg—or at least none cared. Instead, here was a warrior of the Folk among his own again, if only through the kindly anonymity of darkness. Everyone knew, of course, who was singing; no one looked toward neMonn, however. No one mentioned his name in a hushed whisper.

neMonn continued for long minutes, longer than anyone else Erik remembered. But his song, too, ended in sorrow, with a broken line hanging unfinished, spectral in the silence.

There was a extended pause, expectant, as if all present were waiting for yet another voice and yet another Song. Finally, Erik heard the tired rustling of leather tunics and thick cloaks as warriors settled in their robes, most already nearly asleep. neMonn grasped Erik's arm, placed a finger on his lips to indicate silence, and gestured for him to rise. Almost soundlessly, they threaded their way through small clusters of inert forms, crossed the Great Hall, and slipped through the doors into the night. neMonn stopped only long enough to pull the doors tightly closed.

Outside, it was bitterly cold, even colder than Erik had anticipated from the chill that had penetrated the Great Hall. Erik clutched his cloak pulling tightly around his shoulders, but to little effect.

Above, the sky was clear, untouched by even a ragged hint of clouds, its immensity studded with all the stars that Erik had once known on another world, in another time. But even the stars were strangers now, strayed from the meaningful patterns that had made them constellations. Isolated and alone in their incalculable numbers, they were merely flecks of white or blue or distant red. The faintly blue moon just above the rings of trees that formed the horizon was circled by a thin, glistening halo of silver.

"It will be cold," neMonn said, pointing a gnarled finger at the ghostly moon. "Very cold. The cold has come early and will last a long time this year."

They stepped into the small open courtyard in front of the Hall, but as they moved toward the low fence, Erik felt a presence behind him. Suddenly fearful, he turned, half expecting to feel Tir's fist crashing against his cheek again.

Weard stood just outside the great doors, his furred clothing stained silver by the starlight.

He approached and spoke. "neMonn, would you wait for Erik by the gate? Please."

neMonn merely nodded and walked slowly off. Weard waited until the other man was out of earshot. When he spoke again, he kept the sounds low, so that no other possible listeners might hear.

"What happened last night?"

"Someone...I was beaten," Erik finally said, choosing bluntness over obliqueness. "But he...they didn't do much real damage," Erik added quickly. "neMonn says the worst of the bruises will fade soon, and nothing was broken." He smiled—carefully, to avoid pulling on the cut on his cheek but trying to reassure Weard.

He saw something—anger, concern, irritation?—flicker over the man's face.

"Who beat you?"

Erik thought for a moment. The question seemed more statement than anything, as if Weard already knew—or thought he knew—and wanted confirmation rather than information. Still, Erik reminded himself, he had resolved that *he* would handle the problem, that he would allow himself the costly luxury of falling back onto Weard's protection to buffer him from Tir's frustrations.

On the other hand, his decision made sense. This was Weard, his one-time protector and guardian, to whom he undoubtedly owed his life. Even if he identified Tir, Erik could not imagine Weard doing more than increasing his vigilance in Erik's behalf. After all, there had been no lasting damage. Perhaps Tir had even gauged his blows for effect, to frighten Erik rather than hurt him permanently.

But then, they *had* left him alone in the night, cold, helpless, and injured. How would the Folk—especially Æthele and Weard—respond to an overt and ultimately cowardly attack on one, even a non-man, patently incapable of defending himself and equally obviously under their protection?

Weard stood patiently, waiting for Erik's answer. "I don't know. It was dark and I...." Weard nodded, cutting off further explanation. An unreadable expression settled in his eyes, replaced quickly by the blank coldness Erik had begun thinking of as Weard's "official" look.

"Go now, with neMonn." The words were curt and totally emotionless. Erik had no clue as to what Weard was thinking, nor did he have time to consider the multitude of possibilities, since the man abruptly turned and, without looking back, strode toward the hall. Just as Weard's hand reached out to pull the door open, however, Erik spoke.

"Thank you."

Weard looked over his shoulder at Erik, his face still unreadable. Then he turned away and closed the doors, sealing Erik and neMonn out of the warmth inside.

Erik walked toward neMonn, hoping that he had not alienated Weard by lying. He joined neMonn at the low fence, and they made their way toward their hut, the only movement in the Festburg. Fires had died to gray coals speckled with dusky red. Erik shivered uncontrollably once, twice, but he could not force himself to hurry. He sensed the same hesitance in neMonn but did not mention it. He could only imagine what memories the experience of the night had stirred in the other; for him, the walk back to the hut seemed merely another irrevocable acceptance of his outcast state.

"The men...the warriors...sleep in the Great Hall tonight," neMonn said suddenly, his voice flat and formal. Beneath it, Erik felt rending a sorrow. Without further words, neMonn drew ahead, as if now anxious for the darkness and coldness and loneliness of the hut.

Erik thought he understood. Once, not long before, neMonn had had a Name, had been a warrior, proud and stern, worthy to share the lord's fire. Now he was a less than a herdsman, less even than a servant, another non-man, a withered and unwhole shadow sharing a cold hut with an one whose own otherness made him equally invisible.

Impulsively Erik reached out and—for the first time since, well, he couldn't precisely remember how long it had been—he touched another to give comfort. In the starlight, neMonn's face cleared momentarily, his eyes reflecting the eternal fires of a thousand suns.

neMonn did not shrug away from the hand on his shoulder, as Erik half expected that he might. Instead he merely said, "Let's go. We too must sleep."

* * * * * * *

Erik slept well that night, slept in spite of the icy voices that invaded the hut through chinks in the walls to whisper and to pinch at his ears. He dreamed of warmth and openness and hospitality, framed in images he did not consciously understand and would not remember upon awaking, but the effect was a momentary, lulling comfort for all that he had lost. And yet more—beneath that comfort pulsed wild rhythms, disorganized and incoherent, that he could almost grasp before they faded again into nothingness.

He did wake once, or nearly awakened, just enough to feel neMonn's body-warmth at his back and feel the thin fur creased along his shoulder. His left arm was exposed to the night and chilled, almost numb, but he could not dredge up the energy to move it. Instead, he drifted insensibly back into sleeping and half-dreamed that he reached to his nightstand and withdrew a sheaf of paper, holding it closer and closer. Without raising his head from his pillow, without turning on more light than filtered through the ice-frosted window, he began writing, rhythmical half-lines pounding through his brain and onto the paper in a poem that rang with strength and defiance and challenge to the Great Hall and those sleeping in it.

He thought. Or dreamed.

Because only a few breaths after he woke he was asleep again, his arm beneath the covers, his ears hidden, only his nose exposed and breathing figment puffs of vapor into the darkness.

* * * * * * *

Erik woke stiff and cold. Before he opened his eyes, he heard neMonn's breath, even and deep, beside him. The man was still asleep.

Erik rolled away from neMonn, trying to force himself deeper into a dissipating dream of warmth that tantalized just beneath his memory. His hand slipped from beneath the fur and fell on something hard and cold and slightly wet.

He sat up abruptly, only to discover that the inside of the hut was gray with morning light and glistening with a thin crust of snow that had filtered through gaps in the thatching.

Erik shivered as he rose and dressed, then leaned down to neMonn and touched the man's shoulder, no more, but neMonn immediately opened his eyes and grimaced.

"A new day, huh?"

Although he was chilled to the bone, Erik felt floods of warmth. He was not sure how or why, but he had somehow been accepted by neMonn, and that acceptance meant much to him.

Dressed in all of the rags and remnants they could scavenge in the hut, they walked out into the sunlight. The Festburg lay several inches deep in new-fallen snow, the first of the season. The huts wore slouching caps of snow, thin enough in places for the roofing to show through, slashes of black against unmarred white. Even the thorn barrier was crowned with glistening snow that had filtered through the tightly packed branches and formed thin layers on small twigs and black-tipped thorns. Erik could do no more than stare.

"It will not last," neMonn said, as if reading Erik's thoughts. "But, yes, for the morning, it will be beautiful."

Beautiful, Erik added to himself. *But also deadly. For* us *at least, for both of us.*

They spent the morning tearing apart haelo sheaves and spreading the branches in thin layers over the stable floor, providing both food and bedding for the animals huddled close along the interior walls. The boys, apparently still neMonn's charges in spite of the weather changes, did not arrive until almost noon, and by that time, true to neMonn's prediction, most of the snow had melted. In fact, the sun seemed quixotically almost summer-warm as it gleamed on random patches of water and mud.

When the boys did finally arrive, it was only briefly, to inform neMonn that they would be accompanying some younger warriors outside the palisade to begin learning winter hunting skills; so neMonn and Erik worked by themselves most of the day, not talking more than necessary, but growing closer as they shared a pitifully inadequate meal of hard cheese and even harder bread.

By that evening, all of the snow had disappeared, but the cold returned that night and grew more extreme as the days passed. As if as recompense, the herdsmen's duties were relatively light, since the animals barely stirred beyond the shadow of the shelter, but the meager rations were already beginning to tell on both of them. Erik felt the strain more each day and knew that it would only get worse. For his part, neMonn never spoke of his hunger or complained of his pains. He was too much of the Folk to complain, in spite of the fact that the increasing cold and what was tantamount to slow starvation made his injuries noticeably more painful. Even Erik could see that he moved more slowly each morning, that his arm and leg stiffened in the intense cold each night. Still, neMonn struggled on, impassive, focusing his concentration on his job, on the animals. Each night they would eat, sit for a few moments in the darkness, then sleep, their shared bed the only illusion of warmth in the hut. Each night, it took longer and longer for neMonn's shivering to calm to relaxed sleep; it took longer and longer for him to awaken each morning. But he never uttered a word in complaint.

Slowly, Erik began to understand what it was to be one of the Folk. Through neMonn, the least of them, he began to understand the loyalty, the wholehearted commitment, the undying service even in the face of death that it must take for a warrior to become a Weard or an Æthele.

Three weeks later, the snow returned, this time much deeper than before. The night had been clear and harshly, starkly cold. In spite of his shivering and the deep circles of hunger and fatigue around his sunken eyes, neMonn had not even tried to eat; he had looked over at Erik and slowly slid the wooden trencher and its thin scattering of scraps toward the younger man.

"Shit," Erik muttered bleakly, "what would it hurt them to give us...?"

"More for us would mean starvation for many," neMonn said. "The summer was hot, and the harvests not as plentiful as we had hoped. The Elders know what it will take for the Festburg to survive until spring. They have planned and apportioned wisely, but this winter will be harsh and it is possible that many may starve."

Erik shifted uneasily and pushed the trencher back toward neMonn. neMonn seemed not to notice.

"Many may starve," he repeated. "And if this cold invades the lowlands, fell beasts may hunger also, and will come, and our warriors must be strong to fight them off. Our women must be strong, too, to bear children in the spring who will become wives and warriors. Only the old, who are past their time of usefulness, and the infirm, who have no usefulness any longer, can easily be sacrificed."

He looked directly across at Erik.

"*We* are among those who may die in order that the Folk survive. I, because of these..."—he indicated his crippled limbs—"...and you, because of what you are."

Erik stared back. This was more than all that neMonn had said to him in the past few days combined. He started to remonstrate, to argue, but neMonn would have nothing of it.

"No, Erik. I speak the truth. And you know that I do. If we die, it is only that the Folk might endure. And in that is our warrant and our reward."

He pushed the trencher again toward Erik, then turned his back and hunched his shoulders as if in deep thought. Erik tried not to look at the pitiable scraps, tried to convince himself that his half would be more than enough to satisfy his gnawing hunger, tried to call out to neMonn to turn around and share with him. But he could not. He reached down, lifted a bit of hard cheese and placed it in his mouth.

He fully intended to speak again to neMonn, but the taste of the cheese caressed his tongue and its texture seemed to fondle his throat as he swallowed; and his stomach urged him to send more and more and more. And without knowing what he was doing, he did.

Finally, as if coming out of a trance, he stopped, his hand, bearing the last of their meal, already nearly to his mouth. His eyes widening in shock and something like horror, he dropped the morsel to the ground at the same instant that neMonn turned to face him.

"Eat it, Erik. You must. I have no hunger tonight."

"I…I'm sorry. I shouldn't have…."

"Eat it. Then let us sleep."

In a few moments, as soon as darkness was complete, neMonn retreated to the shadows and disappeared beneath his ragged coverings. Erik waited, chewing the last piece slowly, deliberately, even though he did not consciously register the taste—or even the nature—of what he was eating. Nor was he thinking of anything in particular, except for hunger and cold and death. He simply marking time. Across the room, he heard neMonn's breathing, ragged and shallow, as he slept.

When he finished, instead of going to sleep himself, he walked to the door and looked across the silent Festburg. Nearby, everything was still. Further in, at the heard of the compound, he could see distant shadows flickering as men—as Warriors—entered the Great Hall. From where he stood, he could see the rectangle of golden light that was the doorway; he almost convinced himself that he could feel the fire inside.

Finally he shivered and turned and, with a final glance overhead at the piercing stars, went inside.

The next morning, neMonn was awake before Erik, a neMonn more like the one Erik had first met than the one who had seemed so solemn the night before.

"It snowed again," he announced, dropping a handful onto Erik's forehead by way of evidence.

Erik jumped up and grabbed at neMonn's arm, but even so was not able to catch the other man. By the time he was dressed, neMonn was more reserved again, standing just inside the doorway.

"The snow is deeper this time, and now it will stay on the ground. Many months will pass before the earth is bare and warm again."

Erik was about to respond but caught himself. There was something in neMonn's voice. He waited.

"Many months will pass...many. But I shall not see them all. Soon I too will pass."

He turned and faced Erik.

"I was once Ferhth."

It took Erik a moment to understand that the man was revealing his Folk-Name, his Warrior-Name, the core of his identity before the injuries that so nearly destroyed him. *Ferhth, 'Great of mind and spirit'*, Erik translated mechanically, his mind numbed.

"Once. Now I am neMonn. And I must pass." He turned to look toward the rising sun. "But I would have liked to see the spring once more." Erik stepped across the dirt floor and raised one hand as if to lay it reassuringly on neMonn's shoulder, but he pulled it back. There could be no solace, at least none that he could offer. He was *adl, prattling*. He could probably do no more than survive himself—if he could do that much.

Together they watched the sun graze the tops of the poison-thorns of the palisade, imprisoning its light within.

* * * * * * *

The day passed slowly. Again the boys did not come to the shed. neMonn murmured to himself as he worked, limping painfully. For the first time, Erik noted, neMonn had wrapped his feet in narrow strips of hide. And when the work was over, twilight hesitated as the sun itself seemed to freeze at the furthest margin of the crisp skies.

That night, neMonn brought Erik for the second time to the Great Hall. The doors were open, spilling their promises of light and warmth. The two figures approached slowly, isolated in silence and darkness. neMonn pulled his leg up the first low step leading toward the open door, stopping just short of entering the Hall.

"Are you ready to go in?"

Erik did not quite understand what neMonn meant, but the question triggered something else. He couldn't say why, but he knew that it would not be right—tonight, at any rate—for him to enter the Great Hall with neMonn.

"No, please, I want to wait out here a few minutes. Go on in. I will come soon."

neMonn nodded. Apparently Erik had sufficiently answered his question—and Erik could visualize the scene as the crippled man made his way along the Hall. Without the *prattling* at neMonn's side, perhaps a one-time comrade might pull away from the fire, just enough to let him sit that much closer to the heat. Or another might smile and nod, just enough to recognize what had been and was no more.

Erik watched until he could no longer distinguish neMonn from the other shadowy figures inside. He turned and re-traced his steps into the central square.

From there he could see the entire Festburg. Snow silvered the ground, ice hung from the palisade that cast its feeble shadow beneath crisp-cut moon and stars. Huts lay closed, without exception silent and dark, as if all except the warriors gathered in the Hall were already sunk deeply in sleep. Winter closeted all in cold and stillness.

Erik shivered as he looked about. He was so cold that it seemed that he could barely remember being warm, and he was hungry with the gnawing pangs that signaled weeks of meager portions, not just days. He was barely clothed, given the severity of the cold, and he was tired, always tired…tired to the marrow of his bones. Slowly, as the stars gleamed distantly and icily on the settlement, he defined, considered, then finally accepted a bitter truth.

He was dying.

"There is death in your eyes."

On what the Festburg could spare for outsiders such as himself, he was slowly starving to death; and just as certainly, so was neMonn. Neither of them would live to see the brash new growth of spring, neither would survive the more desperate harshness still to come—and by all signs, soon to come. This snow, this chilling, killing snow, with its deadly attendants cold and hunger, was only a foretaste of deep winter. When that arrived, many in the Festburg would probably die—the very young, the very old, the infirm, and the incapable.

Erik and neMonn.

He looked to the stars again, startled to find himself blinking rapidly to keep them in focus through tears that all but froze on his lashes and cheeks. He stared up at them, as if in their cold light he might find either resolution or consolation—he didn't care which. Either would help him in this moment of realization.

Up there, somewhere, unimaginably distant to him in this frozen hell, his world circled a warm, friendly star. There every place would be weather-controlled, with snow an academic memory for most, an incredibly expensive luxury for some. There he could have slipped a credit voucher into a nearby vendo and fed and clothed himself, slept in warm comfort, enjoyed long moments work and study. He could immure himself in the familiar comfort of a disc-library, reading the *Beowulf* as it should be read, as a dim remnant of a barbaric…*something*…lost forever in the backwash of time, not as a blueprint for a perverted, gratuitously isolationist society obviously intent upon destroying themselves...and along with them, destroying him.

Now he closed his eyes against the starlight, inviting the coldness to stab through him as he recalled vivid memories of times not so long past: seeing a microdisc of the age-faded, curling parchment sheaves that were all that remained after all these centuries of the true *Beowulf* fragment; reading beyond that masterpiece into the other literature of that and even earlier periods—reading, almost absorbing the poetry of wandering, the tales of battles, and the gut-wrenching sagas of ancient heroes and warriors.

His eyes tightened as he thought, his lips moving faintly to the rhythm of long-dead poetry.

There were the Sagas, the impossible Legends of Cædmon, for example, the earliest existing singer recorded in pre-Collapse English.

Cædmon....

Erik's eyes flew open, so fast that the movement pained the fragile tissue of his lids. His heart thudded until he was sure that it must be audible throughout the Festburg, its *thrumm thrumm thrumm* startling women and children from dreams of warmth and safety; and he shivered head to toe, but this time *not* from the cold.

He pulled icy air into his lungs, almost numbing them, forcing himself to calmness. Silent, motionless, he considered. He dredged up memories and began to fit them together to complete a puzzle, a picture of a life so long ago that it was nearly less than legend. He strained to see Cædmon in the flesh—Cædmon, who could not sing before the fires in another, far more ancient Great Hall until an angel commanded him to write a poem in praise of God, the Creator.

Perhaps....

Erik spun around, strode up the steps, pulled the massive doors open, and entered the Hall. He almost stumbled in the mustiness of the shadows, then regained his balance and walked purposefully through the center of the Hall and on toward the corner where neMonn and he had sat before. The warriors glanced surreptitiously at him as he passed, their mouths tightening in what might have been grim ill-humor. neMonn was hunched over in the darkness. No one, it seemed, had offered him a spot closer to the fire. Even standing, Erik could feel the waves of cold coming off the walls and fighting to penetrate into the core of the Hall. neMonn did not move. His eyes remained hidden in the folds of fur covering his shoulders. But then, abruptly, he seemed to sense something because he suddenly looked up, his dark eyes glinting in the shadows.

Erik moved closer until he stood next to neMonn's shoulders, then dropped to his knees and leaned back against the icy wall.

"That was not wise, Erik," neMonn whispered from the corner of his mouth. "You should have come through the shadows along the wall, as we did before. I fear...."

"Don't worry," Erik said. "I understand now. I understand everything. I can help us."

"How...?" neMonn began, but Erik raised his hand and touched a finger to the man's lips. They too were cold, two narrowed, compressed lines of flesh that felt like ice against Erik's fingertip

"Not now. Later," Erik whispered back.

neMonn stared at Erik for a moment but did not speak. Gradually, the tension drained from him and, as if he had lost not only interest but the energy to speak further, he huddled back against the wall again, apparently content to wait, lost in the immediacy of his own thoughts.

Nearer the fire, a disembodied voice was stumbling through a fragment of a poem, suddenly familiar to Erik as a bastardized version of one he had studied long before. His pulse quickened as he listened. The voice faltered to silence. Another rose, stumbled, and likewise dropped to nothingness. Erik listened, first to one, then to another, and then another, listened with new ears and new understanding and new hope. Each of the warriors struggled to resurrect the powerful rhythms of words already stored intact in Erik's well-trained mind. But the men were hunters and warriors, not singers.

Patiently—impossibly patiently, it seemed to him—Erik waited as one by one the men fell under the spell of the radiating warmth. Voices droned and died, each more quickly than the last, until there was a long drawn-out silence. Some of the men along the outer circles seemed nearly asleep; further inward, the fire had burned to vivid coals.

Erik looked expectantly at neMonn. As far as he could tell, neMonn was the only one except himself who had not yet tried to sing.

But tonight, neMonn did not even look up as the silence settled over the Hall. He barely moved. If anything, he visibly pulled further into himself, hiding in the shadows, hiding even from Erik.

The silence continued uninterrupted. Erik could not even hear the subliminal scuffing of feet, the occasional cough or whisper that had marred the stillness the first time he and neMonn had stayed in the Hall.

It was as if....

And Erik was somehow on his feet and striding toward the fire, aware of the ruddy glow on his flesh, of flashing cold eyes that followed him as he passed. He felt Weard's gaze, a glance, darting out from beneath lowered brows, that seemed to flay Erik to his inner core. Even Æthele, sitting in his great stone seat on the other side of the fire, cocked an eyebrow as Erik took his place on the stone lip of the hearth, standing closer to the fire than any other.

Before any of the drowsy warriors could think, cr speak, or act, he began.

Nu sculon herian heofon-rices Weard,
Metodes meahta and his mod-gethanc....

Now let us praise Heaven's Guardian,
The Measurer's Power and the thoughts of his mind.
The Glorious Father's works as he established
The beginnings of Wonders, the Eternal Lord—
For the Children of Men he first created
Heaven as a roof, that Holy Creator;
Then Middle-Earth for men the Guardian of Mankind created.
The Eternal Lord, God Almighty.

Erik's face burned as he finished this briefest of ancient songs, and the heat came not entirely from the glowing coals. Even in the growing shadows he had noted an odd look in Weard's eyes, seen an undercurrent of something like anger in Æthele's face. But he had no choice. He had to continue. As he fell silent, the men around him waited expectantly, unwilling to allow him to return to the silence of the corner. Finally, as if on cue, one of the oldest men present asked a question.

"How do you, a stranger here, and not of the Festburg, know such words? You have been silent, you have worked as a beast of burden among the herds, yet now you Sing as only a Singer could. How is that?"

Erik caught his breath. That single, simple, hoped-for question could help him establish the role he had decided to create—or it could hasten his death.

Now that it had been asked, he was ashamed and embarrassed by its directness, by the clear sense in his inquisitor's voice that the warrior waited for, himself hoped for the answer Erik that had already framed.

Even so, he thought in an instant, he had no alternative but to continue. He willingly embraced his deceit.

Dredging his memory, he brought up the words of the ancient Legend. He had been sitting as a herdsman in the silence of the night, he claimed, his voice taking on a ceremonial, rhythmical lilt as if he had unconsciously begun framing his innermost thoughts in poetic structures. He sat in sorrow, bemoaning his inability to Sing, especially now and in light of the Folk's desperate need for a new Singer (his own addition, to be sure, but he was certain it would be a persuasive one). In the middle of his despair, a miraculous being of light appeared and gave him the words he must sing, instructing him to loosen his tongue and stand before the Folk and Sing the Hymn.

As he spoke, he modified the legend of Cædmon to fit his needs, to relate specifically to the Festburg and to the Folk. And all of the time, Weard's lowering gaze never left him, Æthele's glittering eyes never dropped a millimeter from Erik's face. In the distant corner, neMonn remained as before, unmoving, his head hidden in shadows.

They know, Erik intoned to himself even as he spoke. *They know the lie.*

When the questioning was over, Erik was asked to repeat the song. He began again, concentrating on the sounds, shifting from the hypothetical pronunciations drilled into him in training into the actual sounds and rhythms of the Folk. Even through the changes, however, the Hymn radiated its raw, primitive power. He sensed its effects throughout the congregation—for surely that was what the assembled warriors had become. He had wagered that religion would be important to the Folk, and he had won. Along with everything else, they had adopted the rough Christianity interpolated into *Beowulf*—at least enough of it for the Hymn to touch a responding chord in each.

His voice rose and fell in the rhythm of the half-lines, of the alliterative verses straddling the emphatic caesura-breaks in each line. He punctuated each of the stresses, weaving a texture of rough sounds juxtaposed with polished effects. When he finished, he let his voice drop into a final aspiration. He bowed his head as if in humility, his heart pounding, his lungs compressed tightly against his spine.

This was the crucial moment.

Someone moved on the rough floor—the faint *shhht* of tanned hide against hard-packed earth. Across the Hall, a sandal scraped against wood. Then another and another. When Erik finally looked up, a space had appeared in the foremost ranks of the men, a place of honor near the fire. A fur pelt lay rolled up nearby.

They were his, he understood without any words being spoken. They were the freely offered gifts from the Folk to a Singer of Tales.

He raised his eyes to the far corner. neMonn looked at him intently, narrowed his eyes, and nodded once. Even from the distance, and in the miserable light that threw shadows over everything, Erik could feel the warmth of neMonn's half-hidden smile.

He doesn't know, at least, Erik grated to himself, *he doesn't suspect anything. But at least now I can help him, protect him. And protect myself.*

Erik gestured for neMonn to join him near the fire, but the other man shook his head at once, a gracious refusal that acknowledged the intent of the gift. Erik tried again, more emphatically, but neMonn had leaned into the darkness again and Erik could not see his response.

Tomorrow he would decide on some way to include neMonn into his new status. He would bring neMonn out of the flimsy herdsman's hut and somehow see that he would be cared for until the spring. Perhaps he could request a servant. Yes, that might work. Surely they would understand that neMonn, crippled as he might be, could be of use to him. And surely the Folk would consider that a legitimate right for the Singer of Tales.

No, an inner voice raved. *Not Singer of Tales, but Singer of Lies! And a fool if you believe this will really change anything for neMonn...or for yourself!*

Erik raised his eyes again toward the darkness in the corner. He could not see neMonn but tried desperately to communicate through the emptiness. *This is a false face that I assume, I know it is. But it may save us. Nothing else can. Forgive me, my friend, but I am weaker than you, and I must take my chance when it is offered.*

He looked back again, toward the shadows. neMonn was gone. The other man had apparently already retreated to the solitude of the hut, as if unwilling to infringe on Erik's success. He would sleep alone, unmissed by any except Erik, wrapped in his tattered covers against the powdered snow that would filter through the thatching and beneath cracks. Erik wanted to go to him and bring him back to the warmth, but did not dare. At least temporarily, he was one with the Folk, however provisionally. He must not strain that acceptance.

neMonn would have Erik's old rags to augment his bedding, though; that might help a little.

As he moved through the warmth toward the spot which had opened for him, he heard muted whisperings on all sides. One voice, an old man's voice but strong with experience and authority, said, "Well sung, small one."

Another responded with "Sing again soon, Angenga." *Angenga*—"he who walks alone." A worthy name for an alien who must become one with the Folk to survive, but who might never be accepted as one *of* them.

He levered himself slowly to the ground, grateful not only for the flickering warmth of the fire, but also for the steady radiant heat from the bodies that surrounded him. For the moment, the Great Hall was silent—no one else stood to take Erik's place, to follow his song with another. Throughout the hall, heads nodded, eyes glinted tacit approval, a hand or two was raised in mute congratulations to the Singer. Erik tried to keep the smile he felt from forming on his lips. Solemnity seemed more appropriate to the moment. He stared at a spot perhaps a meter in front of him, only briefly raising his eyes to glance around and meet the occasional gaze focused on him.

Someone touched his shoulder. Half-turning, he saw one of the younger warriors—he did not know the man's name, nor did he recognize the face—but he did recognize the warm, salty smell drifting toward him from the wood-burl bowl the man held out to him.

"For you, Singer," the man said, with something approaching respect, perhaps even a touch of awe, in his voice. Even in those few words, Erik thought he heard a familiar cadence; the man had probably attempted a Song earlier, Erik decided.

"Thank you," Erik said as he took the bowl in both hands. The worn wood was warm enough to make the palm of his hands tingle delightfully, but even more appealing was the thick stew it contained. He brought the edge of the bowl to his lips and sipped. Ahhh, there was more flavor, more aromatic richness spilling down his throat than he had enjoyed since the crash. And probably more food in this lone bowl than he and neMonn had shared between them during the past week.

He thought briefly of neMonn, no doubt hungry and cold in the herdsmen's hut. *Tomorrow,* Erik vowed, his cold-chapped lips still stinging slightly from the salty broth. *Tomorrow I will think of some way to bring him back into the Hall. After all, now I am the Singer.*

Again, he almost smiled. He finished the stew, chewing the last bit of meat as long as he could to savor its flavor, then returned the bowl to the warrior.

"Thank you again," Erik said. The man nodded and returned to his place, and a deep silence spread throughout the Hall.

Hiding his face—and even as he did so fully aware of the effect, of his oh-so obvious and apparent modesty and humility on the audience around him—Erik retreated into the silent softness of his cloak, wrapped himself in the warmth of thick fur, and tried to sleep.

In his dreams, he thought he heard a strange and poignant sound, as of a distant, dying voice hidden in a high stone tower. The voice rose with the winter wind, then fell. Erik knew that a Singer had died, stretched naked beneath an open casement, his naked body motionless on cold, naked stones. Even in the depths of his dream, Erik struggled to understand what he now knew, and how he knew it, but as he tried to focus his thoughts, the lingering cry withdrew and faded until it was lost in the whirls of wind and driving snow.

CHAPTER TWENTY

There was warmth the next morning, a delicious and luxurious warmth, coupled with unfamiliar but not entirely unwelcome man-smells: unwashed bodies, uncut hair lank and oily, thick well-worn hides and furs tanned in strong acid and redolent of sweat. When he fully woke, Erik remained still for a moment, aware of others lying around him, aware of the warmth of body heat in spite of a flurry of snowflakes high up against the darkened beams of the Hall. He raised himself on one elbow and looked around.

It was early. Most of the warriors were still sleeping, probably an after-effect of the heady brew they had consumed throughout the singing the night before. Erik had not been offered any and consequently probably had a clearer sense of his surroundings than others might. As far as Erik could tell from a cursory glance around the Hall, Weard was not present, nor was Æthele.

He stretched, reveling in new-found comfort. He was the Singer, the Bard. He had found a place, even if it was based on a lie. At least he would survive, would have food and warmth and a place among the warriors to sleep. He would not starve as long as he could sing.

He tossed back his covering and stood up. The air was crisp and frosty. In the silence of the Hall, he took a quick survey. The fireplace was cold and gray, dead ashes puffing gently in the drafts. Fur-covered bodies lay on the floor, close enough to share warmth, distant enough for some privacy. Erik wondered if, during the winter, the younger, single warriors might not habitually sleep here rather than in their more isolated huts. Certainly men with wives would remain with them in Families, sharing body-warmth with their wives and smaller children; but here, in the cluster of sleeping bodies in the Great Hall, it was more congenial than in the freezing darkness of the outer huts, and certainly warmer. The bachelors' compound was probably all but deserted right now.

He walked carefully toward the closed doors, making every effort at silence in order that he not waken any of the sleeping men around him, half consciously scratching a persistent itch along his ribcage. Part of his mind tried to convince another part that he carried fleas or other such vermin, but he felt too good to worry about that. With a single hand, he shoved at the doors, letting in a puff of icy air.

He stepped into brightness. More snow had fallen. The Festburg was ankle-deep in untouched whiteness; later, the snow would bear the tracks of countless comings and goings, possibly of children playing at games and women moving from hut to hut, but for now it lay like an unmarked tablet, a vast stretch of untrodden potential. The closest huts huddled beneath their weight of snow, their roofs sculpted and polished, as smooth as porcelain. In the distance, the thorn barricade seemed softened and fragile, its poison hidden beneath a shroud of cotton. The interior fences were mounded with ice and almost indistinguishable from the earth itself.

Erik's breath formed a visible vapor as he stood, entranced. He had heard of snow, had even studied vids of it and read monographs about its subtle effects on societies and cultures. But now he was seeing it, really *seeing* it, falling naturally and heavily. The first time it had snowed, only a few days before, he had been too miserable, too hungry, too tired, and too cold to enjoy it. But now.

It was beautiful!

Even so, his breath hissed as he drew it in, and he clutched his cloak tightly against the iciness. To think that only a night ago he had been huddled in darkness, trying desperately to stave off the cold in the hut with neMonn.

neMonn!

Erik shook violently. In his moment of enchantment, he had nearly forgotten neMonn. He moved along the snow-crusted walkway, through the low gate, and—moving as carefully as he could on the wide, slippery path through the center of the Festburg—hurried toward the hut.

How had neMonn fared? For the first time since his performance, Erik allowed himself to consider how bitterly cold last night had been, colder than any night he had experienced yet.

His breath stabbing against his ribs, Erik spotted the snow-mounded hut and ran toward the shadows of the doorway, barely breaking his precipitous progress in time.

It seemed darker inside than it really was, largely because of the brilliant sunshine outside, but even before his eyes had adjusted to the shadows, Erik knew that the room was empty. Everything was neat, everything in its place. neMonn's sleeping roll was stowed carefully on the shelf; the stained food platter leaned against the wall. There was not a hint of disorder—but neither was there any hint that neMonn had even slept there last night!

Erik rushed outside, scanning the Festburg for some sign of neMonn. Perhaps he had been intercepted by an old friend, perhaps he spent the night in Families, perhaps....

But in his gut, Erik knew that the man had not.

He walked around the hut toward the shed. In the early morning stillness, only a few of the animals were moving. The air carried their soft sounds. Erik could smell the accumulated warmth of breathing warm-blooded bodies and moldering bedding straw.

Then he slowed, and stopped, his heart thudding.

Halfway between the hut and the shed, neMonn lay motionless on the ground. Ice crystals glimmered in his hair and a skiff of snow, much thinner than that which blanketed the rest of the Festburg, covered his body. His face was turned upward, toward the sky.

Erik rushed over, his feet silenced by the snow and ice, his breath ragged. He knelt down and touched neMonn's face.

To his surprise, there was movement behind the closed eyelids, and a thin cry that was part pain, part surprise, and part...disappointment. neMonn looked up toward Erik and a frail smile flickered crossed the pale face.

"Is it morning?"

"Yes, but don't talk. Let me get you inside."

He slipped his arm under neMonn's shoulders and lifted the man. The snow covering fell away and Erik saw that neMonn was naked. He weighed very little; Erik could carry him easily toward the hut.

"How do you feel?" he asked, knowing even as the words formed and passed into the air the foolishness of the question. neMonn was deathly pale, his flesh so cold that the chill seeped into Erik's arms and chest as he carried the man. His arm and leg were more twisted than usual, drawn close to his body and shockingly white.

"Well enough. The cold seeps into me, though. I will be stiff until the warmth thaws me."

Erik looked down. Curled in Erik's arm, as if a child, neMonn was smiling. Inside the hut, Erik laid him gently on the floor, then rolled out the bedding and lifted him again. The bits of snow and ice that had not shaken off still clung to neMonn's flesh, signaling how dangerously low his body temperature had dropped. He looked fragile in his nakedness, a newborn child too weak to survive birth.

"What can I do?" Erik said. "A fire? Should I...?"

neMonn raised a hand, slowly but definitely. "No. You are one of the Folk now. I have chosen."

"But I'm your friend, too," Erik said. "You called me by that name."

"Yes. But now you are no longer *prattling*. You are the Singer, the Singer of Tales of the Festburg. My friend, my poor weak friend who had no place among the Folk, is dead. I have no claims on him now."

"That may be, but you are *my* friend, and I will not let you just die."

He lay next to neMonn, willing his body heat into the other. Gradually it worked. The frightening iciness receded, a slow warmth spread through neMonn, and his breathing deepened. neMonn turned his head away to face the wall. Erik reached out and touched his shoulder.

"Friend now and always. Remember that. What I can do, I will. Count on that."

"There is nothing to be done. You cannot remain here. You should not even have returned. Æthele should not have let you come here today. I thought he would keep you at the Hall. That is where the Singer belongs. And that is why I chose. Last night."

Erik chilled further at the word: *chose*. Chose what? Chose to die.

There is death in your eyes. Death. neMonn did not speak the word, but Erik understood it.

It rang true to a memory—somewhere, from one of the ancient texts he had once studied when he was someone else, it rang true. Someone in a high tower, opening the windows to the storm, lying naked on a stony floor and choosing to die: Erik suddenly placed his dream, and shivered. When he had read it, the image had seemed perfect, ideal for choice and freedom as well as for fruition and fulfillment.

But not for neMonn!

Erik couldn't accept it, not yet. Instead he knelt beside neMonn and rubbed warmth into shoulders and arms, chest and thighs, gently pulling damaged limbs away from where they lay curled against themselves, straightening them, massaging them. After a few minutes, neMonn looked up at him. He smiled, but Erik saw a deeper pain flash in the man's eyes.

Outside the animals began calling hungrily, insistently. The pain in neMonn's eyes disappeared—not extinguished so much as clouded over, banked like the dying embers of a nighttime fire that must be preserved until morning.

He sat up, then struggled to his feet. Where he held onto Erik for support his skin was warmer but still cool.

"The animals need food. Let me dress. Then let us go to work."

Erik nodded, far less surprised at neMonn's attitude—and at the change in his physical state—than he would have been a few weeks before. Together they went out into the light, neMonn leaning only lightly against Erik for support as they angled away from the hut and crossed to the snow-covered stacks of haelo. They began working, and soon both were sweating in spite of the cold.

neMonn said little to Erik. Erik could think of nothing to say. Shoulder to shoulder, they worked in silence.

Still, Erik did not hear the newcomer until his voice cut through the air.

"Angenga."

Erik heard the word but did not recognize it immediately. He had forgotten his own naming of the night before, but neMonn looked at him closely as the word echoed across the open ground. His hands dropped to his side and he looked down, even as Erik continued to pull at a stubborn clump of branches.

"Angenga. Singer!"

This time Erik recognized the impatience and urgency in the voice, and knew he was being addressed. He swung around to see Tir standing not a dozen paces away. They had not stood thus, face to face, since the night Erik first went to the Hall. Then he had seen nervousness and fear replacing the fury of the night before. Now the youth's eyes were veiled by his heavy lids. Erik wondered what might lie behind the mask.

"Yes."

"You are wanted."

"Now?"

"Now. Æthele and Weard are waiting."

Erik nodded toward neMonn, not noticing that the other man had still not moved; he stood quietly, his shoulders slumped, his eyes downcast.

"I have to finish here."

"No!"

The imperative rang sharply, but it was neMonn, not Tir who spoke.

"No," he repeated, this time softer. "No, Angenga. You must go. You are responsible to the Hall now. Leave me."

He turned his back to Erik and Tir, and busied himself with sheaves of haelo. Erik dropped the loosened strands he had been pulling and stepped toward neMonn. Something in the set of the man's back stopped him, however, and he turned jerkily in mid-stride, stood motionless for a moment, then followed Tir, walking slowly toward the center of the Festburg. He did not look back.

Just outside Families, Tir stopped, staring ahead but obviously uncomfortable. Erik drew up next to the young man until their fur garments nearly touched and waited.

Finally Tir glanced sideways at him. Erik wasn't certain how to read the youth's expression, but his body tensed, trying to prepare for any sudden, threatening movements Tir might make. When the youth finally spoke, his words startled Erik.

"Angenga. Angenga, I'm...I'm sorry about...."

Erik waited, willing himself not to speak.

Tir glanced away and spoke to the emptiness in front of him. "I acted rashly, Singer. I should not have. I should have thought more deeply about that night...about what happened."

Still Erik refused to help him out.

"I...this morning, I told Weard what I had done. He told me you had not named your...attacker. I...Flan and I owe you...we must thank you for that. Weard made me understand that...what...happened was not of your choosing."

Erik could see the flush creeping into the boy's cheeks. Clearly he still could not resolve his own conflicts, and equally clearly even speaking about such things embarrassed him deeply. To push him further might undo what good had been done.

"Do not speak more of it. That night is forgotten."

Tir looked at him, relief outlined in his face.

"Come," Erik said formally. "We cannot keep Æthele waiting."

Footprints marred the remaining patches of snow near the doors of the Hall, mute evidence that most of the men had long since left for the day's labor. The massive doors were nearly shut.

Tir disappeared from his side as Erik reached out to pull the door open. Inside, the Great Hall lay deep in shadow, with not even a dusky glow from the fireplace to relieve the darkness. Erik walked in, silently glad at the outcome of his words with Tir. He had handled it well, he thought, and had handled the potential crisis entirely on his own.

The Hall was cold. Unrelieved by fire or sunlight, the darkness seemed to hold even more tenaciously to the coldness, as if the two were struggling to merge into one. He walked down the hard-packed floor, staying as much as possible in the dim light filtering down from the openings high in the ceiling above. Even so, he could see no one else until he was within a few meters of the raised dais. Then Æthele abruptly loomed from the deeper shadows behind him, followed, a moment or two later, by Weard.

Erik stopped a few steps from the dais. He waited for the others to speak. It was cold enough inside the hall that his breath was still visible, its fragment movement in the still air the only visible suggestion of life. He stifled a shiver, proud of his ability to do so, to appear impervious and controlled.

Æthele remained silent but after a few moments gestured to Weard, who moved silently closer until he stood midway between Æthele and Erik, slightly to one side. Erik tried to read the expression on Weard's face but could not. There was not enough light, nor was Weard allowing his thoughts to surface.

The silence lengthened as Æthele stared at Erik. Finally, however, the Ring-giver spoke.

"Do you really think that I am such a *fool?*"

Erik was stunned by the words and perhaps even more so by the deceptively soft tone in which they were uttered. Æthele's voice was deep, and low, not at all what Erik had expected. But then neither were the words. He hadn't consciously framed what he thought Æthele would say—but it certainly wasn't that.

"I don't understa...."

"Do...you...think...that...I...am...such...a...fool? Do I speak the language of the Folk slowly enough for you now? Which of my words could you not understand?"

Erik reddened as blood rushed to his cheeks, as much in anger as in embarrassment. He straightened until at attention, his body reacting with lightning-quick tension to Æthele's tone. He had certainly heard its implicit condescension often enough as an Adjunct...as a *Junk* surrounded by the "true" humans of the ExServ. But just as quickly, he realized that this time, the words were no longer addressed to Adjunct 746D42M, half-slave, half subhuman construct whose humility and obedience would be taken for granted. *This* time, he was Angenga, one of the Folk, and he could—he *would*—return an answer.

"I understand your words, sir," he said, and possibly his voice punched the last word a fraction too forcefully for it to suggest unalloyed respect. "I understand them well. But I do not understand what you refer to."

At first, Æthele did not respond. He stood, staring down at Erik as if assessing the figure he saw before him. Then he with a single fluid motion, he turned and disappeared into the solid darkness behind the dais. Weard remained immobile, as much a statue as if carved from marble or granite. Erik wanted to ask what he had done that was so wrong but did not dare whisper to the warrior. Instead, he remained silent and unmoving, almost shuddering again, but this time from more than the ambient cold.

In the depths of the Hall, something clattered, shatteringly loud against the silence, and immediately thereafter a door creaked. Erik dredged his memory for an explanation of the curious clattering but was lost for a long while until finally he remembered—metal. Metal working against metal. Small gears badly in need of oiling, perhaps, or some sort of tumblers.

He blinked his surprise.

Metal? Here? In the Great Hall?

Erik heard muffled footsteps and a scraping sound, this time clearly wood abrading wood. Then the door creaked again, fell silent, the gear-tumblers clattered, and Æthele stood before Erik, one hand bearing a crumbling book. He thrust the book toward Erik.

"Do you really think that I am such a fool?" he repeated.

Erik looked sideways at Weard. A fractional nod allowed— urged—him to move forward.

He took the book, his training insisting that, even in his swelling anger and frustration, he hold it gently. The volume was old, centuries old at least, bound in flaking leather. The pages and binding were reasonably well preserved, however, just as obviously well cared for. Bits of gilt still lingered in the shallow indentations where a title had once marched across the cover, but in the poor light he could not make out any of the letters.

With infinite care, Erik rotated his palms and allowed the book to open to a page marked with a thin scrap of...of *computer print-out*. Startled, he glanced up at Æthele but the man had not moved, was not even looking at Erik.

The incongruity stunned him. The bit of print-out was worn as well, its edges chipped where the paper had simply disintegrated with age. He dared not touch it. It had to be fully as old as the book, he realized. And both must probably to pre-date the founding or the original colony, or at least stem from its founding.

His eyes moved to the part of the page not covered by the print-out. It seemed that he had already known what he was about to see, at least unconsciously, but it was a shock nevertheless to see the familiar works marching neatly across the paper, the ink faded to gray but still legible:

Nu schulon herian Heofones Weard

"Cædmon's Hymn," in a pre-Collapse English print-face that mim-icked perfectly the original handwritten script.

"I do not think you a fool, sir," Erik finally said, almost more to himself than to Æthele. "I found a skill, one which might benefit the Folk. My voice, my memory served me well last night. The others accepted me. I did not plan to deceive. I merely put the words into the form I felt your Warriors would most appreciate." *Another lie*, he thought bitterly, *another victory for the Singer of Lies.*

Æthele did not answer immediately. When he did, he spoke to Weard, not to Erik.

"Weard of the Folk, promised of my daughter Feorm, how long have we hoped for a Singer? Our Singer is dead, and none can tell with such energy and devotion the old Tales handed down from our fathers and those we have formed from our sorrows and our joys. Without a Singer, the fires blaze dimly, the food and drink only par-tially satisfy, and the strength of the Folk diminishes."

He turned to face Erik.

"And now you come. An outsider, a prattling, an *alien*." In Æthele's mouth, the words grew almost venomous, resoundingly contemptuous. Erik shuddered visibly.

"You take our songs and claim them as your own," Æthele con-tinued. He gestured with one finger toward the open page in Erik's hand. "This Song, these words you have stolen, is one of the Sacred Songs. It has never been shared with the Folk; it is—was—known only to the Council. You have made it common and manipulated it for your own selfish purposes.

"And you think us fools." Æthele's voice had grown steadily calmer, milder. His final statement simply represented a fact. There was nothing left of reproachful recrimination.

No! Erik wanted to answer. *That's not the way it was.* But his throat constricted and strangled the syllables. He stood indicted and accepted the Warrior's judgment, himself having and offering no defense.

"Weard," Æthele said, quiet command radiating from the voice.

"Sir."

"What would you have us do?"

Weard appeared to think for a moment then spoke, slowly and deliberately, with a ritual tone in his voice that alerted every nerve-ending in Erik's flesh, and suggested suddenly that Erik had been an actor in a scripted drama without knowing it. Perhaps his response—or lack of response—might determine Æthele's final decision, but he felt instinctively that Æthele and Weard knew well what the probabilities might be.

"I do not approve of what has been done. Yet the *prattling*-Baanfeld has demonstrated unusual skill and knowledge. For months, our fires have grown dim, our food has lingered stale and tasteless in our throats, the night air has lain heavy with silence. And now winter deepens. The trails to other villages are dangerous; soon they will be impassible. We will have no further opportunity now to treat with others for a Singer—and we both know that there are no others trained in the Festburg. During the long evenings, when the snow drifts against the huts, we will need a strong voice to remind us of our heritage."

Weard's voice was lifted slightly in the rhythmic lilt of a born Storyteller. Erik listened, entranced.

"And I know that this small one has shown courage in...in another matter that touches closely upon the Folk and the Festburg. He has suffered much and yet shown great respect for us and for our ways."

Æthele seemed about to speak, almost to ask a question, but he hesitated long enough for Weard to raise his voice again.

"I would take him in and make him one of us. I would make him Singer."

Æthele paused again, as if in thought, but Erik noted that this brief silence lasted almost precisely as long as the earlier one, surely not a second more or less.

"It is well."

Æthele nodded, turned slightly, and addressed Erik.

"Erik Baanfeld, Angenga. I accept you into the Folk. You may serve with us and become one with us. You will be our Singer and our Bard. Your duties will be heavy and you must acquit them explicitly. Much depends upon you during the coming months, lest spring find us diminished and weakened in spirit and in flesh, our fires banked and cold, our strength waning. Do you understand and accept?"

"Yes," Erik said without hesitation, struggling to keep the rising jubilation from his voice. In spite of the little drama they had insisted that he participate in, he had made it, he had established a place for himself. Now, perhaps, he could begin his true mission, preparing the colony for the ExServ contact delayed by his accidental arrival but drawing nearer nonetheless. Many months might pass before a search team might arrive, but eventually one *would* come. And when it did, Erik Baanfeld, Singer of Tales, Angenga among the Folk, would have prepared for it.

"Yes, I will."

"Instruct him," Æthele said woodenly to Weard. With the final word, he disappeared into the darkness. There was no sound this time of metal on metal or wood on wood. The Warrior seemed merely to melt into shadows.

Weard waited several moments before whispering, "Follow me."

Together they crossed the dais and walked toward the darkness. Erik could feel Weard's presence preceding him, could feel his heat in the darkness, but as soon as they entered the deepest shadows, he could see nothing. Weard stopped, and Erik did likewise, alerted more by sound and the sense of Weard's proximity than by sight. Weard manipulated the metal thing—a lock, Erik decided—moving tumblers without the aid of light, apparently guided by touch and memory. He opened a door and stepped into a chamber.

Erik was standing outside the doorway when he heard Weard touch something, click something...and a brilliant surge of whiteness almost blinded him. *A power cell!* Erik would not have been surprised if Weard had lit matches and candles, as the Folk used in the huts. But his utter shock at seeing something so...so *modern* was as great in its own way as his first experience with the matches had been. In an instant, that which one could never have anticipated becomes reality.

He blinked. After a second, he could see again. The stark white light reflected harshly from walls, floor, and ceiling of highly polished metal. The entire room was sheathed in metal.

"This is the Chamber of the Past," Weard intoned. "Only the Elders of the Folk may have leave to enter. Only the Elders...and the Singer of Tales. Here we have retained the Memory of who we once were, and the Knowledge of who we have become."

Erik shuffled into the small chamber. In spite of his initial impression of metal upon metal, the room was actually cramped with shelves and cabinets, each apparently loaded with bits of equipment, many of them most likely non-functional for centuries yet still meticulously polished and preserved. One open case contained fragments of metal, among them his own ExServ insignia and belt—his and Marquette's. Bitterness swept through him, then receded.

Weard motioned for him to follow the corridor that divided the room into two storage areas.

The further along he walked, the further Erik moved back in time, he realized, toward the age of the founding of the colony. At the farthest end of the chamber, he found a bookshelf. Its fabric-lined metal shelves were filled with volumes, all old, all well-used, some battered beyond recognition by the passage of generations of reverent hands. His fingers hesitated along the spines of the nearest ones. Technical manuals, Captain's logs, journals, science texts, romantic novels of a time generations removed from the Festburg—they all stood there side by side, silent, mute, unread, and perhaps unreadable.

On one shelf, set apart from the others, were the original copies of the *Beowulf* and the history he had seen in Weard's hut, along with a handful of other volumes devoted to that long-distant era of Earth's first darkness. He slipped one out, reverently, and turned page after page, awed by the physical feeling of antiquity the book exuded, and surprised by the awe. He carefully replaced the volume on the shelf and turned to Weard.

He did not speak, but Weard answered the question that surfaced in his face.

"You must Know these," Weard said, his voice barely more than a whisper. "In them are the Songs of the Folk, to be Sung to the Folk and to be handed down to them unchanged as the Songs were from the beginning."

"I've studied...that is, I know some of them already," Erik said. "Fragments of *Malden* and *Brunanburh*, and *Finnsburgh*. Bits of *Beowulf*. And, of course, *Cædmon*," he finished, feeling heat creep into his cheeks. "I will learn the others."

He turned back to the case, scanning more of the titles, trying to make sense of the community of which he had suddenly become an integral part and which has just blasted his every presupposition into shreds.

On the top of the case, on its own small box layered with thick fur, lay a single volume, much thicker than the rest, physically much cruder, as if it had been hand-bound by a raw apprentice. It reminded Erik of the other books he had seen in Weard's quarters. He reached for it.

"No," Weard said, his voice rising to a tone of command. "You may not see that book yet."

Erik jerked his hand back and turned.

"The others are books of the past." Weard stepped forward and set his hand lightly on the book. "But this is *our* book, the Book of the Present. In it we have recorded our true names—our lines of descent from the original families. These names are kept secret and revealed only within this room. Only the Elders of each settlement know all of them. And a warrior is told his true name only when he has blooded himself for the Folk. We can trace our descent back to the first ship. This way, we can control the dissemination of the gene pool as well, for example."

Erik's eyes showed his surprise as Weard's last words. The big man laughed—a strange sound in the metal-echoing chamber—and responded to Erik's unasked question.

"Yes, we know about such things. The Elders do, at any rate. And they take such actions as are necessary to build up the strongest lines among the Folk. They control the population—and the movement of population—among the other settlements, all branches of the Festburg."

He laughed again.

"But we *do* also marry for love sometimes."

Erik nodded. Here was another level of cultural definition that he had not anticipated. Perhaps it explained Feorm's relationship with Weard—and why he was nearly killed for inadvertently intruding into it.

He turned back to the books of history and poetry. "I will learn from these. I must."

He stared into Weard's eyes.

"I am now the Singer of Tales."

CHAPTER TWENTY-ONE

The days passed slowly, each as frozen in time and space as the skeletal branches of trees thrusting up, ice-encrusted, along the horizon. Erik officially returned to Weard's hut, this time into a room of his own, small and damp and cold, but a haven of privacy in the closeness of the Festburg. He spent the nights near the great fire in the Hall, sleeping among the men after his Songs ended, sharing their life-extending heat. He saw much of Weard, spoke with him of the Folk, of the history of the Festburg, weaving tales and legends into new songs modeled after the old ones preserved for centuries. Æthele watched Erik constantly, particularly around the fires at night, but never spoke to him. Gradually the Festburg became accustomed to him, to his Voice in the silence of winter.

He worked hard. Most of the day he spent in the inner chamber or in the Hall, reading and reviewing, improving his skills and his repertoire—it was, after all, one thing to memorize lines as a hobby or for a university exam, but quite another to recite an hour-long epic in its entirety before an audience familiar with each breath he should take and the proper nuances of each syllable. Afternoons he spent with Weard in Bachelors, watching the men fashion weapons for the spring or treating and curing hides stored since fall.

Watching and learning, he became in fact as well as in name one with the Folk.

Whenever he could steal the time, he visited neMonn. The man was suffering terribly in the cold. Food was still available but would become scarce long before winter was passed. Already the Festburg was on strict rations. Erik did not starve, nor did he receive an abundance. He saved as much as he could to smuggle to neMonn whenever possible. Once he brought a cloak, a heavy warm fur he had cut and stitched himself under Weard's direction. He threw it over neMonn's shoulders, shocked at the gauntness he felt beneath the man's garments.

neMonn said nothing. In fact he spoke little to Erik now; most of the time they would sit opposite a small fire, neither speaking, both communing without language. Erik worried more and more as time passed, remembering neMonn's words on that morning now weeks ago: "I have chosen."

On the night he gave the cloak to neMonn, Erik sat near Weard in the Hall.

"Where is your cloak?" Weard asked.

"It did not fit well," Erik answered—still the Singer of Lies, he reproved himself. "I will use it for sleeping."

Weard said nothing more. If he knew, he never spoke his knowledge aloud. Erik slept chilled from then on, not daring to ask for additional robes for himself.

Not the least of the benefits of his new position, however, was that he was now allowed to speak with the women of the Festburg for the first time since his arrival. On the second day after his meeting with Æthele and Weard he passed Feorm, smiled at her, and spoke a hasty word of thanks. She smiled in return and, without speaking, continued on toward Families. He stared at her. If he had to remain with the Folk for the rest of his life, if he were forced to make his home in the Festburg and raise a family, she....

He cut that train of thought. Feorm and Weard—promised since childhood. He loved them both, he suddenly realized, deeply and without reservation—and that in spite of the fact that he had spoken only three times with Feorm, and that Weard had murdered Marquette. He should hate them, fear them, condemn them, but he could not.

So the days passed. Winter settled in as great billowing clouds swept from the North. The snow within the Festburg deepened, ankle-deep, calf-deep, finally knee-deep along the northern barricade. The meadow beyond became a featureless expanse of unbroken white, marred only by the occasional tracks of small animals or—more frequently—a cluster of hunters from the Festburg. Game became scarcer, larders emptier. The nights grew steadily colder, the people more silent and withdrawn.

And still winter deepened. It was the coldest season in living memory, Daroth confided to Erik in a rare moment of companionship. Already the forests were barren for miles around. If the cold continued....

It did.

Early in the fourth week of the snows, Erik woke from a deep sleep. He had sung that night, as he did every night now, chanting until his voice cracked. The great fireplace had been cold and dull that night; with firewood growing scarce, only a few twigs had been tossed on the coals. He had sung to silence and darkness, his voice the only source of life and movement in the Hall. neMonn stumbled in just after dark, shivering, thinner than ever, to crouch in the corner and watch Erik. Erik recognized the signs.

He had hoped that neMonn would remain in the Hall. Twice he nodded to the other man, indicating a place near the fire. Both times neMonn averted his face. As soon as Erik finished singing, neMonn slipped quietly away. Erik watched him with gathering pain.

Erik was beginning to recognize his great mistake. There *were* things worse than death. Finally Erik had fallen asleep and dreamed of warmth and cheer. neMonn was whole and healthy, sitting by Marquette at a feast. They were eating and laughing; at one point, neMonn challenged Marquette to arm-wrestling, and his arm was strong and hale again. The two linked arms and smiled and laughed...then looked straight ahead and Erik knew that they were looking at his dream-self and he began backing away from them, not wanting to hear whatever it was they were about to tell him. They pointed their finger at him and the flesh peeled from their bones in rancid strips and a great scream came from their gaping mouths, only it was not them and it was not the dream but something in the Hall itself, something amorphous and shadowy and sinuous. Erik jerked awake.

The last quivering notes of the scream hung on the air. The others were rising, hands unsheathing bone knives. Weard leaped to his feet and now faced the great doors, his legs bent in readiness, his back tensed and ready to strike. Even in the dimness Erik could see the long muscles tightening. Erik wanted to ask what had happened but a nagging half-memory stifled his words.

That sound, that unearthly roar.... And Marquette.

The Grendel!

The beast from the valleys, the shape that had destroyed Marquette. Weard had said they never came this high, but perhaps the snows....

Gradually the warriors relaxed. Several of the older men sank down to the floor and fell into a restless sleep, their knuckles gripping the wooden hafts of drawn knives.

Weard did not sleep. He slipped through the doors, into the night. Erik looked quickly around, then followed.

He immediately regretted doing so. The sky was clear. Stars burned in icy glory, unshrouded by clouds. The air lay like a frigid blanket, colder than anything Erik had ever felt before. It bit through his heavy garments, chapping hands and cheeks. Not three yards away, Weard stood, back to the building, his eyes following the crests of the surrounding hills, the unbroken line of snow-caped trees.

"The grendel," Erik whispered.

"Yes."

The syllable reverberated as if it had been spoken from beneath the earth and had risen through the frozen dust. It rang hollowly, funereally in Erik's ears. He had once hoped to forget the monstrosity, then had learned simply not to think of it. And now it had come to him, to the Festburg.

Weard looked at Erik, starlight glinting in his eyes. He seemed somehow larger, stronger, taller than before, a warrior such as Earth had not seen in a thousand years. But his voice broke in compassion.

"I am sorry, Erik."

He was, in the way of the Folk, both explaining and apologizing—for Marquette's death, for Erik's involuntary imprisonment in the Festburg, for his daily struggle to survive.

"I know," Erik answered, surprised to discover that it was in fact true. "I have known since the beginning, I think. It was the way. Just as it is with neMonn. I should not have stopped him once he had chosen. Since then he does not live, not truly."

He stopped and smiled faintly at Weard. "We can know and hate," he continued, "but we must also understand."

Weard stared at Erik and returned the odd smile. "You are one of us. I am proud of you, Erik Baanfeld, Angenga."

Erik would have spoken in return, but at that moment the piercing cry returned, echoing obscenely from the forests. Again and again the creature voiced its anger, its hunger, its rage.

"The valleys are barren this winter. It has come higher to hunt... to hunt men. The thorn brush will protect us, for tonight at least. But when the beast grows hungry enough...."

A soft crackling as of footsteps on the crusted snow startled both men. A figure approached, wrapped tightly in furs, the head and face hidden from the cold.

"Feorm," Weard said, expressing a tenderness Erik would not have believed even a month before.

"I was awakened by the cry. I knew that you would be out watching. I would stand with you for the moment."

"You shouldn't be out here. The cold. You should...."

"I should, I know, but I could not." She approached Weard, slid her hand from beneath her fur and touched his arm.

"For a while, then."

Erik stepped away, back into the shadows of the Hall. The night was still, as if everything had forgotten the hideous din of only moments before. The men for the most part lay motionless, clustered about the ashes of the fire. Erik wove his way through them until he came again to his place. He sat down, adjusted his robe, and lay back, eyes wide open, mind spinning. He tried to shut his eyes, to force sleep, but all he could see in the darkness of his own self was the black shadowy horror, all he could feel was the anguish of that headlong flight through an alien forest...and Marquette bleeding in the stream. He pushed them from his mind, only to have the images replaced by silhouettes of Weard and Feorm standing side by side against the starlit darkness, hands intertwined, bodies touching, breath blending. Behind them, half-hidden in shadows, a woman swam through warm green waters that changed to white ice as she passed.

He clenched his fists until his nails bit into his palms and the pain interrupted his thoughts.

Later he heard Weard re-enter the Hall and sit quietly along the wall.

* * * * * * *

With the morning, Erik immediately noticed the change in the Festburg. The children—always secretive and shy, even during the warmest days in the fall—never appeared at all, nor did the women. Men left their huts in Bachelors and stood in small clusters near Families, spears in one hand, knives or shields or staves in the other. The Elders were closeted in the Hall, with the great doors swung tightly shut. Weard was among them, Erik noted as he wandered through the Festburg.

Tension screamed from every direction. Even neMonn seemed ill at ease, anticipatory, more alert than he had been for days as he paced back and forth outside the doorway of the hut, never venturing near the main enclosures but glancing frequently toward the warriors.

Erik started to go to neMonn. Perhaps the man could tell him what was happening, what steps the Folk would (should? could?) take against the beast that had invaded the sanctuary of the highlands. But he got no further than the first ring of huts when a youth—Erik did not recognize him—called to him.

"Singer, Angenga. The Elders have called for you." He returned to the Hall.

The council was seated in a tight circle around the fireplace, Æthele at its head, Weard at the other end. Erik heard mumblings as he entered, followed by a deep silence, then again the undercurrent of sound. He approached until he was within hearing-range, then stopped.

"Singer," Æthele said, addressing Erik for the first time in weeks, "Come into the circle of the Council. What we do here will become the stuff of legends and songs. We need you to record for us."

Erik slipped into a vacant spot on the edge of the circle and listened.

Apparently the council was divided. A few, led by Eam, an old man, urged caution. The beast had not approached the Festburg itself. Perhaps it would not do so, perhaps it was merely crossing through this part of the plateau, searching for easier hunting than it had found in the valley.

"Easier, that's for certain," snorted his chief opponent, Anda—young, strong and massive, with two glittering arm-bands and equally glittering, and cold, eyes. "Easier, since it must smell our animals, our stocks of dried meat, ourselves, our wives and children. Do you think that such a beast would hesitate to attack us?"

"But the thorn bushes," Eam answered, as if that were enough to win the debate. "It cannot pass through the bushes. The poison...."

"...is sufficient for the predators of the plateau, that we know. But never in the memory of anyone living have the grendela invaded our highlands. Certainly the thorns are a sure protection against smaller beasts, but against the might of the grendel? And we do not even know if the poison is harmful to it."

A new voice rose from across the circle. Deman stood, a man older than Anda but not as old as Eam. His graying hair was still thick and long, his shoulders broad, his thighs powerful. Yet he was beginning to prefer quiet hours to hunting. His voice carried evenly, a plea for wisdom.

"Perhaps there is a third choice. Eam would have us hide in our huts and hope that the danger will pass. Anda urges action. He would slay the beast and rid us of its terrors. But couldn't we simply drive it from the land. If we haze and harry the beast, if we haunt it incessantly, never letting it rest, perhaps...."

"No," Weard interrupted. Heads turned toward the foot of the circle. Normally one in Weard's position as second to the chieftain would not interrupt, nor would the Chieftain. They would remain silent, awaiting the consensus of the council before declaring their decision. Yet Weard chose to speak.

"Few men living have seen a grendel of the lowlands. Fewer yet have fought one. Æthele did, many years ago, when he was a stripling and restless with the easy life on the highlands. He explored the cliffs and discovered the hidden pathways through the caves. He met a grendel and returned without his spear, leaving it in the side of the still-living monster. He did not choose to return to the valleys, yet none among us would call him a coward."

Æthele turned his face away as Weard spoke, not from embarrassment but to hide the shadow of fear that flickered across his face as old memories rose unbidden. Erik alone could see and interpret Æthele's movement.

"And I have fought the grendel," Weard continued, "or rather fled from it in order to spare the life of Singer Angenga. Even I, Weard of the Festburg, fled before the beast. I would not willingly face it again.

"But I must side with Anda. I must argue that we slay the monster. He is blood-hungry. His cry in the night was filled with hunger and power. He will not stop before a ragged palisade of thorns. He will rip and tear and gouge until he has broken our defenses and stripped us of protection and ravaged our homes, our stores, our flocks, our people. We must kill it."

He fell silent. No one else spoke. In the silence, Erik could hear the infinitesimal dripping of icicles outside the Hall, the pattering of drops of melting ice and snow from the beamed ceiling. And still no one spoke.

Suddenly a piercing cry tore the air. A distant cry, human and despairing. As a man, the council leaped up, hands gripping shields or clutching spears. Weard was the first through the doors, followed by Æthele and the remainder of the council.

Again the cry rang over the palisade. People emerged from huts, staring to the south, straining eyes to see.

Erik ran with the rest, toward the barricade. He saw the open passageway. Someone had left the fastness of the Festburg. Someone had....

The warriors and Elders streamed through the passage as if oblivious to the poison-smeared thorns. They spilled onto the white-sheathed meadow, fanning out from the Festburg. Someone yelled: "There, on the second hill."

Three, four, perhaps five figures emerged from the forest, two supporting a third. Weard set off across the snow, his powerful legs plowing through the drifts. Æthele was close behind, with the remaining warriors stationing themselves as guards at intervals along the way lest danger approach and take them unaware. Erik ran as best he could with the Elders, trailing behind even the oldest. He was winded, the icy air cutting sharply into his lungs, when he crested the first hill.

The figures had made it that far before falling, exhausted and visibly frightened. Æthele, Weard, and the others circled them, weapons at the ready. Erik struggled the remaining few yards and stepped into the line.

Before him stood Flan, Tir, two other youths Erik did not know...and the boys from the hut, Cempa, Cwealm...and Daroth.

The older boys had formed a protective ring around the younger. Flan was bleeding from a hideous rip in his shoulder; Tir was winded and struggling for speech. Kneeling on the snow, Cempa and Cwealm cradled Daroth's body.

Tir spoke first.

"We went...to find...to kill...the beast. Left early...before...the dawn...to catch...to catch it at rest. But we did not know...did not know."

He stopped speaking and stared at the blood-stained snow.

Æthele moved forward and broke through the inner ring and knelt beside Daroth. Flan murmured, "It took us unaware. It was waiting in the shadows...the thickets. We did not see it. It reached out...slashed, ripped.... We could not leave him there, though. We brought him back."

The boy's shoulders straightened with the final words, pride winning through grief and fear.

Æthele did not speak for a long time. When he did, it was in a low, dangerous voice.

"You did well, sons of the Festburg. It was foolish to brave the grendel alone. Foolish yet brave. And you brought back the fallen warrior. You did well. Weard," he continued, his voice raising and shifting in complexity, "take these *warriors*..."—he emphasized the word clearly and precisely—"...to Bachelors. They dwell no longer in Families but are now hunters and warriors."

Weard gestured to the youths. Without a word the six followed him across the trampled snow toward the palisade.

Æthele stood, looking down at the body crumpled in the snow. When he raised his face, his eyes were clear. No tears glinted there, only thirst for revenge against the beast. His voice rolled undiminished across the snow.

"The grendel will die. Either it...or we."

CHAPTER TWENTY-TWO

By late evening, preparations were complete. Scouts had been dispatched and had returned after tracing bloody tracks to the site of the ambush some miles from the Festburg. The beast was no longer there, nor had it apparently followed the boys; a snow slide had obscured its tracks. It had been heading northward: other than that, the scouts had little definite news.

Runners had been sent to the other settlements—but the nearest was over five days' march from the Festburg, perhaps more in the new soft snow. There was not enough time for help to come from anywhere else, but at the least they would be warned should the beast head toward one of them.

The remaining men spent the late morning and afternoon putting weapons in order. Erik noticed glinting metal barely hidden beneath fur folds as the older men brought out prized weapons—steel-headed knives and spears.

With the setting of the sun the Festburg was ready. At first light, the hunting party would set out, most of the men of the Festburg, save only those needed to defend it and the families within. The hunters would track the beast and destroy it before it could kill again. Erik would remain behind.

He was not blooded as a warrior. In his ineptitude—perhaps even in his excessive eagerness—he might prove the undoing of the mission.

But that was tomorrow.

For now, more important business occupied the Festburg. In the center of the settlement, in front of the Hall, a pile of haelo lay heaped, squanderously large, in fact, in view of the severity of the winter and the promise implicit in the recent snowfall that spring would be long in coming. Yet no one begrudged the expenditure of fuel. No one complained as the hide-wrapped form was placed atop the mass. A muted voice cried once...Daroth's mother, perhaps, or a sister. Not a lover. The boy was too young, had not yet proven himself. The cry was for the loss of potential, not of actuality.

With great solemnity, Æthele and the Elders surrounded the bier, hands folded tightly against their chests as they watched. At a nod from Æthele two boys—Cempa and Cwealm, child-friends of the fallen warrior—opened the doors of the Hall. Within, all was dark, the fires dampened, the beams cold and silent.

A second nod and Weard knelt, his knees buried in new snow, and touched a match to the haelo. The aromatic oils that had so scorched Erik's back caught at the first touch of flame, exploding in a shower of sparks and igniting the nearest branches. Within seconds the heap was a raging blaze, melting snow into gray slush, throwing a golden glow through the open doors of the Hall to reflect from the stone mantel, the low dais, the rough walls.

A third and final nod, and Erik began to sing softly. His voice worked as if of its own volition, repeating words composed centuries before man had even dared step beyond the world of birth and become a citizen of the universe. Automatically Erik formed the words of the death chant, but his mind wandered elsewhere, to remember a silver voice piping through still air: *I shall one day be named Freca and Frea. And when I am very old and very famous as a warrior, I shall be Infrod, the old and wise one.*

The fire had burned low as the death chant finished. His eyes brimming, Erik stepped toward the coals and spoke directly to them:

"Be named Freca, the Warrior. The others are not in my power to grant, but that at least you have earned."

Without speaking further, he turned toward the Hall and entered, taking his accustomed place near the fireplace—but now the great gaping maw was cold and dark and the Hall empty. One by one, the others entered, followed at the last by the surviving boys. They too were warriors now and had a place along the outer row.

The Hall was quiet. There would be no singing this night, no tales from the past to entertain and hearten during the long winter evening. Tonight there would be only meditation and preparation.

Finally Erik slept.

And woke almost before he was aware of sleep. The cry that startled him hung threateningly on the air,

Inhuman, eerie, terrifying—it could be but one thing.

Even as Erik leaped from his sleeping bundle, others were already on their feet and running into the darkness, knives and spears at the ready. Soon Erik was also running across the floor and out the doors.

The night was clear and icy. Stars hung in the clearness, competing with the low moon for brightness. The Festburg was starkly outlined, as if in quicksilver, every hut and each filament of thatching shimmering. Even the barricade was transformed into a mist of silver...everything except the shapeless black thing crouching against the northern rim. Erik could see it only dimly, but there was no mistaking it. Sinuous arms flailed at the thorns; the bulk of the thing threw itself against the palisade, wailing as if in pain yet refusing to retreat. It had scented something—man, beast, who knew?—and was come to take its due. And it was being balked, a circumstance probably unique in its experience.

As Erik watched, he saw a shudder pass through the palisade. The poison was either inefficient or too slow-working for such a beast; and given a few more minutes of uninterrupted furor, the grendel would break through. Erik glanced at Families, where mother were struggling with curious children, trying in vain to keep bobbing heads inside window openings, away from the horror that threatened.

The first ranks of warriors reached the palisade. A handful of spears arced over the bushes to embed themselves in the monster's back—to little effect other than increasing the frenzy of the attack. And the warriors who ran behind the first were essentially helpless. Spears had proven useless; knives, short swords, or staves could not penetrate the thorns. The men huddled in clumps, muscles tensed against the bitter cold and the unexpectedness of the attack. Never in all of the tales and songs and stories had anyone heard of a grendel attacking the settlement. Yet here it was, unequivocally here and deadly.

The palisade quavered again. Instinctively the knots of men drew back, then surged forward as if to expiate a moment of all-too-human fear.

Something dark flailed along the top of the barricade, touching hesitantly here and there. The closest men did not, could not see it. But Erik could. He skidded to a halt, feeling the snow slip beneath his feet, nearly toppling him.

"Above! Watch out!" he screamed, knowing that his warning would not be heard above the turmoil. Someone else caught the words and repeated them, then another. The front ranks, startled into watchfulness, sagged back again, only to watch helplessly as the snaky thing—arm, limb, appendage?—shuddered down on a nearby form. A warrior was lifted screaming but hacking at the thing with his knife. In a moment he disappeared over the palisade. Yet in that moment his flesh had caught on the thorns, ripped and bled, and the poison entered his body. Within breaths he was silent; no screams echoed back into the Festburg.

"Like Marquette," Erik thought. And with that memory a strand of his past flickered into his mind.

With a yell he sped back into the hall, crossing the empty floor, mounting the dais, and running toward the door. He yanked at the metal lock with his bare hands, feeling in the darkness as he tried to figure out how to open it. He had never opened the door himself, in spite of having been inside frequently. Only Æthele, the Elders, and Weard knew the secret of the lock.

He dropped the lock and felt along the wall. Perhaps if he could find....

His fingers felt a spear or a staff, it made no difference. He slid the wooden shaft through the lock and wrenched with all his might.

The wooden shaft splintered, shocking Erik's hand against a cold metal door. But there had been some give, he had felt that much. He grabbed the shorter half of the broken length and shoved it through the lock again, pushing downward on the upper part, more slowly this time, letting the force build. Somewhere something squealed, there was the sound of splintering wood, and Erik lurched downward, almost losing his balance and falling as the lock gave way.

He stumbled forward and shoved the door open. He felt for the lock, surprised that it had broken.

It hadn't. But the bolts holding the hasp to the doorjamb had pulled from the wood, so the end result had been the same—he was inside.

He fumbled for a moment before he found the light and switched it on. The sudden glare blinded him, but he continued walking, hands as buffers in front of him, so that by the time he reached his destination his eyes had adjusted sufficiently for him to see.

There on the shelf lay the two weapons neatly wrapped in Ex-Serv belts, apparently untouched since Weard had taken them at the scouter. On the shelf beneath, Marquette's ExServ insignia glittered coldly in the diffused light. The juxtaposition gave Erik a momentary chill, then he reached out and took the weapons.

He thumbed the power switch on one and was relieved at the dim red glow that told him the weapon was at full power and functional.

He thumbed the other switch. It was functional as well. Behind him, there was a quantum swell in the sounds of battle. He could hear screams intermixed with battle-cries, and overlaying all the creaking and groaning of the palisade as the monster's weight pressed against it.

He would have to hurry.

He ran from the chamber, weapons tucked inside his garments, slowing only long enough to shut off the light and pull the door closed.

Outside, the hall lay in darkness, particularly after the light of the chamber. Erik did not see Weard until he had almost run into him.

"Baanfeld!" Weard's voice was sharp and urgent, unlike any tones Erik had ever heard before.

"Weard, let me pass. Hurry!"

"What are you...?"

Weard must have caught something in Erik's tone or stance. He hesitated.

Without thinking Erik pushed by, shouldering against him and catching him enough by surprise that Weard didn't move to stop him. Then Erik was outside and running through the crisp starlight toward the black monstrosity that now lay half atop, half over the palisade.

A hand dropped on his shoulder, almost pulling him to a stop. Weard stepped in front of him, in control now and verging on anger. His eyes bored into Erik.

Before Weard could speak, Erik drew one of the weapons and handed it to Weard. His eyes caught the other man's and held them as he spoke.

"Aim along here. Push this stud and hold it down." Weard glanced at the weapon. His eyes widened but he nodded in agreement. Erik started toward the palisade, but Weard held him back for a second.

"I thought you had run inside for your own safety. I misjudged you."

Erik flashed a quick smile.

"Thanks. Now let's get us a monster." They ran toward the palisade. Erik shouldered a warrior aside, unaware of the man's initial anger and shock, then his confusion, and finally his fear. Erik moved to the line of front warriors, stepping beside Æthele not out of bravado but out of a conviction that the chieftain would be nearest the beast and, hence, nearest its most vulnerable spot. Weard moved up on the other side. Æthele noted them, seemed to understand at once as the metal weapons glinted in the starlight, and moved back a pace.

Erik sank to one knee. Out of the corner of his eye, he saw Weard duplicate his actions. Erik was shaking but not from the cold. He held his breath, willing his arm and fingers to be calm. He was a good marksman—not a crack sharpshooter, to be sure, but good. But he had no idea where to shoot, what to aim at.

A snaky limb flailed out from the beast's bulk and whipped around a man's throat, lifting him bodily from the ground and hauling him toward the poisoned thorns.

Erik swiveled on his knees, changing line of fire as he did so and without thinking pressed the firing stud. A flickering filament of blinding blue leaped out, sizzled wet thorn bushes, and disappeared into the darkness of the grendel's body. At his left, a second beam cut through the darkness as Weard fired toward the beast's bulk.

Erik fired again. His beam hit home this time, squarely at the juncture of the snaky arm and the body. The arm contracted, then whipped outward, releasing the man, who fell limply into the shadows. A bestial scream pierced the night, and a rush of fetid air washed over Erik, as if a refuse pile had been unearthed. Then the blackness slid from the palisade and was gone. So swiftly that none could follow its movement against the darkness, the grendel crossed the meadow and melted into the forest.

Erik slumped onto the snow. Shaking again—this time from the cold as well as from nervous release—he was unaware of arms around him, of hands helping him up. He did note that all of the downed men but one were walking or being supported toward the healing huts. One man lay motionless on a makeshift litter; even in the night light, Erik could see the swathes of blood cloaking the body. He shivered violently, then once again as a chill set out from the base of his spine and invaded his back.

But that was the last one. Gradually he returned to the world, to the smells and sounds of the Festburg, to the faces surrounding him as they entered the Hall. Someone had kindled the fire; blessed warmth billowed through the air.

Æthele stepped forward, taking the weapon from Erik. He already held the second one, Weard's. Erik saw Weard standing in partial shadow along the side of the Hall. In disgrace? About to be punished for breaking the cardinal law of the Festburg and bringing out from the darkness a solid reminder of their technological past? Erik swallowed hard and tried not to look at Weard's face.

He stood on his own, shrugging out of the helping grip of two men. His fingers were stiff and numb. He clenched his fists once, twice, a third time before his fingers moved easily. As he did so Æthele disappeared into the darkness behind the dais. Erik heard hinges squeak once, twice, then a thin bar of light where the door no longer closed tightly against the light in the chamber. The bar disappeared, the hinges squeaked again, and Æthele reappeared on the dais.

His hands hung empty at his sides.

He walked directly to Erik. Erik wanted to open his mouth, to speak, apologize, excuse his weakness in infringing upon the sole command Æthele had laid upon him, to absolve Weard from guilt. It had been his idea, his alone, Erik Baanfeld of the ExServ. And the punishment would be his. Others had seen him wield the weapon from beyond the stars. They knew. He would die now, but he would die alone. Weard would *not* suffer for his errors.

But before he could speak, Æthele stepped from the dais and stood in front of him, looking down at him. His eyes were in shadow; Erik could read nothing in them nor in Æthele's expressionless face. *This is what death is like*, he thought, *cold and impersonal, irrevocable.*

He raised his eyes to Æthele's, remembering Daroth: "*You have death in your eyes.*"

When the chieftain spoke, his voice was soft, gentle, the voice of a father at once proud and deeply loving.

"We are stubborn, Erik Baanfeld. We hold long and dearly to our traditions and customs. Ours is a harsh life, and we meet it with harshness."

Erik nodded numbly, knowing what words must follow. "But we are not fools," Æthele continued. "Our weapons would have been useless to protect our families against the beast. Two men died. Without you many others would have also, and the Festburg would have been a place of slaughter and death before the sun's next rising.

"To save us, you broke your agreement...."

"Yes," Erik interrupted. "*I* broke it, not Weard. He merely did as I instructed. He shares no guilt in this and he...."

"Erik Banfeld, Angenga, *one who goes alone*," Æthele said suddenly, his voice resonant and booming through the Hall. "Step forward."

Erik did. At least his legs weren't shaking, he thought as he stood within a foot of Æthele.

Æthele laid a hand on Erik's shoulder and spoke, this time beyond Erik to the men assembled behind him.

"Angenga and Singer, this warrior is now Ansaca-bana, Beast-Bane."

Erik blinked. Standing here, fully dressed in layers of pelts and hide, he felt more naked and exposed than he had the first time he stood before Æthele.

Swiftly, Æthele removed one of the steel ornaments from his arm and slid it over Erik's wrist. The band was impossibly large; Erik could have pushed it nearly to his shoulder—and suddenly someone did. Erik turned slightly and saw Weard standing behind him, smiling and proud as well. The armband did not fit well, but the honor was sincere.

Erik Baanfeld, ExServ linguist, once-time junk and sole remaining member of the exploration party, one-time Singer of Lies, was now one with the Folk.

"You offered your life twice for the Festburg," Æthele said, more quietly this time, and speaking directly to Erik. "Once by going against the monster at the palisade, knowing how small your chances for survival were. And a second time by disobeying the injunction we had placed upon you, not even thinking that to do so would cost you your life as surely as meeting the grendel face to face would have. You fought twice for the Festburg...and you won both times."

Again he looked over Erik's shoulder and addressed the assembly.

"A new warrior stands for he whose body lies before this hearth. Tomorrow, the warriors will track and kill the beast. The warriors. *All* of them."

His hand came down again and rested on Erik's shoulder and turned him until he faced the men of the Festburg.

CHAPTER TWENTY-THREE

Three hours later, the Festburg was quiet. Æthele had presided over a funeral pyre for the fallen man, Haele. Weard spoke of the man's courage, several others related incidents from his life, and then Erik Ansaca-bana sang the lament. Near the flames, Haele's widow knelt on a thick fur pad, a dark cloak about her head and shoulders. Twice during the lament she had looked up and stared at Erik, examining him so closely that once he forgot his place and had to fill in with formulaic lines until he remembered what came next. Although he could not see her face, he felt her gaze on him, and it disturbed him more than it should have.

But for most of the ceremony, she stared into the flames, as if to find consolation in the light and warmth.

When the flames burned down, the people retreated to their homes while guards built fires around the Festburg and watched should the creature return in the dead of night. The warriors entered the hall to sleep in preparation for the coming hunt.

Erik watched the activities with wonder. Many of the men had been in mortal danger only hours before, yet now they moved and talked and worked with a calm that belied all reason. The women and children, whose lives had also been at stake and who had just watched the funeral ceremonies for one who was killed savagely by the same beast that threatened them, now walked silently toward their huts in Families, and one by one the candles glowing through cracks in shuttered windows died. Erik could not hear the crying of a single child. Haele's widow passed him, her head down as she followed the others into Families. Whatever grief or fear she might feel now would be silent; she had gone through the formal, public acknowledgment of her loss, and now life would begin anew. Haele would remain a memory, no more.

Erik didn't realize that he was himself behaving with the same equanimity, the same control as everyone else, helping where he could, singing the lament strongly and confidently. He had changed more than he knew.

Nor did he see Haele's widow turn just before she entered Families and watch him for many minutes before finally returning to her home...and her empty bed.

Erik remained for a few moments on the Hall steps listening to the silence, thinking about the sudden reversal of his own status. Men had slapped him on the back as they entered the Hall for sleep. Women had glanced at him and smiled, and one little boy had run to his side and tugged at his cloak until Erik reached down and patted his head.

As difficult as it was to believe, he was a hero. And he had done nothing that anyone else would not have done in the same situation.

"Erik," Weard called from beyond the Hall enclosure. Erik walked over to the man, passing through the gate in the fence and leaving the environs of the Hall. For the first time, he felt a tugging. The Hall was his home now, he belonged there, he would have a place at the fire waiting for him when he returned. No matter what happened, he was Erik Baanfeld, Angenga and Ansaca-Bana.

Weard took Erik's arm and guided him into the open space between the huts and the palisade. Behind them, the Festburg slept. In front of them and to each side, small fires flickered as warriors stood guard.

For a long time, Weard did not speak, but Erik didn't mind the wait. It was cold, but he barely noticed it. The air was clear and clean; the grendel's stench had filtered out as the night breezes had picked up. It was quiet, and fresh, and...and wonderful, Erik realized with a start.

"Erik," Weard said finally. "I'm sorry for what I thought tonight."

"It's all right. Don't worry."

"But I have to. When I saw you running away, I assumed that you were running to hide from danger, like a coward. I should have known better. Everything you have done since you came here should have told me differently. But I listened to the part of my mind that judges on appearances. You are small. Therefore you must be a coward."

"Weard, stop. Don't talk like this. Anyone could have...."

"No, *anyone* should have known better. Then, when I saw where you were coming from and what you had, *I* should have taken the weapons. *I* should have thought of them in the first place. I knew they were there. I knew what they were and how they worked, even though I had not yet handled them.

"But I didn't even think of them. We were facing something that I knew was unbeatable, it was attacking the Festburg for the first time in the history of the colony…"—Erik started at the word, at what it implied about Weard's thinking at the moment—"…and I stood there with my spear and wooden knife and thought I could do something. It took you…"—he looked directly into Erik's eyes—"…an outsider, to see what was wrong with us.

"For that, and for the pain you have suffered among us, I apologize. In my name and in the name of the Folk."

Erik stood silent for a long time. He simply didn't know what to say. Nor did he want to hear any more. He had done what he had to do. There was nothing special in that, nothing heroic. Weard and the others had treated him with fairness—they were hard and rigorous and disciplined, but they were fair. What more could be said?

So he said nothing.

He stood in the silence and watched the stars.

Low over the trees, a streak of light glowed for a moment, then died.

"A falling star," Erik said absently. "People used to believe that stars fell in honor of a dead hero. Maybe that one is Haele's."

Weard watched the light intently, then began walking back to the huts.

Erik followed Weard, catching up with the other man just as they reached the fence surrounding the Hall. The great doors were closed and the building silent. Erik could see only a whisper of smoke from the chimney.

When they entered, most of the men were lying around the floor, close to the hearth. Some slept already, but many watched Weard and Erik as they threaded their way through the room. Erik expected Weard to stop at the nearest open space, but the other man continued, mounting the dais and striding toward the closed door. When they reached it, Erik saw that the lock had been repaired, but the door was open. Inside, Æthele and three of the oldest of the council waited.

The two men entered and Weard closed the heavy door behind them. Æthele and the others had laid worn but carefully preserved polymer coats across their shoulders, the modern material jarring with their other garments. Æthele turned to the oldest man, who held the thick book Erik had never been allowed to open or touch.

Æthele lifted the cover and turned several pages, past blank front sheets, and stopped at the first page with writing on it. The handwriting, though faded, was still legible.

Æthele motioned him forward.

"This is the Book of the Colony. In it are the names of the original settlers, their matings and their children. When our children come of age, they enter this room and are enrolled in the Book. Later, when young men become warriors or women marry, they return to receive a new name, known only to those here present—the chieftain, the eldest of the Council, and the sponsor."

Erik glanced back at Weard. The man did not smile, but there was a glimmer in his eyes.

"Only a few—those called to the Council itself—even know that the names are taken from the first page of the Book, from the names of the first colonists. In this way, we keep our heritage, yet also retain the traditions we have chosen to insure the survival of our world. In this room, you will be called Robert Scott XVIII, named for the second in command of the first vessel to reach this planet."

Erik understood the honor as it was intended. Second in command. Not the captain, but important to the Folk.

"But," Æthele continued, "we do not speak of these things outside. No one but one may know your Colony name. We speak it only once outside, to those we choose as wife or husband."

Erik nodded. He would have no worry there. "Please go now," Æthele said. As Erik passed Weard, the other man put is arm around Erik's shoulders.

Outside, Erik found a place near the fire. It was as if the others had known what was to happen and left the best spot open—perhaps that had indeed occurred. At any rate, he rolled up in his cloak and tried to sleep.

Too soon—certainly too soon for it to be dawn and time to set out on the hunt, someone shook Erik. Even as he opened his eyes, he knew that he had not yet slept. It was only a few moments later.

"Come, Erik," Weard said. "I must take you to your home." *An odd way to put it*, Erik thought. *And besides*, "I'm okay here. I want to sleep in the Hall tonight."

"I understand, but you must come with me." Confused, Erik left with Weard, assuming that for some inexplicable reason they would sleep in Weard's hut. But they passed Bachelors and continued on into Families, moving along dark paths from hut to hut.

Finally Weard approached a door and opened it. Erik did not recognize the place; he had never been this far in Families and had no idea who might live here.

As Weard swung the door open, a faint golden light spilled onto trampled snow. Inside, several candles flickered on wall shelves, and a small fire burned in the central pit.

On the other side of the fire pit stood a woman, her back to the door as she busied herself with some chore. She straightened as the door opened and the night air swirled over the fire, but she did not turn.

Weard entered, then gestured for Erik to follow. He did so, feeling ill at ease.

As he stepped into the room, Weard reached around him and pulled the door closed.

Inside, it was wonderfully warm. Erik hadn't realized how cold it was outside. The woman turned and—still without looking at the men—placed a pot on the fire pit.

Then she straightened; but in her movement Erik saw something of her grace...and he knew that she was familiar, that he knew her without having known her. The feeling was so strong that for a moment the room swayed and blurred.

Then Weard spoke.

"This is Triewth."

She nodded to Erik and smiled. "And this is Erik Baanfeld, Anganga, Ansaca-bana, Singer of Tales for the Festburg," Weard continued, his voice formal and controlled.

Erik felt his cheeks reddening as Weard related the names. More than one name meant increased status. For him to have four— even one as negative as *Anganga*—made him uncomfortable, even more so since the woman—Triewth, he reminded himself, *Truth, loyalty*, and *troth*—continued to stare at him.

Weard fell silent.

The woman remained silent.

Obviously, it was up to Erik to say something. He started to speak. "I am pleased to meet you, Triewth, although I would have preferred more pleasant circumstances."

She turned away as if she had been slapped, pulling her robe over her face. Her shoulders trembled as if she were weeping. Erik assumed that her grief had overcome her and wished that he were out of there. After all, it was his fault that Haele was dead. If he had been a better shot, if he had remembered sooner, if he....

But Weard was speaking, softly, with the gentleness that always startled Erik.

"He doesn't understand our ways, Triewth. He meant only the death of Haele."

The woman turned back and uncovered her face. Her skin was pale and her eyes large, but she seemed controlled.

"Erik, I must apologize again. I have assumed something that I had no right to assume."

"What...?" Erik began. Obviously he was missing some essential point.

"Among the Folk, we have strict laws concerning responsibility. The men must protect the Families—our wives and children, who are the future. When a husband dies, someone must assume the role of provider and protector."

Unbidden, a bit of linguistic history rose in Erik's mind. *Lord*, from *hlaef-weard*, "loaf-protector"; and *lady*, from *hlaefdige*, "kneader of bread."

Lord and Lady.

Husband and Wife.

He swallowed. Triewth watched him closely. Weard spoke again in that oddly formal tone, speaking to Erik but looking at Triewth. "You tried to save Haele's life. You could not—no one could have, because he had been pulled against the poison thorns and was dead even before we shot."

Triewth paled even more, but did not weep. Weard continued. "And you are a warrior, Ansaca-bana and Singer." He reached across the fire pit and took Triewth's left hand. With his other hand he drew Erik's left hand until it was over the fire as well. The heat was strong but not painful as Erik expected. Weard laid Triewth hand in Erik's, then closed Erik's fingers over hers.

The room grew infinitely hotter. Erik could feel sweat breaking out on his forehead and down his back.

Surely Weard didn't...couldn't mean that.... "Do you accept this responsibility?" Weard asked.

Erik could not find his voice. His mind raced, considering the meaning of the ceremony and the commitment Weard was asking him to make. To become one of the Folk—truly and always.

Erik looked into Triewth's face and saw there a reflection of a woman in icy green water, tall and dark and beautiful. When he spoke, it was solemnly and clearly: "Yes, I do."

"And do you accept Erik Baanfeld, Anganga and Ansaca-bana, Singer of Tales for the Folk, as your protector and provider?"

Triewth nodded. "I do."

"That is well." Weard laid his hand lightly on top of theirs and left it for a moment.

Then he turned and walked toward the door. "But what...?" Erik stammered.

Weard looked back at him and smiled—an interesting smile compounded part of love and part of a good humor that Erik suddenly found irritating.

"Sleep well," Weard said, smiling more broadly as he slipped out the door and closed it against the night.

The fire seemed to have burned down to coals before Erik looked from the closed door back to Triewth. She looked down at the floor, than let her hand drop from his as she moved quietly across the room and pinched out the candles. The light faded to a dim glow, but the air still seemed unnaturally warm to Erik.

Triewth pointed to one of two doors in the far wall. "My sons, Bryne and Magan, sleep there. They will awaken tomorrow and meet you. We sleep in here."

She took his hand again and led him through the second doorway and across to a bed covered with deep, soft furs. Without speaking, she knelt down and undid the laces on his sandals. As the thongs slipped down his calves, he pinched out the single candle burning on a table beside the bed.

Erik had thought he was tired, but before they slept, the fire in the outer room had died to cold, gray ashes.

* * * * * *

Sometime during the night, Erik woke. Triewth's head lay against his shoulder, her arm across his chest, her flesh warm against his. Briefly he wondered at what had happened, what they had shared in the darkness of the room. He put his arm around Triewth and tightened it, as if afraid that otherwise she might disappear, disintegrate into a fleeting dream and he would be alone again before the great hearth in the Hall, or in the freezing chill of the herdsmen's hut. He kissed her forehead.

This was not dream—but this was what he had dreamed about. Triewth was his, and he hers forever.

She stirred and woke.

"I'm sorry, I didn't mean to...." She laid her finger against his lips. "It's all right. I am glad to be awake." They lay silently, warm and secure. Once Erik tried to ask her how she could love him so soon after Haele's death.

She interrupted his question; then, after a long silence, she answered.

"I did love Haele. We were children together, then friends, and finally husband and wife. He gave me two fine sons. I loved him, and will always love him.

"But that is the past. We cannot live for what is gone. I have mourned him; now I must live for the future. I have watched you, I have spoken with Weard about you."

Erik raised one eyebrow. She laughed, a bright, happy laugh.

"Don't be so surprised. Many women have watched the young stranger. At first we didn't know what to think. After all, you were so small, in spite of being handsome and well formed. Then we noticed how carefully Weard watched you...."

"He...what?"

"Almost every day, almost every hour, he would be where you were, out of sight perhaps, but watching. So we understood that you were important. We still don't know everything, of course, but we know that you come from...from somewhere else."

Erik laughed to himself. So much for security and secrecy!

Triewth grew serious. "We also know that you will change our lives.

"Then tonight, when the beast came and Haele ran with his spear toward the palisade, I....I don't know how or why, but I knew that he would not return. As I watched his back that I have caressed, his straight legs that have lain so often over mine, as the darkness swallowed them, I knew he would not return. I came into this room and wept and tried to block out the sounds of fear and pain.

"Later, at the pyre, I heard Æthele speak of you as Ansaca-bana, as a warrior, and I saw you pouring your soul into the death-lament and I knew. When I left the fire, I returned here to make a fire and prepare a hot meal for you."

Suddenly she laughed.

"What's wrong?" Erik asked.

"It's still out there, on the ashes of the fire! The stew. Oh well, we'll just warm it for breakfast."

She curled closer.

"When the door opened and Weard stepped in, I knew. And then you walked through the door and my heart told me that it was right and I said *Yes* when Weard spoke the words."

"But.... But someday, I may have to return to ..to my place," Erik whispered. "What would happen...?"

"Then I would mourn for you as if you were dead, and would remember you and Haele with fond love and look forward, as I must."

"What about tomorrow...this morning, I guess it is now? I will be going with Weard and the others."

He felt her hold on him tighten.

"I know. You may not return. I am not sure. Sometimes I know things, and sometimes I cannot see beyond the moment. This is cloudy. I think you will return, but there is something.... I don't know. But I am happy. If only for this night, I am happy. Now sleep. Warriors must sleep before the hunt."

She curled against him, sliding her leg over his thighs and dropping her head against his breast. She felt warm against his nakedness.

For a while he ran his fingers through strands of her hair.

Then he leaned his lips close to her ear and whispered, "I am Robert."

In the darkness, in a disembodied whisper so faint as to seem almost a dream, Triewth answered.

"I am Mary."

Then they slept.

CHAPTER TWENTY-FOUR

The hunt began at dawn. Æthele and his group left before first light, spreading in a thin line across the meadow before disappearing into the forest. They would be trail-breakers and scouts. They would find the path of the beast and leave markers for the others to follow. Erik was up to see them off, standing near the palisade with one arm around Triewth. Her small sons stood on the other side of their mother from the strange man that now lived with them. Gradually, they would understand more about what had happened during the long and tragic night.

The second, larger group left two hours after dawn. They would progress more slowly, laden with supplies for wilderness survival... and with Erik and neMonn.

Actually, Erik thought to himself, neMonn would probably be less a burden than he. The man was crippled, to be sure; but his body was used to hardship. Erik was tougher and harder now than ever before in his life. He could begin to compete with the others, but was still not their equal. He wore his ExServ weapon, given him by Æthele earlier that morning. It was strapped round his waist by his own ExServ belt, but both felt alien and unfamiliar.

At least he was going. He vowed that he would not allow himself to hinder the party in any way.

He tightened the metallic belt where it cinched against his clothing. Then he and the others of the second group were off.

As he left her, Erik looked deeply into Triewth's eyes for an answer to his unspoken question, but saw none. He saw only love and fear.

The trek progressed without incident for the first day. By late afternoon, the trail began swinging away from the interior toward the cliffs. By sundown, as Erik's group finally came upon the scouts' encampment, there was no doubt in anyone's mind. The grendel was returning to its own territory. They would soon have to fight it on its own terms.

Night fell with a terrifying suddenness for Erik, used as he was to the constant fires of the Festburg. Here, in the deep wilderness, there was no gradation from light to darkness. One moment, he could see clearly; the next, all was shaded in mists and icy blackness. A spark or two struggled against the encroaching enemy, but to little avail. Within minutes, the early stars were hidden by thick cloud cover.

There would be no singing this night, no camaraderie. As Erik huddled into his sleeping robe and hunched against a tree trunk for some protection against the north wind, he could sense the tension among the men. Guards were appointed; yet they were superfluous. A hundred eyes, a hundred ears would be straining for the least sound, the least hint of a shadow deeper than others hunkering among the trees.

Erik found it difficult to sleep. His body was fatigued but his mind retraced each step of the day, each moment among the Folk— back to the instant that Weard's knife sliced through the air to embed itself in Marquette's body. The circle was nearly complete. Tomorrow, or the next day, or the next, Erik would face that nightmare monster...this time with Weard as ally, not as captor.

A soft slipping sound in the snow drew Erik's attention. He strained his eyes in the blackness, picking out the approaching form. neMonn.

Erik sat up, pulling a loose corner of his robe back over his shoulder. The breeze was light but bitter. neMonn's breath cut in icy spurts as he settled heavily next to Erik.

For a long time, neither spoke. Finally, Erik whispered, "Are you all right?"

"You mean this hike?" neMonn's voice was rich with humor. "I may be lame, but it will take more than this to slow me. I am a bit winded, though. I haven't followed a hunting trail since...."

He fell silent. Erik wanted to ask him questions, to draw him out, but decided against it.

Through the barren branches overhead, shards of shattered winter light filtered through occasional breaks in the clouds, outlining men lying in clumps among the knotted stumps and oak roots. Erik looked about, identifying each man by his stance, his weapon, his clothing. Most were familiar; he belonged to them now, and they to him.

He looked over at neMonn. Deep furrows lined the other man's cheeks, darkness roiled his eyes. Erik laid a hand on neMonn's arm.

"You are sure, my friend?"

"I was born for this. I and my people. You are different. But I am of the Folk, no matter what this arm and leg may say. My death awaits me here, in this darkness. But for you, it would have crept up on me and taken me unawares as I cared for cattle in the Festburg."

"But I didn't...."

neMonn laughed softly, a silver tinkle in the wintry night.

"You asked Weard to allow me to come." It wasn't an accusation or a question. It was a simple statement of fact.

Erik tried to deny it. "No, I...yes, I did."

neMonn didn't respond.

"Are you angry?"

"How could I be? I don't know what you did or how you did it, but something has changed since yesterday. You are different, Ansaca-bana, and more than just fighting the monster would allow for."

Erik thought of his talk with Weard, of the council meeting in the chamber...and of Triewth. Mostly of Triewth.

"Yes," he agreed, "things are different."

"So. And I am here. If I should die here, so much the better. I am with my own."

neMonn turned his back to Erik, but even in the movement Erik sensed no withdrawal, no repudiation of Erik or his company. neMonn was simply too full to speak further. Erik recognized neMonn's need and fell silent.

The night passed. Erik slept fitfully, waking hourly, or so it seemed, to brush away light snowfall from his robes, to see the others gradually disappear into the whiteness of the earth itself. Finally, he woke to grayness that grew to rosy pink and blended into full light. The camp stirred into action as warriors stood, stretched cramped muscles. At the other side of the encampment stood Weard, tall and powerful, seeming impervious to the cold and discomfort of the night.

Erik rose as well. Already the vanguard was moving out. There would be no hot meal this morning.

By noon, the party reached the western extremity of the highlands. The grendel's movements were obvious here: thickets of young growth uprooted viciously, thoughtlessly, by the creature's mass as it forced its way toward the lowlands. Erik and the others found themselves standing on the top of a low line of cliffs overlooking the immense valley. Erik did not recognize the topography. Apparently the creature had led them south of the cave-studded cliffs where Weard had saved Erik's life...and sacrificed Marquette's.

One by one, the hunters descended the treacherous cliff face, their feet straining for toeholds in icy crevasses, their fingers torn by frozen, knife-sharp facets of granite. Erik and neMonn descended last. The crippled hunter climbed with great care, slinging his weight to his good arm and leg, hugging the cliff as closely as possible. To Erik, perched steps below, it seemed as if the other must surely plunge to his death at any breath. Yet the good arm held, the good leg braced securely in impossible places, and neMonn finally reached the churned-up snows at the base of the cliff, only seconds behind Erik.

The remaining men had already fanned out, searching for signs of the monster, forming serendipitous bands as they worked into the thick undergrowth.

Erik followed neMonn's lead as they moved into the forest. Gradually the blinding whiteness of the snow was replaced by dusky shadows, alternating white and black as the sun pierced the lacy crown of terran oaks now inured to alien seasons. The two continued along their chosen track. Erik was certain that they were close behind Weard, although probably falling further behind as minutes turned into an hour or more. Yet they continued, the crippled warrior and the Singer of Tales, on the trail of the monster.

Suddenly, ahead and to the left, they heard thrashings and thundering, as of a huge form careening through unwavering trees. As one, Erik and neMonn sped up, Erik running at full speed, arms tight against his sides to avoid the underbrush, neMonn swinging along with an awkward but surprisingly fast rolling gait, accommodating his lame leg, occasionally even turning it to an advantage in the uneven terrain.

The thrashing sounds grew stronger, nearer. Now they were coupled with human yelps and cries. Seconds passed, seconds of frantic passage among barren trunks, deeper into the heart of the forest. The trail veered sharply to the north. And now individual voices carried through the air, hunters shouting in triumph...and in death.

Erik and neMonn mounted a low rise, much like the one on which the Scouter had crashed, and slid to a halt.

Below, a narrow meadow opened. Undisturbed, it would have been beautiful, with soft, unblemished drifts wrapping smooth trunks and ice garlands glittering from lacy crowns. But now it was a scene of horror.

At the far end, beneath overhanging trees, the grendel thrashed at bay. Even now, in the light of late afternoon, Erik could not see the thing distinctly. He struggled to keep from averting his eyes, trying to define the shape. Black, sinuous limbs entwined about a solid, massive body supported by short, stout legs—as many as six it seemed, although Erik had no leisure to count them. Surrounding it in a ragged half-circle, hunters battered at the thing.

Weard was there, as Erik knew he would be, and Æthele, every inch the chieftain protecting his people. The two were foremost in the circle, thrusting spears at the grendel, striving for the one opening, the one possibility that would allow them to sever a limb or pierce a vital organ—if the grendel had any. Erik realized with a shock that he had no knowledge of how to battle the thing at all.

Erik never knew how long he stood on the brow of the rise watching. It might have been minutes; more probably it was only seconds, because almost before he became aware of himself, he heard a choking cry from one of the embattled hunters, echoed by a cry nearby. The creature had struck, savagely and lethally, slicing away the man's forearm, returning with lightning ferocity to rip through his chest coverings and lay bare bone and flesh. The man cried once in agony then stumbled to the russet snow. Even before he lay still and silent, the grendel flicked the same tentacle-like arm toward a second victim—and neMonn uttered a hoarse cry, pushing his way down the slope with the same curious gait that had brought him so far. He brandished a short spear in his good arm—he had used it as a staff until now. His cry echoed above the clamor of the battleground, even distracting the grendel momentarily. The creature swung around to counter this new threat.

As it did so, Æthele slipped in beneath the largest of the limbs, planting his feet firmly in the snow and thrusting upward with his metal-tipped spear. As the spear ripped into the black fetidness of the monster, neMonn sliced with the edge of his spear, aiming for a knot of muscle obtruding on the thing's body.

Erik's breath stopped. He would be able to see the kill, to sing about this hunt in the warmth of the Hall. He would....

But he didn't. Instead he screamed and hurled himself down the slope.

The grendel swiveled, faster and more laterally than Erik would have imagined possible. With crushing suddenness, it twisted away from the point of Æthele's spear, even as the metal shard penetrated the first layer of armor-plate scales and tissue. The tip of the tentacle retracted, writhed and swirled, disengaging the spear and shattering its ash shaft. It crushed Æthele's wrist in one coil then thrust the intrusive body away with another. Æthele flew through the air and struck a granite outcropping. He moaned, tried once to rise, then fell against the stone, blood spreading beneath him, melting the snow and steaming in the chill.

At the same instant, the knot of fiber neMonn had chosen as target shifted, deflecting his thrust as a section of scaly hide slid around to cover it. Whatever the mass was, the creature acted as if it were vulnerable.

Erik had already slid down the drifts toward the scene of battle and was only a few feet from neMonn.

A spidery tendril dropped from nowhere and encircled neMonn's waist. The tentacle did not rip or slice as it had done before. It merely picked up its victim and crushed the life from the man, impassively, smoothly, as if neMonn were an indigenous Antaeus who could only be killed when held above the earth that bore him. By the time Erik could think, the skirmish was over. The grendel withdrew into the trees. Erik twisted about, yanked the weapon out and leveled the barrel at the glittering blackness of the grendel and fired. As he did so, he felt the sting of tears.

A tell-tale shaft of killing light pinioned the grendel. Tentacle limbs contracted, contorted. Hideous jaws opened near the lumpy mass on the body, revealing a throat cavernously deep, black and glistening. A sudden stench swept over the broken circle, nearly blinding them with its acrid intensity. Erik blinked once, twice, then sighted for a second shot.

And the thing was gone.

As if it were a shadow, it disappeared into the forest. Wounded and, if possible, more dangerous than it had been before. Erik's futile attempt at helping had apparently been too little, too late.

A hand gripped his shoulder. He turned away from the monster's trail, his eyes red and watery.

Weard looked down at him.

"What happened?" Erik asked.

"It came suddenly. We had little warning. And the weapon failed today."

Weard held out the blaster. Erik depressed the stud; instead of a red light, he heard only a whine. It was uncharged, and he had forgotten to check it before Weard left. Erik dropped it to the snow.

"I'm sorry. I should have...."

"There was nothing you could have done. It is as it must be."

"neMonn is dead."

"I know. And there will be time for mourning soon. Now we have other duties."

Erik glanced around. Four knots of men clustered around inert forms in the snow. In the center of the clearing, two young men lay where they had fallen. At the far end, three men lifted Æthele's body and carried it toward the center. From the opposite side, a second group of three bore neMonn to lay him beside the others.

Weard knelt and retrieved the weapon, shoving it out of sight beneath his cloak. He left Erik's side to walk slowly toward the bodies, where he stood silently for a moment before facing the remaining hunters.

"We will not proceed tonight. Darkness falls quickly and we are in the enemy's land. It knows these lowlands. Most of us do not. We will wait here for the others of our party. And we will sing the death-chant for fallen heroes."

The others nodded. Immediately, without a word of command, six men broke away from the main group and disappeared into the undergrowth, returning with what dry wood they could find. Another group had already begun preparing the bodies for cremation, straightening shredded robes and blood-matted furs, covering slashed flesh. Weard slipped the metal bands from his upper arms and placed one on Æthele's chest, the other on neMonn's.

With a gentleness Erik would not have believed weeks before, the men laid the bodies on the pyre. One by one the survivors passed by. Last of all, Erik walked to the mound of wood, his eyes wet...with the cold, he assured himself, with the bitter cold and the sudden release of tension after the battle.

He shook his head. *No! For once, be honest!* They were tears for friends...for brothers. He reached beneath his cloak and removed two small metal insignia from his belt. One was his; the other Marquette's. He placed one on Æthele's breast, one on neMonn's, then stepped back. No one else present recognized the symbols engraved on the bits of metal, but all understood intuitively their significance.

Someone kindled a flame. It sputtered, a fragile warmth in a world of cold. At a word from Weard, the man holding the brand touched it to the branches. Acrid smoke muffled the bodies, swirling in passionate heat. Black clouds billowed through the glade. The snow beneath the bier hissed and steamed, melted away, and the makeshift structure of branches settled, almost throwing the bodies out of reach of the flames.

Erik turned his back to the pyre. He tried to close his ears but could not. The sounds tore through him. The smell of burning flesh anguished him.

And he began to sing.

Softly at first, to himself, allowing the months of pent-up fears and frustrations to escape, he sang of Æthele's justice, of neMonn's patience and courage, of his memories of each, and of his hopes.

Without knowing it, he began to chant, casting his rough images and emotions into powerful alliterative lines. He drew on the wealth of formulae he had studied...but what emerged was not imitation or deriviative. *He* was singing—to *his* people, on *his* world, at the death of *his* friends.

His voice grew louder, vibrant, stirring the hunters circling him, closing out all other sights and sounds and smells and feelings. He rose with his words, a vapor of smoke in a distant sky, and grew.

Finally, minutes or hours later, he returned. His voice broke on a syllable and stopped. There was silence all around, except for the sibilant hissing of dying flames. Gradually the others moved away, grouping beneath the overhanging trees on the margins of the glade. Only Erik and Weard remained near the pyre—the new Guardian, and the Singer.

Erik looked at Weard but saw only a blur. "That was real," he tried to say, but the words would not come.

Weard nodded.

That was enough.

CHAPTER TWENTY-FIVE

Throughout the rest of the afternoon, the fire burned, never again attaining the ferocity of its early moments but continually replenished by branches and twigs. Finally, as the sun settled behind the lattice-work trees, the pyre was allowed to burn down.

In its place, several smaller fires rose around the perimeter of the glade. Each sputtered a dozen feet from its neighbors, throwing the area into relief and bathing ice and snow in febrile red. In the center, the warriors clustered, sharing heat and protection. Guards watched the perimeters, their backs to the fires to protect their night vision. Ears tested each whispered sound, eyes focused on suspicious shadows. Nothing would approach without their knowledge.

Erik sat near one fire, exhausted by his singing even though several hours had passed. He was burdened by the discomfort of his damp clothing and by an irritating sense of guilt. Two good men were dead. He might have saved one—even both—had he acted in time. He worked through each second of the battle as he remembered it, trying to isolate precisely where he could have stepped in, should have stepped in, what he might have done. Finally, he drifted into a troubled sleep.

He dreamed...dreams that muddled reality and fantasy, fear and guilt, blending the worst of each.

And then his dream screamed—the dream itself, as if it were a living thing.

No—not the dream!

He threw himself from his icy cocoon and stood up, almost losing his footing.

The moon filtered through bare branches, reflecting midnight on the snow. There was no movement, no sound except echoes of the shriek...and a slow, ponderous, measured rustling to the left.

He swiveled toward it, just in time to catch a wispy glimpse of shadow among the naked trunks. And a dark form shattered on the snow.

Then the thing was gone, leaving death and confusion behind. Men slipped across the icy crust toward the body, their hands grappling with spears and shields, fingers stiff in the cold. Erik crossed the clearing, not noticing the faint orange smudges of watch fires still gleaming among the shadows.

Weard was already standing over the body, his hand clenching and relaxing, only to clench again on the smooth ash-shaft of his spear. A narrow passage had opened through a circle of men as Weard approached, and it had not yet closed. Erik slipped behind Weard and stood nearby.

The dead man was Reoc (*savage, fierce*, Erik translated to himself). One of the younger warriors. He had been tall, rivaling even Weard in strength and promise, a handsome man with laughter in his eyes.

Once.

Now he was a broken ruin, his blood steaming in tiny puffs on the snow. Erik remembered minute details about the man, remembered his fierce pride in his prowess, in the sureness of his aim, in the bands of metal ringing his forearms. Erik glanced down, fighting a swirl of nausea. One of the rings was missing. Indeed, the arm itself had been ripped away at the shoulder. Reoc's throwing arm, Erik noted dully. The man's spear was nowhere to be seen.

Weard knelt to straighten twisted limbs, then stood. "Another death."

Erik noted the tone. Weard was not just vocalizing a fact already known to all. He was laying another charge against the beast, speaking one more indictment for which the grendel would have to account.

A few men surrounded the body, preparing it for funeral rites.

Erik looked up.

It seemed that only moments had passed, but the unbroken darkness of the night sky was fading. The moon had set, the stars were disappearing, and unmistakable threads of morning light arced the sky. The tremulous morning breezes had risen, blowing from the north across their backs as the men looked into the thicket where the shadow had disappeared. Already it was light enough to see the knots of muscle in Weard's jaw and the bunched sinews of his arm as he gripped his spear.

Without warning, he strode through the blood-stained snow where Reoc had lain and on toward the underbrush.

Voices called to him, arguing that he should return, wait for full light and complete the rites for the dead before hazarding another encounter with the beast. Erik heard subtle hints of hysteria in several of the voices. The men were no cowards, but neither were they used to making such decisions. Æthele had been the chieftain; now they were without a chief, and there was no council of Elders to choose the new leader. Their structure, based on loyalty to a proven leader, was breaking down in the present crisis. Even among the younger warriors, Erik detected hesitance, a desire to forestall the next battle. After all, how many had the monster killed already, without receiving any substantive wound in exchange?

Still Weard strode across the snow, neither slowing nor halting until he stood on the edge of the shadows. Then his voice echoed back to the assembled men.

"Our brothers have died. Their bodies have been burned unavenged, The monster survives which has already killed and which will surely kill again. I hunt that beast. Alone, or with those who dare, I care not. I am Weard, the Guardian, and I must act according to my Naming."

There was a silence so deep that Erik could hear men breathing. Across the glade, Weard disappeared into shadow.

Suddenly a second voice called...and Erik recognized it as his own.

"I am Baanfeld." He shuddered as he mouthed the syllables; sounds of death and destruction echoed through the name. "I am Baanfeld," he repeated more strongly, still wondering what he was doing, what he would say. "And I am Angenga, the one who walks alone. I am Ansaca-bana, beast-bane. I am the Singer, until now the Singer of Lies.

"I have lost a friend, a chief, and now a fellow. I will follow the Guardian that I might sing of his great battle. I...."

His voice cracked. He walked across the snow, aware that a handful of others trailed behind him. Soon the others would follow. Reoc would be cremated, or perhaps borne by one or two back to the Festburg.

Before the sun stood mid-sky high, most of the warriors would be following Weard's track through the forest.

But he was the first. Alone among all, he had spoken first.

CHAPTER TWENTY-SIX

The next few hours stumbled along like nightmares, a reminder of Erik's first encounter with Weard...and of Marquette's death. Weard moved forcefully among the naked trunks, quickly but quietly, without concern for any who might follow. Erik ran until his lungs burned and his side pinioned him on a needle of pain. But he kept on. When he could not breathe, when his legs refused to move, when his head throbbed...he kept going. He didn't know why, except that he had to.

So he continued, slipping on ice, throwing himself against the rough bark of trees, into the hostile embrace of thorn bushes. But he managed to keep sight of Weard and ahead of those further back.

Then, mercifully, Weard halted. Without warning, he simply stopped, waiting, his back against a trunk, until Erik caught up. Erik saw him, nearly stumbled, then covered the few yards between them, bracing himself against the ragged bark, breathing deeply and hoarsely. The throbbing of his heart settled to a thunderous roar. His head spun, but he could see. Gradually the stabbing in his side relented and became merely a constant flame. He looked up.

Weard was staring at him.

"Why?"

Erik heard no strain, no hint of fatigue in the voice. But he did hear deep humor. That was his own word, his agonized reaction that night in the cave overlooking Marquette's death scene. And now Weard threw it back at him. *Why?*

He pulled air through burning lungs before trying to answer.

"I...had to...lived enough...on lies. Must help...somehow."

The syllables gasped into silence. Weard did not move, but a smile played around his lips.

"Why?" he repeated, this time with a totally new inflection. It was a different question entirely.

"Because...because I must...live honestly." Erik breath came more easily now. "I can never be...a true warrior. We both know that. I have not the strength, the stamina. I can sing...but that is all. Yet if I call myself a Singer, must I not know that which I create? Can I live forever on the reputations of generations dead...dead for centuries when this world was first colonized? I owe you everything, Weard, and I will repay it in the only way your...*our* world will allow."

Weard nodded.

"Come," he said, all humor drained from his voice. "We have a monster to kill."

"There are others, close behind...."

"I know. But they will not be with us at the end. The grendel is mine...and yours. That I know."

Erik heard the certainty, the same certainty that he had heard in Triewth's voice as well.

Together, they started again through the forest mazes, slower this time, more methodically.

The trail was easy to follow. In his killing desire to keep Weard in sight earlier, Erik had not paid much attention to the signs of the monster's passage. Now he could see them clearly. Yearling stands of oak were crushed, thorn bushes uprooted and cast aside, and a recurrent smudge of slimy, black ichors stained rocks and bark and snow. The thing was hurt, but how badly? How near to fatally?

Gradually, Erik became aware that the creature was circling and that Weard was no longer simply following its tracks. He would lurch into the unbroken snow to the right, always northwesterly, and each time intercept the creature's trail within a few moments. During one painfully short breathing period, Weard explained.

"The grendel is circling north, in the direction of where we first met. I don't know if this is the same beast or not, but probably it is. We know little of them; we avoid them whenever possible." His voice dropped, indicating the present impossibility of such a course. "But we do know that they are intensely territorial. They are isolated creatures, never living within a week's distance of another. In all likelihood, this one has its lair near the cliff face, near the river where...."

He fell silent.

"I'm sorry," he said finally.

"Let's go on," Erik said. "We can't just wait here for it to come to us."

The hunt continued, both men speeding through the desolation, stopping only long enough for Erik to regain his wind when necessary. Weard seemed unbothered by the pace.

Gradually the cuts became shorter as the grendel straightened its flight. The hunters were closing in on its home ground. The signs of violent passage were fresher now. The angry splotches of ichors were still warm, melting into the snow and pungent with the beast's stench.

Day was passing, too quickly. If they did not spot the beast soon, night would fall, and with the night all advantages—such as they were—would return to the grendel. Weard increased his pace and Erik matched it.

Then Weard stopped, his face cold and pinched. Erik started to speak but Weard gestured for silence. Erik held his breath, trying to muffle his raging heartbeat.

"It's near," Weard whispered at last. "It waits. It feels us on the trail and waits."

They continued, more circumspectly than before. Weard's spear angled clear from his body; Erik's weapon was drawn, its red glow assuring that it was functional, even though it still felt awkwardly alien. The two men spread out, within sight but wary, keeping to the cover of the mottled shadows.

Weard seemed as incapable as Erik of scenting the enemy. He moved with studied caution, stopping constantly, listening, shaking his head as if angry at his own inability.

A thunderous crash to Erik's right brought him up short. With a reflex precision he would not have though possible, he spun and fired.

The beam seared through the forest, scoring half a dozen trunks and slicing solidly into a darker spot of shadow. The spot lashed out convulsively then faded into the depths, leaving only the rancid smell Erik associated with the grendel and a scattering of small tendrils of flame struggling to survive in the damp undergrowth.

Erik felt himself shaking, then a hand on his shoulder. "Good shooting. You hit it dead center. It was not enough to kill it, though. Not enough."

The hand dropped and Weard forged ahead. "The thing is wounded and angry. Careful." He didn't need the warning. He was already on guard. They passed through a close clump of barren trunks, across a small glade similar to countless others they had traversed since setting out from the Festburg.

At the far edge of the glade, they came upon the first concrete evidence of the beast's recent passage, great clots of acrid gore settling steamily into the snow. The trail was clear, cutting violently through copses strewn with splintered trunks and twisted boughs. Both men sensed the nearness of the grendel.

Man or beast—one would soon die. They hurried as they followed along a shadowed swale between two low ridges. Abruptly the trail angled upward, disappearing over the crest. Erik followed Weard, slipping in his haste, almost sliding back down the slope. Finally he reached up, grasped a broken branch, and hauled himself onto the ridge.

And stopped in stunned surprise.

He had not recognized the area, although Weard had warned him.

Erik gripped a nearby tree trunk, reassuring himself by rasping his fingers across the rough bark.

Below, a glade opened, ringed by tremendous trees and abutting against a granite outcropping. Canting against the stone, the scouter lay half hidden in snow.

Erik had returned to his own world, suddenly, unexpectedly, irrevocably. Pangs of loneliness and memory tore at him, threatening to disrupt the precarious balance he had constructed with such effort over the past days, months. Everything was so familiar...and yet so alien. He was no longer wholly a part of the world that devised the structure below.

He had no idea how long he might have remained standing there if Weard had not whispered, "Over there, in the shadow of the ship."

Erik followed the spear-like, pointing finger. The scouter was not as he remembered it, not quite. He shook his head, as if to clear away the visions of memory and make room for objective reality. A dark scar disfigured the ship's metallic skin, stretching evenly aft and stern from the open hatchway. Erik studied the sight, filtering out as much of the glittering reflection from the snow as he could. That dark line, what was it?

"The beast has riven the ship to make its lair," Weard said.

"But that's impossible. The hull is impervious to...."

"The grendel has great strength. It is itself virtually impervious."

"Then why didn't it destroy the Festburg? Surely the thorn barricade wasn't enough to keep it out."

"No, it wasn't, not by itself. Perhaps the poison was enough of a deterrent...I don't know. But I do know that we are protected there not by our strength but by its weakness—and that is a limited one."

The two men circled warily, spiraling down the slope. Nothing moved in the glade. They approached the craft.

Weard had been correct. The hull was split along a jagged line circling horizontally from the hatchway. Centimeter-thick sheathing was peeled back, expanding the opening into the control center.

In that opening, Erik saw a flicker of movement. "It's in there," he whispered.

Weard motioned for silence, then began a slow, circuitous approach. Hunched over and silent, he drew nearer and nearer. Erik followed only a step or two behind.

Shrieking, the grendel expelled itself from the darkness. Erik whirled, slipping on the snow as he aimed his weapon at the animated shadow snaking toward him. Ahead, Weard crouched against a small drift, steadying himself as he raised his spear and waited.

The beast advanced, roiling like a great wave from the scouter, limbs retracting and extending medusa-like, starkly black against the snow. The stench was over-powering; everything Erik had smelled until that moment had been a prelude, diluted and distant. Here, at the beast's own lair, the odor was a physical assault. Erik reeled as the thing approached.

The limbs coiled purposefully toward the intruders. Erik held his fire, waiting for a clear shot. Weard crouched in front of him, not moving as the beast came closer.

Then Weard moved. Shimmering in the sunlight, the spear glistened as it hissed through the air. Deep within the clotted mass of darkness and writhing appendages, Erik caught a single glimpse of red malevolence—an eye or some other organ. That was Weard's target. The spear flew swiftly and unerringly...almost. At the last possible second, a limb flicked fortuitously into the path of the spear, diverting it fractionally. The metal tip embedded itself in the monster's flesh but missed the vulnerable organ.

The shriek, deafening already, crescendoed to a new pitch as the monster constricted in a great shudder then slithered more determinedly toward the source of its pain. Weard shot a hand beneath his cloak and drew out a long, wickedly sharp, gleaming steel blade Erik had not seen before.

Weard leapt forward, returning the grendel's shriek with his own high-pitched battle cry.

It's useless, Erik screamed to himself. A man can't pit himself against such a thing. But Weard was doing it. The battle-fever was on him; he couldn't be deterred.

Erik shifted to the right. From where he had stood, Weard blocked his aim. *Just a little more to the right*, he thought, moving quietly and quickly, in place almost before Weard made contact with the grendel. Dropping to one knee to steady his aim, Erik fired as the steely glitter of Weard's knife disappeared into the creature's bulk.

Both weapons struck true. The red malevolence flared, flickered, and died beneath Weard's blade. Sinuous tendrils whipped, surrounding Weard in a mesh of dying fibers. Tendons tightened, and Weard was being drawn toward the creature.

Erik's second bolt hit. The grendel stiffened, tottered, rolled silently onto its side, releasing Weard. Ichor clotted the trampled snow.

Weard rose to his knees and stood only an arm's length from the grendel's body. Erik moved closer.

In the distance, a murmur of voices carried through the forest—the rest of the warriors, arriving seconds too late.

Erik reached up and laid his hand on Weard's shoulder. Before them, the grendel sprawled in the darkness of its own death.

CHAPTER TWENTY-SEVEN

An hour later, the scene was unrecognizably placid. Although it was nearing noon, the day had dimmed as the sun withdrew behind a bank of charcoal clouds—another storm was on its way. Erik shivered, only now aware of the sheen of sweat that had drenched him during the chase.

He glanced about, curiously, as if the entire thing were new to him.

The others had arrived some time ago. A small group dragged the grendel's carcass into the shadows; its flesh was fetid and unwholesome. Nor would it provide furs or cloaks. Erik watched the thing disinterestedly as they dragged it past. The flesh was slick and shiny, like plastic, an unalloyed black and overtly distasteful. He shivered violently just looking at the creature and felt relieved when it disappeared into the forest.

Another small group clustered about Erik and Weard, assuring themselves that they were uninjured. In spite of the men's attention, however, Erik realized with a sinking feeling that Weard would now replace Æthele, and that whatever relationship might have developed between them would be irrevocably altered.

A third group stood in open ranks around the wreckage of the scouter. They viewed it with awe—so much metal in one place. There was enough here for spears and lances and knives; who could imagine the weaponry that might be forged from the side panels alone? One or two older men shuffled forward a step or two, as if to touch the artifact, then returned, defeated by generations of superstition...and the stench of the grendel's lair.

Another hour passed and already Erik could hardly believe his memories of the last battle. The glade was peaceful now, except for an occasional murmur or the muffled crunch of feet on snow. And the sun, faded behind a cloud, seemed distant and cold, as distant as the worlds Erik had once belonged to.

He looked up, shaking his head as his name carried over the undercurrent of voices.

Weard was standing by the scouter. "Erik, come here."

He made his way through the men, pungently aware—for the first time in months—of the riot of odors the men carried: the sweat of the hunt tinged with an acrid hint of fear and loathing for the beast; the too-sweet heaviness of furs and rudely tanned hides; an occasional whiff of diseased flesh, of old age unaided by medicines, of recent wounds festering and sore. Each odor struck Erik with dizzying force.

Suddenly, he seemed an alien again, the only one who recognized the canting ruin against the rocks. He was the interloper who had manipulated the people by lies and memories. His head throbbed—excitement, adrenalin, an inexplicable sense of loss compounded by the thick atmosphere.

He walked toward Weard.

A voice rose behind him.

"Singer, sing us the death of the beast."

Erik did not turn or acknowledge the request. He looked instead at Weard, loss and pleading unmistakable on his face. Weard looked over Erik's shoulder and shook his head in the direction of the voice. The request was not repeated.

Weard reached out and took Erik by the upper arm, drawing him nearer, almost into the shadow of the imploded scouter. They turned to look upon the ravaged steel walls.

"This is yours."

"Yes," Erik said. *That* was his, that mangled, useless mass of technology which had neither place nor function on this world.

Erik shrugged out of Weard's grasp and walked toward the craft, seeing it doubled—it was at once the shattered hulk lately inhabited by a loathsome creature killed by Erik's hand, and the sleek vessel he had boarded a lifetime ago with Marquette.

His footsteps faltered, strengthened, and continued. A wind rose from the north, forerunner of the onrushing storm. It swept before Erik, thrusting back much of the grendel's stench. Erik steadied himself as he stepped into darkness.

The inside was impossible. He had never understood the strength of the beast until this moment. It was as if fingers of ice had insinuated themselves into minute cracks in a granite wall, frozen there, and ruptured the living stone. Bulkheads hung in shredded filaments, panels and consoles lay twisted out of any semblance of function. Erik glanced only briefly into the control room. It was hollowed out, as if tremendous pressure had compacted everything into glittering smudges along the wall-panels. The floor was littered with splotches, lumps of unrecognizable matter redolent of the grendel. Erik backed out. He could trust his stomach no further.

He turned and followed the corridor. Before, the passage had been choked with wreckage; now openings appeared. The creature had probed the depths of the vessel, forcing ways where none existed.

And destroying as it passed.

The medical cabinet was open, the door ripped off. Canisters, containers, packets were crushed, their contents ground into filth on the metal floor. Nothing remained. Nothing could be salvaged.

Any half-formed plans he had of bringing supplies to the Festburg died stillborn.

Deeper in the ship, the destruction was less complete but unnerving nonetheless. The creature had not disturbed the personal quarters, but heavy beams still blocked the hatchways. No entry—no clothing, no personal records...nothing.

The computer terminal was crushed beyond repair, its delicate internal mechanisms ripped out and scattered. It seemed as if the grendel had acted with human intelligence, casually but knowingly depriving Erik of any link with worlds he would never see again.

His eyes flickered to the switch controlling the emergency beacon. The knob hung limply from a silver wire, dead, useless. His final hope died. There was no way to contact the ExServ. This world of snow and cold and death and savagery was all he would ever know.

He edged back outside, toward the clumps of huge, fur-wrapped men waiting to...to what? He stood for a moment, adjusting his eyes to the blinding whiteness. A light snowfall had begun. Already many of the traces of the battle disappeared as the glade resumed its neutrality.

The men were gone; none were waiting for the return of the small warrior, the strange one, Angenga, Ansaca-bana.

Someone had kindled a fire in a protected niche by the granite ridge. Erik wrinkled his nose at an odor, once alien, now familiar and tantalizing. A sweet herb tea, with the spiciness of pine-needles and the acrid smoke of damp wood.

Weard stood nearby, holding out a steaming cupful of the tea. He took it.

The metal cup burned his fingers as, stiff and chilled from the snow and icy metal, he gripped the handle. He did not react to the pain. Slowly he drank, savoring the warmth that flooded through him. The sun broke briefly through a thinning in the cloud cover.

"We must leave now," Weard said as Erik finished.

"Of course."

The sun faded again, and the bitterness from the north spilled into the glade. "I've sent the others ahead. The Festburg will be awaiting my return. We will feast, and sing, and triumph...and mourn. Come, Erik."

Part of Erik's consciousness noted the awkwardness of Weard's words. *My return*, not ours. And he had said Erik, not Angenga or Ansaca-bana. Erik was an alien again; he had lost.

Already Weard was striding out of the opening and into the forest...as he had done before, so long ago.

Erik ran until he caught up with Weard. "Why are we going alone? And the others did not come this way. There are no tracks here."

It seemed as if Weard were not going to answer. Then, finally, he said, "We must see the place."

Erik had known. It had to be met and faced, or the shadow of a dead man would remain to darken his life. He had long ago forgiven Weard—if *forgiven* were the right word. He had understood the fatal necessity. He had acceded to the crisis of the moment. He had accepted, on one level at least. But had he entirely?

They made their way among trees stiff and swathed in ice and snow. Before, they had been green and living, growing things. Erik did not recognize any landmarks in the crystal maze, but then he had not exactly paid strict attention to the scenery the last time he had passed this way. Occasionally a tree, a peculiarly shaped clump of brush, a jagged outcropping of granite jogged his memory, and images of heat, pain, and sorrow intruded into his mind. But for the most part he moved unconsciously a step or two behind Weard, unaware that he was now following the man easily, at a pace exceeding the one he had set before. Outwardly Erik was the same person, Erik Baanfeld of the ExServ—perhaps a bit thinner, rangier, clothed in outlandish garb—but the same. Inwardly....

They broke through the brush and stood by the stream. Its shallow flow was solid ice now and would remain so until the thaws still months of darkness away. One moment they were in the forest; another, and they stepped into a gray openness. The streambed was obvious as it meandered through the flats, but what had been a silver ribbon singing among rocks was now a silent bed of white. Everything was white—water, banks, even the brittle skeletons of reeds encased in ice and standing sentinel along the creek. Erik could hear a faint crystalline tinkling as ice-sheathes moved in the wind.

It was unendurably beautiful. Gray skies lowered from the north, threatening ice and snow unmarked by man or animal, streaked by shadows flowing from gray to black without margin.

Appropriate for a place of death, Erik thought. Weard did not speak. He led the way across the frozen streambed, perhaps over the spot where Marquette had died. Erik did not look down, half-fearing to see a ribbon of red spreading through glistening waters, a sky-blue tunic edging its way into his field of vision. Instead, he raised his eyes, following the line of black openings which defined the caves.

And then they were across the river, across the bank, and half-way up the cliff face. Erik's toes felt jutting rock, ledges impossibly narrow, shale faces made even more dangerous by the dusting of new snow. His fingers froze on knobs, scraped into cracks, held him over nothingness. His eyes remained on the figure just above and ahead of him.

Weard was climbing without looking back.

He trusts me, Erik thought. *He knows that I can do...anything he asks. He will not help me because he does not need to—and by doing so gives me the greatest compliment in his power.*

They passed the lower caverns, following the ledge along the cliff and finally ducking into a narrow opening. It was not the same cave; Weard was bent almost double as they passed into darkness.

They crept through the interior of the cliff, angling upward easily but steadily. Erik lost track of time, content to follow the slight sounds of Weard's climb.

Then the glow began, intensifying to a glare. They stepped through an opening and were behind the cliffs, on the highlands.

"The Festburg lies only half a day's march, over there." Weard pointed, then turned and began climbing the slope behind them, away from the Folk.

In a few moments, they stood on the crest of the cliff face, their feet only inches from fractured planes sheering toward the streambed.

The lowlands stretched for miles, disappearing into gray gloom. The sky was shrouded, the pines mantled in snow.

"He is dead," Erik said. "Finally dead. I know why you had to do it. If there is any guilt, it is mine for misunderstanding, or the grendel's, who would have killed us all.

"I didn't know then what this world was like. I judged you by standards of worlds you will never know, and found you wanting. Now, I can understand and accept.

"Marquette is dead, and so is Erik Baanfeld of the ExServ, Angenga survives, and Ansaca-bana."

Weard seemed not to listen. Instead, his eyes searched the expanses below them. As Erik fell silent, he gestured, stretching arm and finger and thrusting downward, toward a break in the forest just beyond the riverbed.

Erik followed the movement.

Four...no, five figures dotted the whiteness of a tiny glade.

They wore the sky-blue uniforms of the ExServ.

CHAPTER TWENTY-EIGHT

Darkness had long since fallen. The storm that had been threatening that morning had swept through, piling new snow on top of old, then had blown itself out with unnatural haste, dissipating southward. The sky was unusually clear, the crisp, freezing clearness of deep winter. What wind there was seemed as icy as death as it fingered through the ruff of fur over the man's shoulders. His eyes were distant, focused on the stars shimmering coldly through the night. Worlds. Suns. With people, cities, nations. Incredible, but unavoidably true.

He shivered, less from the cold than from the awesome visions passing through his mind. It would take getting used to, but now that the door had been opened, it could never be closed again. Too many had seen the ship; almost everyone had seen the weapon.

Perhaps they should never have tried to close the door in the first place.

But *perhaps* was useless now. The world would change. There was no help for it.

He dropped his eyes to the valley floor. The night was bright, but even his sharp eyes might be confused in the disarray of light and shadows. He looked long and carefully. Nothing.

He shut his eyes, indulging in a moment of light sleep leaned against a cleft boulder. When he opened them, he looked downward again.

There it was. A movement. He pulled his cloak tighter as the wind caught at it. There, along the base of the escarpment, one figure. It moved slowly, as if burdened.

Weard spun around and began to descend the cliff, following a path he had marked out that afternoon. Nearly fifteen minutes passed before he dropped the final few feet and crouched in the shadowed snow.

The figure in front of him stopped suddenly, aware of the intrusion of something into the silent night. Weard saw a hand slither toward a holster, heard a distant thud as an awkward bundle slipped to the snow. He straightened and stepped out of the shadows into full starlight.

"Ansaca-bana, Angenga," he said.

Erik ran forward, laughing.

"How did you know I would come back?"

"How could you not? You are *Ansaca-bana*, the Beast-Bane. You are *Angenga*, he who walks alone. You share Triewth's hearth-fire. You are the Singer, without whose voice our fires will be cold and cheerless."

He put his hands on Erik's shoulders. Bands of silver metal glinted against the night.

"And you are my friend, without whose warmth my life would be cold and cheerless. You had to return. You are of the Folk."

"Yes," Erik replied simply. "I am." Then he glanced over his shoulder. "We must hurry back. We have much to do. They can't move against us yet, at least I don't think Kopeck will go against direct orders. I have brought a few weapons. We must...."

At that moment, the sky to the west lit up with a cold, brilliant scarlet. A shining pellet burst from the trees and arced skyward.

"They must have discovered that I was gone and that I had taken some light armaments. They probably won't miss these for a while, though."

He pointed to a heavy bundle wrapped in a blanket. Weard knelt down and pulled back the cloth. He stared at the small square box ad the flat discs stacked neatly inside it.

"What is it?"

"Microtexts, and a reader. History, economics, physics, mathematics...everything I could lay my hands on. When they come back, we'll be ready. We'll know more and understand more. And we'll be able to dictate our terms, not have to accept theirs."

"How long?"

Erik grew somber.

"I don't know. We have three months before Kopeck can return to command—and I made a few adjustments in the computer that should keep them from contacting ExServ for a few days at least. An expert could repair it in an hour or so, but I don't think they have anyone that expert on board.

"So, perhaps as few as five or six months. With luck, as long as three years. I don't know, but every day will help."

He watched the streak of light until it disappeared and the sky was again black studded with stars.

"No matter how long we have, we have much to do." He faced Weard.

"They wanted me to become a Singer of Lies for them. To betray and destroy. But I could not."

"Of course not. You are one of us. Come, Ansaca-bana, Singer of Truth, let's go to the Festburg."

"And to Triewth," Erik said, then added one word: "Home."

ABOUT THE AUTHOR

Michael R. Collings is an Emeritus Professor of English at Seaver College, Pepperdine University, where he directed the Creative Writing Program for over two decades. He has published multiple volumes of poetry, novels, short fiction, and scholarly studies of such contemporary writers as Stephen King, Dean R. Koontz, Orson Scott Card, and Piers Anthony. He is now retired and lives in his native state of Idaho.

www.ingramcontent.com/pod-product-compliance
Lightning Source LLC
Chambersburg PA
CBHW050420260626
47156CB00003B/1092